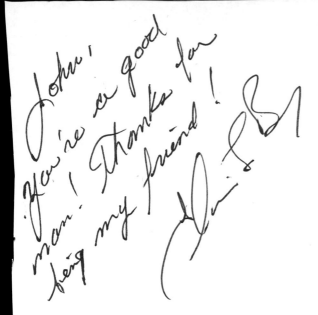

John!
You're a good
man! Thanks for
being my friend!

Well... I am on only a few hours of sleep thanks to you, Elvis! But I just finished your book and it was an EXCELLENT read! I seriously enjoyed it! And I love the way it ended.. you did so great:)) You tell a very captivating story-- you weave all the various plots together so well.. I thoroughly enjoyed learning about each character and their adventures as the main plot developed. It was like living another life and seeing the world through another's eyes.. I LOVED it. You are very accomplished and a great writer. :) Kelley Hutta

THE PRESENCE OF JUSTICE

OF JUSTICE

Fiction Murder Mystery book

Elvis L Bray

Congratulations, you wrote a real winner.

It's a modern-day Western. (I kept thinking about *Shane*, for some reason.) You've got all the elements: cowboys, Indians, Arizona location, horses, a fine upstanding hero (Andrew), a pure but hurting heroine (Shayla), criminals, lawmen, rifles and gunfire, coyotes, etc. But you've also got modern things no Old West western ever had--tape recorders, football games, trucks, drugs, kids texting each other and taking photos with their telephones!.

You know I read a LOT. The birthday party for Shayla in the barn is one of the most romantic and moving scenes I've ever read. Imagine the movie version of that scene!

I really like the one chapter from the coyote's POV. Consider adding another one or two from animal POVs.

Paul Sodeberg

Peace is not the absence of conflict, but the presence of Justice"
    -Reid C. Pixler

I would like to make a shout out about the book I just read. The Presents of Justice, by Elvis Lynn Bray. It was captivating and kept me on edge. I couldn't put it down. Anyone who enjoys mystery and makes you feel part of it will love this new author about to spring on the literary world. Keep up the good and exciting work Mr. Elvis Lynn Bray. Thank you for letting read it!

Harold Gentry

To Sherrie

For answering this question at least a million times:
"Honey, how do you spell...?"

CHAPTER ONE

I inhaled a slow deep breath through my nose. The smell was unique and unforgettable. There's no other like it. The scents of cheap bar soaps, shampoos, aftershave lotions, sweat, blood, pads, helmets, jocks, dirty socks and ointments combined to create the aroma of a football locker room.

Banging locker doors and metal cleats echoed off the windowless gray block walls as my teammates and I got dressed for the big game. In about four hours from now we would be either elated or crushed depending on the final score. But for now, we were living the moment. Why not? The next day would be the same for them, same house, same school, same friends, same church, and same girlfriends. But it won't be for me. *Hell, Andy, what are you afraid of? Think of it as a great adventure. Embrace it.*

Coach Dunn interrupted my thoughts by yelling; "Everybody on the bus in ten minutes!"

I removed the photos from my locker one by one. Janie at Six Flags, Heather in her cheerleading outfit, Sara on the beach in California, Susan on the boat at Lake Powell. I removed the photos and placed them in my gym bag. The last photo was an outline of a girl with a question mark in the center. *Who are you?* Removing the outline, I placed it in the gym bag with the others and shut the door for the last time.

"You nervous, Andy?" Cody Johnson asked as he sat on the metal bench beside me.

"You're kidding right?"

"Hardy is nervous. Look at him. He looks like he's going to throw up."

"He will before the game starts. The dumbass needs to stop chewing tobacco."

Cody shook his head. "Are you ready to kick some ass, big guy?"

"I was born ready."

"Well let's do it!" Cody said as he stood up. Cody and I had been best friends since Junior High School. He's my counterpart at right outside linebacker. He stopped when I didn't follow. "What are you thinking about, Andy?"

"Nothing really. Just cleaning out my locker."

"Bummer."

"It'll be worse if we lose this game."

"That ain't going to happen."

"Nope."

Cody sat on the bench next to me. "I hear the team you'll be playing for next year really sucks."

"Yeah. And in the 3-A division." I didn't want to think about next year's team. Today was the highlight of my life and I didn't want anything to spoil it. I wanted to enjoy every moment.

"Everyone on the bus!" yelled Coach Dunn.

The whole team responded in unison, "YES SIR!"

"Come on, Andy. Let's go win ourselves a championship."

The coach's real name was Milton Dunn but his friends called him Mel. His players called him Coach or Sir. Anything else would get you extra laps or push-ups after practice. He expected perfection, and didn't want excuses. If you screwed up, the only thing Coach Dunn wanted to hear was, "No excuse Coach! It won't happen again." If anyone was foolish enough to make excuses, they'd have plenty of time to think about it while the rest of the team was showered and they were running laps or doing push-ups. I would miss Coach Dunn.

I stopped for a moment to look at the motivational posters one last time. "You won't get any more out of it than you put into it!" "The heart is the strongest muscle in the body." "If you are not hurting, you are not gaining." "What doesn't kill you will make you stronger." and "The more you sweat, the less you bleed." borrowed from the Navy Seals. Above the posters hung eight 5-A state championship banners. It was our job to increase that number by one.

I didn't buy the adage, 'what doesn't kill you' part, but I got the message. We all did. You either bought into the Coach Dunn's system or you quit. He said that if a player quits, it made the rest of us stronger because the person who quit was the weakest link on the team. Few players quit, and if they did, it was early on.

On the bus ride to ASU stadium, the players talked on their cell phones, listened to i-Pods, or talked about the pending game. I closed my eyes and thought about my parents. I couldn't share their enthusiasm about moving. I hated unknowns.

"Worried about the game?" asked Harold Hardy as he scooted into the seat beside me. Harold was our center. Not the smartest fortune in the cookie by a long shot, but one tough kid. He was built like an oak stump, stout and quick for his size. If you planned on running up the middle against the Bulls, you had to go through Harold Hardy first. Few ever did.

"Of course not. Should I be?"

"Did you read the paper this morning?"

"No, why?"

"One of the reporters claims there's no way we can stop the Tiger's running back. He's gained over two thousand yards and has U of A, ASU, Alabama, and Oklahoma recruiting him."

"Yeah, well how do you suppose he's going to get past you, Cody and me?"

Harold thought for a moment. "He won't."

"So what's your point?"

Harold frowned. "I ain't got no point." He put his head back, and closed his eyes.

Car horns sounded as soon as our bus exited the 202 Freeway. Many vehicles had signs painted on the windows supporting their favorite teams. A few had the football numbers of the owner's sons painted on the window. I didn't see number 48 on any windows and I knew I wouldn't. Things like that embarrassed me. Coach Dunn had always emphasized the team and never the individual. But, parents are proud of their sons and coaches have little influence over parents.

Two small mountains guarded the ASU Stadium like Greek gods guarding a holy temple. The Sun Devils played here on Saturday nights and the Arizona High School 5-A state football championships were played there once a year.

"Will you get a look at that?" Hardy said as he took his headphones off. "I've never seen this many people at a football game before."

All the players started looking out the windows. This was what we had sweated for, bled for and dreamed of. The bus stopped at the north end of the stadium to more cheers from the crowd. Thousands had shown up for the game and more were arriving all the time. Most fans were wearing red and black for the Bulls or yellow and black for the Tigers. "I think I'm going to throw up," Hardy said as he ran off the bus and into the tunnel.

After exiting the bus, I stopped for a few moments before entering the tunnel. It was a cold and windy winter day even for

Arizona. I wanted to experience every moment knowing it would be a miracle if I ever got another chance like this again. My moment of glory would have to be at this stadium on this day. I knew there would be no second chances for Andrew Hanson.

"Come on Andy, get in here," Coach Dunn said. He locked the doors behind me and made everyone sit down. He held up his hand to silence the team and began his pre-game speech. "Respect your opponents at all times and never underestimate them. If you do, you will lose! There is never a time for gloating, and I won't stand for it. I don't want anyone celebrating until the game has ended and we have shaken hands with our opponents. Then and only then can you lie on the field of glory. This will be the time to celebrate and to remember. Let us pray."

We bowed our heads and the Coach prayed: "God, thank you for the opportunity to be here this day. May all players and coaches represent you and honor you at all times. Please keep each and every player safe on both teams. Amen."

"Amen."

"Now, let's get out there and kick some ass!" With an overwhelming roar from the team, we ran to the door and lined up for the grand entrance into the stadium.

The teams were introduced to the crowd one team at a time. When the Tiger's team was announced, they ran to their end zone and when the Bulls were announced, we ran to our appointed end zone for warm ups.

We lined up in straight lines looking more like soldiers than football players. Every step, every up and down, every command was in sync. All players were in unison. A marching band couldn't have orchestrated a better drill if they had practiced all year. This type of discipline is seldom seen on any football field and we knew it had a physiological effect on every team we faced.

After the warm ups, we ran back into the tunnel and waited as the Tigers were announced first. Coach Dunn reminded us to, "Just do your job and the team will take care of itself."

The names of the players were called in alphabetical order starting with the seniors. I took slow breaths attempting to calm myself as I waited, but I couldn't stop pacing. The caged animal inside of me wanted out. The agonizing wait seemed endless. My heart pounded in my chest as I paced back and forth.

As the names were announced over the loudspeakers, the players ran onto the field to cheers from the crowd. When my name was called, I ran out and saw myself on the big screen located at the opposite end of the stadium. It seemed as if I were running in slow motion as I watched myself trot to my teammates. The experience was incredible and I wished I could have captured the moment forever.

Coach Dunn and the assistant coaches were the last to run onto the field. The team gathered one last time prior to the start of the game. Coach Dunn only made one statement, "Let's do it!" The Bulls broke the huddle with a thundering roar.

As the senior team captains walked to the center of the field for the coin toss, I turned to search the bleachers for my parents. I knew the approximate location where they would be, but the crowd was too large for me to make them out. Smiling, I waved in the general direction I knew they were. Then I turned my attention back to the field. I couldn't stop pacing the entire time. We won the coin toss and the Tigers would be receiving the ball. I slowly put my helmet on. The animal inside me growled. Show time!

We kicked off and the Tiger's star running back caught the ball at the 15-yard line. He was tackled at the 16-yard line. Six Bull tacklers piled off of him and I was one of them. He didn't know it yet, but it was going to be a long night for their famous tailback. I couldn't help but wonder if the reporter who wrote that article was at the game.

We lined up for the next play and their big offensive tight end moved up close to the guard. I figured they would be running around my end so I moved over right in front of him. He glared at me and said, "You get in my way boy and I'll run over you like a Mac truck!"

He had at least two inches and 40 pounds on me. I moved closer. Just before the ball was hiked, I asked, "Hey, are you a Libra?"

He got a dumb look on his face. "Huh?" He hadn't noticed the ball had been hiked. I hit him so hard his feet left the ground. He was still there when I tackled the running back in the backfield. He was just getting to his feet when I walked past him. "I'm a Gemini, asshole," he said. I had definitely gotten his attention.

Smiling, I said, "Go figure." The rules of engagement had been established and there would be no taunting for the rest of the game.

The first two minutes stood at a deadlock with neither team gathering momentum. The next five minutes set the pace for the rest of the game. The Tigers only completed one first down during the first quarter of the game while the Bulls drove down the field on every other possession and scored. The rally was fast and furious. By now, anyone watching knew the Tigers were a mismatch. We scored twice more in the second quarter within a 30-second time span. Once on a 30-yard pass completion and again when I intercepted a swing pass intended for their big-mouth tight end and ran it back 23 yards to the end zone.

Like all the games we'd played this year, this one was a romp. The Tiger's heavily recruited running back gained less than 20 yards the entire game. He got very tired looking up at Harold Hardy and me. The Bulls intercepted four more passes and two of them were run back for touchdowns. I became a spectator by the end of third quarter, as were all of the starters.

I wished the game could have been closer but that was the way it was with the 2012 Bulls. As a team, we were complete, and one could argue, one of the best high school football teams Arizona has ever fielded.

The buildup to the game was better than the game itself. The Tigers scored a touchdown late in the game but everyone watching knew it was a gift. The final score was 51 to 7.

We lined up and walked to the center of the field to shake our opponents' hands. As I walked down the line, I was saddened by the bitter defeat and shame I saw on faces of their players. Their big tight end wouldn't even look at me and some of the players had tears in their eyes. I felt sorry for them.

After shaking hands, we returned to the center of the field for the presentation of the 5-A state championship trophy. When the ceremony was over, our entire team ran out and laid down in the center of the field to celebrate.

Security was useless in attempting to stop the crowd as students, cheerleaders, parents and spectators rushed to join us on the field. They stood around us like guests at the Oscars congratulating the winners. Some of the mothers and girlfriends wore the letter jackets of their sons or lovers. Cheerleaders huddled together in the cold night air. Young boys looked on in awe daydreaming that someday they might play here. People snapped photos like paparazzi's.

As we handed the trophy back and forth to each other, a reporter snapped a photo of Cody and me holding it high in the air, capturing the moment forever. In the photo, smiling cheerleaders and parents stood surrounding the team. This was the happiest moment of my life.

It was a defining moment for all the players. We knew we could never be denied the fact that we were now state champions. I didn't want this day to end. To me, it would not only be the ending of a season, but the ending of a dream. Knowing I would never get another chance like this again, I hated to let it go.

I searched the crowd for my parents. They were standing at the bottom rail of the stadium, as I knew they would be. My parents would never come onto the field because you weren't supposed to and they would never break the rules.

Heather caught up to me, grabbed my arm and we walked together. She was gorgeous in her cheerleader's outfit. She was as close to a sibling as I would ever have and I loved her like a sister. I had introduced her to her boyfriend, Cody Johnson, while we were in Junior High School. They had been dating ever since. She looked up at me with sad eyes. "I'm going to miss you so much, Andy."

I hugged her. "I'm going to miss you too."

"Why don't you stay? You could go visit your parents on the weekends. You know my parents will let you live with us until you graduate."

"I'm sure they would."

"Then stay with us."

Her eyes were red. She was trying hard not to cry. I stopped to face her and held her by both shoulders at arm's length. "Think about it, Heather. Then I would always be missing someone. I love my parents and they need me."

"I know. I know. But I don't want you to go."

"I don't want to go either, but I don't really have a choice. My parents have always been there for me. I need to be there for them."

"You're right, but you have to promise you'll call. I need to hear your voice. I want to know how you're feeling and what's going on in your life. I need to know you're all right. Promise me, Andy that you'll never forget me. Ever!"

I hugged her. "How could I forget my little sister?"

Sniffling through tears, she slugged me in the shoulder. "I'm a month older than you, remember. And if I don't hear from you every week, I'll come up there and kick your butt."

"I'll call. I promise."

"And promise me something else."

"What?"

"Please fall in love."

"I already love you."

"Yes you love everyone. That's not the same. I mean really love someone. Open up that big heart of yours and let someone special into your life. Okay?"

I hugged her. "You just can't tell yourself to love someone and it happens." I kissed her on her forehead and we walked to my parents.

Mom and Dad hugged Heather and congratulated me on the win. My parents were leaving the game to go to my dad's retirement party and Heather and I were going to celebrate with my teammates. The dream was over but I had bigger problems to think about. Life, as I knew it, would soon become a distant memory.

CHAPTER TWO

The older part of Clarksville looked like a movie set from the 50s. Most of the newer buildings were older than I was. Antique gas stations, empty dirt lots cluttered with trash, old hotels with cracked sidewalks. It depressed me.

The downtown area was a mixture of old and new. Faded paint under a missing sign advertised where an old Five-and-Dime Store had once been. A newer Dollar Store sat next door. A McDonald's sat on the left side of the street and a rustic restaurant named Skeeter's was located across the street. I wanted McDonalds, Dad pulled into Skeeter's.

The large sign in front of Skeeter's read, *BEST HOMEMADE FOOD IN THE STATE!* Below that sign was another smaller one that read, *Profits from the sale of pies goes to charities.*

"After breakfast, we'll drop Andy off at the high school before we meet the realtor," said Dad.

We exited the truck to the smell of bacon and fresh baked pies. If we weren't hungry when we got here, the smell alone would have changed our minds. As we entered, a redheaded woman in her thirties with the nametag "Skeeter" greeted us.

"Welcome to Skeeter's. Will you be having breakfast with us this morning?"

"Yes, please," answered Dad.

The restaurant reminded me of a Cracker Barrel without the souvenir shop. A large Native American sat by himself at a small table in the corner working on a Kachina doll. He looked like a body builder. I had never seen an Indian that big in my life. His leather vest was opened in the front and he wore armbands on both arms. His black cowboy hat sat in the chair next to him sporting a snake headband and feather. His leather pants were tucked inside his high-top moccasins with leather straps hanging from them. His shiny black hair hung below his shoulders. I noticed several other Kachina dolls for sale displayed on a shelf above the cash register.

Most of the kids in the in the restaurant wore Western clothes and either cowboy boots or work boots. Even little kids wore straw hats like the farmers. The one thing I didn't expect was that everyone seemed happy. Perhaps eating at Sheeter's was the highlight of their week. I half expected Andy Griffith and Barney Fife to be sitting at one of the tables.

A gorgeous young lady about my age caught my eye. She had the brightest emerald eyes I'd ever seen. Her long brown hair was worn in a ponytail. Her body was to die for. Well, maybe not to die for, but to break a little finger for anyway. She'd been sitting with several others girls in a booth on the west wall and was about to leave. Things were looking a little more interesting in Hicksville.

We made eye contact. I smiled, she didn't. Maybe not so interesting after all. She walked out without giving me a second look. I watched her drive off in a white pick-up truck. I kicked myself for not following her outside and introducing myself.

A waitress came to take our order. The food was excellent. After breakfast, Dad paid the bill and got directions to the high school from Skeeter.

"I think I am going to like this town," Mom commented as we walked out.

"Me too," Dad said.

I didn't share their optimism and wasn't sure if I would ever feel as if I belonged. I already missed Mesa.

The high school was a two-story stucco building fronted by four tall thick columns. It looked more like a museum than a school. Vines crawled up one side and huge oak trees shaded the front lawn. Several cement steps led up to a large foyer with tall heavy wooden double doors guarding the entrance. The windows on both floors were over six feet tall with light green wood frames. Some were standing open on the second floor, letting the air in. I assumed these were offices.

"They don't build them like this anymore," Dad stated as we studied the building.

I hoped not. I doubted if it had running water let alone air conditioning. I walked around to the side of the main building expecting to see several rows of outhouses marked male or female. There were no outhouses. Several newer buildings sat their instead. The coach's offices and weight room were next to the football stadium. Several cars were parked in the parking lot next to the offices and another one was parked next to the stadium.

The stadium was much larger than I had expected. It was constructed of cement with metal fencing surrounding the sides and top to keep people from falling off. The press box ran almost the length of the stadium. Above the stadium a large sign read: "WELCOME TO THE HOME OF THE CLARKSVILLE COUGARS." It had a painting of a large cougar getting ready to pounce. Grinning, I looked at the big cat. *Here kitty, kitty.*

The parking lot was a lot larger than I expected. I wondered if it filled at game time. If it did, there would be as many spectators here as there were at the Bulls' football games.

"Do you want us to go with you to see the coach?" Mom asked.

"No thanks, I'll handle it. If I need anything I'll call you."

"Do you need any money?" Dad asked.

"No, but if you are giving it away, I'll take it." He didn't offer again. "Take your time and if you're running late, don't worry. I'll walk to Skeeter's restaurant, grab some lunch and hang out until you're done."

When they left, I walked to the stadium and out onto the football field. The grass was so green it hurt my eyes. The visitor's bleachers were larger than the ones we had in Mesa and they had their own bathrooms and concession stands. Farming and ranching might be the lifeblood of Clarksville, but football was its heartbeat. I could almost feel the pulse.

I walked into the gym area and smelled the unmistakable essence of a locker room. To my right sat a man at a desk typing on a computer with his back to me. I guessed he was Coach Ford or one of the assistant coaches. On a wall straight ahead were three photos of three football players in their uniforms. On the wall above the photos was painted, "In Memory Of" in large letters. The names on the photos were, Jimmy Turner, Dave Keller and Bobby Patterson. Above the photos were eight 3-A state championship banners. I heard voices down the hall and the sounds of weights being placed on the metal bars.

I knocked on the office door and the man turned in his chair to face me. He motioned for me to enter. He was about 60 years old, tall, thin, with a full head of salt-and-pepper hair.

He stood as I entered. "Hello, I'm Coach Ford," he said as he extended his hand. "What can I do for you young man?" He was soft-spoken, unshaven and looked tired.

"I'm Andy Hanson," I said as we shook hands. "My family will be moving to Clarksville and I wanted to know if you could use another football player?"

"We can use all the football players we can get. Where did you play this year?"

"Superstition Mountain High School in Mesa, sir."

The Coach smiled. "Were you a starter?"

"Yes sir."

"What position?"

"Mostly linebacker, but some back-up quarterback."

He raised his eyebrows. "What position do you want to play?"

"I like playing defense."

Coach Ford rubbed his chin. "I darn sure could use a quarterback. How's your arm?"

"It's alright."

"Good. If you play quarterback, you can still get a little time at linebacker or defensive end if you want. A lot of the team players go both ways in 3-A."

I didn't really want to play quarterback, but I wanted to play. "I'll play wherever, Coach."

Coach Ford sat back down and looked back at me. "I wish more guys had that attitude. What was your number this year?"

"Number 48."

"I was there."

I wasn't sure I understood him correctly. "You were where?"

"At the game, Andy. I was in the stands."

"Small world isn't it?"

"What does your dad do for a living, if you don't mind me asking?"

"He's going to be the new Assistant Police Chief here in Clarksville."

"Hum," he said nodding. "I heard we were getting a new Assistant Chief."

"When is the gym open?"

"Every day after school, and half days on Saturdays. During the summer, we're open every morning from 6:00 A.M. to 10:00 A.M. and again from 4:00 p.m. to 6:30 p.m., except Sundays. I'm normally here later than that if there's anyone working out. A lot of players have summer jobs so I try to catch them before or after work if I can." Coach Ford paused for a moment, and then asked, "Do you have any idea when you'll be moving?"

"I'm not sure. My parents are out looking at houses as we speak."

"Have a look around if you want. If anyone asks, tell 'em I said it's all right! Here, let me give you a padlock. Take any locker you want that doesn't already have a lock on it."

"Thanks Coach," I said as I took the lock. "I'll let you know when we get moved in."

After leaving the office, I stopped in the hallway and peeked back around the corner. I thought I had smelled liquor on the coach's breath while we were talking. Coach Ford removed a brown bag from his drawer and took a swig. He put the cap back on the bottle and put it back into the drawer. He stared up at the championship banners and photos hanging on the wall for a long time, shook his head, and turned back to his computer.

The locker room was different but also the same, especially the smell. I closed my eyes and took a deep breath. Some things don't change with location.

I heard a loud banging noise and someone yelled, "Damn it!" I walked in the direction of the sound and looked around the corner. A large black kid was leaning on his locker looking down at a piece of paper. He was shaking his head as if he couldn't believe what he was seeing. He hadn't noticed me standing there. He slammed his palm against his locker again and turned to leave when he noticed me. He waded up the paper and asked, "Who are you?"

"I'm Andy Hanson.'

"What are you doing here?"

"I'm looking for a locker. I'll be on the team next year."

He looked me up and down, sizing me up. "What position do you play?"

"Linebacker."

He nodded. "The locker next to me is empty if you want it." He walked past me and threw the waded-up paper in the trashcan on his way out.

I put my lock on the empty locker next to his. I stopped at the trashcan and picked up the piece of paper he had discarded. It was an algebra test with a failing score. I wadded it back up and threw it back in the trash.

About twenty boys were working out when I entered the weight room. A big kid with a shaved head, no neck and very hairy arms and legs was using the squat machine. Several boys stood around watching him. They all looked at me except the kid with the shaved head, he glared at me. I walked over to the water fountain and took a drink.

"No one is allowed in here except football players," said the big bald guy.

His lame attempt to intimidate me bothered me. I hate bullies.

"He's going to be on the team next year," said the black kid I'd talked to in the locker room.

A small grin spread across the bald guy's face. "Oh, he must be the new water boy."

The boys with him laughed. He got back under the bar still watching me and started doing squats.

The black kid added weights to the bench press. His clothes were old and his shoes had holes in them. I counted his weights and there was 250 pounds on the bar. He appeared to be a guard or center, and a good one if he had any speed. He noticed me watching him and nodded. I walked over to where he was working out. "Need a spotter?"

"Sure," he said as he positioned himself under the bar. "I'm Jared Label." When he raised the bar to its full height, I lowered my hands and watched as he did full ten reps without need of assistance.

When he finished, he sat up and asked. "I don't remember seeing you around here before."

"I'm new. We haven't moved here yet."

"Where did you play this year?"

"In the valley."

He paused and licked his lips as if thinking of something. "What position did you say you played?"

"Mostly defense."

He nodded. "We weren't very good this year but we should be better next year. We're getting a lot of our starters back."

"Mind if I do a few reps?" I asked.

"Sure rotate in. I'll spot you. How much you want me to take off?" Jared said as he started to remove some of the weights.

"Leave them," I said.

"There's 250 pounds on here. You sure you don't want me to take some off?"

"No, that's good."

Jared shook his head, "Okay, but don't hurt yourself."

I positioned myself under the bar. The other boys stopped talking to watch me. I placed my hands on the bar. Jared grabbed the bar to help assist it to the up position. After pushing the bar to its full height, I told Jared I was good. I did ten full reps. I heard whispers but I couldn't hear what they were saying. After completing the reps, I sat the bar back on the stand.

"You're stronger than you look. I figured you for 200 at most," Jared said. "The Coach will want to meet you."

"I've already met him."

A tall man who was built like Tarzan entered the weight room. He wore a new matching workout suit. He walked over and offered me his hand. "Hello, I'm Bernie Baxter, the weight coach. I don't think we've met."

I shook his hand. "I'm Andy Hanson."

"He's moving to Clarksville and will be on the team next year, Coach," Jared said.

"That's great. If you need anything, come see me."

"Thanks, Coach."

Coach Baxter left to assist other players. "Seems like a nice guy."

"He's a great guy," said Jared. "He owns the local gym in town and volunteers as our weight coach. He donated most of our weight equipment in here."

After we finished with the bench press, Jared asked, "Want to do some squats?"

"Sure."

The big bald hairy guy had finished his squats but was still sitting on the bench when we got there. "We need the bench, Larry." Jared said.

The guy slowly stood up and moved off the bench and stood to the side. "Go ahead, Boy."

Jared ignored him.

I moved under the bar. "I'll go first."

"Let me help," Larry said. "How much weigh do you want me to take off?"

I counted the weight and there were 300 pounds on the bar. I smiled and said, "Fifty pounds."

He smiled and started to remove a 25-pound weight from one end of the bar. I put my hand on the weight stopping him. "Add, not subtract."

He looked confused. "What?"

"Add 50 pounds. Don't take it if off."

Larry smiled. "Yeah, right pussy. Who are you kidding?" He shook his head walked away. Jared added two 25-pound weights to the bar and stepped back. The bald guy had a big grin on his face. "Don't hurt yourself, Water boy."

"Maybe I should go first." Jared said.

"No, I'm good."

Everyone in the weight room stopped what they were doing to see what was going to happen. Coach Baxter walked over, counted the weights and said, "I'll spot you."

Larry stood next to the squat machine grinning like a possum eating shit. After folding up a towel and placing it across my shoulders, I positioned myself under the bar. When I raised the bar off the rack, Larry's grin disappeared. I completed ten squats as if I had been doing it all year, which I had. Larry was gone by the time I sat the bar down.

Jared proved to be a wealth of information. He told me Larry had been the center on this year's football team last year and had been their best player. He said Larry wasn't going to play football next year. Jared played right offensive guard and was hoping for a football scholarship after high school. He'd lived in Clarksville all of his life and was an only child. He said he never knew who his father was. He claimed his mother was a baker.

"Where are you trying to get a football scholarship?" I asked.

"Anywhere I can. But I need to gain about 30 pounds first."

"How's that coming?"

"Not worth a shit. I eat like a pig and I can't gain an ounce. Doesn't matter though. If I don't pass algebra, they won't take me anyway."

"I can help you with the math if you want. I'm pretty good at it."

"That'd be great man. I sure could use some help. Algebra looks like chicken scratches to me."

"Give me your phone number and I'll call you when we get moved in."

Jared looked down at the floor, hesitated and shook his head. "I don't have a phone." Then he looked up and said. "But, you can go by Skeeter's and ask for me. I live right behind the restaurant. You know where Skeeter's is, don't you?"

"Yeah, we ate breakfast there this morning."

"I'd sure appreciate the help, Andy."

I liked Jared immediately and that was rare for me. I'm normally guarded with strangers. But there was nothing fake about him. He was neither false nor pretentious. He was an open book and kind of reminded me of the kid in the movie, Blindside. I was hoping he would be watching my blind side next year if I ended up playing quarterback.

Overall, my day had been productive. I'd seen one of the prettiest girls I'd ever seen, met the coach, and made a new friend-and an enemy. Football at Clarksville might not be as bad as I thought.

My phone rang. Mom advised she was outside waiting to pick me up. Jared walked out with me. It had turned cold and was raining.

I introduced Jared to Mom and asked, "Where's Dad?"

"I dropped him off at the police station. He wants to talk to Chief Baker and fill him in on our progress." Mom was beaming from ear to ear. "Guess what, Andy? We found the perfect house."

"Already? That was quick."

"You're going to love it. I want you to see it while Dad's busy with Harvey. We're going to meet them at Skeeter's for dinner when they're finished."

"Boy, that didn't take long. Are you sure it's the house you want?"

"It's perfect, Andy! You'll see. It's the house I have always dreamed about. The barn is bigger than the house. I can't wait to show it to you."

Jared asked, "Where is it located, if you don't mind me asking, Mrs. Hanson?"

"Call me Sherrie, Jared. It's located on Canyon Road."

"Hey, that's where I live. On Canyon Road just behind Skeeters."

"You want to come see the house, too?" I asked. "Is that all right, Mom?"

Before Mom could answer Jared said, "I can't. I have to go to work. But you could give me a ride home if you want. It's on your way."

"We'd love to, Jared," Mom said. "Hop in."

"You can drop me off at Skeeter's" Jared said. "I've got to talk to her before I go home. I need to know how many eggs she needs in the morning."

Mom dropped Jared off in Skeeter's parking lot and he went inside. I noticed a small house at the rear of the restaurant and guessed it must be his home. There were chicken coops near the back of the property.

Mom started telling me about the house as soon as we let Jared out. I hadn't seen her this excited in years. Mom was the impulsive one but it wasn't like Dad to make up his mind so quickly. If Dad had agreed to the house, then it had to be a good deal.

"The house is the last one on this street and borders the National Forest," Mom said as we drove south. "No one can move next to us on the south side. It has four bedrooms with a large kitchen with granite countertops, plus a double oven. It's single story, red brick with white shutters. You're going to love this house!"

"Ok, Mom. I'm sold and I haven't seen it yet."

The house was exactly as Mom had described. I wasn't thrilled about the size of the front yard I'd have to mow, but the rest was great. While touring the house, Dad called and told us to meet him at Skeeter's.

I didn't like the fact we were moving, but I felt I had no choice but to suck it up and make the best of it.

When we got to the restaurant, Dad and Harvey Baker were already sitting at a table.

Chief Baker stood up we shook hands. "Congratulations on the state championship, Andy. I wish I could've been there."

"Thanks, Chief."

"Maybe some of that championship stuff can rub off on the Cougars," said Chief Baker.

After dinner, we said our goodbyes and headed home. Larry, the bald guy from the gym, was coming into the restaurant as we were walking out. He bumped into me as we were leaving. "Sorry," he said while grinning at me. I knew we were bound to meet again.

CHAPTER THREE

A s I carried boxes of *treasures* to the driveway, I thought of the old saying, "One man's junk is another man's treasure." I watched Mom collecting money from the strangers going through our stuff. It saddened me to see them picking through our belongings like vultures. Seeing my old toys and clothes being carried away brought back memories of a happier time. I felt violated. I didn't expect most of the junk to sell but it disappeared almost a quickly as I put it out. It was odd to see what people wanted more than money. What didn't sell, we donated to Goodwill.

You never knew who your friends were until you moved. Several of dad's police buddies and half of the football team showed up to help us. We loaded the Penske moving van in record time. I drove Dad's truck pulling the horse trailer and horses. Dad drove the moving truck towing my car and Mom drove her SUV. We had planned on getting out of town by noon if we were lucky, but with all the unexpected help, we were on the road by 10:00 a.m.

It was 1:00 p.m. when our little caravan pulled into Skeeter's parking lot. We parked in a dirt lot next to several semi-trucks. We seated ourselves in a booth next to the window so we could keep an eye on our vehicles. Not expecting any help at this end, we didn't want to start unloading on empty stomachs.

Jared Lobel walked in and sat at the table next to us. "Hey Bro, you made it. I didn't expect you to get here until later this afternoon."

"Hi Jared. Are you working today?" I asked.

"I will be. I'm going to help unload your stuff."

"Thanks, Buddy. How did you know we were here?"

Jared nodded over his shoulder at Skeeter and said, "A little birdie told me."

Skeeter smiled and waved from the hostess counter. "Looked like you could use some help," She yelled. "I have to work but I'm sending you home with a couple of pies. That's normally good for a few volunteers!"

On the way out of the restaurant, Mom stopped and hugged Skeeter while Dad and I picked out pies. When we pulled into our new driveway, a tall Native American got out of his truck. Jared introduced him as Colonel Lightfoot, his Scoutmaster and a volunteer football coach. "Skeeter told me you could use some help."

Dad shook his hand. "We won't turn good help away," he said, and then introduced us.

Mom showed us where to put things as we brought them inside. It took all afternoon to unload the trucks and we were exhausted. We assembled the beds first and left most of the boxes unpacked.

Mom ordered pizza delivered and Skeeter showed up with a bottle of wine and a case of cold beer and sodas. The move from Hell we had expected to last two days had been completed in one. I decided to drop the "Hicksville" title for Clarksville. These seemed to be good people.

Dad tried in vain to pay Jared and Colonel Lightfoot for helping but they wouldn't take a cent and acted insulted by the offer.

We shook their hands and thanked them for their kindness and hard work.

"Do you ride, Andy?" asked Colonel Lightfoot.

"A little. I don't own a horse but I ride Dad's."

"We're going on a round-up tomorrow if you want to join us."

"I'd love too but I better stay here and help unpack."

"Go ahead, Andy," Mom said. "The only thing I'm unpacking is the kitchen tomorrow and I don't need help with that. I need to think about where everything else is going before I unpack the rest."

Dad nodded that it was okay. "Alright, Colonel. Where do I meet you?"

"Meet me at Skeeter's at 5:00 in the morning."

I didn't like getting up that early, but was excited about the cattle drive.

After Jared and Colonel left, we sat on the back porch in lawn chairs, tired and relieved. Mom opened the bottle of wine and Dad popped a cold beer. We watched in contented silence as the horses ran around in their new pasture. My parents cuddled close watching as a crimson sunset appeared in the western sky. I turned in early to give them privacy.

After going to bed, I couldn't go to sleep. The quiet was deafening. I wasn't used to the lack of noise. I sent Heather a text. *First night in new home. Lonely, miss you!*

She answered me within a minute. *Miss you too! Tears.*

The noise of a vehicle approaching could be heard outside of my bedroom window. A moment later, a white pickup truck drove south on the dirt road. Thinking about the girl I'd seen at Skeeter's, I wondered if it could be her.

CHAPTER FOUR

C olonel Lightfoot pulled his pickup truck into Skeeter's parking lot at 5:00 a.m. I had just walked in and was waiting for him. Thermos in hand, he walked over and offered me his hand.

"Morning, Andy."

"Good morning, Colonel," I said as we shook.

Scarlet Manson, a.k.a Skeeter, hugged him and took his thermos. "Good morning, Colonel. You're early."

"Mornin' Skeeter. Has anyone told you how beautiful you are today?"

"Not a soul. You're the first!" she said as she filled his thermos with black coffee.

"She's lying, Colonel. I've been here for 30 minutes and you're the tenth customer to tell her that, including me," said a Highway Patrol sergeant sitting at the counter.

Colonel looked at the patrolman. "Mornin' Bob. You're not hitting on my girlfriend are you? I don't want to have to rough you up!"

That got several laughs from the other customers. Apparently, they had known each other since their high school days. Colonel later told me they had played football for the Clarksville Cougars.

Bob laughed, "We going to get any snow today?"

"Nope, just rain later. Unless you're headed to the rim country."

"No, I am working the New Mexico border and back. What brings you out so early?"

"Some of John Stevenson's cattle got out in the upper ranges. We gotta ride up there and help them find their way home," Colonel replied as he walked over and picked out an apple pie.

Bob nodded at me. "Who's your sidekick?"

"Andy Hanson. He's the new assistant chief's son," answered Colonel. He looked at me. "Don't believe anything he tells you, Andy."

Bob grinned and kept eating.

Colonel paid Skeeter and we headed for the door. "Don't make any moves on my girl while I'm gone, Bob. I'll tell your wife and kids."

"Blackmail is against the law."

Skeeter smiled, "Bye, Darling," as she pushed Colonel towards the door. "Bye, Andy. Have fun."

Colonel blew Skeeter a kiss and pointed two fingers at his eyes and then at Bob. "I'm watching you!"

We pulled out of the parking lot and headed south. The houses faded away after we passed our house and the road turned to dirt. The city gave way to National Forest, dotted with a few ranches where cattle grazed year-round. The Double J Ranch was the second ranch after leaving the pavement and apparently our destination.

A light was on in the kitchen as we approached the ranch. Pulling his truck past the main house, Colonel parked next to the barn. A Ford truck was already hooked to a stock trailer and three horses were tied to the side. One was already saddled. The owner of the ranch was nowhere in sight. Colonel placed the apple pie and his thermos on the dash of the Ford.

A red mare whinnied from one of the stalls as we entered the barn. "Morning Ruby," Colonel said as he handed her several apple treats and rubbed her between her ears. He grabbed a saddle and blanket and told me to do the same. We walked back to the gooseneck trailer. After brushing our horses, Colonel saddled them.

Colonel went back to the barn, retrieved several flakes of hay and put them in the feedbags already hanging in the trailer. We loaded the horses and got in the truck. As Colonel poured us a cup of coffee, a man appeared at the truck and placed two .30-30 rifles in the gun racks mounted over the rear window. The man said, "Morning, Colonel. Who's this?"

"Mornin' John. This is Andy Hanson, your new neighbor. He volunteered to help us find your lost cattle."

"I'm John Stevenson," he said as he shook my hand. "Nice to meet you, Andy. We might need your help."

"Nice to meet you too, sir."

"Call me John," he said as he got in the truck.

"Want some coffee?" asked Colonel.

"Got some, but I'll take some of Skeeter's pie if you'll cut me a slice. Want a piece, Andy?"

"Sure."

Colonel placed his coffee cup in the cup holder and took the pie off the dash. He handed John and me a slice and took one for himself.

"You weren't flirting with Skeeter this morning, were you, Colonel?"

"Hell yes I was, and she gave me a kiss too!"

John laughed, "In your dreams. She's one hell of a women, ain't she?"

"Sure is! But you wouldn't trade her for Donna!"

"No way. Donna and I were made for one another."

We ate pie and drank coffee in silence as we drove up to the dirt road. Small patches of fog hovered above the fields and in the lower ravines. The sun wasn't up yet, but there was enough light to see a few deer feeding in the lower ranges and saddles. Mule deer fed in the flat lands while whitetail Coues deer fed in the higher ranges and steeper slopes. A red-tailed hawk circled high above. The smell of mesquite trees and fresh winter grass filled the morning still morning air. It appeared as if it was going to be a beautiful winter day, but the weatherman had predicted thunderstorms this afternoon. John turned up a steep side road that wasn't much more than a jeep trail following a creek.

Huge white trunked sycamore trees lined the creek bed reaching high into the sky. Steep rocky hillsides contained patches of cholla cactus and brittlebush with a few ocotillos mixed in with the barrel cactus and desert highland grasses. As we climbed higher, hedgehog cactus appeared with a few junipers and desert ironwood.

The road ended at a line shack. "This is private land that's part of the Double J Ranch," Colonel said. "The line shack was built in the early 1900s when it took the cowboys all day to ride up here from the ranch."

It appeared the walls of the shack had never seen a coat of paint and the old planks showed years of weathering. The only noises in a vast void of open space were the slight whisper of wind and banging of the loose tin roof. No effort had been made to replace the rusted hinges and the door sat open at a slight angle. Creaking porch boards warned the rats of approaching visitors. Their droppings were the only signs of recent occupancy.

We walked inside the shack. The main room served as a kitchen with a wood burning stove and a built-in table along the south wall. The only door from the outside led into this room. Small windows opened inward in both rooms. There had been glass in them at one time but plank shutters now covered them. The shutters were held in place by rusted hinges, allowing the windows to be pulled shut to block out the cold and wind. An old metal bedframe still supported sagging springs in the bedroom. The mattress was missing.

"John leaves the shack standing for emergencies," Colonel said. "A small amount of canned food and bottled water used to be left in here. More often than not, it would be missing if there were ever an emergency. He stopped putting anything in here years ago because of vandals and illegal aliens."

"I think it's cool."

"He's considered tearing it down but won't. If someone gets lost in these mountains, they could build a fire in the old metal stove to stay warm. Someone will steal that stove in a matter of time."

"How many cattle do you think are off the ranch, John?" asked Colonel.

"Bill Thornton said he saw three head yesterday with my brand including a small bull. It could be just the three or a dozen or two. We need to find that break in the fence and get it fixed before the whole herd wanders off."

Colonel unloaded the horses while John checked to see what, if any, damage had been done to the shack since his last visit. Satisfied nothing had changed, he returned and retrieved the two rifles out of the back rack and slid them into his and Colonel's saddle scabbards. Colonel adjusted my stirrups and we mounted our horses while John stared at the large mesquite tree about a hundred yards north of the shack. A small white cross with wilted flowers marked the spot.

Colonel looked at me and whispered, "That's where Bobby Patterson Jr. was found shot to death. The murder hasn't been solved. John, and almost everyone else in Clarksville, believes the murderer was a local. So far, the police have few if any clues and no suspects. They aren't any closer to solving the murder today than they were the day it happened."

John shook his head. "What a shame. I wonder if it's Maggie or Peaches who leaves these flowers?"

Colonel didn't answer. He later told me he didn't want to upset John by telling him his daughter had been coming up here alone. After a few moments of silence, John mounted up. "Do you have wire cutters in those saddlebags, Colonel?"

"Sure do."

Riding up and away from the shack, we climbed higher up the steep slope. John noticed a slight change of color on the hillside grasses. Upon closer examination, both Colonel and John said they were ATV tracks not more than a day or two old. The tracks zigzagged back and forth across the side of the ridge, climbing higher on each pass heading toward the top of the mountain. We didn't need to follow the tracks because we would be crossing them several more times before reaching the top. As we neared the top of the ridge, Colonel stopped. He focused to his left, staring at the stillness.

"What's wrong, Colonel?" asked John as he followed Colonel's gaze.

"I heard something. Not sure what. But it was something."

John stared in the same direction for a few moments, "We had better take a look. If anyone is poaching my cattle, I'll put a bullet in him."

I didn't think John would shoot anyone. But, apparently they took poaching seriously.

As we reached the area where the sound had come from, we saw the carcass. The small white-faced calf hadn't been killed. Puncture wounds along the neck and large scratches on the sides of the calf were clear indications of a cougar kill. It had been part-ly eaten at the underbelly. Blood was running downhill from the carcass. Colonel dismounted and placed his fist over a track. "This is a big cat, John. Bigger than any I've seen before. He's close, prob-ably watching us now."

John pulled his .30-30 rifle out of his scabbard. "We better get 'em while we can. He'll kill a lot more if we don't. Can you tell which way he went?"

Colonel studied the bloody prints for a moment and pointed up a steep ravine to the southeast. "He went up that way."

John started walking his horse towards the ravine while Colonel mounted up and followed. I stayed at the rear. The farther up the ravine we went the steeper and narrower it got. A small cliff appeared on our left and the brush became thicker and denser as we climbed. The catclaw bushes pulled at our clothes as we slowly maneuvered the increasingly rocky ravine. The cliff got higher on the left with every step. A small opening appeared near the top of the gorge allowing just enough room for a horse to pass through.

As we walked into the gap, John's mare suddenly froze and her ears went up. A blood-curling scream could be heard as John raised his rifle. Before he could aim, a big cougar leaped from the ledge above and onto him. He ducked to the side attempting to avoid the cat as his horse reared and spun backwards in the rocks. The cat's big claws caught his left arm tearing flesh as his boot came out of the stirrup. As he came off his horse, he held on to the saddle horn to keep from hitting headfirst. Thankfully, my horse startled but didn't bolt. He backed up a few steps and held steady.

John and the cat went down hard. John landed upright but his right boot got wedged between two small boulders. He continued spinning to the side and hit hard on his right shoulder. His rifle flew a few feet away, bouncing off the rocks and landing in the thick brush. The big cat rolled over and turned to face John who was still wedged between the boulders. The cat hissed and growled, exposing its razor sharp teeth. Just as the cat started to leap again, I heard a shot and saw rocks exploding under the cat as the .30-30 round ricocheted off them. The big cougar paused for a split second, looked at Colonel, then leaped over John and up over the ledge. Another thundering round echoed through the canyon as the second bullet shattered rocks just below the cat's stomach.

"Damn it!" yelled Colonel. He wasn't pleased about missing the cougar. I couldn't believe he was able to get a shot and stay mounted on his frightened horse. He quickly dismounted, tied his horse to a small tree and ran to John's aid. I did the same wanting to help.

"Damn, I thought that cat had me for sure," John said.

"I thought you were going to be his lunch!" Colonel said. "How bad are you hurt?"

We knew by the look on John's face it wasn't good. His leg just above the ankle was not supposed to be bent that way. It was obviously broken. Blood poured from large gashes on his left arm and he had a large knot on his forehead. He had other minor scrapes and scratches but his leg and loss of blood from the arm were of the most concern. He was lying slightly downhill with his boot wedged between the rocks. He would have to be moved uphill to remove the pressure before we could get the boot lose. Colonel took his handkerchief and wrapped it around the wound to stop the bleeding. John was as tough as they came, but a broken ankle causes a lot of pain. We hoped John wouldn't go into shock before we could get him off the mountain.

"Can you help me slide him up a little, Andy, so we can get his boot loose?" He looked at John. "It's broken and this is going to hurt."

"Hell, it already hurts," answered John. "It won't get any better until we get me to a hospital. Help me slide up."

John placed a stick between his teeth and bit down hard. Colonel paused for a moment while looking at John. John nodded. Colonel lifted John under his arms while I held his leg the best I could. We scooted him uphill to release the pressure. I slowly lifted the leg and boot upward. John gritted his teeth to keep from screaming. His arms started shaking and his eyes watered, but he never cried out. After he was free, Colonel got his canteen from his saddlebag and brought John some water. Finding two straight limbs, Colonel splinted the leg so it couldn't move. He tied it tight.

A cold gust of wind hit us. Dark clouds hid the top of Mount Graham. The temperature was dropping fast as a steady breeze blew in from of the east. We needed to get John off this mountain before the storm hit.

"We have to get you to a hospital. I'll walk up on the top of this ridge and see if I can get phone service so we can get a chopper up here," Colonel said.

"I've never had phone service in this area. Get my horse, help me in the saddle and we can make the call when we get close to the line shack."

"I don't think you can ride with that broken foot."

"If you two can get can me in the saddle, I can ride. Tie the boot to the stirrup so it doesn't flop around. I won't put any weight on it."

"Damn it, John. It's going to hurt like hell bouncing around in that saddle like that."

"Quit saying that. I know it's going to hurt, but we'll take it easy. Help me off this mountain before I pass out and you can't help me!"

I got John's horse while Colonel helped him to his feet. John wrapped his arm around Colonel's neck to help support the broken leg to keep pressure off of it. They limped to the horse and Colonel helped him stand on a large flat rock so he could help him mount his horse. He helped lift John by his good leg as John pulled with his arms. Once he had his good leg up in the stirrup, Colonel slowly lifted his broken foot over the saddle. I knew this caused a lot of pain but it couldn't be helped. John took several deep breaths. The bandage on his arm started dripping blood. Colonel readjusted the bandage and tightened it, then removed his jacket and used it as padding to tie John's leg to the stirrup.

"Don't fall out of that saddle, John. If you do, you'll be hanging from your broken leg and it'll cause a lot more damage, especially if your horse spooks. If you feel faint, or start to pass out, let us know. I'll either climb up there with you or walk your horse."

John said, "Give me that canteen and get on your horse before I leave you here. Andy, can you get my rifle?"

I retrieved the rifle and slid it into the scabbard on my horse. We mounted up and Colonel started to take John's reins.

"I got it, damn it! Lead me out of here."

We slowly worked our way off the mountain. Every step of the horse had to shoot pain down John's leg. The bleeding from the arm dripped blood from his elbow. Colonel stopped twice to adjust the bandage. John started turning pale from blood loss as we neared the bottom. I felt it was only a matter of time before he went into shock.

Dark clouds had eased their way down the mountain and the air smelled of rain. It got colder with every step and the wind was picking up as we neared the shack.

The line shack came into view as we topped the ridge and so did the bars on Colonel's cell phone. He called the Clarksville Police Department and explained what had happened. An ambulance was dispatched and it wasn't long before we could see the flashing lights and dust trail as it pushed its way up the mountain. The ground flattened out and Colonel rode on one side of John with me on the other side to help support him so he wouldn't fall.

Ominous clouds hovered above us and the wind became eerily still. By the time we got to the truck, we could hear the sirens. Another dust trail followed the ambulance and Colonel recognized it as his truck. "Donna must be following the ambulance up the mountain."

I gave John water but he remained in the saddle until help arrived. It started raining. John's wife was almost pushing the ambulance up the mountain as they pulled up next to the line shack.

Donna ran to John's side with tears streaming down her cheeks. He looked down and smiled, "Hey, Honey, stop crying, I'll be alright."

"Oh, John, I love you," was all she could say.

The ambulance crew gave John a shot for his pain and helped us lift him off his horse. They loaded him on a gurney and slid him into the ambulance. One medic dressed the injured arm while the other started an IV. They didn't remove his boot. It helped to support the broken ankle. As the doors to the ambulance were being closed, Donna jumped inside to be with John on the way to the hospital.

As the ambulance pulled away, Chief Baker and Dad pulled up in an unmarked police car. Colonel briefed them about the cougar attack and the accident. Satisfied no crime had occurred, Chief Baker asked him to stop by the office sometime in the next day or two for a written statement for the report.

Colonel asked me to drive his truck back to the Double J ranch. We loaded the horses into the trailer and drove back to the ranch. After unloading them in the rain, I removed their saddles. Colonel grabbed the remaining pie and his thermos and headed to the hospital. I drove home a little sore and disappointed about my first cattle drive.

CHAPTER FIVE

M om entered the kitchen as I finished breakfast. "Morning, Honey. How'd you sleep?"

"Not good. What was that God-awful noise that kept waking me up?"

"Neighbor's rooster. They do that."

"Yeah, well if he keeps it up, we'll be having chicken for dinner!"

"You'll get used to it. People who live next to train tracks will tell you they don't even notice the trains after a while."

"I sure hope so."

"What have you got planned for the rest of today?" Mom asked.

"Do you need help unpacking these boxes?"

"No. I haven't decided where I'm going to put everything yet."

"It is a beautiful day and I need some exercise. I think I'll take a run up the road."

Mom looked at me like I was nuts. "You're kidding, right? You can't need exercise after riding all day yesterday."

"I need to run some of the kinks out. I'm not used to riding horses. What are you going to do?"

"I'm thinking about going for a horseback ride myself. Maybe I'll see you on the road."

As soon as the pavement ended the road turned to dirt. A sign announced I was entering the Coronado National Forest. It wasn't much of a forest at this level, mostly rangeland where a few cattle could be seen grazing in the distance. The road ran slightly uphill curving gently back and forth with the general direction heading south towards the Pinaleno Mountains. It was the same road I was on yesterday morning but it looked different now that it was light and I was on foot.

The clean air and higher altitude felt great in my lungs. I picked up the pace. About a mile in, a truck approached from the opposite direction. I crossed over to the right side of the road to avoid the dust. The truck slowed as it passed and a man in his late 40s or early 50s wearing a white straw hat waved and I waved back. The truck was a new Ford Kings Ranch edition and had a black horse rearing up painted on the side with a sign that read: *The Diablo Ranch.*

I came to the first ranch and stopped to admire it. It had large poles supporting an oversized front porch looking more like a small resort than a ranch. A sign that read, *Diablo Ranch Quarter Horses* hung above closed gates. A life-size statue of a black stallion rearing up on his hind legs was mounted to the left of the gate, and a life-size man on a horse roping a calf stood on the other side of the gate. Whoever owned this place obviously had money.

A long metal barn sat back from house and had the doors opened at both ends. It had at least 15 stalls on each side with a wash rack located at this end. Several horses had their heads sticking out of the stalls. Beyond the barn were grass pastures.

A big black stallion was in one of the pastures behind the old barn. He was prancing around with his head and tail held high. He reminded me of Black Beauty except he had a white blaze on his forehead and one white stocking. He was truly a magnificent animal.

A woman I hadn't seen at first sat in the shadows of the porch. She stood up and walked out to the edge staring at me. I waved and started to go on when the woman yelled, "Who are you?"

"I'm Andy Hanson. I just moved in down the road."

The woman's smile disappeared and she slowly lowered her arm. Her head sank to her chest. She walked back to the wood swing and sat down. I waved again but she didn't acknowledge me. I continued on my way.

The ranch next door had a sign hanging above two wood poles framing the driveway that read, *Double J Ranch.* This was John Stevenson's ranch. I wondered if he was home from the hospital yet. His ranch was more of the typical type of working ranch I expected to find in this country. The front yard had a white wood fence. Two large oak trees shaded a front porch with a hanging swing and several chairs and tables. A white sign hung on the front gate that read, *Welcome.* A stone sidewalk led up to the house and the mailbox had the name Stevenson painted on it.

The red wood barn stood behind the house. Two wooden doors swung outward and both were open to let the air flow through.

A long lean-to-type garage with a tin roof sat on the south side of the property house facing the barn. A riding mower, a tractor and other farm equipment was parked inside the garage. Attached to one end of the garage was a building that appeared to be a workshop or tack room.

An old gray truck was parked under a tarp at this end of the garage. I was surprised I hadn't noticed it yesterday. I could only see the front grill, bumper and part of the front fenders. From the shape of the grill, I believed it was either a 1955 or `56 Ford. Dad and I had talked about fixing up an old truck like this someday and I thought I might have just located it.

A big red retriever dog greeted me with his head down wagging his tail as I walked through the gate. I patted the dog, walked onto the porch and rang the doorbell. Donna Stevenson answered the door. She looked to be in her late 20s or early 30s. She wore jeans, cowboy boots, an oversized cowgirl belt buckle, and a western shirt. Her hair was pulled back into a ponytail and she had very dark green sparkling eyes. She was strikingly beautiful. "Hello, how can I help you?"

"Hi, I'm Andy Hanson. My family just moved into the second house down the road. I was with your husband yesterday when the cougar jumped him. I was wondering how he's doing,"

"Oh, yes. I'm sorry I didn't recognize you. Come on in, Andy. You can ask him yourself. He's resting in the family room."

"Thank you," I said as I, and the dog stepped inside. She led me into a large family room with high ceilings with exposed wood beams and an oversized rock fireplace at the far end. The room was warm and inviting.

Several deer, elk and javelina heads were mounted on the walls and a mountain lion skin rug adorned the floor in front of the fireplace. Large paintings of cowboys, cattle and horses decorated the walls. John was sitting in a big overstuffed leather chair close to the fireplace. He had a bandage on his left arm and his foot was in a cast propped up on the footstool in front of him. A set of crutches leaned against a TV tray next to his chair. He turned off the TV with a remote as I walked in.

"John, Andy Hanson came to see you. His parents bought the Miller's place down the road."

He looked me over while folding his newspaper. "Sorry for not getting up, Andy." He offered me his hand. "Thanks for all your help yesterday."

I crossed the room and shook his strong calloused hands.

"Pull up a chair," he said.

"Would you like a glass of water or iced tea?" asked Mrs. Stevenson. "You look like you need it."

"Thanks, Mrs. Stevenson. Water would be great."

"Please call me Donna," she said as she turned towards the kitchen.

Turning my attention to Mr. Stevenson, I asked, "How are you feeling?"

"Much better. They gave me some strong pain pills. What brings you a way out here?"

"I was jogging by and noticed that old truck parked back next to your barn and was wondering if it was for sale?"

"That was my farther-in-law's truck," Donna said as she returned from the kitchen and handed me the glass of water. "John pulled it in here a few of years ago after his father passed away."

John looked at his wife but didn't mention the truck. "Andy, tell your dad thanks for us will you? I didn't get a chance to meet him yesterday. Ask him to stop by for a visit if he gets a chance."

"I sure will, sir," I replied as I took the water. "What did the doctor say?"

"Darn lion got my arm, but that wasn't the worst part. My ankle is broken. I'm afraid I'll be laid up for a spell."

"That's too bad. If you need any help around here while you're hurt, don't hesitate to call. I'll leave my number."

"Thanks Andy. I may just take you up on that. Know anything about ranching"

I shook my head, "Not much."

Mr. Stevenson paused and rubbed his chin. "So you think you might want that old truck, do you?"

"My dad and I have been looking for one for a year or two. It's a `55 Ford isn't it?"

"You know your trucks, Andy. It's `56 but there isn't much difference in the two. It has that big wrap around rear window.

Can you believe that was only a twelve dollar option in the 1956 model?"

"I didn't know that, sir. What a deal."

"I'm not even sure if it runs anymore. It was blowing smoke when I parked it and I'm sure the tires are shot. The upholstery isn't in good shape either. What would you do with the old truck anyway?"

"My dad and I would work on it together as a father-son project. We would make it look and run like new."

"That's quite a project."

"Sure is. Dad's real good with mechanical things and I'm going to study mechanical engineering in college. I'm sure we can do it."

Mr. Stevenson rubbed his chin as he studied me. "Well, I hadn't thought much about selling it, being it was my father's. What do think it's worth?"

"I'm not sure," I replied. "Those old trucks are getting harder and harder to find every year, especially if they aren't all rusted out."

"I had a guy stop by here last year and offer me fifteen hundred for it."

"I think he was lowballing you, Mr. Stevenson, they're worth at least twenty five hundred or even more."

He looked at his wife for a few seconds and took a deep breath. "Why don't you go remove the tarp and have a look at it, Andy? Give it some thought and make sure it's what you're looking for. If you make up your mind you want it, we'll talk price."

"Yes Sir!" I hurried out the rear door and ran to the truck. I could see Donna watching me from the kitchen window as I pulled the tarp off. The truck's paint was faded and it looked lonely sitting there with flat tires, but in my mind, it was all new and shiny. It was beautiful. I covered it back up after a few minutes and returned to the rear door and knocked. "Come on in," yelled Donna, "It's unlocked."

I walked over to Mr. Stevenson. "It's all there, very little rust and almost no dents. The bumpers and tailgate are in great shape and there's no broken glass. I'd like to buy it if it is for sale."

"So, do you think it's worth twenty five hundred, do you?"

"That's more than fair, sir. I'll have to talk to my dad first but I'm sure he'll say it's all right."

"I'll tell you what, Andy. I'm going to need some help around the ranch, being laid up with this broken foot and all. If you're willing to work it off for ten dollars an hour, I'll sell it to you for two thousand dollars."

I couldn't keep the grin off my face. "That's even better yet! That way I can keep the money I've saved to help fix it up. Thanks, Mr. Stevenson."

"Deal then, but please call me John. You're making me feel old. Mr. Stevenson was my father." John held out his hand and we shook.

"Yes sir, I mean, John. And thanks a lot! I can work every day after school and on Saturdays and Sunday afternoons. We go to church on Sunday mornings and I need to be done by 4:00 p.m. on Saturdays so I can get to the high school for weight training. When do you want me to start?"

"Weight training? Are you a football player?" he asked.

"Yes sir...I mean, John."

"That team could use some help. They stunk this year."

I smiled, "We'll do our best next year. When would you like me to be here?"

"Then it's settled." John said. "Be here at 5:00 a.m. tomorrow morning since it's Saturday? We seldom work on Sundays, except for round-ups."

"I'll be here!" I replied as I headed to the door. "I can't wait to tell my Dad about the truck."

Mrs. Stevenson walked me to the front door and yelled good-bye as I hurried out to the gate. I stopped and yelled back. "If you see a blond haired woman riding a palomino come by here, that's my mom. Her name is Sherrie."

"I'll look for her!" Donna yelled.

I couldn't wait to start working on the old truck. I hoped I could have it paid for by mid summer. The lady sitting on the porch at the Diablo Ranch wasn't there when I passed. I saw Mom riding towards me and a white truck approaching her from the rear. The truck slowed as it passed her then picked up speed again. It slowed again to pass me. I recognized the driver as the girl I had seen at Skeeter's. I waved, she didn't. Realizing I was looking at a much younger version of Donna Stevenson, I looked back for a second look.

Not paying attention to where I was running, I angled off the road, tripped and fell into the mud and bushes in the bar ditch. When I stood up, I had mud and weeds all over my face and arms and in my hair. The girl in the truck had come to a complete stop. She was laughing while watching me from her side mirror. She waved out of her window as she sped up and drove away.

The only thing injured was my pride. I felt like a complete idiot. You only get one chance at a first impression and that wasn't the one I was hoping for. I wondered if the new job might turn out better than I anticipated.

Mom galloped up on her horse. "Andy, are you all right?"

"Yeah, I'm fine."

"What was that all about? You're going to break your neck."

"I don't have a clue, Mom. Guess what? I found an old truck at the Double J Ranch down the road. I bought it and I'm going to work the payments off at the ranch. Isn't that great?" I jogged off towards the house before she had a chance to reply. I yelled back, "I've got to go tell Dad! Bye, Mom!"

She smiled and shook her head. When I looked back again, she was riding away from me. I wondered if she would meet the girl from Skeeter's.

CHAPTER SIX

D ad wasn't home when I got there. I went to the barn to make
sure we had room to put the truck so we could work on it.
There was plenty of room where the farm equipment used to be. I
went back in the house and waited until Mom came home.

"Did you meet Mrs. Stevenson?" I asked.

"Yes I did, and her husband and daughter too. They were very
nice. Did you get a chance to meet their daughter, Andy?"

"No. I didn't know they had a daughter when I was there. I
think she was the girl driving the truck when I fell into the ditch."

Mom grinned. "Well, that explains a lot."

"No, Mom. It was just that she looked just like Mrs. Stevenson.
I did a double take, that's all."

Mom kept grinning and nodding her head. "Yeah, right. I guess
you didn't notice that she is a very pretty young lady."

Mom stood grinning while waiting for an answer but I couldn't
think of one.

"Mrs. Stevenson said you were on your best behavior. They
seemed to liked you."

"I liked them too. What do you know about their daughter?" I asked.

Mom raiscd her eyebrows. "Well, now you're curious. Let's see. She's a junior in high school, competes in barrel racing, and gets good grades."

"Is that all?"

"No, she's an only child, like you. I got the impression she was kind of shy. She was working her horse in the round pen while we visited. She didn't talk much. Her mom told me her best friend got killed three years ago. His name was Bobby Patterson and he was like a brother to her. He lived next door at that other ranch. Her mom claims her daughter hasn't been the same since."

I recognized the name Bobby Patterson from the photos on the wall in the football office. "How was he killed?"

"Murdered. Someone shot him when he was up in the mountains." I remembered the flowers at the line shack and what Colonel had told me.

"Wow! That's weird. I wonder who killed him and if Dad's looking into it?"

"I doubt it. I've never heard him mention anything about an unsolved murder."

"I saw Bobby Patterson's photo on the wall at the gym. He was a football player. Two other photos of other football players were on the wall with his."

"What happened to the other two?" she asked.

"I don't know. Did her mom say anything else about her daughter?"

"Yes. Mrs. Stevenson told me a funny story about her daughter if you want to hear it."

"Sure."

"When Peaches was a little girl, the only girl toys she ever played with were Barbie dolls that her grandmother gave her."

"Who's Peaches?"

"Donna's daughter. That's her name."

"You're kidding me, right?"

"No, that's what her mother called her. I think that's her name. Anyway, Peaches insisted on dressing Barbie in cowgirl clothes that her grandmother made for her. Her father carved her a wooden horse and Peaches played Barbie rodeo in the back yard."

"Barbie rodeo?"

"Yes, you know, like you playing war with your toy soldiers. Anyway, one day she was playing Barbie rodeo and her mother called her in for lunch. After lunch, she asked if she could have some lettuce for her pet lizard. Her mom gave her some lettuce and she went back outside to play. Donna started wondering what kind of lizard she had and went outside to take a look. Peaches had a Gila monster dressed in Barbie doll clothes inside her dollhouse. Donna screamed, slammed the door shut on the dollhouse and took Peaches inside to check her for bites. Fortunately, she hadn't been bitten."

"Oh my God, that must have been scared her half to death!"

"Donna said she almost had a heart attack. When Mr. Stevenson and Colonel Lightfoot got home, she told them what had happened. They didn't believe her. They went out and opened the dollhouse and the Gila monster hissed at them. They slammed the door shut and took the doll house out into the desert and turned the Gila monster loose."

"Wow, that's scary." I said.

"The funniest part was later that evening when John and Colonel were sitting on the front porch having a beer and laughing like a couple of schoolboys. Donna asked them what was so funny. They had seen a couple of hikers walking down by the creek. They could just imagine the hikers trying to convince the people in town that they found a Gila monster dressed in drag.

"That's funny. But I still can't believe her name is Peaches."

Mom thought for a moment. "We weren't formally introduced, but that's what Donna called her. I think that's her name."

I had a hard time thinking anyone would name their daughter Peaches. I hoped to meet her tomorrow.

CHAPTER SEVEN

The rooster began rehearsing his obituary at 4:15 in the morning. Remembering my new job, I fought the urge to go back to sleep. Forcing myself out of bed, I crawled into the shower. I've never been a morning person. It was still dark when I zombie-walked into the kitchen. It didn't surprise me to find Dad sitting at the table drinking coffee and reading the newspaper. He's always been an early riser. What did surprise me was the breakfast he had made.

"Morning, Son. How did you sleep?"

"Not good. That rooster kept me up again." I yawned. "Why are you up so early?"

"I want to get to my office and set it up. And I need to read some reports. Chief Baker seems to enjoy wasting my time by introducing me to the local businessmen, ranchers and politicians."

I pointed to the breakfast. "For me?"

"Yep."

"Thanks, I didn't expect this."

"I thought you might get hungry with that new job. Do you know what you'll be doing today?"

"Don't know yet. I have to meet Colonel Lightfoot this morning. He'll let me know what we're doing."

Dad folded his paper and headed for the door. "Have a great day and make your mother proud."

"How about you, Dad? Don't you want me to make you proud too?"

He stopped at the door, looked back and smiled. "I'm always proud of you, Son."

I smiled back. "Thanks, Dad. When are you going to stop and see the truck and meet Mr. and Mrs. Stevenson?"

"Get their number and I'll call to make an appointment."

"Okay, have a good day!"

The ranch was only five minutes away and I had 15 minutes to get there. I didn't want to be late. The lights were out in the farmhouse when I got there but a dust-to-dawn security light lit up the barn and garage area. I parked next to the barn and turned off the engine. The Stevenson's dog barked a couple of times and came to investigate. He approached cautiously with his head down and tail wagging. "Hey boy, remember me?" I bent down and let the dog smell my hand and then rubbed him behind the ears, "Good boy." He responded by jumping up and licking my face.

The white ford truck the girl had been driving yesterday was parked in the garage next to the tractor. I walked over to the `56 Ford and started looking at it when I heard the sound of a vehicle approaching on the dirt road. Colonel's truck pulled into the driveway and stopped next to my car. Colonel Lightfoot sat inside drinking coffee and eating something. He rolled the window down and turned his truck off. "I heard you're the new hired hand."

"That's right."

"Want some coffee?

"No thanks."

"A piece of pie?"

"No, I've already had breakfast."

Colonel sat there for a few minutes. When he finished his pie, he took his thermos and pored himself another cup. "I expected you to be late. Sure you don't want some coffee?"

"No, I don't drink coffee very often."

Colonel Lightfoot stepped out of the truck. He looked more like an Indian than a solider. But not like any Indian I'd ever seen before. His cowboy hat had a snakeskin hatband with a feather on the side. His jeans were tucked inside his high-top cowboy boots and the upper half of the boots had colorful Indian designs. He had a thick head of salt and pepper hair, light grayish-blue eyes, and he was tall and thin. He had a hard looking face and a gentle smile.

"I heard you want to be a rancher."

I shook my head and laughed. "I don't want to be a rancher. But I do want that old truck and I'm willing to work for it."

"What do you have against ranchers?"

"Nothing sir. But I want to be an engineer. I'm trying to get into one of the military academies."

Colonel studied me for a minute rubbing his chin. "Military academy, huh? Those are not easy schools to get into you know. Few make it." He paused for a moment. "Call me Colonel."

He reached into his truck and removed the remaining pie off the seat and took it into the barn. I followed him. He put the pie in a refrigerator and walked over to the stalls. A reddish- colored sorrel greeted him and he rubbed her between the ears and on the forehead. "Good morning, Ruby."

He walked to the next stall and greeted another horse he called, Santana. He rubbed her forehead. "How are you this morning, old girl?" Entering the stall he lifted one of her legs and looked at the hoof. "You're going to need a new set of shoes soon, Santana."

"What branch of the service were you in, Colonel? I asked.

He sat the hoof down and turned to look at me. "Army. I was in the U.S. Army during the Vietnam war."

"When did you retire?"

"I didn't retire. I was only in for two years."

"Two years? You can't make colonel in two years."

"I didn't. Colonel is my God-given name, Colonel Lightfoot."

"Oh, I thought you were a real colonel."

He grinned, "Well, I was the highest ranking private and the lowest paid colonel in the whole Army."

I chuckled. "Are you Native American? If you don't mind me asking."

He stretched to his full height and raised his chin. "I'm Choctaw. Full-blooded Choctaw!"

"I've never heard of a Choctaw before except maybe in the movies. I thought there were extinct."

"They are. I'm the last one," he said.

"Where did they come from?"

"We were originally in the southeastern part of United States but were relocated to the Oklahoma Territory."

I wasn't sure if he was pulling my leg or not but decided to let it lay. I'd look it up on the computer when I got home. "What are we going to do today?" I asked as we walked outside.

He looked up at the sky. "We were going to ride up in the mountains and find those lost cows. Maybe fix a broken fence or two, but we can't do that now."

"Why not, that sounds like fun?"

He frowned. "That's not fun, kid. That's hard work." He turned and faced northwest and pointed at the horizon. "See that dark line of clouds between those peaks?"

I followed his gaze. "Yeah, what about it?"

"Rain, Andy. It's going to rain today." He said with the conviction of a preacher quoting the Bible.

There wasn't a cloud in the sky. "How do you know it's going to rain?"

He lifted his chin higher and stared at the horizon. "Indians knows these things. It will be pleasant until about noon then the wind will pick up. It will turn cold this afternoon and rain. We could get a little snow tonight."

I still wasn't sure if he was kidding or not but he sure acted as if he knew what he was talking about. "So, what are we going to do?"

"We're going to get that load of hay stored in the barn before it gets wet. That's what we'll do." Tossing me a pair of leather gloves, he said, "Time to get to work kid."

Colonel brought the tractor around with a large pallet on the forks. He drove the tractor to a large stack of hay and we loaded bails of hay onto the pallet. When the pallet was loaded, he told me to go inside the barn and climb up into the loft. He lifted the hay up to the opening in the loft from the outside. I unloaded the hay and stacked it to one side. I climbed onto the empty pallet and Colonel lowered me back down and drove back to the haystack. We repeated the process for the next four hours until all the hay was in the barn.

"That didn't take long," Colonel said. "Looks like you've stacked hay before."

"My parents have horses, remember."

"Yeah, I forgot. We're going to need some hay next to the stalls. Can you throw eight bales down and stack them next to the four stalls that have horses in them? I need to go see John."

"Sure," I answered as Colonel headed towards the house.

I climbed up in the loft. It was warm and stuffy. I had worked up quite a sweat and the wind and cooler weather Colonel spoke about hadn't showed up yet. After removing my shirt, I hung it on a nail. I moved eight bales to the opening of the loft near the center of the barn. Glistening with sweat I looked down to make sure no one was below me. I tossed a bail of hay down. Just as it hit the ground, I heard a woman scream. "Hey, watch it nitwit! You're going to kill somebody!"

I looked down but couldn't see anyone. "Sorry! I didn't see you."

The girl from Skeeter's stepped into view and glared up at me. "Sorry my ass! You're supposed to yell 'clear' before throwing any-thing from the loft!"

Her hands were on her hips, her nose was wrinkled and her eyes narrowed. Her long auburn hair was in a ponytail with a green ribbon that matched her sparkling eyes. She was the spitting image of her mother. Her faded jeans had holes in them and she wore cowboy boots. Her blue western shirt had the two top buttons undone and was tied around her waist. She wasn't wearing a bra.

She realized she was exposing herself and moved closer to the horses so she could get a better look at me. "Who are you and what are you doing in my barn?" she said as she buttoned her blouse.

"I'm Andy Hanson, I work for your dad."

She crossed her arms and tilted her head to one side. "Since when? I've never seen you around here before."

"You saw me yesterday running on the road. My family just moved here from Mesa. We bought the Miller's place down the road."

The girl was silent for moment, and then smiled. "Oh yes, I re-member you. You're the dummy that ran into the ditch."

I probably shouldn't have reminded her of that. I smiled but didn't reply.

"Why would my father hire a flatlander to work on a ranch? I bet you don't know anything about ranching," she scolded.

"Not much, but I learn quick."

"Waste of good money if you ask me."

"I'm not getting paid. I'm working for that old truck your dad has parked next to the shop."

"Oh my God." She said shaking her head, "You're even dumber than you look. Who in their right mind would want that piece of junk? You're another dumb jock football player, aren't you?"

"Obviously, you don't know me."

"And I don't want to either." She poked her nose in the air, walked over and retrieved the pie Colonel had left I the refrigerator. "Don't get to close to these horses, they bite!" she said sarcastically before turning back towards the house.

It wasn't my nature to avoid conflict, physical or mental. I watched her heart shaped ass strut towards the house. Determined to get the last word, I yelled, "Looks like the only thing that bites around here is you!" I was sure she heard but she didn't acknowledge me.

As soon as she left the barn, Colonel walked in grinning from ear to ear. "I see you've met Peaches."

"Peaches my ass. More like persimmons, if you ask me."

"What was she in a fuss about?" asked Colonel.

"I almost hit her with a bale of hay and she chewed my ass."

He laughed. "You startled her, that's all. Give her time; she doesn't warm up to strangers easily. As a matter of fact, she doesn't warm up to most boys at all."

"I don't think she has any intentions of warming up. She's as cold as polar bears paws."

Colonel laughed, "If you want to make up to a woman, take her flowers, say you're sorry and ask for forgiven. It works every time, even if you don't mean it."

"Why do women always want flowers anyway?" I asked.

"Because they are singled mined and emotionally driven."

"She didn't look singled-minded to me, just emotional."

"You should apologize anyway."

"Why should I?"

"Because she makes our lunches."

"Oh, good point."

He nodded. "It'll make you feel better."

"How do you know?"

"Believe me, Indians know these things."

I saw Peaches going back to the barn while we were in the shop. Colonel walked behind the shop, picked a hand-full of wild flowers and handed them to me. "Here, take these to her, apologize and all will be forgotten. You'll thank me later."

I didn't want to apologize but I was getting hungry and thought it best. I took the flowers and walked back into the barn. She had changed into a new pair of jeans and a light jacket. She was coming out of a stall with the reddish-colored mare named Ruby as I walked in. She stopped when she saw me.

"Can I offer you a peace offering? We didn't get off to a very good start this morning. I'm sorry I frightened you."

She eyed me for a moment, paused and took the flowers. "No we didn't." She looked at the flowers. "I guess I was pretty hard on you."

"Thanks, Peaches. I... "

She cut me off mid sentence, "Peaches! Who told you to call me Peaches? Don't every call me that again. My name is Shayla." She threw the flowers in my face and stomped out of the barn pulling the horse behind her. I exited the barn brushing petals and leaves out of my hair.

"You sure have a way with women, Andy!" Colonel said grinning from ear to ear.

"Yeah, well I wouldn't start a dating service if I were you. Why didn't you tell me her name was Shayla?"

"I thought you knew her name. Peaches is a nick-name her father and I gave her as a kid." Colonel slapped his leg, laughing as he walked back into the shop. I watched Shayla load the horse into a trailer and drive away.

"What do we do now, Colonel?"

"We're going to go up to the water tank and try to plug a leak. Water is coming out faster than it goes in. The Stevenson's don't have much water pressure."

We gathered tools for the repair and a tube of silicone. Colonel handed me a sheet of aluminum and a rivet gun. The water tank was located south west of the ranch about two hundred yards up-hill. It had a cast iron pipe at the top with water flowing into the tank. Another pipe came out of the bottom of the tank that ran downhill towards the ranch. Colonel asked me to follow the top pipe further up the hill to a spring and shut the valve off to stop the water flow.

After I shut the valve, Colonel opened the bottom valve and drained the tank. "I don't know how many times I'm going to be able to keep patching this." Colonel said. "It won't be long before I'll be putting patches on top of patches. The water pressure is so low the Stevenson's have to run around in the shower just to get wet."

The thought of Shayla running around naked in the shower made me grin.

"What are you smiling about, Boy? Get your mind out of the gutter."

Colonel drilled four holes in the tank while I cut a patch from the aluminum sheeting. He put silicone on the patch and riveted it in place. We repeated the process several times.

"Let's leave the tools here and go grab some lunch, Andy, while the silicone dries. By the time we get back, it should be dry and we should be able to fill the tank back up."

"Sounds good to me, I'm starved."

Donna had lunch waiting for us. I didn't see Shayla and wondered if she was running around in the shower trying to get wet. She'd have a long way to run with a drained tank.

"What are you smiling about, Andy?"

"Nothing, just thought of something funny."

After lunch, we finished fixing the tank and filled it back up with water. We fixed a sagging gate and tightened some wire fencing. I didn't see Shayla the rest of the day. But I couldn't get her out of my mind.

CHAPTER EIGHT

J ared and I sat in the cold parking lot waiting for the bell to
ring. We were early and class wouldn't start for another 15 minutes. The main building looked like a dinosaur that didn't know it
was extinct. Most of the people entering it appeared to be teachers
or employees. I wasn't looking forward to my first day of school at
Clarksville High. It was just something I had to do.

For some unknown reason, Jared felt obligated to be my guide
for the day, as if I would be lost without him. He hadn't stopped
talking since I picked him up this morning. He told me he would
introduce me to all the good-looking girls and let me know which
ones had boyfriends and which ones were available. I wasn't sure
why he thought this was the most important information I should
know on my first day at a new school, but he did. "Jared," I said to
get him to stop talking, "the first thing I have to do is go see a guid-
ance counselor named Miss Rigby, to get registered."

" She's a nice lady. You'll like her." He then continued to tell
me everything he thought important for me to know about my new
school. None of which was on my priority list for day one.

"We have some codes at school you need to be aware of and you can never tell any of the girls. One is emerson."

"Who is Emerson?"

"Emerson stands for "em-r-some nice tits!"

"Jared, I don't think I will be using that expression to describe girls."

"That's cool. Just wanted you to know what it means when you hear it. You know, so you can be on the lookout."

As we sat watching other students arrive, I saw a kid get out of a car, kiss his mother on her cheek and start walking into the school. He had a backpack with the name ALEX sewn on the back in big letters. He was tall, thin and had bad posture. His glasses were so thick you could have started a fire with them. His black slacks were too short and his white socks showed above his black shiny shoes. He had his shirt bottomed all the way up and his out-of-date tie seemed to be choking him. Curly brown hair framed a bad complexion around the boy's bony face. Nature hadn't been kind to Alex. He carried enough books in his backpack to start his own library.

"You don't see that every day," I said.

"See what?"

"That kid," I said pointing to Alex. "Who's is he?"

"Oh, that's Alex. He's a nerd. But real smart."

I watched him walk up the stairs and another kid slapped him on the back of the head as he walked pass. The kid that slapped him and another boy started laughing. Alex continued walking with his head down. It was obvious Alex was used to being bullied.

Jared looked at his watch. "We better get in there, the bell is going to ring in a few minutes. We started towards the front door when Jared nudged me in the ribs. "Emerson."

Several girls were standing on the lawn in front of us talking and we walked up to them. One of the girls was definitely an *emerson* in Jared's book and she was obviously proud of them.

"Hi ladies." Jared said with a big smile on his face. "Let me introduce you to a new student. This is Andy Hanson. This is his first day at Clarksville High." He said as if he were introducing a prize-fighter at a championship fight. "Andy, this is Stacey Miller, Kelsey Garner and Cricket Pilone. Three of the prettiest girls in town."

The girls seemed immune to Jared's bullshit, but he was right, they were all good- looking. Stacey Miller was a natural blond, tall, thin and athletic-looking. Kelsey Gardner looked like a dancer. Cricket Pilone was the 'emerson' Jared had described earlier. She wore a revealing sundress short enough to accent her long legs and a white coat with a white fur collar. It opened in the front revealing her glowing cleavage. She had blue eyes and blond hair that may or may not have been her real color. All three girls smiled and said hello.

"Welcomed to Clarksville High, Andy," said Cricket with grin on her face while batting her eyelids. Kelsey and Stacey just said "Hi." Neither seemed impressed.

"Nice to meet you," I said as Jared and I started to leave.

"Glad to meet you, Andy Handsome," Cricket said.

Jared, Kelsey and Stacey started laughing. I could feel my face getting flushed. "It's Hanson; Andy Hanson." I said over my shoulder.

Cricket smiled, "Oh, I must have been mistaken. See you later, Andy." All three girls were giggling as we turned to leave.

We walked into the main building. I saw Alex at his locker about half way down the main hall. The two boys I'd seen earlier were making a nuisance of themselves teasing him. One was messing up his hair and the other one was flipping Alex on the ear. As we approached them, one of the boys took Alex's book. Alex tried to get the book back but the kid wouldn't give it to him.

"Give him the book," I said as I walked up to them. The boy looked at me but didn't respond. "I don't want to tell you again, give Alex his book back."

That got their attention and the boy handed the book back to Alex.

"Now apologize."

The boy looked at his friend and back at me. Neither boy was half my size. "Sorry, Alex, we were just kidding around."

"Yeah, just fooling around, that's all," said the other boy as they walked away.

I turned to Alex. "Hi, Alex. I'm Andy Hanson."

He didn't make eye contact. "Thanks," he said. He turned to leave as if he were in a big hurry. When he got to the end of the hall he turned and glanced back at me. He waved and disappeared around the corner. Alex may have become accustomed to being picked on, but he wasn't used to having someone stand up for him.

As I turned to go to the office, I noticed a man in a shirt and tie with his arms folded across his chest at the end of the hallway staring at us. "Go up those stairs and make a right." Jared said. "Mrs. Rigby's office is right down the hall." He turned the other direction and left for class.

I walked up the stairs and found Mrs. Rigby's office. She was talking on the phone when I arrived so I stood in the hall waiting for her to finish. The man in a shirt and tie from downstairs came up to me. "Who are you and why aren't you in class young man?"

"I'm Andrew Hanson." I said as I stuck my hand out. "I'm here to see Mrs. Rigby about signing up for classes. I'm transferring from Superstition Mountain High School in Mesa."

The man paused for a moment and then shook my hand. "I'm Henry Rudd, the Principal. I heard we were getting a new transfer. Welcome to Clarksville High School."

"Thanks."

"Have you met Coach Ford yet?"

"Yes, sir. I stopped by and introduced myself."

"Are you going to be our new quarterback?"

"I'm not sure. I'll play where Coach Fords wants me to play."

He nodded his head. "I like that attitude, just keep your nose clean. I run a tight ship around here."

"Yes sir."

"I see Mrs. Rigby is off the phone. I'll see you around."

Mr. Rudd left and Mrs. Rigby motioned me into her office. "Hi Andy, I'm Mrs. Rigby."

We shook hands and she offered me a seat.

"Andy, I got you records from Superstition Mountain High School and must say, I'm impressed. Your grade point average is very impressive. I'm going to have to check the rules, but I think you might be in contention for valedictorian next year."

"Valedictorian?"

" Yes. You will be competing with Alex Dehaan and Shayla Stevenson."

That got my attention. "What do you mean check the rules?"

"Well, it used to be the student with the highest grade average was the valedictorian. Some kids who knew they weren't going to be valedictorian at one school would change to another school their senior year so they could be valedictorian at that school. The school district changed the rules so students have to have attended the same school for more than one year to be eligible for the valedictorian award. Since you transferred halfway through your junior year, you still may be eligible for the award."

"Mrs. Rigby, I don't think it would be fair for me to be the valedictorian at Clarksville High. These students have gone here all four years. I wouldn't want to be considered for the award."

"That's considerate of you, Andy, but you don't understand. If you are the valedictorian, you get extra money for college scholarships."

"I wouldn't have been valedictorian at Superstition Mountain High School if I had stayed there, and I don't want it here. Please, let someone else have that honor. They deserve it, not me."

"But what about scholarships, Andy. Don't you want them?"

"No ma'am. I'm trying to get into one of the military academies. Grades are important, but they pay for everything and I won't need a scholarship."

"All right then. I'll make sure your name doesn't come up for the valedictorian award if you're sure you don't want it. But let me know if you change your mind. I'll check the rules for you just in case."

"Thanks, Mrs. Rigby. Do you know what classes I need to take?"

"Well, looking at the credits you've already taken, you won't have to take many this year. You've already taken so many accelerated classes you wouldn't have to attend Clarksville the rest of the year if you don't want to. Clarksville doesn't have many accelerated classes like Superstition High School does. You'll probably get bored here. Of course, you can take as many electives classes as you want."

"I need to finish the year at Clarksville. If I am correct, I have to be attending a certain amount of classes this year to be eligible to play football next year."

"That's correct. You'll need a full load to play sports. I'll put you in sixth hour physical education so you play football. We only have two math classes you haven't taken, but it appears you skipped them to take higher AP college classes. You'll still need them here because they are required for graduation. I'll put you in Mr. Payne's third hour class, room 108. He's very good."

"That sounds good."

"I'm not sure what other classes you want to take, Andy. You've already met most of the other requirements to graduate. I'll give you a list of elective classes and you can choose which ones you want. Think about it and come back tomorrow. Then I'll help you get registered. You might ask some of the other kids what they like. We have a shop class that wasn't available at your school. Would you like that?" she asked as she handed me the list.

"Yes, please. I'll take the shop class. I'll check the list and come back and see you in the morning."

Mr. Rudd was standing in the hall when I walked out. He asked me to step into his office and offered me a seat. "What do you think of our school so far, Andy?"

"I don't know. I just got here. It's all right, I guess."

"I saw you taking up for Alex in the hallway this morning. What was that about?

"Nothing. Just introducing myself."

Mr. Rudd tapped his pencil on his desk while he stared at me. I didn't break eye contact. After a few moments, he said, "That'll be all," obviously ending the meeting.

I walked through the main building, out the back door and over to the newer buildings, where I knew Jared had gone. The bell rang and students started exiting the classes. I stopped and watched them. Shayla Stevenson came out a classroom and walked the other way. She stopped to talk to another girl for a moment and then enter one of the classrooms at the far end of the hall. I waited a minute, then followed her into the classroom and sat down in the back row just as the teacher was about to start class.

Other students were helping themselves to cookies at the front of the room before sitting down. I noticed that here were only girls in the room. Cooking stoves, pots, pans and mixing bowls were in the adjoining room. Then I saw CREATIVE COOKING written on the white board in big letters at the front of the class. The teacher looked at me and asked, "I'm sorry young man, are you in the right class?"

Every girl in the room turned around and stared at me, including Shayla. "I'm Andy Hanson. This is my first day at Clarksville High. I just transferred here," I said as I looked around trying to think of something to say. "I have to take several elective classes and Mrs. Rigby asked me to check out a few so we can determine what classes I'll be taking."

"Well, Andy, are you interested in creative cooking?"

"I'm thinking about it. That is, if you allow boys in the class." Shayla rolled her eyes as if she thought I was gay.

"Of course we allow boys in the class. I'm Megan Wright. You're welcome to stay and if you want to take the class, please do."

I wasn't sure what I'd gotten myself into but it was too late to back out now. I saw Stacey Miller and Kelsey Garner and they both smiled at me. Miss Wright handed out a recipe for quiche lorraine and gave us instructions. The class broke up into groups of fours and walked into the adjacent kitchen area. Stacey walked over. "Come on Andy, you can join our group," she said with a grin on her face.

Stacey introduced me to the rest of the girls in our group who seemed to enjoy having a boy in their cooking class. After mixing the ingredients in a bowl, we put the quiche in the oven. When it was done, we removed the bowl from the oven to let it cool.

Miss Wright came and checked on each dish, adding a little advice and commenting on how well we were doing. She instructed us to let them cool and to place them into the refrigerator until tomorrow when we would sample the results.

I knew this class wouldn't do much to enhance my reputation but I didn't care.

It took me a while to find my math class in Room 108. It was on the bottom floor of the main building. As I walked in the instructor, Mr. Payne, was taking roll call. He saw me come in and commented, "You must be our new student."

"Yes sir," I replied.

"Mrs. Rigby told me you were coming." He addressed the other students. "Class, welcome our new classmate, Andy Hanson."

Most of the students turned to welcome me. Shayla sat in the front row with her back to me. There were no empty seats near her so I took one near the back. Mr. Payne finished taking roll and started teaching Calculus 1. I had already taken Advanced

Calculus so I relaxed and before long, started daydreaming. Before I knew it, I had closed my eyes. I was brought back to reality when I heard Mr. Payne calling my name. Several classmates were laughing. "Mr. Hanson?"

I opened my eyes. Mr. Payne and most of my classmates were staring at me. "Mr. Hanson, you're not sleeping in my class are you?"

"No, sir. I was just blinking slowly. I heard every word you said."

Several students started laughing and Shayla was smiling. She was obviously enjoying my embarrassment.

"Well, Mr. Hanson, since you heard every word I said, then I shall assume you know how to work these problems I've written on the board."

"Yes, sir. You may assume that." More giggles.

"In that case, would mind coming to the front of the class and showing the rest of the students how to work one of them."

"It will be my pleasure, Mr. Payne."

Several snickers were heard as I got up and walked to the front of the class. Shayla had that same smirk on her face that I had seen yesterday in the barn.

"Which problem would you like me to do?"

"Take your pick, Mr. Hanson. I'm sure the class will want to learn how to do all three of them before the class ends."

I studied the problems written on the board, examining each one as if I were attempting to figure out which one I wanted to solve. The third problem was the hardest so I choose it. I waited at least a minute to give Shayla the maximum satisfaction.

"Well, Mr. Hanson, do you give up?" asked Mr. Payne.

"No, sir." I picked up the marker and wrote the answer next to the question and circled it. I put the marker back on the tray and started to walk back to my desk.

"Just a minute, Mr. Hanson," stated Mr. Payne as he picked up his book to check the answer. After making sure the answer was correct, he said, "Well, it appears you were just blinking slow."

Most of class laughed. Shayla didn't. Her smirk was replaced with a look of confusion.

"Mr. Hanson, now that we know you can solve the problems, would mind showing the rest of class how you arrived at your answer?"

"I'd be glad too." I walked back to the board and as fast as I could write, I worked the problem to completion with the same answer. Instead of walking away, I said, "Or, you could work it this way." I did the problem another way and got the same answer.

Mr. Payne walked up to the board and studied the second equation. Satisfied it was correct, he erased it. "I'm afraid the other students won't be using that formula for a while, Mr. Hanson. We don't want to confuse them, do we?"

"Of course not, sir. I apologize."

"You may return to your seat, Andy."

As I walked to my seat, Mr. Payne said, "You may blink as slow as you wish as long as your test results are as accurate as these answers are. Thank you."

I returned to my seat and sat down. Shayla was watching me. I didn't give her the satisfaction of looking back. I leaned back and closed my eyes.

After class, I went to the cafeteria to find Jared. He and several football players were sitting at a table just inside the room. Shayla sat at a table with Stacey Miller and another girl I didn't recognize at the opposite end of the cafeteria. I walked around and sat next to Jared facing Hairy Larry. I held out my hand and said, "Hello, I'm Andy Hanson."

Larry didn't take my hand, "I know. You're the pussy that's taking creative cooking?" All the other boys started laughing except Jared.

"That's me." I smiled at him. "I hear you were the best player on the football team last year."

He nodded. "You heard right."

"I also heard you could play at almost any college in America if you'd put your mind to it." I left out the part that he was as dumb as a mud fence and couldn't pass an SAT test if he were given the answers.

"So?"

"So, I hear you aren't going to play next year."

"Right again, dipshit."

"Well, I'd like to help rebuild the team next year and we need your help. I think we could win the championship."

He looked at me and grinned. "You're dreaming Hanson. These pussies aren't going to go to no state championship no matter how good you think you are."

None of the other boys said anything. One got up and walked away. I noticed Mr. Rudd watching us from across the cafeteria. "I think you are underestimating the team, Larry."

"And how do you think this team is going to win anything with a drunk for a coach, dumbass?"

"Well, we'd start by putting together our own summer work-out plan without the coach. We'll work harder than they've ever worked before. We'll excel in the weight room and we'll be in better shape than any of the other teams at the start of the season."

"Bullshit. You try that and half of these wimps will quit on you. Besides, you ain't got a quarterback."

"I'll be the quarterback. And it doesn't matter if anyone quits. He'd be the weakest link on the team anyway and would only pull the rest of the team down."

Larry narrowed his bushy eyebrows. "Are you saying I'm the weakest link?"

"No, what I am saying is, you could be one of the strongest links. You could run the offensive line, Jared could run the defensive line and I'll run the linebackers, safeties, receivers, running backs and corners."

Larry looked at Jared and then at me. "If I thought this team had a snowball's chance in hell of winning, I'd think about it. But they don't. And I know anyone who takes creative-cooking classes couldn't be much of a quarterback." He pointed at Jared. "You two can play your little coaching gig all you want. I'll come to the games and laugh at you while you're getting your ass kicked."

"Suit yourself, Larry. But, before the season is over next year, you'll be sorry."

"Up yours, Hanson."

I got up from the table and walked to the table where Shayla and her friends were sitting. I sat with my back to Larry facing Shayla. "Hi, Shayla, Stacey and I don't think we've met." I extended my hand to the third girl at the table. "I'm Andy Hanson."

"Hi, I'm Stephanie Miller, Stacey's sister," she said as she took my hand.

She didn't look much like her sister. She had a pleasant intelligent look about her.

"Really, who is older?"

"We're twins, but Stacey was born first."

Shayla looked at me and asked, "What are you doing here?"

"I'm visiting the few new friends I have at this school."

"I'm not your friend, remember. Are you stupid or just suicidal?"

I grinned, "Are those my only choices?"

Shayla shook her head, got up and left the table.

I smelled my armpits. "What, did I forget my deodorant this morning or what?"

"She's not trying to insult you, Andy. She's trying to protect you," said Stacey.

"Protect me from what?"

"It's not what, it's who. Hairy Larry picks a fight with any boy he thinks has an interest in Shayla," Stephanie said.

"She's not as harsh as most people think. She just doesn't want that on her conscience," Stacey said. "She doesn't want anyone to get hurt, that's all."

I looked back and saw Larry staring at me. No one else at his table was talking. I turned back to the Miller twins. "Tell Shayla I can take care of myself. I'll straighten things out with Larry. Nice to meet you, Stephanie."

As I started to get up, both Stacey and Stephanie grabbed my forearms holding me down. Stacey leaned forward keeping her voice quiet. "Andy, please don't do it. That's just what Larry wants you to do. He'll pick a fight and you'll get hurt. He's real mean. The guy's nuts!"

"You girls worry too much. I'll see you later." I got up and walked back to the table where Larry was sitting. "Think about it, Larry. I want you on the team, I'll talk to you later."

"Don't waste your time, pussy."

Jared followed me out of the cafeteria. "You don't take advice very well do you?"

"Who, me?" I said as we walked.

"You're in deep shit, buddy." Jared said.

I smiled. "I know what I am doing Jared. Don't sweat Hairy Larry. I'm just baiting him."   Jared raised his eyebrows and shook his head. "It's your funeral. I'm just trying to help."

After school, Jared and I went to the gym to lift weights. After the workout, I drove Jared to Skeeter's restaurant so we could work on his algebra. I turned on my phone and had a couple of text messages. The first message was from Heather. *Miss U, hope UR ok! Heather.* The next was from Cricket Pilone that read, *Nice to meet you, Andy Handsome!*

"Jared, how did Cricket get my number?"

"I gave it to her, bro!"

"Damn it, Jared. I don't give my number out to just anyone."

"I didn't give it out to just anyone, just her, Kelsey and Stacey. You should be grateful unless you're gay. You aren't gay are you, bro?"

"No, I'm not gay, bro! Who else did you give it to?"

"No one else."

"Did you give it to Shayla Stevenson?"

"No, she didn't ask for it. Besides I figured she has it since you work for her dad."

"I don't need any help with my love life."

"You will if you plan on dating Shayla Stevenson. That girl don't date."

After helping Jared with his homework, I answered Heather text with a simple, *Thanks*!

CHAPTER NINE

Jared and I parked in the school parking lot. He was quieter today than yesterday. I suspected he sensed trouble with Hairy Larry. He also knew I wasn't happy with him for giving my phone number out. I hadn't received any other calls or texts and wasn't upset with him anymore. I asked him if he knew what classes Shayla was taking. He told me she was taking chemistry and a creative writing class but he wasn't sure what else.

Jared left for class and I went to see Mrs. Rigby. I asked her if I could take the creative cooking class. She seemed surprised but didn't hesitate to sign me up for it anyway. I told her I wanted to take a creative writing class. She said they only had one and assigned me to the class. When I asked to be put me the same chemistry class that Shayla Stevenson was in, I got the impression she sensed ulterior motives for the classes I was asking to be assigned to. She knew I had already had AP chemistry. She looked at me and smiled but didn't say anything.

While attending the creative cooking class, I saw Shayla looking at me through the reflection of the oven glass. When I turned to look back, she looked away. I went to Mr. Payne's math class and spent most of the class blinking slowly. Mr. Payne called on Shayla a couple of times during class and she knew the correct answers both times.

When I got to the cafeteria, Jared was waiting outside for me. "Hey, Andy, do you want to go to McDonald's for lunch?"

"No, not really."

"How about Skeeter's? The food in the cafeteria doesn't look good today."

"Yeah, but then I wouldn't get to see Larry, now would I?"

"I guess not. But if you're looking for trouble, Larry is it. If you have to fight him, take it to the O.K. Corral."

"Where's that?"

"It's the big hay stack on the other side of the track. Go to the far side after school hours. No students will follow you and the school can't touch you because it's off campus."

"Thanks. And don't worry, Jared. Larry won't do anything at school. He doesn't want to get kicked out."

We walked into the cafeteria and I walked over and sat next to Shayla and the Miller sisters. I sat facing the bench were the football players and Larry sat. Jared sat at the table with them. The mood was tense and I saw Mr. Rudd was watching the situation closely. Larry was watching me.

"Hi, ladies," I said as I sat down.

Shayla gave me a concerned look but didn't respond. I assumed she had gotten the message. Stacey and Stephanie both said hello. Shayla said, "You're a slow learner, Andrew. I was beginning to think you were smarter than that."

"I'm just being friendly. What's the big deal?"

"You're going to get yourself hurt. Do you know that?"

"You're not responsible for my safety and I'm not asking you to be. Can't we just be friends? What happens between Larry and me is my business. You don't need to worry about it."

"Andy, we just don't want to see anyone get hurt. That's all," said Stephanie.

I looked at Shayla. "Can't we just be friends?"

I waited for a few moments for Shayla to say something, anything. I could see she was frightened. When she didn't respond, I got up and walked over to the football table and sat down facing Larry. Mr. Rudd moved closer to us.

I smiled. "Hello Larry, change your mind about playing football?"

"Nope!"

"Too bad. I thought you were smarter than that."

"What the hell do you want, Hanson?"

"I want you to play football, Larry. But, I'm beginning to understand why all the girls thinks you're such an asshole."

Larry started to get up. He saw Mr. Rudd staring at him and sat back down. "You know, Hanson, when I first saw you wearing those pussy cargo pants and baggy t-shirts, I figured you were queer."

Smiling I said, "The first time I saw your forehead I figured your parents were first cousins."

Larry rose out of his seat again and Mr. Rudd started walking towards us. He slowly sat back down. His face was red and his blood veins were popping out on the side of what little neck he had. I smiled.

Larry smiled back. "You know I'm going to stomp your dumb ass, don't you Hanson?"

"Really. If bullshit was electricity, you'd be a walking powerhouse, Larry!"

"This powerhouse will run over your ass like a Mack truck, asshole!"

"I don't think you're smart enough to get a driver's license, let alone drive a Mack truck."

"You won't be smiling when I knock your teeth out."

"That'll be a cold day in Hell, Hairy Larry."

You could hear several groans for the other boys when I called him, Hairy Larry. I'd definitely hit a sore spot. His knuckles turned white from grabbing the table so hard. "Where do you want to meet, pretty boy?" asked Larry satisfied that he had suckered me into a fight.

"I suppose we should go to the O.K. Corral after school. We need to come to some type of enthusiastic agreement."

"You won't be enthusiastic while I'm pounding your face, pretty boy!"

"Sounds wonderful, Larry. Maybe we can talk a little football strategy while we're at it."

I got up and walked out of the cafeteria. Jared followed me. "You aren't going out there are you?"

"Why not?"

"Because the guys nuts, that why."

"He's just misunderstood, Jared. He needs a friend to help him change his ways. If you want to worry about someone, worry about Larry if he doesn't get smart real quick."

Jared threw up his hands, "Okay, Buddy, it's your funeral. But I sure hope you know what you're doing."

No one in Clarksville had any clue about my involvement in the martial arts since I was five years old. I figured Larry as a brawler with little knowledge of fighting. He had bullied himself through life with his large size and natural strength. I needed to get his attention if I was going to be successful at Clarksville High. I needed him on our team.

After school, I met Larry by the track. A large group of kids had gathered. Everyone had heard about the fight and knew the new kid in school was going to get his ass kicked. They gathered like sharks smelling blood in the water.

"Ready to go have our friendly little chat, Larry?" I said as he approached.

Smiling, he said. "Never been more ready in my life, Dipshit! After you." He extended his hand to the fence inviting me to go first. I climbed over the fence and Larry followed. The crowd stayed on the school side of the fence.

"You surprised me, Hanson, I didn't think you had the balls to show."

"Hell, Larry, I didn't have anything better to do. Besides, I think it's time we get a few things straightened out while we're still friends."

Larry laughed, "Yeah, friends! I hope you still feel that way when you get out of the hospital."

I smiled. "We'll still be friends, Larry."

We walked behind the haystacks and Larry started rolling his shoulders and warming up. He took off his shirt. I stood there watching him. Jared had been right. He was as hairy as a caveman. The hair pored out of the top of his sleeveless t-shirt like a waterfall. "It's ass-kicking time punk!" he said.

"Before you kick my ass, Larry, we need to talk about that enthusiastic agreement I told you about."

"What agreement? I didn't agree to anything but to give you a good ass-whooping!"

"I'll tell you what, Larry. You kick my ass and you can have Shayla Stevenson. If I kick your ass, you stay away from her and play football next year. What do you think of that?"

A big grin spread across his face. "Fine with me. Cause you ain't got a chance in Hell, asshole!"

Larry stepped forward with a large roundhouse swing at my head. I sidestepped it and hit him in his ribcage while his hand was fully extended exposing his side. I heard the air expelling from his lungs and he staggered. I stepped around him and stood a few feet away while he caught his breath. "You alright, Larry?"

"Lucky punch, Hanson!" He lunged at me attempting to tackle me. He knocked me into the haystack but I was able to remain standing. He grabbed mc around the waist and lifted me off the ground in a bear hug. The air was being squeezed out of my lungs but my arms were free. My ribs felt as if they were going to snap. I raised both arms high above my head and brought my elbows down hard catching Larry on both sides of his shoulders next to where his neck should have been. The shock wave vibrated through him and he dropped me. He stood back with his arms hanging straight down by his sides momentarily unable to raise them.

I spun away to my left and caught Larry with a spinning round kick to his chest. His feet left the ground and he landed flat on his back unable to breath. As he staggered to his feet, I caught him with a wicked left hook to his other ribs. He fell back to his knees clutching his ribs and chest still attempting to stand up. He stumbled to his feet and reached out trying to grab me by the throat. I grabbed his wrist with my left hand and pulled him towards me. Placing my right hand on top of Larry's fist, I threw my elbow over his arm turning his body away from me and went down to one knee. I put all of my weight on Larry's twisted arm, which forced him down and away from me. As I lowered myself, he had no choice but to follow me downward or his elbow would break. At the same time, I added pressure to his bent wrist causing excruciating pain. He cried out as I held him in this position. He was helpless and couldn't move.

I spoke in a calm, clear voice, "Larry, if you haven't noticed, your face is in the ground facing away from me and you can't get up. You know I can break your wrist with just a little pressure." I applied a bit more pressure on his wrist and he cried out in pain. I released some of the pressure and said, "I can also break your elbow by putting my weight on it and it will snap." I added weight to his arm and he again cried out in pain.

"Stop it, damn it! You're breaking my fucking arm."

"That's the idea, Larry. I could break both the wrist and the elbow at the same time if I wanted to, or you could just give up and keep our agreement. What's it going to be?"

With his face in the dirt and out of breath, he stopped trying to move. Snot ran out of his nose. I didn't want to break his arm because I needed him on the team. But I would if I had to.

For the first time in his life, Larry Muller realized he had been defeated. He was helpless to do anything about it. Pain and fear overcame him. "Alright, alright, I give up, you're killing me man, you win."

"What was that, Larry, I didn't hear you?"

"I said you win. You beat me. I'll play football!"

"And, Shayla?"

He hesitated for a slight moment and I added a little more pressure. He cried out, "Her too. I'll stay away from her."

I eased up on the arm. "I'm going to let you up now. God help you if you try anything. I won't give you a second chance. Do you understand?"

"Yeah, yeah, Andy. Just please don't break my arm!"

"All right" I released him. "Get up."

I stepped away ready to do battle. I knew he was humiliated and wanted revenge, but I doubted even he was that stupid. He rubbed his wrist and elbow and put his shirt back on. He didn't try anything.

"Larry, I'll tell you what. We'll keep this between us. No one else has to know, agreed?"

He looked at me as if he wasn't quite sure what I was saying. Holding his ribs and wrenching in pain, he said, "Well, sure, if that's what you want. What do you want me to do?"

"I want you to help me re-build the football team."

"Alright."

As I was telling Larry what I needed him to do, Shayla came running around the haystack out of breath expecting to see a fight in progress. "What's going on out here?" she demanded as she rounded the corner. Seeing me with my hand on Larry's shoulder, she stopped in her tracks.

"Hi, Shayla. What's up?" I asked.

"What are you two doing out here?" she yelled.

I smiled. "We're trying to figure out how to win a football championship next year."

Shayla threw up her hands. "Is that all you think about... football? Oh... men!"

She shook her head and started back towards the school.

"Hey, thanks for saving me," I yelled. She didn't answer.

Larry and I followed her back to the school. Larry moved gingerly as he climbed through the fence. Coach Ford met us when we entered the schoolyard. "What's going on, boys?" he asked.

"Larry decided he wants to play football next year and we were just discussing strategies."

The crowd looked as dumbfounded and confused as Shayla and the coach were. None of them understood what had happened behind the haystacks.

Coach Ford shrugged and started walking towards his office. Mr. Rudd stood close by watching us. I heard him say, "If that don't beat all," as he turned to leave.

I headed for my car and Jared caught up with me. "What happened?"

"Larry decided to play football."

"I know that. How in the Hell did you do that?"

"Pain. It's a great motivator."

Jared stopped and looked back. Larry didn't look happy. Jared caught back up to me. "This isn't over, you know?"

"I think it is. He knows I could have hurt him real bad if I wanted to."

Jared shook his head. "What about his brother?"

"What brother?"

"He has a big brother, even bigger and meaner than Larry is. You better watch your back, dude."

"What does he look like?"

"Just like Larry but a lot bigger. He doesn't shave his head and has a full beard. He has a very nasty disposition. The whole family's nuts."

I shook my head. "If Larry was my brother, I'd sue my mother."

Jared didn't laugh. "I'm serious man, his brother will be gunning for you. Family pride and all that bullshit."

I kept walking. "I'll cross that bridge when and if I get to it."

CHAPTER TEN

I sat at the rear of my creative writing class bored to death. Mr. Webb was a complete nerd who believed it was his duty to unlock the subconscious creativity within all students who took his class. If you didn't work hard, you wouldn't do well.

English is the subject I liked least and my handwriting resembled that of a doctor's scribbling. I had gotten A's in English classes but I never took English AP classes. Creative Writing was one of the few classes offered at Clarksville that I had hadn't already taken. Mrs. Rigby felt it would be beneficial to my future. She might have been right, but I knew I would be bored out of my mind. Alex, Kelsey, Stephanie and Shayla were also taking the class. I was beginning to think Shayla thought I was a stalker.

Mr. Webb began, "Students, our next assignment is going to be fun. It will be a poem. I'll give you two topics to choose from. You may use any of the two topics for your poem or a combination of the two topics. The topics are romance or humor. This assignment will be due next Monday." The rest of the class was spent on writing styles.

"Damn it, that's all I need." I left the class rejected.

Overall I was adjusting to life at Clarksville High. Hairy Larry wasn't wreaking havoc anymore and the tension level was way down. Most of next year's football players started showing up at the gym. I kept busy by developing a computerized workout program for each player. They would be able to set goals in the weight room and the program would track their progress. If a player started falling short of his goals, he would be able to modify his weight workout program to get back on-track. The biggest problem the football players seemed to be having was gaining weight. I told them to add slim-fast to their meals. It was a trick I had learned at Superstition High. If you eat a healthy high protein meal and drink slim-fast with protein power, you gain weight and build muscle. The other players were skeptical at first, but it works and soon many of them were loading up on the slim-fast diet. Even Jared was gaining weight.

School rules forbade the school from having organized football practices out of season. There was nothing preventing us from training on our own after school hours. Larry brought two huge semi truck tires to school and had the lineman flipping them end over end up and down the football field. Running stadium steps was unofficially added into our summer workout plan. All members of the team were encouraged to participate. Isometrics were introduced into the program to improve our speed and agility. With Larry involved, encouragement came easy. No one wanted to get on his bad side. A couple of wannabe players quit. But other athletes joined the team after noticing the team's improved attitude. We were definitely making progress.

Larry had been a little heavy handed on some of the players. I had a "come to Jesus" meeting with him. I told him players would work harder for us out of respect than out of fear. Larry backed off and everyone seemed to be getting along. I feared my biggest problem was going to be Coach Ford if he didn't give up the bottle. He had a good track record in the past and I didn't want to give up on him.

CHAPTER ELEVEN

My alarm woke me at 5:15 a.m. I groaned, forced myself out of bed, showered and got dressed. Dad was in the kitchen drinking coffee. He had a large police file and several photos on the table.

"Morning, Son. Going to work?"

"Yeah, you're up early. What's this?"

"It's the Bobby Patterson murder case. I'm going over it to see if I can find anything they may have missed."

"I thought that was the Sheriff's case."

"Yeah, it is. This happened up in the mountains three years ago. But Donna Stevenson mentioned the murder to Mom so I got a copy of their report."

I picked up two photos. "What are these?"

"That boot print belongs to the suspect. The other one is a photo of a 270 shell casing from the murder weapon."

"Do you think the suspect would still own the same boots after all this time?"

"I doubt it. You can wear out a pair of boots every year if you use them for work. If you only use them for hunting, he may still have them."

"Do you have any ideas who did it?"

"No, but I think he was someone familiar with the area and wears a size twelve or thirteen boot. There's not much to go on from what I see."

I finished breakfast, grabbed a sandwich for lunch and headed out the door. It was 6:00 a.m. when I got to the Double J Ranch. Shayla had a rope around Ruby's neck in the rear pasture attempting to get a halter on her. Ruby was excited and wouldn't stand still. Colonel was also in the pasture with a rope around Thunderbolt, the black stallion from the Patterson's ranch next door. Thunderbolt was running in circles and rearing from time to time attempting to get loose. When Shayla saw me she said yelled, "Open the gate and get in here, Colonel needs help!"

Colonel didn't look like he needed help to me. I started walking towards the gate. "I'm not sure I should, I hear these horses bite."

Shayla gave me a disgusted look. "Damn you, Andrew, get in here or I'll come out there and bite you myself!"

I stopped and put my hands up. "If that's the case, I'm staying here."

"Andrew Hanson, my daddy's not paying you to sit around on your lazy ass! Get in there and help Colonel!" she replied getting more irritated by the moment.

I smiled, gave her my best imitation of the smirk she had given me in the barn. I wanted to remind her that I wasn't getting paid but didn't want to push my luck. I entered the pasture. "Need a hand, Colonel?"

"Sure, Andy. Open the rear gate so I can put Thunderbolt back where he belongs."

I opened the rear gate and Colonel led Thunderbolt through it. I opened the second gate leading into the Patterson's property. Colonel walked Thunderbolt into his own pasture. He didn't want to go home. Colonel checked him over to see if he had any injuries before setting him free. Thunderbolt ran back and forth along the fence prancing with his head and tail held high. He was a spectacular sight. I marveled at the magnificent animal.

"What happened, Colonel?" I asked as wc walked back to the barn.

"Thunderbolt wants romance. He had jumped the fence and I found him in Ruby's pasture when I arrived this morning."

I looked for Shayla and Ruby but they were nowhere in sight. Colonel leaned on the fence to watch Thunderbolt and I joined him. "He's a beautiful horse, isn't he, Colonel?"

"He's more than that. His bloodline is pure champion and cowboys have won millions on him over the years. He's famous in the quarter horse circles. Bob Patterson paid a fortune for him. He gets request for breeding from as far away as Britain, Canada, Australia, New Zealand and South American. Breeders of quarter horses dream about horses like that. It would cost at least thirty thousand for breeding rights."

"That's a lot of money."

" No kidding. Most breeders would breed him to any horse for that amount of money. But not Bob Patterson. He only breeds Thunderbolt to champion pedigreed mares. If the mare doesn't meet Bob's expectations, no amount of money will convince him to breed Thunderbolt to her. That's one of the things I respect about Bob Patterson. He's not in it just for the money."

"Was the boy who got murdered his son?" I asked.

Colonel looked over at me. "Yeah, what a tragedy."

"Did you know him?"

Colonel thought for a long time before answering. He paused as if he was deciding what to say. "I knew him most of his life.

When Bob and his wife Margaret moved here, little Bobby was about three years old. Bob bought the old Bar 4 Ranch with the intent of turning it into the finest quarter horse ranch in the country. He built the new home, the barn and all the new fencing. He brought in a good stock of breeding mares, mostly champions who were too old to compete anymore. All with good bloodlines. He didn't want to raise cattle, so he made an agreement with John Stevenson. John could use his grazing rights if John would let him use some of his steers for roping."

"Sounds like a good deal for both of them."

"It was. They became close friends. Donna was pregnant with Shayla at the time. When Shayla was born, Meg drove Donna to the hospital because John and I were rounding up cattle and couldn't get off the mountain in time. The Patterson's son, Bobby Jr. was three years older than Shayla. He became a big brother to her. Anyone who didn't know the difference would think they were brother and sister. She followed him everywhere on her pony and pestered the hell out of him most of the time. When Bobby started playing football, she attended all of his games. She was a funny, cute and a delightful child back then."

"She's not funny or delightful anymore."

Colonel laughed, "Yeah, but she's good-looking." I didn't comment.

"When Bobby got killed, she took it hard. She cried for weeks and has never been the same. It hardened her and she withdrew. She doesn't trust strangers. Never dated like most girls."

He paused for a moment, turned and looked at me. "I think that's why she's so hard on you. She doesn't want to get close to anyone and is afraid of getting hurt. She wouldn't admit to that even if it were true."

Colonel paused again. "After Bobby got killed, Meg had a breakdown. The pressure of losing her only son was more than she could bear. It almost killed her and destroyed their marriage. Bob has learned to live with the death of his son… but he will never rest until the suspect is caught. It's almost as if Bob lost a son and a wife at the same time. He's been taking her to counseling, but I don't think it's helping."

I remembered the first time I saw Mrs. Patterson sitting on her porch. "That's tragic and sad."

Colonel looked down at the ground and then at me. "I think you remind Shayla of Bobby. He was a good-looking kid, big, strong, played football and had brains. Maybe that's why she avoids you. She can be a real hard ass at times."

"No kidding." *And, that's one of her better qualities!*

"I know one thing," Colonel continued, "If your father solves that murder, he'll be the most popular man in Clarksville."

We watched Thunderbolt for a little longer. "Alright Andy, help me saddle those mustangs and get loaded. We have cattle to round up and fences to mend. We're burning daylight."

Shayla was brushing Ruby when I walked into the barn. I approached her but she acted as if I wasn't there. "Shayla, I'm sorry I almost hit you with that hay. You think we could start all over? I'm not really as bad as you think."

"Forget about it, Andrew. I've already forgiven you. Hand me a hackamore from that rack behind you."

I handed her one of the items hanging on the wall. She shook her head. "That's a bridle, dummy." She stepped around me and got a hackamore. "Does someone have to tie your shoes for you, Andrew? You're completely useless."

"No. I tie my own shoes. And my friends call me Andy."

She gave me the same smirk she gave me when we first met. "I know."

Cute! I put my hands up in surrender and backed away. "Which saddles should I take for the mustangs?"

"The two on the far left," she said and then added, "Andrew."

I let her have the last word this time and considered it a draw. I took a saddle and pad to the horse trailer. I came back to get the other one and carried it to the trailer. Colonel saddled the horses. We loaded them in the trailer and headed out. Donna walked out of the back door and greeted us as we approached the house. She handed us a paper sack with sandwiches in it. "Did you take the rifles?" she asked as she handed the bag in through the window.

"I got `em. Thanks for the sandwiches." Colonel replied.

"You two be careful and keep your phones on," she stated with a concerned look on her face.

CHAPTER TWELVE

W e parked next to the line shack and unloaded the horses. Colonel adjusted my stirrups.

"Keep your eye out for anything suspicious." Colonel said.

"Like what?"

"Broken fences, dead cattle, mountain lions. Stuff like that."

"Alright."

Riding away from the shack, Colonel asked, "Ride much?"

"Not much. Between school and football, I haven't had much time for riding."

"If you're going to ride, I'd advise you to get yourself a good pair of cowboy boots. The heel won't let your foot slip through the stirrups and drag you to death if your horse spooks."

"Thanks."

"A good cowboy hat will keep the sun from burning your face and keep the rain from running down the back of your neck."

"Alright." I hadn't given any thought to cowboy boots or hats. I'd always thought they were for looks.

We spooked up a mule deer doe with a yearling and a coyote on the way up the mountain. At the very top of the ridge, we turned slightly west and followed the fence line.

"That's where the cougar jumped John Stevenson." Colonel said as we passed a steep ravine. We rode another mile and didn't find any broken fences. We came to a very large canyon. Colonel used his binoculars to follow the fence line towards the bottom and up the other side. "I can't see to the bottom. That might be where the fence is down. There's an old horse trail down there and a gate. We'll have to go down and take a look."

We followed the fence line to the bottom of the canyon. It was steep and rocky. We busted a lot of brush on the way down. By the time we got there, I was feeling very uncomfortable from sliding forward in the saddle. We stopped at the gate where the old trail was supposedly located. It could hardly be called a trail. I wouldn't even have known it was there if Colonel hadn't told me. The gate was shut. Colonel got off his horse to re-check it. Convinced the gate was secure, he studied the ground.

"What are you looking at, Colonel?"

"Hoof prints. Someone has come through here with two horses, both ways, and within the last few days."

"Who do you think it was?"

"I have no idea. This trail is seldom used. Most people don't even know it's here."

"Where does it go?"

Colonel stood up, covered his eyes with his hand and stared into the canyon. "This is one of the original trails used by the Apaches during the Indian wars. Geronimo used it to get to the Chiricahua Mountains and then into Old Mexico."

"Really?"

"Did you know Geronimo hated the Mexicans more than he did the whites?"

"No. I didn't know that."

"It was because they killed his family."

Colonel remounted. "I haven't seen anyone on this trail in years. It's overgrown and hard to follow. John and I used it when we were white tail deer hunting as kids. We never saw any sign that it was ever used."

He looked back and caught me with my hand down the front of my pants adjusting myself. "What you doing? Playing with yourself?"

"Just putting the family jewels back in the safe."

"I wouldn't worry about `em boy. They're only costume jewelry."

"Costume or not, I want to protect them. I'd like to have kids someday."

Colonel laughed. "When you're riding down hill, put more heel pressure in the stirrups and sit up straighter. That way you won't slide forward and you'll have better balance."

We rode back up to the top of the mountain and backtracked along the fence the way we had come. We continued following the fence for another couple of miles. A large watering hole came into sight and we stopped to water our horses. Colonel dismounted and walked around the pond checking for tracks. He knelt down on the other side and studied the ground. Placing his fist over something, he looked around.

"What is it?" I yelled.

"Cougar tracks. Big ones."

"Are we going to hunt him?"

"No, they are at least a week old. No telling where he'll be."

"To bad. I've never seen a mountain lion before the one that jumped John."

"If you ever find a fresh cougar track, stay on it or you'll never see that cat again. They have a large roaming area and hunt more at night than during the day." Colonel remounted.

"There's another gate up here about a mile. We need to check it, then we can go on the other side of the fence and find John's cows."

We found the gate lying on the ground. Colonel again searched for tracks. "This is where the cattle are getting out. One of them may have rubbed his horns on the gate causing it to unlatch. If someone had opened it, it would be left standing open instead of just laying here."

We rode through the gate and Colonel shut it. He dismounted, got down on his hands and knees and looked in both directions. "Someone has been through this gate on an ATV. The dumb ass may not have gotten the gate closed all the way."

"I didn't think anyone is supposed to be riding ATVs up here."

"They're not."

After going through the gate to the other side of the fence, Colonel shut the gate. He remounted and led us to a big water hole close by with lots of fresh cattle tracks. "This is the only water on this side of the fence. We should find the cattle close by."

Four cows, a small bull and a calf with the JJ brand on them were near the water hole. We drove them back through the gate and re-latched it. Following our own tracks, we rode back to the watering hole on the downward side of the fence and dismounted. I was hungry, stiff, and sore. Getting off my horse was a strain and it took me a while to get my legs to straighten out. I now knew why Colonel had said this wasn't fun.

We had lunch and relaxed for a half hour. When it was time to leave, I looked around and found a large rock to use to get back on the horse. Colonel watched me with a smile on his face as I pulled my aching bones back into the saddle. He remounted from the ground and we started the long ride back to the truck. By the time we got there, I wasn't sure if I would be able get off my horse by myself. I groaned as I lifted my leg over the saddle and almost fell down when my feet hit the ground. My balls hurt, my butt was sore and my legs were shaky. I'd found a new appreciation for cowboys. We loaded the horses into the trailer and headed for the ranch.

"Nice little ride today. Wasn't that fun?" Colonel said sarcastically.

I was too tired to answer and slept all the way back to the ranch. Colonel woke me up when we got there so I could help unload the horses. Getting out of the truck was painful and I ached all over. I noticed Shayla loading Santana into the two-horse trailer. I was able to get out of the truck by myself but my leg refused to move and my back didn't want to straighten. I didn't want Shayla to know I was hurting so I forced myself upright and began to walk. I unloaded my horse and tied it to the side of the trailer. I unsaddled the horse and carried the saddle into the barn trying to hide the pain.

"How did it go today, Andrew?" Shayla asked.

"My friends call me Andy... and it went fine." She ignored my statement.

"How far did you ride?"

"Not far, just to the top of the mountains and back." *A thousand miles!*

"Did you find the lost cattle?"

"Yep!"

Shayla thought for a moment then asked, "Have you written your poem yet?"

"Nope, I can't seem to get motivated."

"You better get motivated, it's due Monday," she said as she took Ruby out of her stall and headed for the trailer.

I followed her outside. "Have any suggestions on how to get motivated to write a poem?"

Shayla ignored me until she put Ruby into the trailer. "I wouldn't have a clue how to motivate you, Andrew."

"You could start with a kiss."

She got that smirk on her face again, reached over and lifted up Ruby's tail. "Kiss this!"

She dropped the tail, walked to the door of the truck with her back to me. She pushed her butt outward and gave it two small pats on her right hip. She got into the truck and drove up to the house and her mom got in. I could still see the smirk on her face through the side-view mirror as they drove away.

I limped back to my car and drove home, very motivated!

CHAPTER THIRTEEN

S hayla had that same smirk on her face when she approached me outside our creative writing class Monday morning. "Hey, Lover Boy. Did you get motivated enough to write your poem?"

It seemed everyone in school knew I had put the moves on Shayla. I was too embarrassed to answer. She stuck her nose in the air, smiled and walked into the classroom. I swallowed hard and followed.

Mr. Webb took our homework and told us we could use the rest of the time to work on the next assignment, a poem about nature this time. I felt brain-dead.

As we worked on the assignment, we heard laughing at the front of the class and looked up. "I'm sorry class," said Mr. Webb. "One of the poems turned in today is quite humorous. The author combined the two subjects, romance and humor, and wrote a very clever poem. I won't disclose the author but I'd like to read it to the class. It is called: The Cowboy Kiss."

"Going down to Tombstone, just my old donkey and me.
No particular reason, just wanted to see what we could see.
Met up with an outlaw, he'd just broke out of jail.
He stuck his pistol in my face and raised up my donkey's tail.
"Have you ever kissed your donkey?"
And he said to tell him true.
"Nope I never have. But I've always wanted to!"
About that time a dust devil blew dust in the outlaw's eyes.
I quickly grabbed the outlaw's gun to the outlaw's surprise.
There we stood in the middle of that desert, staring face to face
The outlaw's smile turned upside down when he realized, we just
traded place.
A many a year have now gone by and we have traveled a many
mile.
And every time I tell this story, my old donkey smiles!

Everyone in the class clapped except Shayla. Mr. Webb encouraged the author to write more poems. Shayla turned in her seat and glared at me. I pushed my butt a little to the side of my seat and patted it twice. I imitated her smirk as best I could. She quickly looked away.

After class she walked up to me. "Having fun yet?"

"I am. Are you?"

"Should I be? You're making fun of me."

"You asked for it."

"No I didn't. Maybe you should use some of your talent for something more serious next time."

"Maybe you should reconsider."

"That's absurd. You asked for it when you asked for a kiss."

"You're right. Anyone asking you for a kiss would be absurd."

She put her hands on her hips and tilted her head to one side. "What's that supposed to mean?"

"You know what it means."

"No I don't. And don't write any more poems about me, Andrew." She turned to walk away.

I yelled to her, "Keep motivating me and I might just do that."

She stopped and turned to face me. "I'm serious, Andrew. I bet everyone in school will know what's behind your poem before the day's out."

"You shouldn't have told them I hit on you. At least, I don't kiss and tell."

She paused and studied my face. "I really don't want to be the butt of your jokes."

"Hey, this is just between us. And it was just a joke."

She looked down and bit her lower lip. "All right. No harm done."

"So, are we still friends?"

"I didn't know we ever were."

"Oh, come on." I wanted to change the subject. "What was your poem about?"

"I'd rather not say. But yours was better. What are you going to write about next time?"

"Mountains."

"I'm warning you, Andrew, it better not have anything to do with me or my body parts, all right?"

I laughed. "I'll think about it."

She looked as if she was going to say something else, but instead, turned and walked away.

CHAPTER FOURTEEN

J ared, Sonny Turner, Darrel Abney and I made a mad dash to McDonald's. If we didn't hurry, Sonny, Darrel and I ran the risk of being late for our math test. Mr. Payne had strict rules about tardiness, especially when he was giving a test. He'd deduct one point for every minute you were late unless you had a solid excuse for not being there. A note from God wouldn't work, but one from Mr. Rudd or the school nurse might get you a pardon.

An ugly gray Ford diesel truck with oversized tires and chrome smokestacks pulled into the parking lot as we were eating. It parked and an extraterrestrial crawled out of the cab. He wore an orange and white striped sleeveless t-shirt too small for his body with his belly hanging out of the bottom. The stripes ran horizontal, making his barrel body look even rounder. His spiked multi-colored Mohawk displayed every color of the rainbow. His long hairy arms were covered with tattoos with enough color to rival a male peacock in heat.

"Lets get the hell out of here." Jared said. "That's Larry Muler's brother, Bruce." We left our trays and headed for the door.

I was halfway across the parking lot before I heard him growl. "Hey, are you Andy Hanson?"

Pretending not to hear him, we picked up our pace. "Hey, Dickhead. I'm talking to you, City Boy."

We kept walking but I could hear him advancing. By the time I got to my car, he was right behind me. My retreating options had vanished. I turned to face him.

He was huge, well over 6 foot and 300 pounds. Like his brother, he didn't have a neck, but unlike him, he had a nose ring and large holes in both ears big enough to stick your finger through. A shaggy beard framed small beady eyes below one large hairy eyebrow. Tan cargo shorts hung halfway between knobby knees and his oversized feet, adorned in leather sandals. He looked like the poster-boy for the cover of Redneck magazine.

"Are you talking to me?" I asked as I backed up next to my car.

"Damn right I'm talking to you, Hanson. I hear you think you're a tough guy." His fists were clenched and his breath smelled of leftover anchovies.

"You must be Hairy Larry's brother."

He grinned. "How'd you guess, Dipshit?"

"You don't have a neck. What did your mother do, drop you guys on your heads? You look like Jabba the Hutt."

He shifted his weight and I knew what was coming next. I waited a split-second before ducking. His giant fist brushed my ear before smashing into the roofline of my car where the doorpost met the roofline. I heard bone cracking. I pushed off the car and head butted him in the face. Cartilage crunched and his nose poured blood. I jammed my knee up into his groin and watched him grow three inches instantaneously. He receded six inches like an accordion as the heel of my boot slammed down on his yellow toenails. I sidestepped two paces to my left. My right foot smacked into his knee and I heard it snap. He fell like a giant redwood. His good hand flipped back and forth like the arm of an octopus between his toes, his groin, his knee, and his nose. His groans sounded like a bear with his balls caught in a trap moaning in soprano.

A police car came to a screeching halt. Sgt. Ortiz got out with his radio in one hand and his side handle baton in the other. He looked at Bruce and called for paramedics and an ambulance. "What's going on here, boys?"

"Bruce jumped Andy, officer!" Jared said. "He didn't have a choice but to defend himself."

"Bruce tried to deck Andy," Sonny said. "We were just trying to leave."

Sergeant Ortiz eyed Bruce. "Is that right, Bruce?"

Bruce answered in a foreign high-pitched non-understandable dialect.

Sgt. Ortiz turned to me. "Are you injured?"

"No, sir."

"What did you do to him, run over him with your car?"

"He broke his hand when he hit my car."

"Hum, and you did the rest of this damage." Sgt. Ortiz looked at Bruce and then asked me. "Do you want to prosecute?"

"Not really."

"Looks like he may have a few broken bones. I'm going to have to make a report."

Jared asked. "Can we leave, Sergeant? We have a math test and we don't want to be late."

"Yeah, you can leave but I'm listing you as witnesses." He looked at me, "You'll have to stay. I need your statement for the report."

"Andy drove us here." Sonny said.

I handed Jared my keys. "Take my car. I'll get a ride to school."

They left as the ambulance arrived. Bruce continued to moan, as he was loaded for his trip to the hospital. Dad showed up and I explained what had happened. After I completed my written statement, Dad drove me back to the school. Mr. Rudd gave me a note excusing me for being tardy.

Students were walking out of the class by the time I got there. Shayla gave me a, *where the hell were you look,* but didn't say anything. I went inside and handed Mr. Payne the note. He told me to take a seat at the rear of the class. Sonny and Darrel were sitting in the first row. Sonny sat at one end and Darrel at the other end. Mr. Payne brought me my test and told me I could begin.

He told Sonny and Darrel that their test was slightly modified. He handed them the test and a blank piece of paper.

"Forty percent of your grade will be the first question and sixty percent will be the rest of the test. Write your answer to the first question on the blank page and hand it back to me before continuing. Since a flat tire caused you to be late for the test, the question should be very simple. I'm sure you'll both know the answer. There will be no talking or looking at one another during the test. Is that understood?"

They nodded indicating they understood. Mr. Payne said, "The first question is; which tire had the flat?"

To keep from laughing, I buried my head in my test. I don't think Sonny and Darrel found humor in the question.

After school, I drove to the hospital to see Bruce. He was asleep when I walked into his room. His right leg was propped up on pillows and wrapped from his toes to his thigh. His eyes were black and his nose stuffed with white gauze, giving him the appearance of a raccoon eating a snow cone. His right hand was in a cast and something was packed between his legs.

I cleared my throat and he opened his eyes. His expression was shear panic. His octopus arm franticly fumbled the call button. "I'm not here to harm you, Bruce."

He held the control with his thumb on the button, but I wasn't sure if he had pushed it or not. He mumbled, "What do you want?"

"I want to know if this is over between us."

"You broke my hand, my knee, my nose and two toes."

"You started it and you broke your own hand."

He didn't say anything so I took a step forward. "Yeah, yeah, it's over Hanson."

"It better be, Bruce. I don't like looking over my shoulder."

He tried to nod but the expression on his face told me it hurt too bad. He gritted his teeth for a second, "What about my brother?"

"What about him?"

"You're not going after him, are you?"

"This is between you and me. I need Larry on the team."

He paused for a moment then said, "Okay, we're square."

A nurse walked in and asked if everything was all right. Bruce told her it was. I turned and walked away wondering if Larry would still play football.

CHAPTER FIFTEEN

The aroma of biscuits and gravy, bacon and hot apple pie filled the air as Jared and I entered Skeeter's. Sunday mornings were normally slow until the church crowd let out at 11:00 a.m., then there would be a waiting line for the rest of the morning. Skeeter and Henry Spillman drank coffee while looking at a large folder when we walked in. "Hi Skeeter, Mr. Spillman," we said at the same time.

"Well, who's the new cowboy?" said Skeeter. "You look so handsome, Andy. Where did you get the hat?"

"Colonel gave it to me."

"When are you getting cowboy boots?" asked Mr. Spillman.

"I don't know about that," I said as I looked down at the travel brochures. "Someone planning a vacation?"

"No," replied Skeeter, "I'm showing Henry my bucket list."

"Bucket list, as in Morgan Freeman and Jack Nicholson's bucket list?" asked Jared.

"One and the same," said Skeeter. "I got the idea from the movie."

"You're not sick are you, Miss Skeeter?" asked Jared.

"No, not at all. But I want to see all these places before I'm to old too enjoy them."

I started naming them. "That is the Eiffel Tower, that's The Leaning Tower of Pisa, The Great Wall of China, The Taj Mahal, The Coliseum in Rome, and The Pyramids in Egypt."

"How do you know all these places?" Jared asked.

"We studied them in World History."

"Are you really going to all these places, Miss Skeeter?" asked Jared.

"I sure hope so. I want to go see them all before I die. That's why I work so hard and why you guys need to eat more."

"Are you going to go to all those places too, Mr. Spillman?" asked Jared.

"I'm thinking about it boys. I'm truly thinking about it. What are you two up to today?"

"I'm helping Jared with his math and we're going to go sight in our rifles."

"You getting ready for hunting season?" asked Skeeter.

"Not me," Jared said with a disappointed look on his face. "I didn't get drawn this year. But Andy did and I am going to find him a big whitetail come January. I'm his guide. Ain't that right, Andy?"

"Yes, Bwana." I replied.

"You're lucky, Andy. Jared kills a big deer almost every year," Henry said.

"I sure hope I get one," I said as we left for our table. "We'll see you later."

We had lunch and started working on Jared's homework. Bennett Nahche had been working on Kachina Dolls at one of the tables and approached us. "Hi guys. I like your new hat, Andy."

"Thanks Bennett, it was a gift."

"Well I have a gift for you," Bennett said as he removed a hatband and a feather from his pocket and handed them to me. "The hat band is rattlesnake. It will ensure you will be victorious. The eagle feather will give you knowledge and wisdom."

"Thanks, Bennett." I said as I examined the hatband. "How do you know these will make me victorious and wise?"

"Trust me. Indians know these things."

I nodded. "I should have known," I replied. "Thanks a lot."

Colonel Lightfoot walked in and saw us talking to Bennett. He walked to our booth and sat next to me, leaving Bennett standing. The two men locked eyes immediately. After a few awkward moments, Colonel spoke. "Hello, Bennett."

"Hello, Colonel."

"Eat any dog lately, Bennett?"

There was a long moment during which the men just stared at each other, neither blinking.

"No, but I see that bitch of yours had puppies. We shall have plenty of food in the spring," Bennett replied and then turned and walked out of the restaurant. Colonel's eyes never left Bennett until he was completely out of sight.

"It appears you don't like Apaches, Colonel."

"Apaches are alright. Just not that one."

"If that's true, why do the Apaches put up with him? Indians should know these things," I said.

Colonel smiled, then he got serious. "They don't put up with him. That's why he cannot live among them. Avoid him at all times."

CHAPTER SIXTEEN

Since I'd never been to a rodeo before, I didn't know what to expect. I took my own car in case I didn't enjoy it and wanted to leave early. Mom advised me to wear my cowboy hat and the new boots she had bought me. Looking in the mirror, I felt like an imposter.

When we arrived, I knew she was right. Everyone wore cowboy hats and boots. All I was lacking was a big fancy belt buckle with a horse or bull on it. My shirt was mild compared to most of the others. Many of the men wore cowboy belts with the owner's name engraved on the back. Convenient if you wanted to meet someone.

The cowgirls were even more colorful. They wore boots with colorful designs and patterns. Their belt buckles sparkled and were shaped like horseshoes or hearts. Some wore buckles they had won in competitions.

The program brochure claimed Clarksville's first rodeo had been held in 1894. It has been an annual event ever since. Shayla would be competing in barrel racing. An event her mother had competed in when she was in high school on her horse, Santana, winning the Junior National Barrel Racing Championship twice.

The program showed Shayla currently in second place behind a girl named Haley Lofgren in the current state standings.

It appeared that more people were at the rodeo than lived within the city limits of Clarksville. Some of the horse trailers looked like houses on wheels and were pulled by semi-trucks. I'm sure they cost more than our house. Plenty of old beat up pickup trucks and rusty horse trailers were mixed in among the elite.

Vendors sold everything from saddles and tack to horse trailers. The air smelled of popcorn, hot dogs and hamburgers. The beer booth already had a line and it was only 9:30 in the morning.

We located John and Donna Stevenson, Bob Patterson, and Colonel in the stands. I sat down next to Colonel. "Colonel, who is the best rider, Shayla or Haley?" I asked after reading the program.

"Haley has the better horse and Shayla is the better rider. The irony is that Haley's horse was one of Thunderbolt's fillies. Mr. Lofgren paid a lot of money for her training. John Stevenson couldn't afford that much for a horse and Shayla does most of her own training."

Shayla wore a bright green and white shirt with fringes. Her boots were white and green with silver spurs and she wore her hair in a ponytail with a bright green ribbon.

After Shayla left for warm-ups, Colonel and I went to the warm-up arena to watch her.

"Colonel, what are the rules for barrel racing?"

"Each competitor crosses the start line at a run. They have to decide if they want to go to the left barrel first or the right barrel first. If you go to the left barrel first, you go around once to the left and twice to the right. It's the reverse if you go to the right barrel first. Some horses turn better to the right and some horses turn better to the left. Each rider knows which way their horse turns best and chooses the course that they think will give them the fastest times. If a rider knocks a barrel over, five seconds is added to his or her time. If they fail to run the course properly or come off the horse, they are disqualified. Each rider runs the course twice. Prizes are awarded for the fastest time in each barrel race but the overall winner is determined by averaging their times from both races. Speed is the name of the game. A winning time is normally about thirteen to fourteen seconds."

"Why aren't there more boys racing barrels?"

Colonel smiled. "Because they don't like getting their ass beat by all these pretty little girls."

"Do riders ever come off?" I asked.

"Not many, but they do once in a while. A horse can trip or loose its footing and go down, or a rider will lose their balance and come off."

Shayla entered the practice arena and ran the course flawlessly. I thought she was flying but Colonel said she was only going about three-quarter speed because she's just warming up.

"She sure has a good seat, doesn't she?" said Colonel.

I looked at Colonel and he looked at me. I didn't say anything. "Get your mind out of the gutter, boy. Saying someone has a good scat while riding a horse means she sits the saddle well and is a good rider."

"You're right, she does have a good seat." *And a great ass!*

After watching the warm ups, we returned to the stands and waited for the start of the competition. Shayla would be the sixth rider and Haley Lofgren would be seventh.

"Do you think Shayla will win, Colonel?"

"Hard to say. She's a more experienced rider than Haley, but we have a ten thousand dollar horse running against a fifty thousand dollar horse. It will depend on how clean their runs are. If I were placing a bet, I'd have to bet on the horse. Haley would have the edge."

Shayla's hat came off as she entered the arena. Her horse shot out of the gate at a full run. Her ponytail trailed straight out behind her. She had good speed and her turns were quick and smooth. I thought she was much faster than the girls who had gone before her. After the last barrel, she sprinted back to the gate with a time of 13.46 seconds, a full second faster than any previous rider. The crowd gave her a big applause.

Haley Lofgren ran next on her horse, Mindy. The well-defined black horse with a white blaze had great muscle tone. She resembled Thunderbolt. Haley came out of the gate as fast, if not faster, than Shayla had. She rounded all three barrels without knocking any over. She wasn't as smooth in the turns as Shayla had been. Mindy sprinted back to the gate faster than Ruby had. The clock read 13.54 seconds. Shayla was ahead by a mere eight one hundredths of a second.

Donna and Sherrie jumped up and down cheering, while Scott, Colonel, Bob Patterson, and I stood and clapped. Shayla and Ruby had had a great day.

Shayla came back to the stands and sat next to me. "Well, Andrew, what do you think of your first rodeo?"

"I love it. This is great!"

"What did you think of my ride?"

"That was exciting. You ride a lot faster that I thought. You have a great seat."

She searched my face for a double meaning, "Are you talking about my riding or my ass?"

"I'm talking about the way you ride."

"I'm warning you now, Andrew. If you write a poem about my ass, your parents will never have grandchildren."

"I didn't know we were getting married."

"We're not! You won't be able to have children--with anyone." Shayla noticed her mother looking at her.

"What are you two talking about?" asked Donna.

"Andy is quite the poet, Mom. We were just discussing our creative writing assignment due next week. It's a poem about nature. Sometimes, Andrew needs motivation to help him get started. Isn't that right, Andrew?"

"That's right, Mrs. Stevenson." *And, I'm motivated not to write a poem about Shayla's ass.*

Shayla gave me a nudge with her elbow. "Coming to the dance tonight, aren't you?"

"Sure, if you want me to."

"I don't care if you come or not, but you might as well. It's a lot of fun. I won't be staying late because I want to get plenty of rest for my ride tomorrow."

"I'll be there."

After watching the calf-roping and bull-riding events, we went home to get ready for the dance. Mom had bought me a new shirt and told me to shine my boots. I didn't know what to expect at the dance either. I was nervous because I didn't know how to dance to country western music. I would have stayed home except Jared was going and Shayla asked me to go. Well, hinted that I should come anyway.

When my parents and I entered the hall, it was half full. The DJ played "Amarillo by Morning" by George Strait. Only one couple was dancing. Mr. and Mrs. Stevenson sat at a table close to the dance floor. John had his broken ankle propped up in one of the chairs. Shayla, Skeeter, and Henry Spillman were talking at the next table. John motioned for us to join them. Mom sat next to Donna and I sat next to Mom. Dad sat on the other side with John.

"Do you and John dance often?" asked Mom.

"Every chance we get. But with John's leg in a cast, we won't be dancing tonight. Do you and Scott like dancing?"

"Are you kidding me? Square dancing was a required class at my high school. I grew up with country music. Scott wasn't much of a dancer when I first met him but now he's actually quite good."

"Scott and Colonel will have to take up my slack tonight," John said. "I have as much fun watching her dance as I do dancing with her. You wouldn't mind, would you Scott?"

"Hell no. I'll dance with both of them. Only a fool would pass up an opportunity like that!"

"Andy can help too," said John.

"I don't know how to dance country."

John shook his head. "Boy, you better learn or you'll be missing out on lot of pretty girls."

"I'll teach you," said Donna. "It's not that hard."

Dad ordered a round of drinks for the table. Shayla came and sat next to me. "Nice shirt, Andrew. You clean up well for a city boy."

"Thanks, nice pants."

"We're not going there again are we?"

"Nope, I want to have children someday."

She laughed, "Are you going to dance?"

"I don't know how to dance to country music."

"Just watch. It's easy. You'll get the hang of it soon enough."

Skeeter came over and whispered something in Shayla's ear. Shayla smiled, got up and left the table. She walked to the DJ's table and said something to him, then returned to our table but didn't sit.

When the song he was playing finished, the DJ announced, "We have a request for 'Pontoon' by Little Big Town. Let's get some movement out there on the floor!"

I didn't recognize the song but it had a great beat and there were no horses, dogs, or trucks in the song. Shayla and Skeeter walked out on the floor and started dancing. Dad took Mom and Donna out on the floor at the same time. Skeeter motioned for Henry Spillman to join them and he did. A tall cowboy in his mid twenties walked out onto the floor and started dancing with Shayla. Her body swayed to the music and her feet appeared to float just above the floor. She was a great dancer and looked gorgeous. Sexy, yet innocent.

Many others joined them and before long the dance floor was full. I noticed Kelsey Gardner and Stacey Miller dancing with some boys I didn't recognize. For one of the few times in my life, I felt out of place.

The same cowboy kept asking Shayla to dance and she did several more times. I figured him to be one of the bull riders. He stood at the bar with several other cowboys drinking heavily. They watched every girl in the place, but he had his eye on Shayla.

After a few dances, the DJ announced he would be taking a short break. Shayla left our table to talk to Stacey and Kelsey. The cowboy who had been dancing with her headed for the restroom and I followed. I walked up to the urinal next to him and started taking a leak. The cowboy noticed me and said, "Hey kid, what's the name of the girl sitting at your table."

"Who, Peaches? The one you've been dancing with?"

"Peaches, is that her name?"

"Yeah, she's my cousin. She's only sixteen."

"You're kidding me, aren't you? She looks nineteen or twenty."

"Nope, she's jail bait and her father is the Chief of Police."

The cowboy had a disappointed frown on his face when we left the restroom. I returned to my seat and saw him talking to his friends and looking in Shayla's direction. When the music started, he didn't asked Shayla to dance. He asked another girl to dance.

Shayla grabbed my arm and led me out to the dance floor. "I'll lead and you follow." I awkwardly stumbled my way through my first country and western dance.

"Not bad for a start," she said.

We danced several more times. Shayla was a good instructor and I enjoyed the lessons, especially the slow songs. None of the other cowboys asked Shayla to dance the rest of the night.

During the next break Shayla walked up to the bar and ordered a soda. The cowboy she had been dancing with said something to her and she attempted to slap him. He caught her wrist to stop her. She attempted to slap him with her other hand and he grabbed that one also. "Hold on there, tiger," said the cowboy. "Let's not get rowdy."

John was hobbling to his feet and Colonel was already up but Dad was one step ahead of them, "I got it boys. Just relax." His voice sounded official and both John and Colonel sat back down. Dad approached Shayla and the cowboys. I followed but stood back out of the way.

"Let her go, cowboy," Dad said.

The cowboy let her go and raised his hands, "I'm not looking for trouble."

Shayla tried to slap him again but this time Dad grabbed her arm and told her to go have a seat. "He called me Peaches!" she said. She wasn't happy, but returned to her seat.

"Alright, what's this all about?" asked dad.

"Nothing really. I danced with her a couple of times. I found out she was only sixteen and stopped. The next thing I know, she's attacking me."

"Who told you her name was Peaches?"

He pointed at me. "Her cousin."

Dad looked at me and I wiped the grin off my face. He frowned and turned back to the cowboy, "Yeah, she's jailbait for sure but her name's not Peaches. That's her nickname. Only her family can call her that."

"I didn't know that. Like I said, we're not looking for trouble."

"Alright boys, just stay clear of her and I'll try to keep her on a leash."

"Thanks."

Dad started to leave and then stopped to face the cowboys. "By the way, if you're riding tomorrow, you might want to slow down on the booze."

The cowboy who had been dancing with Shayla started to say something but his buddies grabbed him by the arm and started walking him out. "Come on, Bart. You know better than to argue with the law."

Shayla was fuming when we got back to the table.

"What was that about?" asked John.

"Nothing really. He got her mixed up with someone else." Dad looked over at me and winked.

He then leaned over and whispered in Mom's ear. Mom smiled and looked at me, "Devious little shit, just like his father."

"Got to give it to him," Dad whispered.

The DJ started playing music and Shayla grabbed me by the arm and led me out on the dance floor again. After a couple of dances, she asked, "Andrew, will you drive me home? I don't want my parents to have to leave the dance just for me."

"Sure." We told our parents we were leaving and my mom winked at me.

The three cowboys from the bar were in the parking lot standing next to an old faded pick-up truck drinking beer as we walked to my car. One of them whistled and Shayla yelled, "Jerk!"

The one they called Bart said, "What's the matter, Peaches? You know you like it."

The other cowboys laughed. Shayla started towards them and I grabbed her arm. "Oh no you don't." I pulled her towards the car.

Bart started stumbling towards us, beer in hand. "Come on, baby girl, give me a good night kiss."

Shayla responded over her shoulder. "You can kiss my ass!"

Bart kept coming. "That would be a good place to start, sweetheart."

"We don't want any trouble, Bart." I said.

He was almost to us. "Fuck you, pussy. I'm talking to the bitch."

Before Shayla could react, I spun with a roundhouse kick, hitting Bart in the center of his chest, knocking him flat on his back.

The other cowboys came over and lifted him off the ground. He clutched his sternum, trying to catch his breath. "Anyone else?" I asked.

"We ain't got no dog in this fight," said one of the cowboys laughing as they dragged Bart back to their truck, trying not to spill their beers.

Shayla stared at me, mouth open. I asked, "What are you looking at? Let's go home."

We got in the car and Shayla asked, "Is that how you got Hairy Larry to change his ways?"

"Something like that."

She smiled, "Thanks, Andrew."

"You're welcome. And my friends call me Andy."

CHAPTER SEVENTEEN

I had a great time at the dance and looked forward to the second day of the rodeo. Shayla smiled as she joined us in the stands. "Good morning, Andrew," she said as she sat next to Colonel and me. Mom and Dad sat visiting with Donna and John. We watched the rodeo events for a while. I thought anyone wanting to ride a bull, had to be insane.

When Shayla left to get ready for her ride, Colonel and I went to watch her warm up. After a few practice runs, Colonel and I returned to the stadium to wait for the competition to begin.

Haley Lofgren would be riding in ninth place and Shayla would follow in tenth place. Haley came out of the gate very fast and made a clean run. Her horse looked outstanding and Haley rode a cleaner ride than she had yesterday. Her time was 13:38, which meant Shayla had to ride at least as fast as she did yesterday just to tie. The pressure was now on Shayla and Ruby.

They came out of the gate fast and rounded the first barrel. Ruby sprinted to the second barrel and rounded it flawlessly. Their turns were quick and smooth. Ruby sprinted to the third barrel.

Shayla cut the barrel too close. Ruby hit the barrel causing her to trip and fall. Shayla came off hard and hit the ground. Ruby went down, rolled, and stumbled back to her feet. She tried walking but had a bad limp. Shayla lay motionless in the dirt.

I sprinted down the stairs and jumped the fence. When I got to Shayla, she was dazed but conscious, trying to stand up. I grabbed her shoulders and held her down.

She had a large lump on her forehead and her right arm was scraped and bleeding. "Are you all right?"

She looked around as if she didn't know where she was. She didn't answer me. Colonel, Donna and Dad joined me along with several of the rodeo employees. Dad asked Shayla to follow his index finger as he moved it back and forth in front of her eyes. She followed his finger without hesitation.

"Do you know where you are?" he asked.

She looked around. "At the rodeo."

"How do you feel?"

She sat up. "Fine, were is Ruby?"

Several cowboys were holding Ruby on the other side of the arena. She was holding her right front leg up off the ground. Dad and I wanted Shayla to stay down but she forced herself up with Donna's help and walked to Ruby. Ruby could hardly put any weight on her right front leg. She was limping badly as Shayla led her out of the arena while Donna, Colonel, Dad and I followed.

When we got to the gate, the rodeo workers told us no spectators were allowed in the stall area except for her parents. Donna went with Shayla.

We returned to the stands and met John at the bottom row. Dad told him Shayla had a knot on her forehead but it didn't appear she had a concussion or any broken bones. John went to be with his wife and daughter. Dad went back into the stands to get Mom and I followed John to the stall area.

The rodeo personal let John in to see Shayla but I wasn't allowed in. I walked around to the wood fence and watched through the cracks in the fence. I could hear John and Donna talking to Shayla and a veterinarian named Dr. Olsen. Shayla told her parents that she wasn't hurt. They obviously saw the knot on her forehead and the scrapes on her arm.

Dr. Olsen examined Ruby, and said, "It's the digital flexor tendon. I'm not sure if she tore it completely or just stretched it badly. I won't be able tell without x-rays, but I can tell you right now, this horse will never race barrels again."

"No Doc," Shayla cried. "That can't be true!"

"Shayla, the very best you can hope for is that she might make a decent trail horse if that tendon is not completely torn."

Tears ran down Shayla's cheeks. "No Doc, it can't be! Tell me she will be able to race again! She has to be able to race again!" She was sobbing now.

Doc Olsen put his arm around her. "Honey, I wish I could, but I can't. Once that tendon is damaged like this, she can never support the pressure she would need to barrel race. If it is completely torn, she may have to be put down. I'm sorry, Shayla."

John asked Colonel if he would load Ruby and take her home. Her parents said they were going to take Shayla to the doctor to make sure she was all right. Shayla protested and didn't want to leave Ruby, but her parents insisted. Colonel said he would give Ruby some pain medication, ice the leg and wrap it before taking her home.

I felt terrible for Shayla and Ruby but there was nothing I could do so I rejoined my parents in the stands hoping Ruby and Shayla would be all right.

CHAPTER EIGHTEEN

Mondays were never my favorite day of the week, but having a spring break from school made this one better than most. Being able to work at the Double J Ranch made it even better. I wanted to get the truck paid off as quickly as possible. I also wanted to see if Shayla was all right. I parked my car next to the barn and went inside.

Shayla was in Ruby's stall. Her eyes were red and puffy. She looked as if she hadn't slept much. She had a bucket of ice and several towels, tending to Ruby's leg. She didn't notice me enter the barn as she changed the ice pack. "How's she doing, Shayla?"

"Hi, Andrew. Not good. She can barely put pressure on her leg."

The bruise on Shayla's head had turned a light shade of yellow and purple overnight. She had a bandage on her right arm and scraps on her hand. "How are you feeling?"

"I'm fine, just sore. I didn't get a chance to thank you for helping me yesterday."

"You scared the hell out of me. I was afraid you broke your neck. I'm just glad you could walk."

She didn't reply.

"Do you think Ruby will be all right?"

"No, she won't!" Shayla said as she tried to hide the tears. "She'll never run barrels again." Shayla paused and took several deep breaths while looking at Ruby. "She will be lucky if she can even make a decent trail horse. It's breaking my heart. I raised her from a foal."

"If there is anything I can do, please let me know."

"You know nothing about horses, Andrew. And even if you did, there's nothing you could do. Just go away, will you?"

I hated to leave her but knew she wanted to be alone with Ruby. And, she was right. I didn't know much about horses and there was nothing I could do to help her. "I'll catch you later."

I left to find Colonel. We were supposed to be replacing rusted pipes from the well on the hill to the Stevenson's ranch. Colonel had hauled the PVC pipe the up the mountain with the quad and connected them to the water tank. He dug a trench with the tractor. We would not be covering the pipes until we were sure they didn't leak. I had already installed the pressure regulator at the pipe going into the house from the barn. Today, we planned to connect all the pipes together and secure them to the new bladder inside the tank. If all went well, the Stevenson's should have all the clean water and pressure they desired. Mr. Stevenson told me I could take the truck as soon as this job was completed.

I walked to the shop to find Colonel. I saw John Stevenson walking towards the barn. His walking cast made things slow but at least he was able to get around with a cane.

"Good morning, Colonel. What do you want me to do?"

"Morning Andy. Go around behind the barn and find me another piece pipe? I only need about two feet. Find any piece longer and I'll cut it to length."

I walked to the rear of the barn and started looking for the pipe. I heard Shayla and John arguing inside the barn. Shayla was becoming hysterical and crying loudly. I couldn't help overhearing their conversation.

"Dad, I raised her from a foal, you can't just send her off to the auction!"

"Shayla, you know the rules. We don't feed animals that can't produce. You need another horse and I can't afford to buy one. It's hard enough trying to keep from loosing this ranch without feeding horses that are useless to us. Someone will buy her and give her a good home."

"No they won't! Some jerk will buy her for next to nothing and send her to the slaughterhouse! No one wants a lame horse."

"She's too good a horse to be sent to the slaughter house and you know it. I'm taking her to the auction tomorrow and that's that. Bob Patterson is going to loan you another horse until I can afford to buy you one."

"I hate you!" Shayla screamed as she ran from the barn crying.

I found a short piece of pipe and waited for John to go into his house before rejoining Colonel in the shop. He was unusually quiet today. He kept looking back at the barn as if something was wrong. We walked to the water tank and connected the well pipe to the shut off valve. Colonel went to where the last pipe needed to be connected to the pressure valve and had me open the top valve at the well. A small stream of muddy water started flowing through the bottom pipe and then it tuned clear. Colonel told me to open it up.

I opened the valve all the way and water sprayed fifteen feet out of the pipe. John Stevenson had joined Colonel at the bottom valve by the time I got there.

"Damn, Colonel, that will blow the facets through the roof. That's what I call pressure. I can't believe it could be this easy."

Colonel told me to turn the valve off. I turned the water off and re-joined them at the bottom of the hill. John Stevenson was smiling, "We've been suffering with low water pressure for years. I had no idea we could get rid of that old rusted-out tank. Andy, you earned that truck. You can take the truck anytime you want."

"Thanks Mr. Stevenson. But I still want to work off the rest of the money. I'll see when Dad can help me get it home. I can't wait to start fixing it up."

"John we'll get this last pipe hooked up in the next hour or so and start turning the water back on. Tell Donna I'll call her on the phone and she can let us know when she has the right amount of pressure," Colonel said.

"Alright. And when you're done, can you hook up the small horse trailer to my truck? I have to go to the auction tomorrow."

Colonel nodded, "All right."

After John left, Colonel took a deep breath and shook his head. We connected the last pipe and Colonel called Donna on the phone so he could adjust the water pressure. I walked back up the hill to check for leaks. Colonel said he would cover the pipe tomorrow with the tractor if everything was all right. Convinced the job was completed, we picked up the tools and put them in the shop. It had been a short day.

I saw Colonel hooking up the horse trailer as I was leaving. I hadn't seen Shayla again since she left the barn this morning. I hoped she'd gotten some desperately needed sleep.

Went I got home, I told Dad we could bring the `56 Ford home anytime we wanted. He told me to hook up the trailer and grab a come-a-long and an air pump and we'd go get it.

We drove to the Ranch, filled the tires with air and hooked a come-a-long to the truck. Then, I cranked it onto the trailer. John and Donna came out and watched us load it up.

"Scott, Andy sure earned that truck. We haven't had decent water pressure for years and now we have all we want. He's a bright kid."

Dad smiled, "He has a gift for figuring things out. He's going to do most of the work fixing up this old truck."

"Andy, you bring that truck by when you get it finished," said John. "We want to see how it looks."

"I'll do better than that Mr. Stevenson, I'll let you drive it. I want Shayla to see it to, she thinks it is a piece of junk."

Donna replied, "I kind of agree with her. I can't imagine it ever running again. But if it does, I want a ride also."

"It'll run again! Mr. Stevenson can take you for a ride then I'll take Shayla for a ride."

"We'll be looking forward to it," John said.

As we drove home, Dad asked, "How much money do you have to fix it up?"

"I'm not sure yet. I'm thinking about buying a horse. I'll let you know when I get back from the auction on Wednesday."

Dad looked confused, "Going to get yourself a horse are you? I'm glad to see you're taking an interest in riding, son." He paused and scratched his head. "Need any help finding a good horse?"

"No thanks, Dad. I already know the one I want. I just don't know how much she'll cost."

"Well if you need any help, let me know. Now let's get the truck in the barn so we can start taking it apart. Are you still thinking of painting it blue?"

"I've changed my mind. I'm going to paint it green."

CHAPTER NINETEEN

Colonel Lightfoot and I arrived at the Double J Ranch about the same time. John Stevens hobbled out of the house in his walking cast carrying a cane. "Colonel, will you load Ruby in the trailer for me please?"

"Sure,"

After John turned to go back in the house, Colonel starting walking toward the barn, stopped, turned and opened his mouth as if he was going to say something. But he caught himself and turned back around shaking his head.

I saw Shayla standing in the kitchen with her mother looking out the window. Donna had her arm around her. Tears streamed down Shayla's face as she watched Colonel walk Ruby towards the trailer. Obviously in pain, Ruby favored her left front leg. Her left font leg had been wrapped for support. I expected Shayla to come outside to say goodbye, but she didn't.

By the time Colonel got Ruby into the trailer, Shayla was shaking her head back and forth. She pulled away from her mother and disappeared from sight. With Ruby loaded, John got into his truck and drove away.

After John left, I approached Colonel, "How much do you think he'll get for Ruby?"

"Normally eight to ten thousand dollars with her papers and training. But with that limp, he'll be darn lucky to get five hundred. She'll probably go to the slaughterhouse."

"You think John's making a mistake, don't you?"

Colonel looked at me. "You ask too many questions kid," then he walked away.

John returned about an hour later and went into the house. I didn't see any of the Stevensons for the rest of the day.

Eight hours of mending fences left me worn out, but I still wanted to work on the truck. When I got home, I removed the bolts holding the truck bed on and unhooked the gas tank from the back of the seat. After dad got home, we removed the bed and sat it aside so we could take it to the body shop. It was late by the time we finished. I hadn't been much help because my mind wasn't on the job.

I couldn't forget the pain in Shayla's face watching Ruby being led into the trailer. I checked the drawer in my bedroom where I kept my money. I had $580.00 in cash.

The next morning, I hooked up the horse trailer and drove to the auction. After checking in at the office and getting my number so I could bid, I went inside to watch.

Two Hispanic men were buying all of the old and lame horses. They spoke Spanish and were paying anywhere from fifty to a hundred fifty dollars per horse. Those horses were bound for the slaughterhouse in Mexico. The healthier sound horses were being purchased by local residents at much higher prices.

Ruby was one of the last horses to be brought out. She could hardly walk and looked sad as she limped into the arena. I heard several people commenting on what a shame it was for such a fine animal to be lame. The auctioneer said Ruby might make someone a fine broodmare. Apparently, even he had given up on her. I wondered if I would be wasting my money.

The bidding started at a hundred dollars. One of the Hispanic men took the bid. I waited until I was sure no one else would bid on her. I bid two hundred dollars. They immediately raised the bid to three hundred. I raised the bid to four hundred thinking I'd scare them off. The two men whispered to each other while looking back at me, then raised the bid to five hundred fifty dollars. I stared at them. Pausing for a moment, I remembering how much money I had, I raised the bid to $580.00. One of the Mexicans shook his head as if he didn't want to bid any higher. They waited until the auctioneer said, "Going once, going twice, going th…."

"Six hundred," The other Mexicans said in broken English.

My heart sank. I didn't have that much money. I took a deep breath knowing I'd failed. The auctioneer said, "Going, once, going twice, going th… " From somewhere behind me a voice yelled, "Seven hundred!"

The Mexican quit bidding and Ruby sold for seven hundred dollars. I attempted to see who bought her but couldn't see above the crowd.

I went to my truck in the parking lot and sat in the dark thinking. I couldn't believe someone would pay that much for a lame horse. When I started to drive away, Colonel appeared at my driver's window. "You like that girl a hell of a lot more than I thought, Andy."

"What are doing here, Colonel?"

"Thinking about buying a horse. But I didn't want to bid against you."

Then I noticed he was leading a horse. I took a better look. "You?"

"Yep. Interested in buying a horse? She's for sale."

"I did, but I only have $580.00."

"Would you have paid $700.00 for her if you'd had it?"

"Of course."

"She's yours if you want her. Pay me what you have and you can owe me the rest."

A smile spread across my face. "Sold Colonel! And thanks."

Colonel helped me load Ruby in my trailer. I gave him the $580.00.

"Drive slow so she doesn't bounce around any more than she has to. I'll meet you at your house and show you what to do."

I couldn't keep the smile off my face. "Thanks again, Colonel."

When we got to my house, Colonel helped unload Ruby. I put her in a stall. Colonel took a large white syringe and squeezed something into her mouth while holding her head up.

"What are you giving her?"

"Bute, it's for the pain. Can you bring me some ice and ask Sherrie if she has any wrap and some towels?"

Mom came out to assist Colonel when I brought the ice. They wrapped Ruby's leg with an ice pack and Colonel showed me how to change it. I placed two new bags of wood shavings in her stall so she would be more confortable when she laid down. Colonel told me the correct amount of food he wanted me to feed her and warned, "If you overfeed her, she'll gain weight, adding more pressure on the leg, making it harder for her to heal."

"I'll change the ice pack several times a day." Mom said.

"Keep her calm and hopefully we'll see improvement within a week or so. If you think she's in a lot of pain, Andy, give her more Bute, but not much. We want her to feel some pain so she keeps her weight off that leg. I'll stop by every few days to check on her," Colonel said.

I walked him to his truck. "You're a good man, Colonel Lightfoot." He smiled and got in his truck and started to leave. "Can you do me a favor? Don't tell anyone I bought Ruby. If I can't get her healed, I don't want Shayla to know I bought her. If I can heal her, I want it to be a surprise."

"I'll tell her a local bought her and that she'll have a good home. She'll sleep better knowing Ruby didn't go to the slaughter-house." He offered me his hand and I took it. "It was a good thing you did today, Andy."

"Thanks, you too."

I walked back to the barn and Ruby was lying down. I'd never owned a horse before and felt a strong sense of responsibility.

CHAPTER TWENTY

I'd been working on my truck all day and was running late. When I arrived at the gym, Coach Ford was in his office reading a Sports Illustrated magazine. Hairy Larry passed me in the locker room but didn't make eye contact. I could never figure him out, or what his hidden agenda was. Sometime, I wondered if he even thought at all.

Most of the football players were done with their workouts by now. It seemed the players were staying longer lately, which was a good sign. The usual laughing and horseplay was less obvious. The gym closed at 6:30 p.m. but everyone knew the coach would stay as long as anyone was there. Jared had told me Coach Ford's wife had died of cancer three years ago and that he didn't have any children. He never seemed to be in a hurry to leave.

When Coach Ford saw me, he motioned for me to come into his office. "Andy, I added you to the roster as the quarterback if you're still willing."

"Sure, Coach, wherever you need me. Will we be having a football camp this summer?"

"No, we tried that a few times but it never seemed to work out. Most players have summer jobs or are working on their parent's farms. We didn't get much of a turnout and money was always a problem."

"Can we run our own program at the school?"

"The rules are pretty strict about organized practices at the school."

"But, we could run one at the park as long as none of the coaches were involved, right."

"Sure. You can practice as much as you want on your own. Are you thinking of doing that?"

"I'm going to try. My dad might help us."

Coach Ford rubbed his chin for a moment, "Well good luck with that. Hope it works out."

The coach walked into the weight room with me and watched the players for a while. Everyone was wet with sweat and was either on the weights or spotting their partner. As soon as one finished, his partner replaced him. Each player had a white card with him that he wrote on it after completing his reps.

I had my laptop computer sitting out and some of the players were checking it against their cards. The Coach looked at the back wall where I had place a new poster which read; *THE MORE YOU SWEAT, THE LESS YOU BLEED!* Just below that was: *U.S. Navy Seals.*

Coach Ford rubbed his chin. No one acknowledged him or even acted as he were in the weight room. He turned and walked back to his office.

The rest of the team had left by the time he returned around 7:00 p.m. Jared and I were the only ones still working out. "Last rep, Coach," I said as he entered.

"Take your time boys, I'm not going anywhere."

I noticed the coach counting the amount of weights we were squatting. He smiled, shook his head and walked back to his office.

Ten minutes later Jared and I left. We told the coach good night in unison as we passed his office.

"Good night boys. Drive careful," Coach Ford yelled as he locked the door behind us.

"The coach looks kind of bummed-out today, Jared. You have any idea what's going on?"

"Today is the third anniversary of his wife's death. I'm not sure if that has anything to do with it or not. Rumor has it that some parents have asked Mr. Rudd to replace him as our coach."

"Why would they do that?"

"This town is tired of losing, I guess. If we have another losing season, I know he's a goner."

I drove Jared home and returned to the stadium to run the steps. Coach Ford's truck was still parked in front of the office when I got there, but the inside lights were out. I was running my last set steps when I heard, "What the hell?"

Coach Ford stood at the bottom of the steps staring at me as I came down. I stopped and caught my breath. "Hi, Coach. What are you still doing here?"

"What am I doing here... what are you still doing here?"

"Isometrics, Coach. And running stairs."

"But why? It's almost nine o'clock."

"I know, but if you do squats and don't run or do isometrics, you'll get stronger but slower. The goal is to get bigger, faster and stronger."

The Coach shook his head. His words were slurred. "You fail never to amazzze me, Andrew. Still dreaming about another championship are ya? Be careful what you wish for boy. There's more important things in life than wining... winning football champion... ships."

As he turned to walk away, he stumbled, caught himself and then walked towards his truck. I followed him. "Hey Coach, can I give you a lift home?"

He waved me off. "I appreciate your concern but I'm al… alright, just tired. I'll see you tomorrow."

"Come on, Coach, let me give you a lift. It's on my way home."

Coach Ford kept walking towards his truck. " Go on home, Andy. I'm alright."

"You won't be alright if the police stop you."

Coach Ford got to his truck and turned to face me. He paused for a minute and then said, "Andy… you're a good kid and I like you. I wish I had twenty more just like you. If we did, we might take that state championship next year. But to be honest, we ain't got a snowball's chance in hell of beatin' Safford! They beat us like a red-headed stepchild this year. It was downright embarrassen. Next year they'll have more starters returning than we will. You keep right on dreaming kid. But we don't have that caliber of players on this team. I'm sorry."

"I think you're underestimating the team, Coach, I think they have grit. We need a lot of work but we're coming around. With the best coach in the state, I think we can find a way to beat Safford."

"Now you're over estimating me. Go on home, Andy."

Coach Ford turned to get into his truck. I grabbed him by the arm. "I can't let you drive, sir. You might hurt someone. It could even be one of your players."

He jerked his arm away. For the first time, I saw he was angry. I had hit a nerve.

"Leave me alone, damn it. I don't need a babysitter."

"Bullshit." I grabbed his keys. "You're not driving Coach. And that's final."

He looked at me as if he was going to argue, but didn't. He took a deep breath and stared at me. His eyes began to water. "I wouldn't hurt one of my boys, Andy! Not in a million years! If my wife were here, she'd tell you. She'd tell you, Andy. I never would."

I put my hand on the Coach's shoulder, "I know you wouldn't hurt anyone on purpose, Coach. I wasn't saying you would. I was just explaining what might happen if you drive when you've been drinking. Now let me drive you home."

Coach Ford took another a deep breath, dried his eyes and gathered his composure. A few awkward moments of silence followed as he hung his head in thought. "Oh hell, Andy. I guess there's no use arguing with a cop's son. You're right. I don't want to chance hurting nobody. You take me home. But what about my truck?"

"I'll drive you home in your truck and jog back here to get my car. It's not far and I haven't finished my workout anyway."

Coach Ford scooted into the passenger's seat and I strapped him in. I drove to the front of the school and turned to exit onto the street. I noticed a white car parked in the parking lot with its lights off. Steam rose from the tailpipe. The headlights from Coach Ford's truck illuminated the inside of the car just long enough for me to see Lt. Reinhardt sitting behind the wheel.

I looked over at the coach. He had his head leaned back on the seat with his eyes closed. I turned onto the street and drove away from the school watching for movement from the unmarked police car. It never moved. I drove Coach Ford home and helped him to his front door. "You're not going anywhere, are you, Coach?" I said as I handed him his keys.

"Yes I am. Straight to bed! Thanks, Andy, I owe you one," he replied as he stumbled into his house.

After he closed the door, the living room light came on. I waited for a few more moments and a bedroom light came on. The living room light went out and a moment later the bedroom light went out. Satisfied the coach had gone to bed, I turned and started jogging down the road towards the school. Half way down the block, I spotted a white vehicle parked in the dark shadows of an old oak tree facing up hill towards the Coach's house. It was parked on the opposite side of the street and not running. I couldn't see inside the vehicle, and was unsure if Lt. Reinhardt was there or not. I jogged back to the school, got in my car and drove home.

CHAPTER TWENTY-ONE

D ad was going to work the swing shift so he could get better acquainted with the swing and graveyard shift officers and get a feel for what went on weeknights in Clarksville. He asked me if I wanted to go for a ride-a-long. Clarksville's small police department had only a Sargent and four officers working the swing shift. They only had three officers working the graveyard shift.

We pulled into the police parking lot and sat there. An older `60 model pickup pulled in and parked in the employee parking area. The truck appeared stock but in immaculate condition. It looked as if it had just come off the showroom floor.

We sat in Dad's truck and watched as an officer exited the truck. His shoes were shined; his hair was cut short and his clothes were pressed. He looked like a poster child for a police recruiting poster except he was about forty pounds overweight. He got out of his truck, pushed the door lock down and reached inside to get his gear. He retrieved his bulletproof vest, a flashlight, a briefcase, a nightstick, a radio, a lunch pail and a thermos bottle. He used his rear end to shut the truck door and waddled into the station with both arms full.

I asked, "Is this his first night on the job, or does he take his equipment home with him every night?"

"I don't know. They have lockers."

We entered the station and Chief Baker asked us to step into his office. We walked in and he shut the door. "You going out with your father tonight, Andy?"

"Yeah, I'd like to see what happens around here."

"Not much I'm afraid. I heard you bought a horse."

"I got her at the auction. She's lame now but I think I can get her healed up."

"What's up, Harvey?" asked Dad.

"I think you'll have a visitor pretty soon."

"Who's the visitor?"

"Bernie Baxter. He's been asking about you."

"Isn't he the weight coach for our football team?" I asked.

"That's him."

"What does he want?" Dad asked.

"He claims he just wants to get to know you. But with elected officials, you never know. Most of them have hidden agendas."

"It sounds as if you don't trust him."

"No, that's not it. He's one of the Police Department's biggest supporters."

"Tell me about him."

Chief Baker lit a cigar and blew smoke rings into the air. "Bernie is a three time elected councilman. He took the position when another councilman retired and no one else wanted the job. He was unopposed in the next two elections. I think he has his eyes on the Mayor's job if the Mayor ever retires. It's rumored he may take a shot at the State House of Representatives."

"He sounds ambitious."

"He is. He comes from a good family and his parents own the largest farm in the valley. It runs all the way from the Apache Indian Reservation east for five miles and all the way from the state highway down to the river. His parents are retired and his brother, Harold, runs the farm. Harold is probably the best farmer in these parts."

"What does Bernie do for a living?"

"Andy," said Chief Baker, "I wouldn't want anything I tell your father to be repeated."

"I won't say a word, Chief"

"Good." Chief turned to Dad. "He owns the Iron Man Gym. He's divorced and I hear his ex-wife did a number on him financially. He's never had an interest in farming. He played football for Coach Ford, and as Andy said, he volunteers as a high school football coach. He's also the president of the high school's Booster Club."

"Anything else?"

"Yeah, there were two no votes from the city council members on bringing in an outsider for the Assistant Chief's job. Bernie was one of them."

Dad paused for a moment. "Isn't the Iron Man Gym the name of the health club Bobby Patterson was working at on the night he was killed?" Dad asked.

Chief raised an eyebrow and scratched the back of his neck before answering. "One and the same. The only health club in town. Bernie is a body builder. He was runner-up for Mr. Arizona once, I hear."

"Anything else I should know about this guy?"

"One other thing, but you didn't hear it from me. After Bernie got out of high school, he joined the Army and told everyone he was going to be a Ranger. He didn't make it through boot camp and told everyone he had some medical problem and the Army wouldn't let him stay in. Years later, another soldier told me he was kicked out of the Army for fighting. He apparently got into two fights with other recruits. Then, made the mistake of hitting his drill sergeant. He got his ass kicked and they threw him out of the Army. I'm not sure if that story is true or not."

"Thanks for the heads up."

Dad and I went to the briefing room where Sgt. Ortiz was briefing the swing shift officers. Ortiz stopped the briefing when we walked in. He introduced Dad and me to the officers. Dad shook hands with the four patrol officers which he knew by name. The officer who had carried all of his equipment into the station was named Gordon Goff, but the officers called him Gordie.

The 15-minute briefing could have been a five-minute briefing if Sgt. Ortiz hadn't stretched it out. There apparently wasn't much to brief about in the town of Clarksville. Sgt. Ortiz was good-natured and told two funny jokes which I hoped I could remember.

After briefing, Dad and I got into the police cruiser with Sgt. Ortiz. All of the patrol officers were already gone except Officer Goff, who was at the gas pumps washing the windows of his patrol car. "Tell me about Officer Goff," Dad said.

"He's a bit on the anal side and meticulous as hell and can't help himself. He always goes to the pumps after briefings to clean his windows, throw out any trash, empty the ashtrays and check the air pressure in the tires. He's the kind of officer that if he were talking to you in your office and saw a stack of papers that weren't straight, he would straighten them without realizing he was doing it."

"How is he as an officer?" asked Dad.

"Officer Goff is the best marksman on the Department. His reports are always complete and he never misspells a word. Over all, he is a good police officer. He has great sense of humor and he never gets citizen complaints."

Dad told Ortiz about him bringing in all of his equipment to work. "That's Gordie. Takes all his equipment home every night and brings it back the next day. Claims he wants to clean it."

Sgt. Ortiz told us we needed to wait for a tow truck that was coming to pick up a vehicle out of the police vehicle compound lot. When the truck arrived, Sgt. Ortiz checked over the paperwork, had the driver sign the release forms. He released a car to the driver who towed it away. Dad noticed a brand new Ford 150 pickup truck sitting in the lot with a burned out cab and asked Sgt. Ortiz about the truck.

"A couple of local boys stole that truck off a car lot in Show Low. They drove it around for a couple of days, then took it down to the river and set it on fire. The fire burned the inside of the cab. With the windows and doors shut, it couldn't get enough oxygen to burn the truck completely. We got a call of a car fire down by the river. The fire department was able to get the fire out before the gas tank blew.

"Did we catch the suspects?" Dad asked.

"Yep. Several kids had seen the boys driving the truck. We arrested them the next day and they confessed."

"Were they convicted?"

"Would have been, but the father of one of the boys is a big-time rancher and the Bishop of the LDS Church here in town. He went to the Ford dealership and told them he would pay sticker price for the truck if they dropped the charges. That was more money than they would have gotten from the insurance company, so they took the deal."

"Who owns the truck now?"

"Technically, the father who paid for the truck owns it. He holds the title but he doesn't want it. He's trying to keep the theft quiet and hopes it doesn't make the paper."

"Can you get me a copy of the report?"

"Sure. It'll be on your desk tomorrow morning, Chief."

I couldn't believe the transformation that took place on a week-end night as we patrolled the downtown area. The place was hopping. Groups of kids gathered at different spots all along Main Street. A steady stream of cars drove back and forth along Main Street, all within a six-block area. Most cars were filled with kids who were yelling and waving at the kids parked on the side of he road. Every type of vehicle imaginable was driving back and fourth, mostly filled with teenagers. There were a few street rods on the road and more parked in groups along the sides of the street. McDonald's seemed to be the largest group and several nice street rods were parked facing Main Street. They had their hoods up and people were walking around looking at the cool cars. A speaker blared `50s music from a loudspeaker. Another group of older men parked their old cars in Skeeter's parking lot facing Main Street. Most of them were stock from the 1930s and 1940s.

"What's this all about?" Dad asked.

"Cruising Main. They do it every Friday night. On Saturdays, most of them move to Safford. It's an unofficial traveling car show. Been going on for as long as I can remember."

"Do we get many problems down here."

"Not really. Once in a while a couple of guys butt heads but we're on top of it and send them packing. We keep a couple of officers in the area to keep the speeding to a minimum. There's not much else for the kids to do and it's easy to keep an eye on them since they are all in the same place."

As we passed McDonald's, I saw Shayla and two girls I didn't recognize standing in the parking lot. I made a mental note to be here next Friday night.

At 10:00 p.m. we stopped at Skeeter's for lunch. Almost everyone in the place knew Sgt. Ortiz. After lunch, Ortiz said he wanted to show us some of the back roads around town. We drove north towards the river. An old paved road followed the river, curving back and forth. Traffic was light to non-existent. Sgt. Ortiz informed us that this road used to be the main highway through the area before the new highway was built. He explained you could get from one end of town to the other by using this road and never go into town. We came upon an old gray pickup truck headed east driving about five miles per hour. It hugged the right side of the roadway.

"That's Claud Anderson," said Ortiz. "He owns a garage on the eastern end of town. His son was the tow truck driver I released the car to earlier at the station. He's retired and his two sons, Ray and Larry, now run the shop. It's a good place to get your vehicles worked on. They do good work, back it up, and don't overcharge."

Sgt. Ortiz followed the truck but never turned on the overhead lights or tried to pull him over. After about a mile, Dad asked, "So what's the deal with Claud?"

"He's drunk," replied Sgt. Ortiz. "He gets that way a couple times a year. This is the back way to his house."

A few minutes later, Dad asked, "Are you gong to pull him over?"

"I was going to just follow him home, but if you want, I'll pull him over."

"How do you know he's drunk except for the fact he is only going five miles per hour?"

"When Claud gets drunk, he knows he's drunk. He's driving slow so he doesn't hurt himself or anyone else. If he were sober, he would be doing five over and taking the Main Street. See how he's bent over the wheel of his truck staring out the windshield. He doesn't even know we are back here."

I knew this wasn't normal police procedure and guessed Dad didn't want to tell Sargent Ortiz how to do his job. I wanted to see what Sgt. Ortiz was going to do when we got to Claud's house. We rounded a sharp curve and Claud's truck got too close to a short wooden guardrail and drove up onto it. The truck high-centered on the rail. The rear axel slid up about two inches off the ground and Claud's truck came to a gentle halt. The rear wheels kept spinning. Claud kept staring over the steering wheel as if nothing happened. He kept turning the front wheels back and forth as if he was still driving. Sgt. Ortiz stopped and put the patrol car in park. We sat there for a few minutes and Sgt. Ortiz said, "I guess I better go talk to Claud." He turned on the overhead blinking light and started to get out of the patrol car.

Dad said, "Stay here. I'll see what he's up to."

Ortiz seemed disappointed. Dad walked up to Claud's driver's side window. Claud didn't even notice that he was there. Dad started running in place as if he was chasing Claud's truck.

"Pull over, Claud," he yelled.

Claud looked over at Dad, hunched over the steering wheel and gave his truck more gas. The tires started spinning faster. Dad started running faster in place. "I said, pull over Claud," Dad yelled again. Claud gave the truck more gas and Dad ran faster in place. Claud kept increasing the RPM's and Dad kept running faster and faster in place without moving. Both Sgt. Ortiz and I were cracking up.

"You can't outrun me, Claud." Dad yelled. "Pull over or I'll have to take you to jail!"

Claud put his foot on the brake to stop his truck and put it into park. He turned the motor off, looked out the window at Dad who had now stopped running. "What the hell are ye? Some kind of Olympic runner?"

"You know you can't outrun the law, Claud. Now get in my patrol car so I can take you home," Dad said.

Not expecting the ground to be so far below him, Claud tripped as he stepped out of the truck. Dad grabbed his arm to steady him. Claud turned back and stared at his truck, realizing for the first time that he was high centered. He shook his head and walked back to the patrol car. When he saw Ortiz, he asked, "Gosh darn it, Ortiz. Who you got in the back?"

"Andy Hanson. He's the new Assistant Chief of Police's son."

"What'd he do?"

"Nothing. That's his father behind you."

Claud's eyes got wide and he tipped his hat to Dad. "Nice to meet you, Sir."

He walked behind the patrol car and took a leak. Dad patted him down and took his keys. Claud got in the back seat with me and Dad shut the door. Dad locked Claud's truck and walked back to the patrol car with a big grin on his face.

Claud's sons thanked us for bringing their father home. They said they would go get his truck. Ortiz and Dad didn't say another word about the incident.

The dispatcher advised by radio of an accident on the main highway just inside the city limits. Officer Goff was assigned the call. Sgt. Ortiz drove us to the scene of the accident to see if Gordie needed any help. It was a one-vehicle accident where a lady attempted to avoid hitting what she thought was a dog and ran into a ditch. She hit the dog, which was really a coyote, and killed it. There was minor damage to her car but we were able to push her out of the small ditch.

Officer Goff stayed to get the information for the accident report. Before we left, he asked, "What do you want me to do with this dead coyote?"

"Throw it in your trunk and unload it at the station for the humane officer," said Ortiz. Officer Goff looked disgusted at the suggestion. It was time for the shift to end so we drove back to the station.

All in all, it had been an interesting evening. They sure did things differently in Clarksville than they did in the big city. Apparently, Dad didn't seem to find any reason to change it. We went to his office where he checked his e-mails and responded to a few. On the way out of the station I noticed Officer Goff working on the accident report. He didn't look happy.

Dad and I went outside and saw Sgt. Ortiz and the other three officers walking away from Officer Goff's truck laughing. When they saw us, Ortiz approached. "We're playing a practical joke on Officer Goff," he said. Apparently they had taken the dead coyote and sat him in Officer Goff's truck and shut the door. They had taped his front legs to the steering wheel and opened its mouth so it looked as if it were growling. They turned the coyote's head facing the driver's window. The parking lot was dimly lit and Officer Goff's truck windows were tinted. He wouldn't be able to see the coyote in his truck. The officers were now getting ready to hide and wait for Officer Goff to complete his report and come out to go home.

Dad decided to wait to see what would happen. About ten minutes later Officer Goff came out of the station loaded to the gills with all his equipment. He had his keys in his hand and looked like an overloaded porter at the airport. He walked to his truck while balancing all his gear under is chin. He placed the key in the door and opened it. He was now face to face with a coyote sitting in his truck growling at him.

Officer Goff screamed and his stuff went everywhere. His equipment landed all over the parking lot. He jumped back, grabbed his gun with both hands and pointed it at his truck.

"Don't shoot, Gordie. Don't shoot!" yelled Sgt. Ortiz as he and the other officers roared with laughter.

Gordie looked at Sgt. Ortiz and then back at the coyote. He slowly lowered his gun and put it back in the holster. The others went to assist him in picking up his gear. They removed the dead coyote. Officer Goff wasn't amused at first, but soon joined in on the laughter as the other officers imitated him drawing down on the coyote. Dad started his truck and drove out of the parking lot smiling. "I sure miss the good old days in patrol."

CHAPTER TWENTY-TWO

S aturday had been reserved for working on my old truck. Dad and I went to Skeeter's for breakfast to let Mom sleep in. We sat down and Skeeter poured Dad a cup of coffee. Bernie Baxter approached our table. He wore a matching jogging pants and shirt with Nike sneakers.

"Hi, Andy."

I stood up. "Good morning, Mr. Baxter. This is my father, Scott."

Dad stood up and shook Bernie's hand. "You want to join us for breakfast, Mr. Baxter?"

"Alright, I think I will if you don't mind." Bernie pulled up a chair. "But please call me Bernie. I've been meaning to come by your office but haven't found the time."

"I heard," Dad said as he studied Bernie's face.

Bernie looked at my dad for a moment. "How you liking Clarksville so far, Chief?"

"We like it. But please call me Scott," Dad said.

"Clarksville is a friendly little town and we want to keep that reputation."

"What did you want to see me about?"

"I just wanted to clear up a few things before you got the wrong impression of me."

"I've heard nothing but good about you, Bernie."

"I don't know if you know it or not, but I was one of two city council members who voted not to hire you." Bernie paused for a response. When Dad didn't give him one, he continued. "I wanted to explain my vote."

Skeeter took our orders and Bernie only wanted coffee.

"You don't owe me any explanations," Dad said. "I'm sure you did what you thought best for the town."

"You're right, I don't. But I'm always upfront, especially with voters. Most people don't trust politicians, and for good reasons. Most politicians are more concerned about getting re-elected than the people they serve. I'm not like that and I wanted you to know why I voted no."

Bernie paused again for a response but still none came. "There were two reasons I voted no. One, we have always promoted from within the police department at Clarksville. You're the only certified officer on the force that hasn't grown up here. We like officers who care about our town and know the people they serve. It's worked well for us for many years and it's good for morale within the department. I voted for Reinhardt for that reason. I've known him all of my life and felt I owed it to him to try to make sure he got the job."

Dad smiled. "Loyalty is a good trait. I admire that in a man. I also understand wanting to keep morale of the police department as high as possible. I'd probably have done the same thing if I were in your position."

"There is another reason I didn't vote to bring you aboard."

Dad didn't answer. He drank his coffee and ate his breakfast as if he wasn't interested. Bernie shifted in his chair as if he was in a hurry. When Dad finished eating, he said, "Let's hear it." A frown creased Dad's forehead.

Bernie cleared his throat. "I thought it was an unreasonable expectation to think anyone could come in here and solve a three-year-old cold murder case that the Sheriff's Department and our own Police Department couldn't even come close to solving."

"Bernie, to tell you the truth, I didn't even know about the Bobby Patterson murder case when I took the job." Dad pushed his chair away from the table and leaned back. "Chief Baker never mentioned it. He told me there wasn't much crime in Clarksville."

Bernie wrinkled his nose and narrowed his eyes. "That's strange. Mayor Stapley did a great job convincing the council to hire you. He claimed you could solve cases that other detectives wouldn't have a clue where to start."

Dad narrowed his eyes. "I'd never met the mayor until after I was hired. I thought Chief Baker was behind me getting the job."

"Nope." Bernie grinned. "Reinhardt was his man too. Mayor Stapley's sister is married to Mesa's Police Chief. I figure Mesa's Police Chief recommended you for the job."

If Dad was surprised about that information, he didn't show it.

Bernie continued. "Harvey Baker might not have mentioned the Bobby Patterson case to you because he didn't think you could solve it either."

"Maybe."

"But I can tell you, every council member was thinking of that murder when they voted. They all expect you to solve the case, and if you don't, most of them will be disappointed they voted for you."

Dad took another drink of coffee. "I'll do what I can, but I won't make any promises. It's not even our case. And unfortunately, some cases are never solved."

"I know that. I just wanted you to know that if you don't solve it, I won't hold it against you."

"I appreciate that."

Bernie took a sip of coffee and asked, "How are things going for you so far? Making any headway."

"I've learned my way around town and I'm satisfied so far. Andy is having a little trouble adjusting to all the cowboy stuff. He doesn't seem to fit in being a city-boy."

Bernie looked at me. "If he's as good a football player as I hear he is, he'll fit in just fine after a game or two."

"What do you think of Coach Ford?" asked Dad.

"I played football for him in high school and I think the world of him. I don't think his mind is on the game much anymore since his wife died. A lot of townsfolk want him to retire and think we need another coach."

"Andy seems to likes him. Don't you, Son?"

I hadn't mentioned the coach's drinking to my father. "He's alright so far."

"Maybe we can help him back into the game," Dad said.

"Good luck with that. I've been trying for the last three years. Clarksville loves their football team and they're not used to losing. Some of them want him gone and the list is growing. As an elected official, I have to take their concerns into consideration."

"Isn't that the school board's decision?"

"It is. I'm on the school board too."

Dad didn't answer. Bernie took another sip of coffee. "Any progress on the murder case?"

"So we're back to that again?"

Bernie frowned. "Just thought I'd ask."

"Nope. I didn't even know I was supposed be working on it. If Donna Stevenson hadn't mentioned it to my wife, I wouldn't even know about it. There wasn't much to go on from what I've heard."

"Well, if you can solve it, the town will be grateful. If you run into any problems, or if there's anything I can do to help, don't hesitate to call."

Bernie drained his cup, laid his business card on the table. As he turned to leave, Dad picked up the card. "Since I'm supposed to be working this case, do you have time for a couple of questions?"

Bernie wrinkled his forehead again and sat back down, "Sure, what do you want to know?"

"Bobby Patterson worked for you didn't he?"

"Yes he did, one of my best employees. He was a great kid."

"I understand he was working at your gym the night he was murdered."

"Yeah, that's right. But for some reason, he closed early and left. He didn't even call me to let me know why. Something must have happened to make him to leave like that."

"Do you have any idea what that might have been?"

"Not really. It didn't appear he was having any concerns when I left."

"When was that?"

"About 9:00 p.m. It was slow that night. There weren't many people working out. It's always that way during the Christmas shopping season. Besides, everyone in the town was in mourning after those other two football players died."

"Where were you the rest of the evening?"

Bernie frowned. "Well I… I was home. Surely you don't suspect me?"

"I don't suspect anyone in particular. But whoever killed Bobby knew him and knew he was working at the gym that night. I don't suppose anyone could verify that you were home that evening?"

Bernie took a deep breath. "I'm a bachelor, Scott. I was alone that night. But you can say that about me almost every night if I'm not at a meeting. For someone who didn't even know about the murder, you seem to know a hell of a lot about it."

"I read the report."

Bernie stopped to think about that for a moment but didn't say anything.

"Do you remember who was in the gym when you left that night?" Dad asked.

"No, but we keep records when our customers sign in. It won't include anyone who may have stopped by to visit. But I can get the list for you if you want."

"I'd appreciate that. I'll drop by the gym and pick it up."

"Anytime, I'm there everyday," Bernie said as he got up to leave. After he was gone, I asked, "What did you think of Bernie?"

"Typical politician. It's hard to know what their intent or motives are."

I could tell Dad's mind was somewhere else. "What are you thinking about, Dad?"

"Just reading between the lines, Son. I already know why Bobby left the Gym early that night." He patted me on the shoulder. "Let's go home. That truck won't fix itself. We have a lot to do today."

"Why did Bobby leave?"

"I can't tell you. It's something they kept out of the police report that only the suspect will know. And they kept it out for a very good reason."

CHAPTER TWENTY-THREE

D ad and I needed a break. We decided to take a day off from working on the truck to go for a trail-ride. We saddled up Big John and Pharaoh and rode into the mountains south of the Double J Ranch. A clear blue-sky day with no wind greeted us as we rode past the Stevenson's ranch and cut back west along a creek bed. We followed a creek bed lined with sycamore and cottonwood trees.

We spotted a camouflaged colored quad ATV parked in the bottom of the creek bed about a mile in. Dad searched the area with his binoculars for the rider but couldn't see anyone. We waited for a while but no one came to the ATV.

I told Dad about the ATV tracks Colonel and I had found when we were rounding up John Stevenson's cattle. I also told him about the old Indian trail, but couldn't remember where it was located.

Dad thought maybe the quad had been stolen and left here. We approached the ATV. It had an ice chest attached to the front rack and a small Kachina doll hanging from the handlebars. When we got closer, we saw footprints leading up the wash away from the quad. Dad felt the engine and said it was still warm. He started to open the ice chest when we heard a voice, "I wouldn't do that if I were you, Chief."

Bennett Nahche approached us. He had a headband and wore his hair in a ponytail. His leather pants were tucked inside his knee-high moccasins. A big knife hung in a sheath from his side and he carried a stick with a forked end. He had a backpack on.

"Why not?" asked Dad. "What's in there?"

"Snakes. And if you aren't careful, they'll bite you."

Dad looked at the ice chest but didn't open it. Bennett walked up and tapped the ice chest with the stick. The unmistakable sound of rattlers came from inside. Dad stepped back. Bennett opened the lid and a big rattlesnake struck out about a foot above the top of the lid. Then it attempted to crawl out. Bennett took the stick and pushed him back inside and closed the lid.

"What are you doing up here, Bennett?" Dad asked.

"Collecting cottonwood roots and rattlers if I can find any. I know of a den where they hide during the winter months. There's always a few sunning themselves on warm days."

"What's in the backpack?" Dad asked.

"Cottonwood roots," Bennett said as he removed the backpack and dumped the roots out on the ground.

"What do you do with them?" I asked.

"I make Kachina dolls out of them. You should buy a doll some-time, Andy. It'll give you good luck and keep evil spirits away."

"I might just do that." I said as I looked at the roots.

Bennett put the roots back in his backpack and tied it to the back of his ATV.

Dad said, "You know you're not supposed to be off road on a ATV in the National Forest don't you?"

"Yeah, I know." Bennett said as he got on the quad. "But I only ride in the sand washes so it won't hurt anything. One good rain and you'd never know I was here. It's the only way I can find the good cottonwood roots I need."

He started to drive away.

"Hey, Bennett, got a minute?" Dad asked.

Bennett turned motor off. "Got all day Chief. What do you need?"

"I understand you and Bobby Patterson got into some kind of disagreement at the Iron Man Gym on the night he was killed. What was the argument about?"

Bennett hesitated before answering. "I'm not very good at signing in at the front desk when I go in to work-out. Bobby had warned me several times about signing in but I kept forgetting. He was mad that I hadn't signed in that night, that's all."

Bennett waited for Dad to ask him another question but when he didn't, Bennett waved and rode off on his ATV.

"He's kind of strange isn't he, Dad?"

"Yep, and one of the last people to see Bobby Patterson before he was killed."

"You think he killed him?"

"I don't think so. His shoe size is too small. But if he did, I still haven't found the motive."

CHAPTER TWENTY-FOUR

My alarm startled me awake at 3:30 a.m. on a cold January morning in the Pinaleno Mountains. It was pitch dark inside the tent and it took a few moments to clear my head and remember where I was. Fumbling around, I located my flashlight. Jared Lobel was sleeping beside me. I shook him awake, crawled out of my sleeping bag and started getting dressed in my camouflage hunting clothes. We were hunting white tail deer and it was rutting season.

Chilled to the bone, my hands shook as I laced up my boots. My ears and nose were numb by the time I climbed out of the tent. Bright stars and a small sliver of moon greeted me in the western sky. Frost covered the ground.

As Jared got dressed, I ate two power bars and grabbed my backpack out of the truck. I grabbed two bottles of water. The ice chest had kept the water from freezing.

Jared came out of the tent rubbing his hands together attempting to warm them, "Damn, it's cold!"

He grabbed a couple of power bars and got his backpack out of the truck. A Smith and Wesson six inch .44 mag revolver hung from his right hip.

"Get your rifle, great white hunter. We're chasing daylight," Jared said.

He turned on his flashlight ready to lead us out of camp. I removed my rifle from its case, "I'm ready."

Jared led the way down a hiking trail in a southeasterly direction following the ridgeline. We turned down into a draw and headed east for about two hundred yards, then slanted upward to the southeast again, climbing all the time. A slight glow silhouetted the ridgelines. After another half mile, Jared stopped under a large mesquite tree and whispered instructions. "See those small trees and bushes at the top of this ridge. That's where we're going. Before we get there, we need to stop and catch our breath before going over the ridge. Zigzag back and forth until we get to the crest. Go slow and take your time. If we slip, we could scare the deer."

Jared paused and looked around. "When we get to the top we have to be quiet because the deer are only about two to three hundred yards on the other side of this hill below us in a creek bed. The ridge drops off very steep on the other side and flattens out at the bottom."

He checked his watch. "There is a creek at the bottom of the next valley. The water in the creek only goes for about a hundred yards or so, and then disappears below the sand. A clearing is located just before the creek. You should be able to get a good shot if the deer come to my call. Just beyond the bare spot is thick mesquite trees following a small creek. That's why the deer are here. They feed all night and want to water before bedding down. You may not see any deer for a while but keep looking because they'll be there."

"Yes, Bwana," I replied smiling at my guide.

Jared ignored me and started climbing the hill. We worked our way to the top and stopped. Both Jared and I were out of breath. We sat under a tree in the darkness for about five minutes to rest.

Jared moved closer to me and whispered. "When we get to the other side, we'll go down about twenty yards to a big mesquite tree. There's a lots of brush uphill from the tree to help break up our image. A large fallen log is on the downhill side of the tree. Get between the log and the mesquite tree. As long as you don't make any sudden movements, the deer won't see you."

"What are you going to do?"

"While you're getting set up, I'm going to work my way into a small draw to your left. I'll only be about forty yards downhill from you behind several large boulders. I'll set up between the boulders and wait until it's light enough to shoot before I start calling. You should be able to see me from where you are but the boulders will hide me from the deer. Pick out a big one and don't shoot any rag-horns. I don't want you to ruin my reputation."

"Yes, Bwana!"

We made our way over the crest of the hill in the darkness and down the other side to the mesquite tree. While I pulled barbed cactus out of my hands and knees, Jared disappeared into the little draw to my left. The sky showed signs of brightening but it would be another half hour before there would be enough light to shoot. I settled down, made myself comfortable, and waited.

I laid back and bundled up, trying to stay warm. I thought of Shayla. I wondered what she thought of me or if she just didn't like men. Attempting to clear her out of my mind, I concentrated on the clouds above me. Streaks of reds, yellows and grays of the early morning sunrise painted the sky. Clouds changed into multiples shades of colors, each color chasing the color before it moved westward.

Using my binoculars, I scanned the creek below and the hillside beyond. There may have been deer grazing on the far hill but

I wasn't sure. Jared's outline could be seen in the draw to my left as he set up to begin calling.

Lying still, I tried to focus on the hunt. Sounds of horns rattling from the area of the boulders startled me. What I thought I'd seen earlier on the far hill was indeed whitetail deer. Several doe and a couple of yearlings stared in our direction attempting to locate what they thought were deer fighting. Jared stopped rattling the horns after a few seconds and the deer returned to grazing. A few minutes later, Jared sounded the grunt call a couple of times and then rattled the horns again. Again the deer studied the hillside for activity.

Searching the thick mesquite trees, I found no sign of any bucks. Jared stopped rattling the horns and all was quiet. He repeated the ritual several times in 10 to 20 minute intervals. As the sun climbed higher, the shadows crept down the mountain and the deer on the far hill grazed their way towards the creek. They disappeared into the mesquites.

Just when I began to think there were no bucks in the valley, I saw something walking in the shadows near the edge of the creek. I focused my binoculars on a deer looking towards me. There were so many branches it was difficult to tell if it was a buck or doe. After a few minutes, the deer stepped out into the open. It was a small two by three buck. I was tempted to shoot, but remembered Jared's warning, "Don't shoot no rag horn and ruin my reputation!" I kept searching. The small buck kept looking up the hill towards the sound of the deer grunts and then to his right. He stood just outside the thick mesquite trees fully exposed.

Suddenly, he broke and ran to his left as if he was being chased. I couldn't see what had spooked him. The small buck disappeared back into the trees about forty yards away. I focused on the area where the deer had been looking before he ran. There was movement deep in the shadows. Leaves shook just behind where the small buck had stood. The shaking stopped when Jared started rattling the horns again.

A big five by five trophy buck magically appeared into the clearing. He was staring in Jared's direction. He held his head high in the air while licking his nose. His tail was flashing back and forth. He was obviously in a fighting mood. This deer would indeed enhance Jared's reputation.

Lowering the binoculars, I flipped the safety off my rifle and lifted it to my shoulder. The buck was facing me and slightly to the right. I looked through the scope and put the crosshairs on his chest. I waited to see if he would turn and give me a side shot. My heart pounded. Several deep slow breaths calmed me. I used the dead log in front of me to steady the crosshairs and held this position for what seemed like an eternity. Not wanting to risk hitting him in an area that would ruin the mount, I waited. The deer turned sideways and peered into the trees behind him. As I started to squeeze the trigger, a slight movement to my left caught my attention.

A huge mountain lion was creeping across the boulder above Jared. He was low to the ground, muscles flexed and tail twitching ready to pounce at any moment. Jared was well hidden in the brush below unaware of the danger above him.

Aiming my rifle at the cougar, I placed the crosshairs on his right front shoulder and fired. Just as I pulled the trigger, the cougar leaped into the air. I thought I had hit the cougar but wasn't sure. The cougar landed on Jared and they both rolled. The big cat appeared stunned. Jared screamed bloody murder at the top of his lungs. The cougar jumped into the brush and disappeared. The deer below ran up the far mountainside including my trophy buck.

Jared ran around screaming and brushing himself off as if he were covered with ants. Concerned for his safety, I ran to his location to see if he was injured. When I got there, he was still doing the Snoopy dance and screaming as loud as he could. His jacket had several tears where the lion's claws had ripped it but I couldn't see any blood.

"Are you hurt?" I yelled!

"Hell yes I'm hurt. A lion tried to eat me!"

"I don't see any blood. Where did he get you?"

"Everywhere, he got me everywhere!"

Looking him over, I couldn't find any blood or scratches. "Calm down, Buddy and take your jacket off. I don't think you're injured."

Jared removed his jacket. "Damn right I'm injured. I need to go to the hospital!"

"You don't need to go to the hospital. There's not a scratch on you."

"I need to go to the hospital to get my shorts surgically removed from my ass," Jared said. He started to calm down as he pulled out his big .44 magnum pistol and pointed it the direction the lion had gone. "Come back here lion, I'll blow your sorry ass off!"

Knowing Jared wasn't injured, we both laughed until our sides hurt.

"Did you see him, Andy? He landed right on top of me. I thought I was a dead man." Jared's hands were shaking.

"Yeah, I saw him. I gave up the buck of a lifetime to save your sorry ass, Bwana," I laughed.

"Don't worry about it, I'll find you another one. Did you hit the lion?"

"I think so but I'm not sure. I had the crosshairs right on his front shoulder but he jumped just as I was pulling the trigger. Let's track him and see if we can find any blood."

"Go grab your backpack and let's get after him," ordered Bwana. Jared appeared a lot braver now that he had his .44 mag in his hand.

After retrieving my backpack, we pushed through the thick brush searching for any sign of blood or the cougar. I went first and Jared followed behind me at a safe distance. We found a couple of tracks but lost them as the lion headed up the far side of a small wash. I followed the side of the hill where the tracks were last seen and Jared stayed in the wash with his big .44 leading the way.

After walking about fifty yards, Jared yelled, "I got `em, there's fresh tracks down here!" I dropped into the wash and saw fresh paw prints going up the wash. After a few yards, I spotted a spot of blood. As we continued, the blood spots became larger and more frequent. I had definitely hit the lion, but where? We followed the tracks up to the top of the ridge where the dry wash faded out. The lion continued west crossing the hill to the other side. He went to the bottom of that hill and followed another wash upward for another quarter mile. The blood thinned, but a drop could be seen every few steps. The cougar climbed the next ridge to the west and crossed the side road where we were camped.

"Let's go to the truck and go get the posse," Jared said as we got to the road.

"No, we have to stay on his trail. If you ever leave a lion's track, you won't see him for at least another month, if ever again."

"How do you know that?"

"Indians know these things."

"Fool, in case you don't know it, you ain't no Indian!"

"Colonel told me, Bwana, and he's an Indian."

Jared thought for a moment. "Well let's get after him then."

The lion crossed a big wash and headed uphill for another two miles. Jared and I stopped twice, removed our coats and drank water. The blood drops were farther apart now and much smaller. The lion wouldn't bleed out from the amount of blood he was leaving behind, unless he was bleeding internally

We proceeded cautiously wondering if this lion was the same one who jumped John Stevenson. I checked my GPS. We had traveled about a half-mile east of the line shack and a quarter mile higher up in the mountains. While following the cougar, we spotted ATV tracks on the side of the wash. They had been there for a while because water had run in the wash after the ATV was here.

Jared looked around, "Man, this guy was way off the beaten path, that's for sure. Wonder how he got a quad up here?"

"Hell if I know. I've never been in this area before."

We followed the lion across two more washes to the west and up a wide deep canyon. The tracks became more difficult to see because the ground was rockier and the blood had all but stopped. I covered Jared with my rifle while he tracked the lion. He carried his trusted .44 mag in his hand.

The higher we climbed the narrower and steeper the canyon became. The brush became very thick and it didn't appear there was another way out. We were entering a small box canyon. We walked as far as we could without crawling. Small animal tunnels led into the brush. We could only see a few feet into the thickets. As we studied the tunnels, we heard movement about ten yards ahead of us.

Jared moved behind me. We stood perfectly still, waiting and listening. I kept my rifle at the ready. My heart hammered my rib-cage. Quiet footsteps could be heard in the brush not far away. Whatever made them was coming towards us.

Jared took hold of my backpack and whispered in my ear, "He's coming. Let's get the hell out of here." He started backing up. I held my ground with the rifle at the ready. Jared stopped a few feet behind me as if hoping I would come to my senses and leave with him. I raised the rifle to my shoulder and kept both eyes open. The hair on the back of my neck stood on end as my heart pounded. Deep in the shadows, something slowly inched forward. I saw a nose, then teeth, and then an eye. Just as I was about to shoot, a big javelina boar chewing on a prickly pear leaf stepped into view.

Lowering my rifle, I motioned for Jared to join me. He didn't move as if his feet were glued to the ground. I picked up a rock and threw it into the bushes. The gorge came alive with scrambling pigs. At least twenty of them ran in all directions. Jared hadn't seen the javelina and didn't know what was happening. He started running as soon as they scattered. A javelina ran up behind him and he leaped up on a small ledge on the side of the canyon.

Grinning from ear to ear, I walked back to his location. "What are you doing up there, Bwana?"

Jared held his hand above his eyes as if searching for something. "Scouting for lion, Great White Hunter. There's a better view from up here."

"Scouting my ass. Get down here. You know pigs wouldn't be in that brush if the lion was in there. Let's get after him."

Jared regained his confidence. "Yeah, let's go get that son of a bitch. I'll shoot his ass off for trying to eat me!" He climbed down and we walked back to the thick brush.

Jared got down on his hands and knees and studied the small tunnels leading into the brush. After a few minutes he pointed. "He was here. There's a small spot of blood on those branches. You must have hit him high."

"Well let's go get him. He's not going to come to us."

Jared got to his feet and stared at the cliffs above. "He must have gone up over those rocks. We can't climb up there. It's too steep. Maybe we should mark this canyon on the GPS and come back tomorrow. We can come up from the top and track him from there."

"No. I want to make sure he is not already dead. We'd never find him if we leave. We need to check here first."

"You said the pigs wouldn't be in there if the lion was near. I don't think he is in there."

I thought for a minute, "The wind is coming from our back. If they went to the very back of the canyon, the pigs wouldn't be able to smell him. They can't smell very well and they're half blind. Let's go take a look. I'll crawl in first." I got down on my hands and knees. "Don't point that hog iron at me, Jared. I don't want to get shot in the ass!"

Crawling inside the brush tunnel, I kept my rifle in front of me. I figured the lion couldn't jump on top of me because the brush was too thick. If he came from the front, I could get a shot off. We took our time as Jared followed me into the tunnel. After going a few feet, the tunnel opened up and we stood up.

"That's strange," Jared said looking confused. "Pigs don't make tunnels in the brush any larger than they are. And look, Andy, someone has cut these limbs."

"What the hell," I said while looking at the cuts on the branches. "Why didn't they cut them all the way out? That way, they wouldn't have to crawl in and out."

"Hell if I know," Jared said while scratching his head. "Unless they were hiding this place and didn't want anyone to find it."

"Beats me," I said. "I don't know why someone would be in here in the first place."

We made our way along the cliff for about twenty yards and found an old mineshaft going right into the side of the cliff. It was about six feet wide and seven feet tall. "Is this a mine or a cave?" asked Jared.

"It's an old mine. Caves wouldn't be square like this."

Darkness from within the mine hit all but the first few feet. We turned on our flashlights and entered the mine.

"I'll keep my light shining down the tunnel, Jared. You check for tracks."

Peering deep into the darkness, I let my eyes adjust before continuing.

"Find anything?" I asked.

"Hell yes," Jared whispered, "It's a damn freeway in here. Look!"

Human tracks led into and out of the mine. One set of prints had smooth soles. The other was a boot print, much larger than the first. Fresh cougar tracks led into the mine and covered some of the human tacks. The lion had to be in the mine unless there was another opening.

"Shine your light down here and let me have a look at those," I whispered. Getting on my knees, I studied the tracks. I used my knife and made circles around three sets of the better prints.

When I stood up, Jared whispered in my ear, "Why did you do that?"

"Evidence, we don't want to step on them when we come out."

"Evidence for what?"

"In case whatever they're doing in this mine is illegal."

"So, what's the evidence about?"

"This mine isn't far from the line shack where Bobby Patterson was killed. They've never found the killer."

"How do you know they are connected?"

"I don't. But why would someone take the time to hide the entrance?"

"I don't like this, Andy. Let's get the hell out of here and call the Sheriff."

"And be the laughing stock of the whole town if they don't find anything. What about your great hunting reputation, Bwana?"

Jared looked around rubbing his chin. "Alright then, but I'm keeping my .44 cocked and ready."

We made our way about thirty feet into the mine. A large wood table sat against the wall. It was about eight feet long, five feet tall and four feet wide. Covered in dust, it appeared very old. Another shelf sat about halfway down.

Jared shined his light on the bottom shelf. Three flat black lunch boxes were sitting on the shelf. They looked new and weren't covered in dust. I didn't think they had been there very long. Jared reached for one of the boxes. I grabbed his arm, "Don't touch those!"

"Why not?" asked Jared? "I want to see what's in them."

"Evidence, that's why. You'll destroy any fingerprints that might be on them."

Jared thought for a moment and left them as they were. I checked for footprints and found more boot and cougar tracks. There were two sets of human prints. The larger print had a small cut in the right heel. I used my cell phone to take photos of the boot prints and the black lunch boxes.

We continued deeper into the shaft for about sixty yards. Then the tunnel split into two directions at a ninety-degree angle. We found cougar's tracks going into the right shaft and the smaller footprint leading into the left shaft.

"Which way do we go? And what is that smell?" Jared asked.

"The cougar went to the right. I don't know what that smell is, but it smells rotten."

"Maybe it's a dead body."

"I don't think so. It would smell a lot worse than that," I whispered.

I studied the tracks. I was afraid Jared might be right about a body but I didn't want to go into the wrong tunnel and have a wounded lion at our backs. I pointed to the right. We slowly made our way up that shaft. We started finding small caves cut into the walls of the mineshaft as if someone had found something interesting and dug it out. We worked our way deeper into the mine and the holes became larger and more frequent. Jared's flashlight started to dim and we stopped so he could change batteries. While switching batteries, we heard something up ahead. We didn't move until Jared got his flashlight back on.

"Did you hear that?" whispered Jared.

"Yeah."

"What was it?"

"I don't know. But it's close," I whispered.

We eased forward a few more steps and heard a low soft growl. I held the flashlight and rifle pointing forward. Jared kept his right hand on my back and his gun in his left hand pointing it down the tunnel. My heart was pounding. We hugged the west wall concentrating our lights to the far wall in the direction the sound was coming from. I suddenly stopped and Jared bumped into me.

"What is it?" He whispered.

I didn't answer but moved my upper body slightly to the right so Jared could see the cougar's tail. The big lion was hiding in a small cave on the other side of the mineshaft a few feet in front of us. Inching forward, the big cat's body came into view. Jared pointed his pistol in the direction of the lion. It was shaking badly. I hoped I wouldn't have to rely on him to shoot anything. I held the rifle steady and walked the scope up the lion's body as it came into view. The cougar's heart area came into view and I thought about taking the shot, but hesitated.

Jared whispered, "Shoot him. Shoot him."

I started moving again and the cougar's head came into view. The cat was staring straight into the light. It growled at us, exposing his sharp teeth, ready to leap at any moment. One of his canine teeth was broken off. I watched his ribs as he breathed in and out. The remains of a dead rabbit lay on the ground in front of him. Blood stained his left rear hip where I had grazed him.

He looked very old and I felt sorry for him. His fate was now in my hands. Life or death for the cougar was my decision and mine alone. He was trapped and had nowhere to run.

"Jared, I am going to keep moving past the lion. I want you to move with me. Do you understand?"

"Yeah."

We inched forward keeping the light in the big cat's eyes and our weapons at the ready. When we moved past the lion, I told Jared to shine his light back down the mineshaft. Jared followed my instructions.

The lion looked back down the tunnel and then at us. Almost as if the he knew what I was thinking, he struggled to his feet and limped back away towards the entrance. After about twenty yards, he stopped and looked back at us. I lowered my rifle. The Cougar turned and disappeared into the darkness.

Jared was still shaking and in shock. "You let him go, Andy. You had him right in your sights and you just let him walk away. Why didn't you kill him? That lion tried to eat me!"

I stood in silence for a few moments. "No he didn't, Jared. He wanted to kill a deer and thought you were one. As soon as he saw who you were, he ran off. He didn't want to hurt you."

"He tried to kill John Stevenson, didn't he?"

"Maybe, and maybe not. He's old and hungry. This is his home. We are the intruders here. I won't shoot anything that's not trying to kill me or that I won't eat. I don't think he wanted to harm us."

We stood there for a moment. "It's over, Jared. Let's go home." We started walking back down the tunnel.

Jared looked confused and kept shaking his head. I didn't think he understood why I didn't shoot the lion, but somehow he seemed at peace with it. As we got close to the split in the two tunnels, the smell hit us again.

"What the hell is that?" asked Jared. "It stinks."

CHAPTER TWENTY-FIVE

The more I thought about it, the more I thought Jared was right about a body. "I don't know what that smell is, but I have a bad feeling. Let's go take a look."

We noticed flies as we entered the mineshaft. The farther in we went, the stronger the smell and the more flies there were. We covered our noses and mouths with our handkerchiefs to lessen the stench. Something swarming with flies came into sight far down the tunnel. We walked closer. Jared stopped and started backing away. I moved a little closer and saw what was left of a body lying in a small side tunnel. The body was badly decomposed. Mostly bones. One foot was wearing a tennis shoe. The other shoe was lying on the ground next to the other foot. The shoes were small like a woman's. Red toenail polish shown on the exposed toes. I inched forward and more of the body came into view. The body had blue shorts and a pink faded red top. "It's a woman, Jared. She's been dead for a long time."

Jared inched forward and stared at the body. It lay face up and what skin remained looked dark and leathery. The stomach area was flat and caved in. We couldn't see the head from this angle.

"Let's get the hell out of here, Andy!"

"Hold on, I want to see her face."

We took a step forward and the head came into view. It was obvious what had killed her. Her skull had been crushed and maggots were crawling around inside her head. She had short blond hair. All of her teeth were missing and so were her hands. Jared turned around and puked. I used my cell phone and took a photo of the body. Jared regained his composure and inched forward to have another look.

"Do you know who she is?" I asked.

Jared placed his flashlight beam on the skull. "I don't think so. But even if I did, I don't think I could recognize her like that."

While we were staring at the skull, the right eye socket appeared to blink and Jared fell backwards. I took a step back while focusing on the skull. A black beetle come out of her eye socket and then went back inside, giving the illusion the eye blinked. Jared got to his feet and started to leave. I grabbed his arm. "Hold on, buddy, it was just a beetle."

"I don't give a shit what it was, I'm getting the hell out of here," he said as he pulled away.

We hurried to the mouth of the mine attempting to avoid stepping on any of the tracks. Once outside, we walked to the small brush tunnel and crawled through it. I crawled out first and stood up. Before Jared had a chance to clear the tunnel, a shot rang out and the bullet struck the cliffs above my head. I dived for the tunnel and crawled back inside as fast as Jared could crawl backward. When we stood up, Jared started to run back towards the mine. I grabbed his arm and pulled him away from the opening to an outcropping of rocks in the other direction. We were well hidden by the thick brush. Several more rounds splattered off the cliffs above the mine.

"What are you doing? These bushes aren't going to stop bullets," whispered Jared. "Let's get back into the mine."

"Stay behind these rocks and keep still. Whoever's shooting at us will expect us to go back into the mine and then we'd be trapped. If we stay here and he enters the mine, we'll be behind him and may get the drop on him. Or, we'll get away while he is searching the mine."

I used my binoculars and peeked over the rocks searching the ridge from where the shots were being fired. The bullets were hitting close to the mine and bouncing off the walls above the entrance. I spotted a figure in a prone position on the ridge about a hundred yards away. I couldn't see his face or clothing, just a baseball cap and rifle. It appeared the person had turned on his side to reload his rifle. I pointed out the location on the ridge where the man was laying and told Jared he was reloading.

We remained still as I watched him. "He's getting ready to shoot again."

We squeezed further behind the rocks as four more rounds rang out. Then the shooting stopped. Each round had hit the rocks above the mineshaft. The shooter obviously didn't know where we were. I moved back into position to watch the man. I told Jared the guy was reloading again.

Jared jumped up and started shooting his .44 mag in the direction the man was hiding. I couldn't believe what I was hearing as the big gun roared next to me hurting my ears. I watched as the first bullet hit about ten yards below the sniper. Each round climbed higher until the sixth round hit about a foot below him. The man scrambled away and disappeared from sight. Jared ducked behind the rocks and started reloading his 44 mag. talking to himself.

"How you like that sumbitch? Give you a taste of your own medicine! I'll blow your fucking ass off, messing with me," Jared said as he reloaded. His hands were shaking so bad, he dropped half of his bullets.

"Calm down, Jared. He's gone… for now!"

"Calm down my ass. The sum-bitch is trying to kill us. Get your rifle and help me shoot his ass!" replied Jared as he peeked over the rocks trying to get another fix on the guy. "Where did he go?"

"I don't know. You almost hit him with that last shot and he took off. I don't know if he's gone or just moving to get a better angle now that he knows where we are. Keep your head down," I said as I searched for the shooter.

We laid still for about five minutes and nothing moved. There was no more shooting. I broke the silence. "I see him!"

"Where," asked Jared, ready to let loose with another volley of 44 rounds.

"He's hauling ass over the next ridge about two hundred yards away. Let's get the hell out of here!"

We scrambled out of the brush, ran back down the wash and up over the ridge away from the man who had shot at us. We were both out of breath and soaked with sweat by the time we got back to camp. We threw our backpacks in the truck and left the tent where it was. While driving back to town, I called Dad on my cell phone and explained what had happened. The phone service kept cutting in and out and it took three calls before I could explain the entire situation.

Since the mine was located in the County, Dad notified the Sheriff's Department and advised them about the shooting and the body in the mine. Dad, Chief Baker, and Lt. Reinhardt met Jared and I at the Double J Ranch. We drove to the line shack and met several Sheriff's Deputies SWAT team including a K-9 officer and his dog. A helicopter arrived shortly thereafter. The pilot,

Scott Davison, asked Dad and I to fly with him so I could show him the location of the mine.

Davison told us he had been a Warrant Officer in Vietnam. He had been shot down by a mortar while flying medical helicopters and had logged thousands of combat flight hours.

I showed them the location of the hidden mine. Deputy Davidson directed the SWAT deputies to the area by radio. We searched the surrounding mountains for the suspect but we couldn't locate him. The ground officers searched the mine and advised by radio that the lunchboxes were missing. There were fresh footprints over the footprints I had circled. Apparently the suspect had returned to the mine and removed them prior to the deputies' arrival. The body was still in the mine.

Several .270 shell casings were recovered from the location where the suspect had been firing. ATV tracks were located about a mile down the hill. The tracks ran north to the bottom of the mountain into a big wash. They couldn't tell if he went east towards town or west towards the Apache Indian Reservation because there were to many ATV tracks in the area. The suspect was not located.

Jared and I were minor celebrities at school after the story made the front page of the local paper. The story made headlines on the local television stations throughout the state. There were speculations about this shooting incident being tied to the Bobby Patterson murder, which sparked renewed interest in the old case.

Dad told me he was glad the crime happened in the sheriff's jurisdiction because they would be the ones having to remove the dead body. He got the autopsy results back within a few weeks. The cause of death was determined to be from a skull fracture. The coroner thought the murder weapon used might have been some type of small statue because of the imprint in the skull.

CHAPTER TWENTY-SIX

For the next few weeks, Jared and I were treated as heroes at school. Everyone wanted to know every detail about the body in the mine and the man that shot at us. Rumors ran wild as people speculated over who the dead woman might be or who the shooter was. Their identities remained a mystery. Within a few weeks everything returned back to being routine and I was getting bored. Then I got a text from Heather. *Hey bro, want company this weekend?* I hadn't seen her since I left Mesa and I missed my best friend.

I texted her back: *Sure if u don't mind sleeping on couch.*

I'm in your room. ur on couch. Clean the sheets!

Can u come tonight? Want to show u the city lights.

They have lights in Clarksville?

Just a few, but I know where they r.

Already packed, leave right after school. You'll have to feed me.

Meet me at McDonald's.

Which one.

We only have one. Can't miss it.

Tell Mom I'm coming. CU

Jared and I got to McDonald's around seven. The Friday night parade had already begun. No one cruised Main in a Toyota Corolla unless they wanted to get laughed at. I parked at the rear of McDonald's. We walked to the front parking lot where all the cool cars were parked. Unofficially, no one is allowed to park there unless they had something worth showing off.

"Sherry" by The Four Seasons blared over the loud speakers. Girls drove by in droves and Jared seemed to know most of them. Just one of the benefits of growing up in a small town. I was more interested in the cars.

A `57 Nomad, a Bucket-T and a `34 Ford 2 door sedan sat in the front row. A `67 GTO pulled in just as we walked up, followed by a `68 AMX. All in show condition, polished like fine silver. My motivation level soared as I thought of my `56 Ford. Someday, this would be where I'd be parking it on Friday nights.

I only recognized one of the car owners from our school. He wasn't a football player and I didn't know his name. Jared introduced me around. McDonald's was packed and there were kids everywhere. There were so many cars in the parking lot, you had to watch out or you'd get run over. Being a football player at Clarksville High School has its privileges. Like hanging out with the cool crowd.

Cruising rules didn't apply to girls. They could cruise in anything they wanted, and did. The only interest guys had in their cars was their back seats.

My head was under the hood of the `67 GTO when I began to hear catcalls and whistles. I figured Heather had arrived. I looked up to see her dancing across the parking lot to the tune of 'Pretty Woman' by Roy Orbison. And yes, she was wearing a red miniskirt, a white coat with a fur collar and high heel boots.

Heads turned in awe as the unknown princess appeared. Her natural beauty and outgoing personality attracted boys like a magnet. She jumped into my arms and smeared lipstick all over my cheeks and forehead to the groans of a dozen hopeful knights. "Hey little sister. I've missed you."

Broken hearts mended as soon as they heard me say, "sister." Heather was good for my ego and it was good to see her. She had become an instant celebrity.

Heather looked around and yelled above the music. "Wow, is there a car show in town?"

"No," I yelled back. "It's like this every Friday night."

"This is great. Not what I expected."

She surveyed the Detroit artwork and selected a bright red '34 Ford Sedan as her chariot for the evening. After a few moments of complimenting the owner, we were cruising all six blocks of Main Street. Jared and I sat in the back, while the princess and her new servant, Roger, rode in the front. Roger couldn't keep his eyes off Heather. He was hotter than a four-balled tomcat on a hot tin roof. She ignored him while flipping through his collection of ancient CDs. A moment later, we were all singing "Ain't Too Proud To Beg" by The Temptations:

> *"I know you want to leave me*
> *But I refuse to let you go*
> *If I have to beg and plead for your sympathy*
> *I don't mind, coz' you mean that much to me."*

Jared's natural soul flowed to the surface as he and Heather sang every word of the song. Roger and I faked backup. Jared was in his element as he and Heather danced in place. Back and forth we cruised for the next hour. Kids yelling, tires squealing and radios blasting. Heather smiled and waved at all the boys, spreading her magic. Roger's hand brushed her leg every time he shifted gears, which was often.

We were laughing and having a ball. It wasn't long before a half dozen of the nicest rods in town were following us from one end of town to the other, forming our own hotrod parade.

Heather soon tired of Clarksville. "I'm hungry. Let's go get something to eat."

Roger offered to buy our dinner but Heather refused his offer. She had him drop us off back at McDonald's. He hated to see her leave and "begged for her sympathy." She rewarded him with a kiss on the cheek and wrote a phone number on a card and handed it to him.

Roger wasn't the kind to give up that easily. As we started walking across the street I heard him say, "Hey, Heather, wait up a minute."

Heather waited as Jared and I crossed the street. Just as we reached the other side I heard a loud scream. I turned and saw Roger on the ground wincing in pain. Heather had him in an arm bar. I heard her saying, "Be nice, Roger. I don't want to have to hurt you."

"Aren't you going to go help her?" asked Jared.

I smiled, "The only one that needs help is Roger."

Heather released Roger and crossed the street.

One of Roger's friends helped him to his feet and asked. "Who is that Ninja Bitch?"

Roger didn't answer. He handed his friend the card with Heather's phone number on it and walk away rubbing his wrist!

When Heather reached our side of the street, I asked, "Who's number did you give him?"

"Bonnie's. She loves hotrods."

I laughed. "He'll be disappointed."

She held her arms out and palms up, as a grin spread across her face and her eyebrows went up, "Life's a bitch."

"I expected you to give him a round house kick in the chest."

"Not while wearing a mini skirt."

We placed our orders. A few friends stopped by to say hello while we were waiting. Most were Jared's friends but I knew a few of them from school.

"Where's your girlfriend, Andy?" Heather asked.

"I don't have one yet."

"He could have a half dozen if he wanted them," Jared said. "The man's picky if you know what I mean."

"I'm not either. I'm just trying to decide which one I want."

Jared rolled his eyes, "Since when? I give 'em your number and you don't even return their calls. You're not helping my reputation."

"He has always been like that," said Heather as she slugged me in the shoulder. "What do I have to do, come up here and hook you up with someone?"

"I think he's holding out for Shayla Stevenson," Jared said. "But she don't date nobody. She wouldn't even know Andy was alive if he wasn't working for her daddy."

"Knock it off, Jared, You don't know that. Don't listen to him, Heather. He thinks he's a walking dating service. He gave my number to half the girls at school."

Heather high-fived Jared, "I think you hit a nerve, Jared. If you see this Shayla, let me know. I'll hook 'em up."

That's all I needed, another dating service. Shayla would think I was such a nerd. But then again, I wanted Heather's opinion of Shayla.

I saw Shayla and the Payne sisters walking in the door. Shayla glanced in our direction, stopped, said something to her friends and walked back out the door. Stacey and Stephanie continued into Skeeter's. Jared saw them and said, "Hey, there's Shayla now. But, she's leaving."

"Where?" asked Heather as she stood looking out of the window.

Jared pointed outside. "Getting in that white truck."

Heather headed for the door to catch Shayla before I could stop her. This was going to be embarrassing. I wanted to crawl under the table. Fortunately for me, Shayla drove away before Heather got to her.

Heather came back in and sat down. "Darn, I missed her. Give me her number, Andy. I'll call her and tell her to come back."

"No way."

"Coward! Give it to me, Jared."

I gave Jared a stare as if I were going to kill him. He said, "Ah sorry, Heather. I don't have her number."

Heather shook her head in disappointment. I was off the hook for now. We hung out at Skeeter's for another hour and Shayla didn't come back. Heather decided it was time to go. She knew Mom would be waiting up for her. Heather was the daughter Mom never had. As we left McDonald's parking lot, Heather asked, "How are you doing, Andy?"

"I'm fine."

"Are you having a hard time after getting shot at and finding that body?"

I hesitated, not really wanting to talk about it. But, I knew she was worried about me. If I didn't talk about it, she would only worry more. "So that's why you came, to check on my mental health?"

"No, I came to see you, but that had to be very dramatic." She put her hand on my shoulder. "Are you okay?"

"I'm fine. Shit happens."

"We saw it on the news. They had your photo and everything. Everybody at school has been talking about it."

"I'm alright and I'm starting to like this little town. There's a lot of really good people here. But, I have to admit, that was weird."

"Jared seems really nice."

"He's alright. But a lot of strange things have happened in this town that has everyone on edge."

"Like what?"

Well, one of the football players named Bobby Patterson got murdered when he was up in the mountains close to where we found the body. Some people believe whoever killed him might be the same guy who killed the woman in the mine and shot at us."

"Wow, that's strange," said Heather.

"Yeah, and two other football players died the week before Bobby was murdered. And all three of them were good friends. Dad thinks the murder of the football player and the woman in the mine might somehow be connected to the deaths of the other two boys."

"How did the other boys die?"

"One collapsed on the practice field. The autopsy showed he had some type of heart problem from birth that had gone unde-tected. His best friend was the quarterback and he hung himself in his bedroom a few days later."

"Why did he do that?"

"Nobody knows. He didn't leave a note. Then Bobby Patterson got killed a few days later. Dad says they have to be connected, but the Sheriff investigators couldn't find any connection. The whole football program went to shit after that."

"What happened to the team?"

"I'm not sure. They just started losing. I think the deaths of the three players may have been the reason for the team's decline. But maybe it's because the coach's wife died of cancer that same year."

"A lot of unanswered questions," she said. "You need to watch yourself. I don't want anything to happen to you."

"I'll be careful. One more year and I'm outta here."

As soon as we got home, Mom came out and gave Heather a big hug. They went to the barn to look at the horses. I joined them so I could change Ruby's bandage.

"What happened to her leg?" asked Heather.

"She injured it barrel racing," Mom said. "She would've been sent to the slaughterhouse if Andy hadn't recused her."

Heather wrinkled her nose. "How's she doing?"

"She's improving," I said. "But she has a long way to go. I'm going to start letting her out in the back pasture soon."

Mom promised Heather she would take her riding tomorrow while I was working. Heather asked, "Can we ride to the ranch where Andy works? I want to meet his new girlfriend."

Mom looked at me. "I didn't know you and Shayla were dating. Why didn't you tell me?"

"We're not dating, Mom. That's just Jared running his big mouth."

"Well, I don't know why not, she's a lovely girl," Mom said.

I stood up. "Why is every one so interested in my love life all of a sudden?"

"Because you don't have one, that's why," replied Heather.

I shook my head and headed to the house. "I've got to get some sleep. I've to get up early to go to work." Mom and Heather were both grinning at me when I left. I slept on the couch. Heather got my room.

Heather was still asleep when I left the next morning. Colonel wasn't at the ranch when I arrived. I was on my own. Shayla had left early for a barrel racing lesson. I hoped she would get back in time to meet Heather. I really wanted Heather's opinion of her.

Mom and Heather rode up on Big John and Pharaoh while I was mowing the lawn. Donna must have been expecting them because she came out to meet them as soon as they arrived. I finished the lawn and sprayed weeds around the barn and shop. Mom and Heather were still visiting Donna when I left. I wanted to get home and help Dad work on the `56 Ford.

A wrecker was backed up to the barn when I arrived. The burnt-out Ford truck we had seen in the police impound lot had just been unloaded. Dad paid the tow truck driver as I got out of my car. When he finished, he looked at me. "What do you think?"

"I think it's great. How did you pull this off?"

"Turns out, the kid that stole the truck was the local bishop's son. The old man paid cash for it so his son wouldn't be prosecuted, and then quickly sent junior on a church mission to South America. I paid more for the impound fee than I did for the truck. All I had to do was promise not to tell anyone who stole it. Don't ever mention it to anyone."

"I won't. Looks like we have all the running gear we'll need for the `56."

"Yeah, I'm hoping we can modify the frame and put the `56 body on it. That way, the `56 will drive just like a new truck."

"Wow, Dad, this is great. Where do we start?"

"We start by getting it inside the garage and taking it apart. I think we can sell the spare parts and get most of our money back."

We pushed the truck into the garage and started taking it apart. Other than the burnt interior and scorched cab, there wasn't really anything wrong with it. We removed the cab and bed so we could start comparing the two frames to see if we could make it work. "I think if we shortened the frame by sixteen inches, it will work, Andy."

Heather and Mom came back and put the horses away while we were working on the truck. Heather joined us in the garage. "Hi, guys, what's all this?"

"This is all the running gear for Andy's old truck," Dad said.

"Wow, it's all burned up."

"Just the cab, the rest of it is in perfect condition," I said.

She looked confused, "Oh."

"Did you guys have fun?" Dad asked.

"We sure did. I miss you guys so much."

"What's Mom up too?" I asked.

"Starting dinner. She has a roast in the oven and she's making an apple pie."

Dad wiped his hands. "I better go see if I can give her hand."

When Dad left, I asked. "Did you meet Shayla?"

"No, she wasn't there. But if she's as pretty and nice as her mother, she's a keeper."

"She's just as pretty but not near as nice. She has a quite a temper. We got off on a pretty rocky start."

"I heard. You really like her, don't you?"

I hesitated. "I don't know what I think about her."

"Your mom told me about Ruby being Shayla's horse."

"You didn't say anything to Shayla's mom about Ruby did you?"

"No, Sherrie said not to say anything because it's a secret."

"I don't want Shayla to get her hopes up until I find out if Ruby will heal or not. And I'm not sure that will happen. Ruby is such a good horse. It'll be a shame if she's lame for the rest of her life. I'm hoping to make a trail horse out of her."

Heather looked me in the eyes. "You know, I think you're in love, Andrew."

"Don't Andrew me. And, you don't know what you're talking about."

Heather laughed. "Your mom told me Shayla calls you Andrew. Does she know you're a virgin?"

That caught me off guard. "What makes you think I am?"

"Oh come on, Andy, I know you. I know you better than you know yourself. Besides, you don't even have a girlfriend."

"Yes, and we both know you're not a virgin."

"Virginity was an insecurity blanket that smothered me. You need to get laid."

I shook my head. "Cody's a bad influence on you. I should wash your mouth out with soap."

She made a fist and stuck in my face. "Oh yeah. Just try it."

To change the subject, I asked, "How are you guys doing anyway?"

"Great. He wanted to come with me but I didn't want to share."

"Tell him 'hey' for me."

"I will… he misses you. And, you're changing the subject… Andrew."

I stopped working on the truck and wiped my hands. "Alright, why do you think I'm in love?"

"Because, I know why you bought Ruby."

"I bought her to keep her from going to the slaughterhouse."

"No, you didn't. You bought her because you couldn't make Shayla love you, so you wanted to own something she loved."

"I did not."

"Yes you did. I know you, Andy. You think if you could save her horse, she'd love you for it. And she just might. Her mother said she's really hurting over losing Ruby. And she's still doesn't speak to her father after he took Ruby to the auction."

I didn't want to argue. I rubbed Ruby's forehead. "She's a great horse. I sure hope I can save her."

Heather put her arm around me. "If anyone can, big guy, it's you. Let's go see what your parents are up to. And keep me informed about Shayla."

"Will do."

We went to the house. Heather left the next day but I couldn't help thinking of what she had said about me being in love.

CHAPTER TWENTY-SEVEN

When I walked into the kitchen, Dad was going over some notes. Without looking up, he asked. "Andy, would you like to go to Florence Prison with me today? I need to talk to one of their prisoners and he's not much older than you are."

"Sure, Dad. I've never been in a prison before. Who do you want to talk to?"

"A man named Dean Freeman who is serving 20 years for vehicular manslaughter. He killed a woman and her two small children while driving drunk."

"What do you want to talk to him about?"

"He was a close friend to the three football players who had died three years ago. He told Lt. Reinhardt he didn't have a clue why anyone would want to kill Bobby Patterson, but I think he does. The Sheriff's detectives never interviewed him. Having you there might help."

After breakfast, we drove to the prison. After signing in, they took all of our possessions except Dad's badge. After going through three locked doors, we walked down a long hallway with polished concrete floors. We were seated in an interview room and the door was locked behind us. The table and benches were made of cement and bolted to the floor. The walls were bare. Every sound echoed off the solid walls and I could hear the guards approaching before they brought Dean into the room. He wore an orange prison jump suit and handcuffs. Dad was dressed in civilian clothes with his badge hanging on his belt.

"Can you remove his cuffs please?" asked Dad.

The guards gave him a "are you sure look" but didn't argue. They removed Dean's cuffs and left the room.

Dean looked at me as if trying to decide if he knew me. Even though he was three years older that I was, we were about the same size. It was obvious he had been working out. He looked at Dad's badge. "Who are you?"

"My name is Scott Hanson. I'm the Assistant Chief of Police in Clarksville. This is my son, Andy. He plays football for Clarksville High."

Dean looked at me. "I keep up with the games in the newspaper. I haven't seen your name in any of them. Were you a bench warmer?"

"No. I played at Superstition Mountain High School last year. I'll be playing quarterback next year."

"How's coach Ford doing?"

"Alright, I guess."

"Are you guys going be any good this year?"

"I think so. We have a really good summer workout program now. The whole team is working hard."

Dean slowly shook his head as if thinking about that. "Well good luck."

"Thanks."

He studied Dad. "Since when did you become the assistant chief? I don't remember you when I lived there."

"Harvey Baker hired me to solve the Bobby Patterson murder."

Dean's eyes widened and he nodded. "So, have you solved it?"

"Not yet, but I will."

Dean stared at him. "So what do you want from me? I didn't kill him and I don't know who did."

"No one seems to know who killed Bobby. More importantly, no one seems to know why he was killed. I think you may be able to help me with that."

"You're wasting your time, Chief. I don't have a clue who killed Bobby."

"Maybe you do and you don't even know it."

Dean looked down at the table and took a deep breath. "Chief, I've spent a lot more time thinking about Bobby's murder than you ever will. That's all I've got to do here. I don't know who killed him. If I did, I would have already told Reinhardt."

"I believe the deaths of Bobby Patterson, Jimmy Turner and Dave Keller are connected." Dean looked up but didn't say anything. "If I can find that connection, maybe I can find the motive. If I can find the motive, perhaps I can find out who killed Bobby." Again, Dean didn't answer. "I need to know why these boys died. I need your help."

Dean was quiet for a long time. He stared at the table but his mind was somewhere else. Finally, as if he had made a decision, he said, "Sorry Chief, I'd like to help you. But I don't know anything."

"Look, Dean, Bobby was one of your best friends. He was killed in cold blood and whoever killed him is still out there. You owe it to him to help me."

Dean shook his head. "I would if I could. But I don't know who killed him."

Dad studied Dean for a long time. Dean wouldn't make eye contact. Dad must have sensed Dean was holding back. "Did you know Bobby's mother had a breakdown after he was killed?"

"I heard."

"Do you know she never leaves the house? She spends most of her days sitting on the porch staring into space?" Dean didn't answer. Dad waited for a few seconds to let that sink in. "Did you know Bobby's father lost his only son and his wife that day?"

Dean stayed quiet, staring at the table. He picked at his fingernails and remained silent. He looked as if he was hurting.

"Dean, you owe the Patterson family," Dad said. "They need closure so they can heal, and so do you. The whole town needs closure and Bobby deserves justice."

Dean jumped up and slammed his fist against the door. "I know, I know!" he yelled. "We all need closure. We all want justice. But I can't help you!" He was holding back tears.

The door opened and two large guards came in. They looked at Dean. "Everything all right in here, Chief?"

"Yeah, we're good."

The guards gave Dean a threatening stare and told him to sit down. They slowly closed the door and locked it. Dad handed Dean a tissue and he blew his nose. "What do you want from me?" asked Dean.

"I want you to tell me why Jimmy Turner and Dave Keller died."

"So you just walk in here and ask me to destroy my two best friend's reputations so you can go on a wild goose chase. What about their parents? Don't you think they're suffering too?" He paused. "If I tell you what I know, it will just muddy the waters and hurt a lot of innocent people. It won't help solve the murder."

"You don't know that."

Dean shook his head. "I won't betray my friends memory, Chief. I can't, and I won't."

"Do you know Shayla Stevenson?" I asked.

Dean looked surprised. "Yeah, Bobby's little sister. What about her?"

"She has never dated or gone to any school dances. She keeps to herself. She is hurting too."

Dean slowly shook his head. "That's too bad. Bobby really loved her. She was such a good kid." He rubbed his forehead and temples and let out a long breath. There was a long moment of silence. I could barely hear him say, "A lot of people got hurt for nothing."

Dad closed his notebook and put his pen away. "Dean look at me." Dean looked up, "Let's make a deal. We go off record. Whatever you tell me stays in this room. No record of this conversation will ever be added to any report unless it's needed to convict the suspect after I arrest him. If that were the case, you would testify anyway, wouldn't you?"

Dean thought for a few moments. "So if the information I tell you doesn't help solve the murder, it stays here and no one else will ever know?"

"That's right, no one will know what you told me."

"How do I know I can trust you?"

"You don't, you just have to trust us. Think about it, Dean. We all want the same thing, justice and closure. You need it as much as Bob and Meg Patterson. And Shayla Stevenson needs to heal and so do you. I know you're hurting."

Dean closed his eyes. "What do you want to know?"

"Everything."

"Alright Chief, but if you betray me, I'll swear this conversation never happened."

"Fair enough."

Dean looked at me. "Can I trust you to never repeat what I tell your dad?"

"I promise. I won't say a word."

Dean stood up and paced back and forth as if gathering his thoughts. Then, he sat down and began speaking: "We all grew up together, played football for Clarksville High and were good friends. Jimmy, Dave and I were from the poor side of the tracks. Bobby's parents had money. We had a good football team and Dave was our quarterback. We were dominating all of our games that year and were a sure bet to win the state championship." Dean hesitated. I couldn't help but think that I now wanted the same thing these boys wanted three years ago. They weren't much different that I was.

"Go on," Dad said.

Dean continued. "Dave had a lot of scouts interested in him. He was putting up big numbers. His golden arm was his ticket to a college education. All Jimmy and I could hope for was getting a job and taking classes at the Community College."

He paused again. "The scouts who were watching Dave all had the same concern. He was too skinny and not strong enough to compete at the next level. The coach from ASU told Dave's parents that if he could put on twenty pounds of muscle before he graduated, they would give him a full ride scholarship. After our junior year, Dave joined the Iron Man's Health Club. He worked his ass off. He lived in the gym and took all kinds of protein powder and supplements. But he wasn't gaining weight. Then, after about a month, he started gaining weight and began to get much stronger. He added sixty pounds to his bench press and over a hundred pounds to his squats. He knocked a full second off his forty-yard dash time. His golden arm got even better. He kept going to the gym even after we were in full swing with football practice. It didn't make sense that he would continue at the gym. There were college scouts at every game and Dave started getting a lot more attention."

Dean stopped talking as if he was unsure he wanted to continue.

"Let me guess. Steroids?" Dad asked.

Dean looked surprised. "Good guess, Chief. We got suspicious when Dave's complexion started getting worse and he became more and more irritable. Jimmy and Dave were like brothers. Dave's mood swings were causing a lot of tension between them. Dave broke down and told Jimmy he was using steroids. They kept it a secret, even from Bobby and me. If Coach

Ford found out that anyone was using steroids, he would kick them off the team. It didn't matter who you were. Steroids were strictly forbidden. Any chance of a scholarship would vanish. No one else knew."

I couldn't help but wonder if Coach Ford knew any of this. All the signs were there. How could he not have known unless his wife's cancer had distracted him?

"Whoever was supplying the steroids knew," Dad said.

Dean scratched he head, "I never thought of that. I always figured Dave was getting the steroids from Old Mexico. I guess you could be right."

"Did he tell you he was buying from Mexico?"

"No, I didn't even know he was taking steroids."

"When did you find out he was taking them?"

Dean bowed his head and took a deep breath. "Dave told me the day before he hung himself."

Dad nodded, "Go on, what did Dave tell you?"

"Jimmy wanted a college scholarship. He begged Dave to get him steroids. Dave refused at first. It caused even more tension between them. As the season progressed, Dave got strong as hell and kept gaining weight. Jimmy kept pressuring him for steroids and Dave finally gave him some. The next day, Jimmy dropped dead on the practice field. Dave was devastated. He believed he had killed his best friend by giving him drugs."

"So, that's why he killed himself," Dad said.

"Yeah. He didn't know about Jimmy's heart condition at the time. But I don't think it would have made any difference though. Dave would still have blamed himself for Jimmy's death. He quit going to school and wouldn't come out of his room. He wouldn't even talk to Coach Ford. He was depressed, couldn't sleep, and wouldn't eat. I went to see to him. He broke down and started crying. He told me he had killed Jimmy by giving him steroids. He couldn't stop crying. After I left, he hung himself in his bedroom.

I was devastated. I blamed myself for not being able to help him. But it was too late."

Dean had tears in his eyes. Dad waited for him to regain his composure. "Anything else?"

"I don't think Bobby knew about the steroids. That's why I don't think steroids had anything to with his murder. It just didn't make sense. I didn't tell anyone about the steroids. I got depressed, started drinking and stayed drunk as much as possible. I was drunk and stoned when I wrecked my car and killed those people. I can never forgive myself, Chief. This nightmare never ends. That's all I know."

Dad didn't say anything for a long time. After a few awkward moments, he said, "Thanks Dean. If I can find out who was supplying Dave with steroids, maybe I can find out why Bobby was killed."

"And if not, this conversation didn't happen. Right?"

"Right. And if you think of anything else, give me a call. I'll come back to see you."

"If you find out who killed Bobby, let me know."

"You'll be one of the first to know. Thanks for helping. Is there anything I can do for you?"

"Yeah, catch the son of a bitch. I want him as a cell mate."

Dean looked at me but didn't say anything. He just sat there as if he didn't want us to leave. I held out my hand. "It was nice meeting you."

Dean shook his head but didn't say anything. He shook my hand and stood up. He yelled, "Guards."

The guards came in and let Dad and I out of the interview room. Dean's sad empty eyes focused on me as we left. I think he wished he was in my shoes. I guess concrete and steel has a way of making a man think. We kept eye contact until he disappeared behind the sliding metal door. I'll never forget the hollow sound of the door slamming shut echoing through the hallways. I thought of how fragile life can be.

Dad said he didn't know if he was any closer to solving Bobby Patterson's murder or not. There were still a lot of unanswered questions. But at least he had a possible motive.

CHAPTER TWENTY-EIGHT

J ared, Larry and I organized our own summer workout program and encouraged all players to participate. We met every weekday morning during the summer at the city park after weight training and on Saturdays at 4 p.m. at the high school. I worked with the running backs, receivers and tight ends. On weekdays we ran plays and worked on timing. Jared worked with the defensive line and Larry worked with the offensive line. On Saturdays, we worked on speed training and special teams.

Colonel agreed to assist with the workouts. He recruited Lieutenant Reinhardt and Bob Johnson to assist us. It was seldom that all three of them were there at the same time, but at least one of them showed up most days. All three had played football at Clarksville High and wanted the team to return to its glory days.

Coach Ford had given me copies of the films from last year's games. With Dad's help, I was able to identify many of the team's problems. Not having a quarterback who could throw was the most obvious. Using Coach Ford's playbook, I took notes on plays that seemed to work and ones that didn't.

When not practicing football or collecting eggs, Jared spent most of his summer in my barn helping me with the `56 Ford. He knew nothing about cars. But, he helped with disassembling and cleaning up messes. Eager to learn, he did whatever I asked. And, we were making good progress. In return, I kept tutoring him in math and he seemed to be grasping it for the first time in his life.

I kept showing up at the Double J Ranch from time to time even though John Stevenson had told me I had worked enough to pay for the truck. John kept paying me for my work even though he didn't need me anymore. I needed the money to pay Colonel back and for parts for the truck. One day when Colonel, John and I were working, Colonel stopped and looked me straight in the eye. "Andy, I think Shayla has something to do with your decision to say on."

"That girl is a wasted cause, Colonel. I just like ranching." He smiled and I knew he wasn't buying any of it. John Stevenson acted as if he hadn't heard either one of us but he was grinning. To tell the truth, I wasn't sure why I even bothered. Shayla was with her mother most Saturdays either practicing barrel racing or participating in horse events. I'm not even sure she knew I was around anymore.

John Stevenson was getting around without his cane and was now riding a little. They really didn't need me. It had been a busy summer for the most part and I needed a vacation before school started.

CHAPTER TWENTY-NINE

For the first time in my life I wished it would stop raining. Tropical storms from Mexico had already dumped a considerable amount of water upon the state. Some areas got more than four inches one week alone. Flash flood warnings where abundant. The monsoon season had been much wetter than normal that year. Good for Arizona but not for our planned vacation to the Mogollon Rim.

We pulled into our familiar camping spot in the Coconino National Forest right after it stopped raining. We parked in a small meadow surrounded by tall pines located next to several corrals and a large fenced pasture. The fresh smell of pine, along with the cooler temperatures, was a welcomed relief from the triple digit heat in Clarksville.

"Andy, check to make sure the back gate is secure before we turn the horses out. I want to check Ruby's leg," Mom said.

I secured the back gate and went to help with the horses. "How's she doing, Mom?"

"There's no swelling and she didn't hesitate to back out of the trailer. I think she's fine. But keep an eye on her."

The last six months of rehabilitating her leg seems to have paid off. So far, she showed no sign of lameness. After unloading the other two horses, I turned all three loose in the pasture. Dad's horse, Big John, and Mom's horse, Pharaoh, bucked, farted and kicked high in the air as they ran around the familiar pasture. Pharaoh led the way as always, with Big John hot on his heels cutting corners attempting to keep up. Ruby followed at a quick trot. After a few trips around the pasture and through the trees, they settled down to the business of grazing.

After setting up camp we headed to Clint's Wells, a 5-minute drive away. It consists of a gas station with a garage, and a small store, and the Long Valley Café. The café was our destination. They served all you could eat fish or shrimp every Friday night and a prime rib special every Saturday night at very reasonable prices.

After dinner, we turned in early wanting to be on the trail shortly after daybreak. We were riding to a cave located in the bottom of Clear Creek Canyon. The round trip was a little over sixteen miles on horseback.

While we were saddling our horses the next morning, several Forest Service trucks, Sheriff's vehicles and a Highway Patrol car sped by on the dirt road close to our camp with their emergency lights on headed east. Within the next thirty minutes, several trucks pulling horse-trailers with "Search and Rescue" written on the sides drove east on the same road headed towards Jones Crossing. "What do you think's happening, Dad?"

"I suppose someone's lost."

"Maybe we can help find them?"

"We will if we run into them and they need our help," said Mom.

We rode across a long meadow and up the face of a steep rocky mountain to Dry Lake that wasn't dry. We traveled east from there to an elk trail that led us down the other side of the mountain to a large grassy meadow.

The emergency vehicles and horse trailers that had driven by earlier were parked around several campsites in the meadow. Everyone had gathered under a large tent with maps spread out on a picnic table.

As we approached the meeting area, one of the Sheriff's deputies approached Dad. "Are you part of the search and rescue team?"

"No, I'm the Assistant Police Chief for the City of Clarksville. We'll help if we you need us."

"We'll take all the help we can get," replied the deputy.

We dismounted and joined the meeting that was about to start. The Sheriff's Department had the lead in the search and a big Sheriff's Sergeant yelled for everyone to gather around.

"Listen up everyone!" he yelled. "I'm Sargent O'Hara and will be in charge of the search. My deputies are passing out photos of the little girl that's missing. Her name is Carolyn McKay. She's five years old and has a history of sleepwalking. She was missing from her tent when the family woke this morning at 5:30. We have no idea if she left early this morning or has been missing most of the night. She was asleep in the tent at 9:30 p.m. when the family turned in. Our best guess is that she has been missing from somewhere between 3 to 8 hours. The family has searched the immediate area with no sign of the child. She was last seen wearing blue polka-dot pajamas. Her pink blanket is also missing. She has blond curly hair, blue eyes and is missing two front teeth."

He paused and looked around. "We'll search the immediate area again on foot and assign the horse riders to areas further out. We will limit our search to a three-mile radius to start with and expand the search area if she is not located. The weatherman is predicting heavy rains this afternoon, so let's find this little girl. Are there any questions?"

When no one asked any questions, Sgt. O'Hara asked, "Is there anyone here who is familiar with this area?"

My dad raised his hand. "We've been riding this area for years."

"We'll assign you to areas farther out since you are less likely to get lost," said Sergeant O'Hara.

We marked the camp on our GPSs while Dad got our assigned search area of responsibility.

The search and rescue teams, Forest Service personnel and on-duty Police Officers had radios for communication, but none to spare. Everyone else added Sergeant O'Hara's phone number into their cell phones. The search teams were to call if they had anything to report. Phone service was hit and miss at best in this area.

We had a short family meeting. Dad explained that our search area was east of the camp towards Clear Creek and south of the Jones Crossing Road. The area was made up of thick pine and oak forest, small meadows, steep rocky ridges and a few old logging roads. It was home to deer, elk, squirrels, turkeys, mountain lions, and bears. The remote area around Clear Creek had no roads crossing the canyon except the Jones Crossing Bridge. The canyon was very primitive if you ventured far from the main road in either direction.

The little girl's parents watched as the search party departed. The mother had tears streaming down her cheeks and her husband had his arms around her trying to comfort her. I made eye contact with the mother and her eyes pleaded with me to find her daughter. "We won't come back until we find her," I said.

She turned away sobbing and her husband walked her back to their camp.

Dad gave us his instructions; "Andy, I want you to head northeast to Jones Crossing and work your way back south along Clear Creek to the old elk trail leading into the canyon. Sherrie, head due east checking the center area. I'll go southeast to Clear Creek and work my way back to the north and meet you and Andy at the elk trail. We'll ride back to the command post from there."

We divided the sandwiches and bottled water, and checked our flashlights, matches, Power Bars, and rain gear.

I rode slowly stopping every few yards yelling out for Carolyn then listening for a reply before moving on. Ruby wanted to move out fast, but I held her back not wanting to add pressure to her injured tendon.

After several hours, we made our way to the top of the cliffs overlooking Jones Crossing. I turned south along the ridge yelling down into the canyon and listening for a reply. I checked my phone and there were no messages saying the little girl had been located. I knew she must be frightened and wondered if she had been injured. I prayed someone would find her before the afternoon storms hit.

Thunder and Lightning could be seen far away in all directions as the storm neared. Huge thunderclouds were building in all directions and the sky was starting to darken. It appeared we were in for a gully-washer.

Ruby suddenly stopped and stared out into the canyon with her ears pointed in the direction she was looking. "What is it, girl?" I asked as I patted her neck. After a few moments of not hearing anything, I nudged her to move on, but she wouldn't budge. I gave her rein and she started walking to the edge of the canyon and stared into it with her ears pointed forward. "Is there something down there, Ruby?"

I yelled as loud as I could, "Carolyn, are you down there?" There was no answer. I dismounted and tied Ruby to a tree branch, then walked out on a rocky ledge overlooking the canyon. I yelled again. This time, I heard a scream from the bottom of the canyon. It was a muffled scream but I knew it was a child's scream. I yelled several more times but I didn't hear anything.

I looked for a way to climb down into the canyon but the sheer cliffs prevented it.

Checking my GPS, I figured I was only a half mile from the elk trail where I was supposed to meet my parents. I checked my cell phone and there wasn't any service, but I had a text message from my mother. "*Met up with Dad. No luck. Headed back to camp. Will move our camp to the search area before the storm hits. See you in camp.*"

Believing Carolyn was somewhere in the bottom of the canyon, I considered my options. The storm was coming fast, lightning was increasing in intensity and the sound of thunder was getting louder. I knew it would start raining soon. If I rode back to camp to get help, it would be dark before I got there. The thought of Carolyn, cold, wet, and alone in the canyon made my decision for me. I would try to find her while it was still light enough to see.

When I got to the elk trail, I found two sets of hoof prints going west. They belonged to Big John and Pharaoh. The wind was getting stronger and the first drops of rain pelted my hat. Untying my rain slicker, I put it on. We followed the trail slowly as mud began collecting on Ruby's feet. "Careful girl, you don't want to slide over the edge."

After a quarter of a mile, the trail flattened out where an old logging road had once been. Ruby jumped a large fallen tree and we continued. The trail started down a steep rocky slope to Clear Creek. Standing water filed out path. "Easy girl, take it slow," I said as I patted her neck.

I slowed Ruby's pace so she wouldn't trip or injure her leg on the large boulders. She picked her path carefully. If she re-injured her tendon, she would not be able to walk out of this canyon. When we got to the bottom, the trail flattened out again as we approached the creek. I checked her leg and she wasn't limping and appeared to be all right.

I opened a wire gate at the bottom of the trail and closed it behind us. As soon as we got through the gate, the trail dropped off into the creek bottom. I located the small pine tree growing out of a large boulder on the opposite side of the creek that we used as a landmark for finding our way out of the canyon. I wasn't sure if I could locate the tree after dark. There were no other trails leading out of the canyon for another two miles. I started getting worried because everything looked different at night. I tied my handkerchief to the tree hoping I could see it after dark.

Normally, this was a beautiful place for riding, but it looked uninviting and ominous at the moment. The area where I had heard the screams was about a mile north of my present location. Lightning flashes cast eerie shadows along the canyon walls. Rain pounded us as we rode. It kept getting darker and colder by the minute. Water ran off the front of my hat. I strained to see the trail in front of us. Ruby pushed on without protest but was soaked to the bone. The water in the creek was rising.

We traveled for about a mile when Ruby came to a sudden stop. Her ears went forward. I had learned years ago to trust horses at times like this. They could see much better in the dark than people. I patted her on the neck and stared into the darkness looking for movement. "What is it girl?" Ruby felt tense under the saddle. I squeezed her with my legs but she refused to move. She started pawing the ground and snorting. She inhaled and then blew hard which was a sign of danger. I nudged her forward a couple of steps and saw what she was looking at. The hair on the back of my neck stood up. A large black bear stood about twenty yards away. "Easy girl."

The bear was on the same side of the creek as we were. He was milling around a pile of boulders. I expected Ruby to bolt at any moment but she held her ground. I thought about firing off a round or two from my pistol to scare the bear away but I didn't know if Ruby was trained for hunting or not. I couldn't chance shooting knowing she might buck me off. The ground was mostly sand and grass but there were plenty of rocks where I could hit my head or break a leg. I decided to yell for Carolyn thinking it might frighten the bear away. "Carolyn, where are you!"

I didn't hear a reply. The bear didn't run away either. It pawed at us, showing his teeth. Ruby became more agitated after I yelled and started whinnying and pawing the ground, tossing her head up and down. She moved closer to the bear, kicking her front feet upward and snorting as she advanced. A horse challenging a bear didn't make sense.

Ruby pinned her ears back, baring her teeth as she approached the bear. The bear stood on his hind legs and growled at her but she wouldn't back down. The last thing I wanted at this moment was to take a horse to a bear fight. I pulled her hard to the right but she spun completely around facing the bear again. Yanking her to the left caused her to spin 360 again facing the bear. She reared up and pawed at the bear like horses do to when fighting each other. I held on tight trying to stay mounted but I couldn't control my horse. Ruby was relentless and wouldn't give an inch. The bear was now hopping up and down on his front feet and making puffing sounds between growls.

The rain pounded us and Lightning cracked above our heads. It would be completely black if it weren't for the Lightning. The bear's sharp white fangs and long dark claws glistened when the Lightning struck. I couldn't see the bear between strikes. Ruby reared and pawed. She spun and kicked high in the air attempting to kick the bear as I held on for dear life.

My only option was holding on, or dismounting and try to shoot the bear. I decided to dismount and shoot the bear. While attempting to dismount, I lost my balance and fell hard on my right side. Fortunately there were no rocks. I quickly jumped to my feet but had lost my hat. I pulled my pistol to try to shoot the bear, but Ruby was between us. The bear moved towards the boulders but Ruby cut him off every time he went that way as if she were trying to protect me. The bear charged Ruby and she spun to her left and kicked the bear with her rear hooves knocking him over. The bear rolled, got back to his feet. He looked behind himself as if he was deciding what to do. Then he turned and ran northward along the creek with Ruby hot on his heels. They disappeared around the bend leaving me alone in the darkness. My heart pounded in my chest and my hands shook as I was wondered what I should do.

Holstering my pistol, I retrieved my hat and slapped it against my leg to get the sand out. Using my fist, I pushed it back into shape and then placed it back on my soaked head. Standing in the darkness, I considered my options. The big cave was only a short distance to the north. At least I could get out of the weather. Concerned for Ruby, I yelled for her as loud as I could.

A small cry of a child came from somewhere behind me. I turned toward the boulders but couldn't see anyone. I yelled, "Carolyn, where are you?" A small frightened voice answered, "Here, I'm in here."

The sound was coming from the boulders. Getting down on my hands and knees, I looked under the large boulders but couldn't see her. "Carolyn, where are you?"

"I'm in here," answered the child. I looked deep into a small crevice as lightning lit the canyon. I saw Carolyn in a fetal position squeezed far inside. She had tears streaming down her cheeks and was shaking. "Carolyn, can you come out?"

"No, who are you?"

"My name is Andy. Your mother sent me to find you and take you home. Can you come out?"

"No, I'm scared."

"I won't hurt you. Come on out so we can go home."

"No, the bear will eat me."

No wonder she was terrified. Ruby must have known she was there and tried to protect her from the bear.

"Carolyn, the bear is gone. My horse chased him away."

"Are you sure?"

"I promise, he's gone. I won't let anything hurt you. Come on out." I reached my arm inside the crevice as far as I could but I couldn't reach her. "Come on, Carolyn, give me your hand."

"You promise the bear is gone. Promise?"

"The bear is gone, I promise. Now give me your hand."

Carolyn slowly crawled forward and reached out to me. Taking her cold hand, I helped her out of the rocks. She was cold, wet and very scared. As soon as she was free, I wrapped her in my coat. When I picked her up, she wrapped her arms around my neck and squeezed tight.

My only option now was to get to the cave, build a fire and get her warmed before hypothermia set in. As I started walking towards the cave, something came towards us in the darkness but I couldn't see what it was. I drew my pistol out of the holster. Ruby whinnied. She walked up to us when I called out to her. My heart sunk when I saw her limping on her right front leg.

"Carolyn, look. Here's the horse that chased that mean old bear away."

"What's his name?"

"She is a girl and her name is Ruby. Want to pet her?"

"Does she bite?"

"She doesn't bite people, just bears."

Carolyn tentatively reached out and rubbed Ruby's forehead. "She is nice."

"You want to ride her."

"No, I'm afraid," she said as she squeezed my neck tighter.

"Okay, I'll carry you."

I held Carolyn in my right arm and took Ruby's reins in my left hand and started walking towards the cave. When we got there and started to walk inside, Carolyn asked, "Are there any bears in there?"

I shined my flashlight into the cave so Carolyn could see there were no bears. We went inside and I sat her down. She took the flashlight while I went to get some matches to light a fire. The storm raged and Carolyn shook from the cold. The cave already had some firewood. Carolyn followed me with the light while I got a fire started.

Loosening the cinch, I removed the saddle and placed it and the pad near the fire to dry. Ruby didn't appear to have any other injuries other than the limp. I took my sandwich and a bottle of water out of the saddlebags and handed them to Carolyn along with a Power Bars, then threw more wood on the fire.

The rain hadn't let up and thunder echoed through the canyon. The wind howled as I walked towards the opening of the cave.

"Where are you going?" Carolyn cried.

"I'm going outside to get more wood for the fire."

"No! Don't go. I'm scared."

I knelt down next to her and looked her in the eyes, "Honey, we need more wood for the fire so we can stay warm."

"No, the bear might come back. Stay here."

"Carolyn, bears are afraid of fire. They won't come anywhere close. Even if a bear wanted to come in here, Ruby would chase him away. Ruby is not afraid of bears."

"How long are you going to be gone?"

"Just a few minutes. Just long enough to get some more wood."

"Okay, but hurry. Please."

"Carolyn, nothing can hurt you now. You're safe. I promise I will not let anything harm you and neither will Ruby. Do you understand?"

She looked at me, then at Ruby and said, "Okay, but I want to go home. I want my mommy."

"As soon as it stops raining, I will take you to your mom. You can ride Ruby, all right? But for now, you have to be brave until I get back."

"I'll try, but hurry!"

I ran outside to the edge of the tall cliffs supporting the cave. I worked my way around the side to a game trail leading up the steep slope. Slipped several times in the mud, I climbed hand over foot up the steep mountain. When I got to the top of the cliff I was exhausted and out of breath. My phone had a weak signal. Mom answered on the second ring.

"Andy, where are you? We are worried to death."

"I found Carolyn, Mom. We're both all right and we're waiting the storm out in the cave."

"We'll come and get you."

"No, Mom. The trail is muddy and you might slip over the side. We're okay. We have a fire and will be fine until morning and then we'll walk out."

"Walk out? Aren't you going to ride out?"

"No. Ruby chased a bear and came up lame."

"A bear! Are you sure you're all right?"

"We're fine, it's a long story. Mom, I'm getting soaked out here and I've got to get back to the cave. I'll tell you about it tomorrow. Let Carolyn's parents know she's okay and we'll be coming home in the morning. Bye."

I hung up and half-climbed, half-slid, back down the mountain. By the time I got to the bottom, I was a muddy mess. Quickly gathering wood, I re-entered the cave.

Carolyn was crying. "Where've you been? I was scared."

I threw the wood in a pile and picked her up and held her. "I told you I was coming right back."

"You were gone a long time. Don't leave me anymore. I'm scared."

I handed her a bottle of water and asked her to drink. She took several swallows and stopped crying. I sat beside her and threw more wood on the fire. She climbed into my lap and I wrapped her tightly in my coat. Soon, she stopped shaking and fell asleep.

Listening to the sounds of the raging storm and thinking of the bear, sleep came slowly.

When I woke, the fire was out but the coals were still hot. My butt and back ached and I hadn't slept more than a few hours. I placed Carolyn on the ground next to me still wrapped in my coat. She stirred and mumbled a few words but didn't wake up. While tossing wood on the fire, I noticed Ruby was missing. I was worried she may have wandered off in the storm. I found her grazing near the mouth of the cave. She whinnied when she saw me and went back to grazing.

The rain had stopped and the air was still. Thick fog had filled the canyon. I checked Ruby's leg. She had a stone bruise, the tendon had held. I heard Carolyn screaming and ran back into the cave.

"I'm right here." I yelled as I entered the cave.

"Where were you? You said you wouldn't leave me. I'm scared."

"I was just outside checking Ruby's leg. I'm not leaving you." I dried her tears and held her tight. "Are you okay?"

"No, I'm hungry and I want to go home."

I gave her my last Power Bar and another bottle of water. I walked Ruby back into the cave and saddled her. "You get to ride a horse today. Won't that be fun?"

"I don't know how to ride a horse."

"Well I'm going to teach you. It's easy and fun."

Carolyn half-smiled, "Okay."

I picked her up and placed her in the saddle. I wrapped my coat around her to keep her warm. "All you have to do is hold on to this saddle horn. I'm going to walk and we'll be with your parents soon."

"Okay. But don't go fast."

" I won't."

A cool, damp, thick fog kept us from seeing very far ahead. The water in the creek ran deeper than it had yesterday, but was still passable. Uncertain at first, Carolyn seemed to enjoy riding after a few steps. Walking south along the creek bed, we crossed the creek several times before getting to the small pine tree growing out of the big boulder. We turned east and worked our way up to the wire gate and back up the rocky ledge to the elk trail. I took Carolyn out of the saddle while Ruby jumped the fallen log. I put her back on and we continued along the muddy trail. About a mile further, I heard something coming towards us in the fog. We stopped and listened. Several people from the search party were coming to greet us. My parents were leading the way and Carolyn's father, Ronnie McKay, was right behind them riding a mule. They were leading a spare horse.

When Carolyn saw her father, she started crying and reached out for him. He dismounted, wrapped her in his arms and checked her for injuries.

Dad asked, "You okay, Son?"

"I'm fine. Just tired."

Mom said, "We're so proud of you, Andy. Is Ruby alright?"

"Yeah, the tendon held. It's just a stone bruise."

Mr. McKay took Carolyn with him on his mule. I rode the extra horse. He thanked me at least a dozen times on the way back while I explained about finding Carolyn and the encounter with the bear.

When we arrived back at camp, everyone was waiting for us, including a news reporter and a cameraman. They started cheering when they saw Carolyn. Her mom ran to her with tear-filled eyes and wrapped her in her arms.

Tired, cold, hungry and sleepy, I wanted to go back to bed. Everyone wanted to thank me for finding Carolyn. I worked my way through the crowd to our trailer. Just before entering, I looked back and saw Mr. McKay holding his daughter as she hugged Ruby's neck saying, "This is Ruby. She bites bears."

The rest of our vacation was uneventful. I didn't ride Ruby the rest of the week and her stone bruise completely healed by the time we left to go home. Convinced she was a sound trail horse, I now had to decide how I was going to let Shayla know that I had Ruby.

CHAPTER THIRTY

My senior year was a breeze academically. No more poetry or creative cooking this year. I had applied for all three major military academies and was waiting for a call from one of the State Senators to see if I could get a nomination.

Jared and I spent Saturdays at the barn working on the truck. Dad helped most Saturdays and Sunday afternoons. We were making great progress.

I had basically given up on Shayla and quit going to the ranch. We were on speaking terms but that was about it. I had convinced myself that she was a lost cause. Neither one of us had dated anyone during our junior year.

The football team was eager to get started at Clarksville High. The team voted Larry, Jared and I as team Captains. Our summer workout program had not only boosted our confidence as a team, but we were stronger, faster and heavier than we had been last year. I'd put on ten pounds of muscle over the summer and had knocked another tenth off my time in the forty. We couldn't wait to hit the practice field.

During our first meeting, I addressed the team: "The team rules have changed this year. There will be no more walking. Every player will be required to run anytime the team moves from one place to the other. It doesn't matter if we are going to the practice field, to get a drink of water or going back into the locker room, everyone has to run. If we are going to the state championships, we need to start acting and looking like a state champion team."

We made sure all players adhered to the new rules. We required perfection when lining up and dong calisthenics. If anyone was not in unison, we all had the whole team start calisthenics over. It didn't take long for the team to start looking a lot better than they had in the past.

If Coach Ford noticed the changes in the team, he didn't show it. He still showed up to work in wrinkled clothes, uncombed hair and unshaven. His eyes were often bloodshot and I smelled liquor on his breath more often than not. His only full-time assistance was Rowdy Thomas. Rowdy washed and repaired uniforms, acted as part-time trainer, waterboy, and janitor. The players called him Coach, but it was apparent, he knew very little about coaching football.

Bernie Baxter did a good job as the weight training coach and showed up every morning and evening to make sure everyone was doing their workouts properly.

We were wasting a lot of time during practice as the offensive players stood around while Coach Ford worked with the defense and the defensive players stood around while he worked on offense. This caused boredom for the players not involved and they became frustrated. Not much was getting accomplished from practice to practice.

Knowing Coach Ford needed assistance, I discussed the issue with him. He welcomed any extra help he could get. Colonel Lightfoot, Bob Johnson and Lt. Reinhardt volunteered as assistant football coaches for our team. All three of them showed up at the next practice.

The additional coaches definitely helped the team. But Coach Ford seemed to have little faith in them. Despite his attitude, practices improved and the team's enthusiasm, morale and attitude got much better. Our work ethic over the summer had definitely paid off. I kept reminding the team: "Guys, whatever team we play against in the championship game is working just as hard as we are and it all comes down to who wants it the most."

Surprisingly, no one quit. The wannabe players had been weeded out over the summer. This team knew what was expected of them and we wanted to win. Larry and Jared were doing their part and setting good examples for the rest of the players.

CHAPTER THIRTY-ONE

C larksville was a great football town. The local citizens and newspaper strongly supported the team and the newspaper ran several articles about the team's obvious improvement. Everyone in town was excited about the new prospects and had high expectation for us.

The first game was against the defending state champions, the Safford Owls. The Owls had outscored Clarksville 42 to 7 last year. They were Clarksville's biggest rivals and the winner of the game had bragging rights in the Gila River Valley all year.

Another loss to the Owls would be hard to swallow for the residents of Clarksville since most of the families from both schools knew each other and boasting could be brutal. Both towns had high hopes for their football teams this year.

On game day, almost the entire population of both towns turned out for the game. It had a playoff atmosphere even though it was only the first game. The parking lots were full as were both stands.

Coach Ford's pre-game speech was disappointing to say the least and he didn't appear confident. When he was finished speaking, I got up and addressed them. "Guys, if each player will do his part, the team will prevail. Dream big and then make it happen. I assure you our team is as good as Safford's. We can win if each one of you believe we can win. Only doubt can doom us."

As the team entered the field, a large roar erupted from the crowd. I searched the stands and saw Stacey and Stephanie Miller, Kelsey Garner and Priscilla Zayas. Shayla wasn't with them. I located my parents sitting near the 50-yard line with John and Donna Stevenson, Colonel Lightfoot and Bernie Baxter. Shayla wasn't with them either. It disappointed me that she hadn't come to the game.

After warm-ups, Jared, Larry and I walked to the center of the field for the coin toss. Safford won the toss and elected to kick off rather than receive the ball. The game began with the kickoff going into the end zone. I walked out to the 20-yard line for the first play of the season for the Cougars. I was so hyped. I handed the ball off to the running back for a one yard gain.

The next play lost four yards when the tailback couldn't get around the corner before being tackled by Safford's big defensive end. The Coach called for a play action and I faked to the running back up the middle and hit our tight end with a pass for a gain of 14 yards and a first down. We continued to drive down the field for 60 yards, until the drive ended with a pass being dropped by our wide receiver.

Safford came back with their own drive of sixty-four yards, all on running plays, and scored their first touchdown. They kicked off and I received the ball on the 5-yard line and ran it back to Safford's own 48. Coach Ford called for a pass option play again and I kept the ball gaining another 12 yards for another first down. I hit the tight end on a slant pass for another first down at the Safford 24 yard line. We squandered yet another opportunity when our running back fumbled the ball on Safford's own 16-yard line.

The Owls drove the ball back to the Cougars 20 yard line before our safety picked off a pass up the middle and ran the ball back to Safford's 18-yard line. We were held to four yards on three running plays and had to settle for a field goal. The rest of the first half had both teams moving the ball downfield, but major miscues, penalties or costly turnovers stopped either team from scoring. The first half ended with Safford leading with a score of 7 to 3.

The mood in the Cougar's locker room at half time was optimistic. We had held our own against a team that had dominated us last year and we felt confident we could play better in the second half. Coach Ford told us to keep doing what we were doing and we had a chance to pull off an upset. Not the most encouraging half-time speech I'd ever heard by a long shot.

The second half started with the Cougars kicking off to Safford. Safford ran a reverse on the kickoff catching us off guard and was able to run the ball back to our 16-yard line. The very next play, their quarterback hit a receiver in the corner of the end zone for a touchdown. The Owls scored a two-point conversion when the quarterback picked up the ball and ran it around the left end untouched. The score was now 15 to 3.

The score stayed the same until the beginning of the fourth quarter when I hit the wide receiver with a 42-yard pass in the end zone to make the score Cougars 10, Owls 15.

After receiving the ball, Safford was stopped on three downs and was forced to punt. We started on our own 34-yard line and drove down to their 48-yard line on six plays. The drive ended when our tight end was hit by two defenders at the same time after a three-yard gain and fumbled the ball. Safford's middle linebacker picked up the ball and ran it back for a touchdown. The Owls kicked the extra point and the score was now Owls 22, Cougars 10.

We got the ball back on our 18-yard line and drove down to Safford's own six-yard line by completing seven out of eight passes. Coach Ford called for four consecutive run plays and the Cougars turned the ball over on the one-yard line on downs.

It was a hard fought game but we couldn't overcome the deficit. Both teams had costly penalties and missed opportunities but we lost the game to the Owls 22 to 10. The upside was that score was a lot closer than most people had expected. But it was still a loss and hard to swallow.

The team took the loss hard and after shaking hands with the Owls, we assembled in the locker room. It was so quiet you could have heard a mouse fart. The mood was somber, the players were exhausted and no one was speaking. The team had worked so hard and yet we lost.

The silence was broken when Larry threw his helmet against his locker causing a loud bang that echoed off the walls. I looked at him but didn't say anything; I knew this wasn't the time. Everyone was tired, frustrated and disappointed after losing the game. Everyone felt we should have won that game and many blamed the coach.

Larry sat on the bench for a few minutes and then slammed his fist into his locker putting a large dent in it. "Fucking Coach! If he'd get his head out of his ass, we'd have won that game."

Jared looked over at Larry, "There's enough blame to go around Larry, it wasn't all his fault."

" The hell is isn't! We busted our asses for him and he comes to work drunk half the time."

"Knock it off," I yelled when I saw Coach Ford standing in the doorway. "Go home and get some sleep. We'll get better next week!" No one challenged me.

Jared and Larry saw the coach standing in the doorway as did the rest of the team. The coach turned and walked away without commenting. We showered in silence, got dressed and left.

I was the last one to leave the locker room. Coach Ford's door was closed and the shades were pulled down and the lights were out. His truck was still parked in the parking lot. I walked back inside and started to knock on the coach's door when I heard a bottle smashing against the wall. I left wondering if I made had made a mistake by not talking to him.

CHAPTER THIRTY-TWO

Monday morning after the Cougar's opening game of the season was a somber day at school. The newspaper had praised the team for a great effort, commenting on how much improved the team was over last year's team and on how close the score had been. However, the article didn't seem to help the foul mood of the players and no one was talking about the game. Knowing Coach Ford had heard the comments Larry had made after the game, we wondered what practice would be like today.

The team got dressed for practice and went out onto the football field but the coach wasn't there. I called for the team to line up for warm-ups and we went through our calisthenics. Coach Ford did not join us.

Worrying about what the Coach may have done after the game on Friday night, I asked, "Has anyone seen the Coach today?"

When no one answered, I asked, "Has anyone seen or talked to the Coach since the game?"

"He wasn't in church Sunday, and the coach never misses church," Jared said.

"His truck was parked in front of the office when we came in," Larry said.

I told the team to stay there and I sprinted to the coach's office. Just as I was about to open the door, he stepped out. He was clean-shaven, his hair was combed and he had gotten it cut. He had on a new pair of slacks, a buttoned-up shirt and a tie. Coach Ford asked, "Where's the team?"

"On the field, Coach, we've finished the warm-ups."

"Get everyone in the film room, we're having a team meeting."

"Yes sir," I replied.

I ran back to the field and told everyone to come to the film room. Larry was the last one in. Coach Ford was sitting in a chair at the front of the room looking down at his desk. He sat still for a few moments as if thinking about what he wanted to say. Larry interrupted the silence and said, "Coach, I'm sorry for I said in the locker room. I was out of line."

Coach Ford looked up at him, smiled, and said, "No you weren't, Larry. Never apologize when you're right."

The coach walked around and sat on his desk and continued. "Boys, it is I who owe you an apology. Larry was right. It was my fault for losing that game. You deserved better. I haven't been much of a coach and you and I both know it." He paused for a few seconds before continuing. "I was a good coach once. But that all ended three years ago when my wife passed away from cancer and three of my players died. My wife and I couldn't have children. But we felt blessed because the boys on my team became like our children. My wife loved the players as much as I did. Anywhere we went we would run into one of our past players and they would come up to us and thank us for being a part of their lives. We were content with our extended family. We felt blessed and wouldn't have it any other way."

Coach Ford stopped talking and took a drink of water and swallowed hard, then continued. "When my wife died I was devastated.

I had lost my lover and best friend. All I had left was the football program, my players and my memories. Three of my boys died that same year. I turned to the bottle and have been there ever since. I'm a drunk and a lousy coach."

At that point, most of us thought he was going to tell us he was quitting. Several of the players commented that he was a good coach. Coach Ford held up his hand and silenced them.

Coach Ford looked at me and continued speaking to the team. "Then one day this kid walks into my office and starts talking about winning another state championship. He said he would play anywhere I wanted him to if it would help us win. He worked his butt off and on his own started rallying this team together."

The coach paused and took another drink of water, then continued. "I discouraged him and told him we didn't have the quality of players it took to win another state championship. I should have told him he didn't have a coach good enough to win another championship. But, the young man was hardheaded and continued to believe in the team, and for some unknown reason, in me. The problem was, I didn't believe in myself."

There were rumbling through out the room as players whispered to each other about how they believed in the coach too and wanted him to stay.

Again, the coach held up his hand again for silence. "Boys, I'm not here to quit. I'm here to ask for forgiveness and to ask for another chance. I'm asking for you to believe in me because I truly believe in you and believe you can win the state championship if I get my head out of my ass, quit drinking, and stop feeling sorry for myself. I need to start coaching again. If you'll give me another chance, I promise you, I'll never take another drink and be the coach you deserve."

Larry was the first one to speak up, "Coach, we don't want you to leave. I believe in you and with your help, we'll win that state title!"

The whole team started yelling, "Coach, Coach, Coach," over and over until the coach finely held up his hands again to silence us. "Well then, let's get out on the field boys. We have a lot of work ahead of us before we get that trophy."

The team ran out of the room and sprinted to the field. Coach Ford and I were the only ones left in the room. He walked over to me and put his hand on my shoulder. "Thanks for believing in me, Andy. Are you ready?"

I smiled, "You bet, Coach!" I sprinted to the field and Coach Ford followed.

CHAPTER THIRTY-THREE

Ruby's stone bruise healed by the time we got back from our summer vacation and I rode her as often as possible. She was a fine trail horse and showed no sign that she had ever been injured. I wanted to tell Shayla that I had bought her, but I wanted to wait for just the right moment. Ruby had started gaining weight and I was starting to wonder if I was doing something wrong. I wanted her to be in great shape when Shayla saw her.

I called Colonel Lightfoot and told him that Ruby was getting fat. He told me to cut back on her feed. When I explained that I wasn't feeding her any more than I had been and that I was riding her a lot, he decided to come by and check her out.

Colonel parked his truck next to the barn and set up his shoeing equipment. I led Ruby out and tied her to a hitching post. Colonel sat down, picked up Ruby's back leg, sat it back down. "Well I'll be damned! John Stevenson is going to kick himself in the ass over this one."

"Kicking himself over what?" I asked.

"Over Ruby, that's what. One of the biggest mistakes he's ever made."

"What the are you talking about, Colonel?"

"Ruby, that's what I'm talking about. She's not getting fat, she's about to have a foal."

I didn't know what to say.

"Didn't you hear me, Andy? Ruby's pregnant, she's about to give birth. You're going to be a daddy."

"How did that happen and who's the father?"

"Well, since your horses are gelded, it has to be Thunderbolt."

"Thunderbolt? Are you kidding me?"

"Nope, I didn't think he had scored when I found him in Ruby's pasture. But I must have been wrong."

"I gotta tell my parents."

Mom and Dad came out and Mom looked under Ruby. "See the udders, Andy?" She said pointing. "They're starting to drip milk. She will deliver very soon. You'll want to add more wood shaving to her stall and no more riding her until after she gives birth."

———

Three days later, I walked to the barn and found a newborn foal lying in Ruby's stall. I ran back into the house and got my parents. Mom told us to be quiet as we walked into the barn. The foal was attempting to stand up when we entered but fell back down. "Is it all right?" I whispered.

"It's a little colt and he's beautiful." Mom said. "He looks as healthy as a horse, no pun intended. Give him a minute and he'll get to his feet."

Ruby started licking her colt. He attempted to stand up but fell back down to his knees again. After a few moments he got to his feet and remained standing on shaking legs. He attempted to take a step and fell back down but managed to get back up and walked unsteadily towards his mother. After several attempts, he found Ruby's udders and began nursing.

We watched them for the next hour until mom told me I had go to school. I wanted to stay home but she said no. "He'll be right here when you get home and I'll call the school and tell them you'll be late."

I started to argue when Dad said, "You have a son to support now, Andy. Get to school and set a good example."

Both Mom and I laughed. "Okay, Grandpa," I said as I left to get ready for school without further protest.

CHAPTER THIRTY-FOUR

C alm settled over our team after the first loss. Coach Ford came to work everyday in a shirt and tie. He was cleaned-shaven and his eyes were clear and focused. He'd found a new determination we had never seen in him before and pushed us hard. The entire team had to eat lunch together in the film room and discussed strategy while watching game films. The chemistry and attitude of the team had changed for the better. We all started believing we could win, and more importantly, we expected to.

The second game was against Snowflake. Their team had been playing well. The game was supposed to be a close one, but Snowflake was still favored by seven points. The Cougars won by a score of 36 to 7. Everyone in the league realized the Cougars were a team not to be taken lightly.

The Cougars won their next seven games by out scouring their opponents by an average of 30 points. We had the highest pass completion rate of any school in the league with an average of 350 yards a game in the air and well over a 100 running on the ground.

Jared was also having an outstanding year and football scouts from around the state started showing up at the games. Both Arizona State University and the University of Arizona had shown interested in Jared, Hairy Larry, Sonny Turner and me. Other colleges were looking at several other players.

The playoffs were about to start and the only undefeated team was Safford. At 9 and 1. Clarksville was in second place. If both teams won throughout the playoffs, we would be facing each other for the state title.

Coach Ford told everyone not to think about Safford. "If you don't win your next game, you'll never get a chance at them anyway." He wanted everyone to keep focused, one game at a time.

Anticipation ran deep throughout the town of Clarksville as the playoffs neared. The small town was proud of their football team and many of the devoted fans, had played on the team at one time or another. Football dominated the headlines of the local paper and it was all the old timers talked about at Skeeter's.

The first team we were to play in the playoffs was Snow Flake who had gone 7 and 3. Although the Cougars had dominated the first game, Coach Ford didn't want anyone taking them for granted. I saw no reason to believe anything would change this time around, but I also knew it would be a big mistake to underestimate them.

I walked into the film room and found Coach Ford watching game film on Safford. "Hi Coach, thought we weren't supposed to be thinking about them yet."

"You're not, but I am. Did you know their coach was my assistant for many years?"

"No, I didn't."

"Well he was, and that's a problem. We know how each other thinks and that's a two- edged sword. If we win out and get close to the championship game, I want you and I to go over these game films and find out what we can do that Safford will not expect us to do. He may know how I think, but he doesn't know how you think. Maybe we can catch him off guard."

"Sure Coach. When do you want to start?"

"Don't worry about Safford unless we beat the rest of these teams."

"Don't you mean, until after we beat the rest of these teams?"

Coach Ford smiled, "Yeah, right, then we'll sit down and go over what I know about him so you can get into his head. He's a very good coach. I should know, I taught him myself. The problem is, we're both predictable."

"If you're both predictable, then we should think about using the no huddle offense. Even if he figures out what we're going to do, he won't have time to adjust."

The coach thought about that for a minute, "No huddle offense. Hum, that's not something I would do and he would never think I would do it. I'll have to give that some thought."

CHAPTER THIRTY-FIVE

The stands filled up quickly for the first play-off game against Snowflake. They had as strong a fan base as Safford did and it appeared half of Snowflake citizens had traveled to Clarksville to support their team. During warm-ups, I searched the stands for my parents. They were near the 50-yard line about halfway up in the stands. John and Donna Stevenson, Harvey Baker, Bernie Baxter, Colonel Lightfoot, Skeeter, Henry Spillman, and were all sitting together. I searched the student section and located most of my friends sitting together with the girlfriends of my teammates. There was a new face in the crowd and it was Shayla's. She saw me looking at her and waved at me. I smiled and waved back.

Snowflake kicked off and I caught the ball at the 19-yard line and ran the ball back 81 yards for a touchdown. The blocking was outstanding and the extra time the coach had spent on special teams was paying off big time.

The Cougars kicked off and stopped Snowflake on the 18-yard line. Snowflake made two first downs on six plays and then fumbled the ball. We took possession and drove down field scoring again on seven plays. Our team completed three passes in a row to three different receivers. It became apparent the Cougars were going to dominate the game early on and the score was 35 to 3 at halftime.

During halftime, the coach informed the team that everyone would get to play as long as we kept our current lead and no one would be playing both offence and defense during the second half. He wanted the team to concentrate on perfection. He said, "Stay focused or I'll put your ass on the bench," And he meant it.

The second half was not much different but Snowflake did score a touchdown on a long pass late in the game and they kicked the extra point. The final score was 50 to 10.

After the game, Shayla was waiting outside with the other girls as we left the dressing room. The team normally went to Skeeter's to celebrate after the game because Skeeter gave all the players free pie if we won. I asked Shayla if she needed a ride and she accepted. She was more relaxed and talkative than normal and it was good to see her smiling.

I drove her home after we left the restaurant and asked her how she liked the game. She said it was nice to see the team playing well again. She didn't comment on my performance or say if she liked the game or not. I knew going to a football game was a big step in the right direction for her and I didn't want to push it. I walked her to her door and she thanked me for the ride. She stood there looking at me for a moment. It was awkward because I wasn't sure if I was supposed to kiss her goodnight or not. She leaned over and kissed me on the cheek, "Good night Andrew, you played well."

As she turned to walk into the house, I said, "My friends call me Andy."

She smiled and said goodnight again, but left off "Andrew." *Oh well. That's a good start.*

The next playoff game was pretty much like the first and the Cougars won the game by a large margin. The problem was, Safford was doing the same to the teams they were playing. Everyone knew the two teams were headed for a showdown. The tension was high and the newspaper was highlighting the players from both teams. Safford was the number one team in the league and would be favored in a playoff game, but the big question was, by how much.

Shayla kept coming to the games but went home with her parents when the games were over. I kept wondering if I'd get another chance to take her home. There was a two-week winter break before the championship game between Clarksville and Safford and everyone was expecting a hard-fought game with a close score.

CHAPTER THIRTY-SIX

An old coyote kept the wind to his face as he snuck along the thick brush of the river. The half moon gave him just enough light to see the quail and rabbits he sought to satisfy his never-ending hunger. He stopped to listen to the sounds of frogs croaking and crickets chirping when he heard a distant sound far away that caught his attention. He walked to the water's edge and saw a small boat coming down river in the stillness of the night. He moved deeper into the brush as the boat approached and watched it stop at the bank not far from where he was hiding.

The sound of the boat's motor ended and the coyote moved deeper into the shadows. A man got out of the boat and tied it to the bushes. The man removed something from the boat and walked up onto a flat area not far from the river. He removed his jacket, looked around and began digging a hole. He dug for a long time, and then walked back to the boat. He waded out into the water and picked up something from the boat and put it on his shoulder. He carried the object back to the hole and dropped it into the hole and covered it with dirt.

The man took a small branch from the bushes and walked backwards all the way to the river brushing the ground as he walked. He got into the boat, started the noise again and went back in the same direction from which he arrived. The sound of the motor faded into silence and the crickets resumed their cacophonous song. The frogs soon added their deep base and nature's music was once again in harmony.

The coyote cautiously approached the area where the human had been digging and sniffed the ground. He dug in the soft dirt of the hole until he unearthed the human that had been left there. He backed away from the scent and resumed his hunt for food along the river.

CHAPTER THIRTY-SEVEN

D ad came by after football practice and waited for us to finish. He waited outside the locker room for me to come out. "Mom and Donna Stevenson went shopping and we have to fend for ourselves. Want to go to Skeeter's for dinner?"

"You bet, Dad. I'm staved."

We grabbed a seat and Skeeter approached with a concerned look on her face. "Scott, Carrie Campbell hasn't shown up for work the past two nights and I'm worried about her."

"Have you tried calling her?"

"Several times but her phone goes straight to voice mail as if it's turned off."

"Has she done this before?"

"Never, Scott. Anytime Carrie is going to miss work she phones the restaurant and lets someone know. She has been very dependable and not hearing from her worries me. I drove to her house but there was no answer and the door was locked."

"Was her car there?"

"No, it's still parked in the parking lot at the restaurant. I noticed it day before yesterday but didn't think much about it because it's always breaking down."

"Where does she live?"

"She lives in the small house behind Bennett's Indian store next to the reservation."

"Does she live with Bennett?"

"No, Bennett lives in the back of the store. He lets Carrie live in the old house for free."

"Have you talked to Bennett?"

"Yes, over the phone. He told me he's been in Santa Fe for the past week buying jewelry. Bennett said he saw her Monday before he left town but has not heard from her since. She worked Tuesday night and got off work at 6:00 in the morning. I saw her when she was leaving but no one has seen her since."

"Do you have any contact information for any of her family?"

"No, she ran away from home at sixteen after her father had abused her and to my knowledge, she hasn't contacted her family since running away. She never talked about her family and I'm not even sure where she's from. Oregon, I think, but I'm not sure."

'I'll send an officer out to her place to look for her. If the officer can't locate her, he'll stop by here for a missing person's report."

"Thanks, Scott."

Dad called Lieutenant Reinhardt and explained the situation. He asked Reinhardt to send someone out to Carrie's place and check to see if they could find her. Lt. Reinhardt agreed that something wasn't right and that he would send an officer to Skeeter's for the report if they couldn't locate her. He said he would go to Carrie's house himself and try to contact her.

Satisfied that Lieutenant Reinhardt had things under control with Carrie's disappearance, we ordered dinner. Colonel Lightfoot walked in and we invited him to join us. Dad asked him about the

ATV tracks and the old Indian trail that he and I had found when we were rounding up cattle.

Colonel told dad about the ATV tracks high up in the mountains where motorized vehicles are not allowed. He said that he and John Stevenson had found some more ATV tracks the day the lion jumped John."

Dad asked, "What can you tell me about that old Indian trail?"

"It's not much of a trail and most people wouldn't even know it was there if they weren't familiar with it. Not many Indians even know about it. Indians normally used the easiest and fastest routes possible to get from one place to another. Most of the well-known trails are now major roads. When Geronimo jumped the reservation, he had a big problem because the Calvary used Indian guides who knew where the trails were located. He had to find other trails to avoid being captured. It's rumored this is one of the trails he used to travel to Mexico. It was abandoned after Geronimo was captured but you can still see some of the worn paths in the soft sandstone in places. The trail is pretty overgrown in many areas."

"Where does the trail lead?"

"It goes south to the area around Benson and turns east and then south again into the Chiricahua Mountains. It cuts through the mountains into Mexico."

"So, if someone knew about this trail and wanted to ride a horse from Mexico to Clarksville, they could do it?"

"Sure, but it would be the long way around."

"But, it would be perfect if you wanted to make sure no one saw you, wouldn't it?"

"I guess so. What are you getting at, Scott?"

"I'm not sure, it's just a hunch. Thanks for the information, Colonel."

After dinner, we went home and Dad took out his Forest Service maps of the area and studied them for a long time. He took out the police reports about trucks that had drugs hidden on them and compared the dates with the cycle of the moon.

While he was studying the maps, Lieutenant Reinhardt stopped by. He had come back form Carrie's home. "Scott, Carrie is not at her house. The house was locked and there was no evidence of forced entry. I forced a rear window open and got inside, but nothing seemed to be out of place. The bed was unmade and the place was untidy. Her clothes were in the closet and there was food in the refrigerator. Her purse was not there but her checkbook was. It showed $53 dollars in saving and $312 dollars in checking. I couldn't find any phone numbers for any of her family and there were no notes or letters."

"Did you find anything suspicious?" Dad asked.

"There was a very large silver and turquoise bracelet and a squash blossom necklace on the end table next to her bed that appeared to be of high quality. There was no one at Bennett's store but there was a "Closed for Vacation" sign in the front window.

"Check to see if anyone has seen her since the last night she worked or after she left work. And stop by the bank tomorrow to see if there were any banking transactions from her account since the time she left work. Oh, and get a copy of her phone records, will you? You might as well run her through the computer and see what we can come up with, where she was from or where her relatives live."

"Will do, Chief. And I'll enter her information into the computer as a missing person."

"I don't like where this investigation is headed Lieutenant. I'm worried we might be looking for another dead body."

After Rinehart left I asked, "Dad, do you really thinks somebody killed Carrie?"

"I don't know, Son. But there are a lot of things not adding up in this town lately."

A couple of days later, Jared and I saw a lot of smoke coming from the west. I called Dad who was working in his office. He said a call came over the police radio advising there was a house fire at Bennett's store. He said he and Reinhardt were about to drive out there. Jared and I drove out to the scene and discovered that Carrie's house was burning and not the store. The fireman had used their limited water supply to contain the fire from spreading to the store and nearby grass fields. The house was totally engulfed and collapsing by the time we arrived. Officer Goff and Sgt. Ortiz were working traffic control and keeping curious citizens from entering the scene.

Dad and Lt. Reinhardt showed up and came and stood with us as we watched the firemen work. When the flames were extinguished, Dad asked Reinhardt if he would hang around until the Fire Marshall arrived. "Tell him that Carrie Campbell is missing and ask him to look for her and the silver bracelet and squash blossom necklace in the bedroom." Dad told Reinhardt he would catch a ride with us. Then we saw Bennett standing near his store watching the fireman. We walked over to him.

"Hello, Bennett," Dad said. "Mind if I ask you a few questions?"

"Sure, Chief. Have you located Carrie yet? She's going to be pissed."

"Not yet. Do you know how the fire started?"

"No."

"Where were you when it started?"

"I'm not sure because I don't know when it started."

"Well, where were you today?"

"I got up this morning around 8:00 o'clock, stopped by Skeeter's for breakfast and went to the gym at 9:00 when it opened. I left there around 10:30 or 11:00 and drove back to Skeeter's. I delivered two Kachina dolls to Skeeter and was having lunch when someone said there was a fire at my store. Then I came back here."

"Have you heard from Carrie?"

"Not a word, and that's not like her. I normally see her at work or she calls me almost every day."

"Do you rent this house to her?"

"No, I let her stay here for free."

"What is your relationship with her?"

"Just friends."

"Have you given her any Indian jewelry?"

"I've given her a lot of pieces, nice stuff too."

"Have you ever slept with her?"

Bennett paused as if he wondered whether he should answer that question.

"Well, have you?"

"A few times when she was drunk but she's not my girlfriend if that's what you're asking."

"Why not? She's a very attractive woman."

"I know, but she only wants to be friends."

Dad handed Bennett his business card. "If you hear from her, call me." He started to walk away when Bennett asked, "You'll let me know if you find her won't you, Chief?"

"Sure," Dad said as we left.

Dad told Reinhardt what Bennett had said and asked him to check out Bennett's story. Dad had me drop him off at his office. He didn't say anything on the way back. He seemed more worried now than ever.

CHAPTER THIRTY-EIGHT

All talk around school for the last week had been about the upcoming Sadie Hawkins dance. This was the week the girls started asking boys to the dance. I had gone to a Sadie Hawkins dance at Superstition High School with Heather. My mother had asked me why I didn't date Heather more often. I told her that dating Heather would be like kissing my sister. And, that was truly how I felt about her, my little sister.

Most of the other football players were going to the dance, except Hairy Larry who no one had, or would ask. I wouldn't have minded going with Shayla if she asked, but that wasn't going to happen. I wondered who, if anyone, would ask me. I didn't know many of the girls at school but that had never discouraged them in the past. I had been asked to go the Sadie Hawking dances before by girls I didn't even know. Heather had given me safe haven at Superstition High School but she was no help here.

Stephanie Miller had already asked a boy in our Creative Writing class who had said yes and Kelsey Gardner was dating another football player. That left Shayla, Stacey Miller and Cricket

Pilone as the only other girls at school I really knew. Cricket had dropped many, not so subtle hints, about us going out. That could make for an interesting night but could also give me one of two reputations, neither of which I desired.

I had avoided girls all week knowing they could come up with all kinds of creative ways to ask a boy to a Sadie Hawkins dance. Stacey Miller would be a good choice but she was one of Shayla's best friends. But, then again, no one knew exactly what I thought of Shayla Stevenson and certainly no one would have considered us a couple. I wasn't even sure what I thought about her. Maybe Stacey wouldn't ask me to the dance and I would dodge the bullet. I hated to admit it, but that wouldn't be good for my ego.

The week went by and no one asked me to the dance. If I were going to be asked, it would most likely be on Monday because the dance was the following Saturday night.

I went to work at the Double J Ranch on Saturday and didn't see Shayla most of the day because she and her mother had gone to a barrel racing lesson. When I was getting ready to leave for the day, she and her mother arrived at the ranch with their horses.

"Need some help putting the horses away?" I asked.

"Sure, Andy," replied Donna. "I'm bushed and need to get dinner started."

Shayla didn't pay any attention to me and unloaded her own horse. I took Santana into the barn, unsaddled her, brushed her and put her in her stall. Shayla was getting hay for the horses but hadn't said a word to me. When she started to leave, I asked, "Are you going to the Sadie Hawkins dance?"

"You're not supposed to ask girls to the dance, Dummy. They are supposed to ask you."

"I'm not asking you to go to the dance. I'm asking if you are going."

"It sounded to me as if you were asking."

"I wouldn't ask you to the dance."

"Why not? What's wrong with me?"

"Nothing's wrong with you."

"Then why wouldn't you ask me to a dance."

"I didn't mean I wouldn't ask you to a dance. I was just saying, I wouldn't ask you to the Sadie Hawkins dance, that's all."

"Are you asking *me* to ask *you* to the Sadie Hawkins dance?"

"No, I don't want to go to the Sadie Hawkins dance. Never mind, just forget it."

I turned to leave and she said, "Well you brought it up." Then she turned to leave.

I turned back to her and took a big breath. "Shayla, all I was doing was asking you if you go to school dances. You know, like proms and stuff like that."

She faced me and got that old familiar smirk on her face. "Do I look like the prom type to you, Andrew? Why would any girl in her right mind want to go buy an expensive dress that is way too tight, with a slit up the side that is way too short. Then add a push-up bra with an under-wire that kills her all night just so her boobs can play pick-a-boo, making her horny date drool all over himself. Then she paints her face with God-awful make-up, puts on four-inch f-me heels that no one can walk in, let alone dance in, and they kill her feet all night. They go to an overpriced dinner that the girl has to pay for and it's not half as good as a meal at Skeeter's for half the price. Then they go to the dance with feet that's already killing her. After the dance, they sneak out of town to a motel hoping no one sees them so he can find out how fast it takes to get her dress off without destroying it. No, I think I'll pass! How about you?"

I was sorry I'd asked, but Shayla sure knew how to make a dance sound fun. "I'm not into school dances either but these Sadie Hawkins dances put guys at a disadvantage."

"Tell me about it. Now you know how I feel. But, you will be asked. This is a girl-empowered rite. You better be ready to say yes or break someone's heart. I'd go with Cricket if I were you. She'll take the dress off for you and save you a lot of time." She smiled and walked away.

My head was spinning and I couldn't figure Shayla out. I was starting to think she was a complete head case. But the conversation confirmed two things. One, Shayla wouldn't be asking me to the dance, and two, someone else would. The question now was, who would ask, and, how could I say no. Maybe I'd get the flu and be sick all next week. I was starting to think I should take someone else and give up on Shayla.

Monday morning came and no one had asked me to the dance. I felt I might get lucky and dodge the bullet. As I left the weight room, I saw my car and knew I had been targeted. It was full of balloons and there was a big card attached to the rear view mirror. I knew Jared was in on this because they would never have been able to get inside my car without his help. The question was, who was asking?

I looked around to see if anyone was looking. There were no girls in sight. Jared walked out of the weight room and looked at my car.

"Thanks, Buddy!" I said.

"What?" Jared responded as if hurt, "I didn't do anything."

"Alright, who is asking me to the dance?"

"How would I know, why don't you read the card?"

"Jerk!" I said as I opened my car door and balloons filled the air. I guess this was the signal that I now knew I'd been asked to the dance. I read the card and was relieved to see it was Stacey Miller and not Cricket Pilone, even though Cricket would have been fun according to Shayla. I read the card out loud. "Everyone has been wondering if you were going to the dance. If your not already committed, I would love to have the chance! Will you go to the dance with me? Stacey."

"Well how about that?" Jared said.

"I don't even want to go to the dance but I guess it's not cool to say no, is it?"

"No it's not, Bro. And you could do a lot worse than Stacey Miller. If you say no, you'll get asked several more times by other girls. If you turn them all down, everyone will think you're gay!"

"Yeah right. Should I call her or send her a text?"

"Call her Dude, and act excited. You don't want to hurt her feelings."

"Alright, Romeo, as if I should be asking you for advice," I said as I got in the car and pushed the rest of the balloons out.

I called Stacey later that evening and told her I was honored and accepted the date. She sounded excited. I pretended to be.

I went to bed regretting the decision but knowing there was no way out without hurting someone's feeling. Besides, I really liked Stacey. I hated the fact she was one of Shayla's best friends and knew Shayla would know all the details. That was reason enough to make sure Stacey had a wonderful time.

Shayla acted normal on Monday morning and I wondered if she knew I was going to the dance with Stacey. I ate lunch with her, Stacey, Stephanie, Kelsey, Jared and his girlfriend, Priscilla Zajas. The girls were discussing the dance and announced that Stacey, Stephanie, Kelsey and Priscilla had rented a stretch limo for the dance and that we would all be going together. This took some pressure off me knowing I wouldn't be alone with Stacey. The news of Stacey and I going to the dance together didn't seem to bother Shayla, and if it did, she could have gotten an Academy Award for acting.

—≕+ +≎—

I wore a light gray suit with a black shirt with a gray and red tie. A red handkerchief embraced my suit pocket. The limo pulled up to our house and everyone else was already in the car. Mom insisted they come in for a quick group photo and one of Stacey and me.

Stacey had on a beautiful lavender strapless gown that went all the way to the floor. It showed modest cleavage but no peak-boo. She was a gorgeous young lady. I couldn't help but wonder how bad the underwire hurt. Her hair was professionally done and curly. She seemed a lot taller than normal and I wondered if she was wearing the four-inch f-me heels that Shayla had described. All the other girls were dressed similarly and everyone was in a festive mood.

The other boys were also wearing suits and I was not over-dressed. I didn't know Priscilla Zajas well but learned quickly that she was outgoing, funny and witty. I had always considered Jared as the class clown, but with Priscilla around, he was just the straight man in a two-person comedy act. Priscilla was a little uncouth at times but had everyone laughing in the limo before we even got to the restaurant. She had blond hair and green eyes and was quite pretty. It was obvious that she and Jared had been friends for a long time and I wasn't getting some of their inside jokes.

We went to a Chinese restaurant that was quite good and everyone seemed to having a good time. Stacey sat a lot closer to me than she had ever done before. I missed the peek-a-boo show Shayla had described but Stacey was a lady and showed her class and not her ass. After leaving the restaurant, the limo drove us to the dance.

There were a few people dancing to a slow song when we arrived but for the most part, the dance floor was almost empty. It reminded me of a wake I'd seen on TV once and I felt this could be a long night. As soon as Priscilla entered the gym she let out with a very loud, "YEEEEEHAA!" That seemed to wake the dead and everyone started smiling at us, especially at Priscilla. Stacey, Stephanie, Kelsey and Priscilla wasted no time in dragging us out onto the floor and the party was soon in full swing. A lot more kids started dancing.

I was relieved the DJ was playing all kinds of music and not just Country, since I didn't know how to dance Country. The girls were excellent dancers, especially Kelsey. Her boyfriend, Sonny Turner, was one of the football players and I knew him from the weight room. He seemed like an okay guy. Stephanie was dating another football player named Calvin Warner who I knew because he was a wide receiver and I had practiced with him.

As the night progressed, Priscilla got louder and funnier and had most of the people at the dance laughing and dancing too. She and Kelsey organized the students into two lines, boys on one side and their dates on the other side. The idea was to see who could make biggest fools of themselves dancing between the rows of waiting spectators. Once you danced down the line, you went back to the other end until your turn came around again, then you tried to come up with something more outlandish than before.

The DJ and other students were eating this up and almost everyone at the dance joined in. Most, if not all, f-me heels were under the tables by now. Stacey and I were having a blast seeing who could out-dance the others in some silly made up dance. We once danced disco, once like native tribesman and once like a tap dancer, a way out of step. A couple of the teachers joined in the line dance and everyone got a good laugh. Cell phone cameras were lighting them up like celebrities. Everyone was having a ball making fools of themselves including me. I knew this dance would be remembered for a long time at Clarksville High School, thanks to Priscilla.

On cue, all four of the girls excused themselves and went to powder their noses or whatever they powdered. Maybe they needed help getting out of their dresses so they could do their business. I saw Alex dancing with a girl named Sara, who sat next to him in our math class. They were so far apart you could have put another person between them. Sara wasn't bad- looking and if you removed her braces and thick glasses, she was kind of cute. *Way to go Alex.* I noticed Mike and Bucky, the two boys who had bullied Alex in the hallway at school, hugging the punch bowl with their dates. I walked over to Alex and Sara. "Hey Alex, are you having fun?"

"Hi, Andy, we sure are. Do you know Sara?"

"Of course I know Sara, she sits next to you in our math class. Hi, Sara."

Sara commented, "I'm surprised you noticed me since you blink so slow."

We all laughed. "I try to pay attention, sometimes."

Alex said, "You guys cracked us up with that line dancing."

"You should have joined us, it was fun."

"Way too crazy for me."

"Loosen up and live a little Alex, life is short."

"Maybe next time."

I nodded towards the punch bowl. "Those guys aren't giving you a hard time are they?"

Alex looked at Mike and Bucky, "No, they leave me alone after you talked to them."

"Well, if they bother you, let me know and I'll put knuckle prints on their foreheads faster than they can rub em."

"Thanks, Andy."

I walked back to my friends and looked back to see Alex and Sara dancing again. This time there was very little air between them. I smiled. *Confidence conquers all.*

I learned a lot that night about my new friends. Kelsey was on the dance team at school and wanted to go to college and major in fashion design. Stacey and Stephanie were competitive in junior rodeo and had competed with Shayla almost all their lives. They had competed in almost every rodeo event there was but Stacey was now focused on jumping, Stephanie on cutting.

After we left the dance, we went to McDonald's for ice cream. It seemed strange going through the drive-through in a limo. Then the limo driver dropped Sonny and Kelsey off at Kelsey's house, Jared and Priscilla off at Priscilla's house and Stephanie and Calvin off at Calvin's house. Stacey and I were now alone and the limo driver took us to Stacey's house. Somehow, he must have forgotten about the out of-town-motel.

When we got out of the limo, it didn't leave, which was my first clue the limo would be dropping me off last. I walked Stacey to the front door and she turned to face me. "Stacey, I had a blast. Thanks for inviting me."

We stood on her front porch for an awkward moment, and then Stacey pulled me close and kissed me on the lips. Her lips were warm and inviting but I was caught off guard. I didn't return the kiss. After the kiss, she searched my eyes for answers that wouldn't come. Stacey looked hurt and said, "Shayla is a wonderful girl, Andy. She may be worth waiting for, but if you do, you may become the next 40-year-old virgin."

I could see the disappointment in her face as she turned to go. I turned her around, took her in my arms and kissed her on the lips. "Stacey, you are what dreams are made of. I had a wonderful time and thanks for asking me to the dance. I am truly honored."

She gave me a half-grin. "Thanks, Andy. And if you ever change your mind about Shayla, call me."

She turned and walked into the house. I felt like a complete jerk. I didn't even know she knew I had feelings for Shayla, but she had put herself out on a limb anyway. She had a lot of class and I hoped we could remain friends.

While riding home in the limo, I laid my head back on the seat and thought about love verses like, verses lust, verses infatuation, verses desire and just wanting what you can't have. There was no clear line dividing them and I wasn't sure I understood the difference. I wondered how a young girl who had just offered her heart in her hand, and was rejected, felt at his moment. I felt terrible. But situations beyond my control led me to this place. Damned if you do and damned if you don't.

CHAPTER THIRTY-NINE

Shayla never mentioned the dance or asked me any questions about it or Stacey. I knew she knew about the date, but I doubted if she knew Stacey had kissed me, or the conversation we had about her. Stacey had too much class to kiss and tell. But for some reason, Shayla seemed to have changed. She started missing lunches at the cafeteria and hardly spoke to me in class or when I was working at the ranch. I kept thinking she was a lost cause.

While going to lunch at McDonald's with Jared, I noticed a group of kids hanging out at an abandoned gas station talking and smoking cigarettes. There were about twenty kids and several cars. I had seen some of the kids at school before but some I didn't recognize and most looked older than we were. Shayla was standing at the tailgate talking to a tall guy who was wearing a cowboy hat. "Who are those guys, Jared?"

"Smokers or dopers. Hey look, isn't that Shayla?"

"Yeah, who's the guy she talking to?"

"That's Robert Willis. He graduated several years ago."

"He looks like he's in pretty good shape."

"He should be. His parents own the local feed supplies store. He stays in shape by loading hay and grain all day. He's all right."

"Is he a doper?"

"He smokes but I don't think he does dope."

Shayla wasn't with the group at the gas station when we were headed back to school but I saw her in our math class. The next day, we went to McDonald's again and Shayla was at the gas station again talking to the Willis guy. She had a cigarette in her hand. I made a U-turn and pulled into the gas station.

"Hey, where are you going?" asked Jared.

"I need to talk to Shayla." As soon as she saw my car, she flipped the cigarette on the ground. Shayla stood facing Robert who was sitting on his tailgate of his truck.

I got out of the car. "What's up, Shayla?"

"Nothing, why?"

"I didn't know you smoked."

She looked embarrassed. "It's none of your business. What are you, my baby sitter?"

"Why don't you come with us? I'll buy you lunch."

"No thanks, I'm staying here."

Almost everyone was smoking cigarettes except Robert Willis.

"You don't belong here," I said.

Robert smiled and spat tobacco on the ground next to his truck. "Why not?"

"Stay out of this. It's none of your business."

"I'm making it my business. You heard what she said."

I reached for Shayla's arm, "Come on Shayla, let's get out of here."

Shayla pulled away and Robert slid off the tailgate. "Let her go, kid. I don't want to hurt you."

I started towards him when Jared stepped between us. "Come on, Andy. You don't have a dog in this fight and Shayla's a big girl."

I took a deep breath, turned around, walked back to my car and got in. Jared shut my door, walked around to the passenger's side and slid into the seat. "What's the hell wrong with you? You can't tell Shayla what to do."

I put my car in gear and sprayed gravel all over the parking lot on the way out. "Damn her. What the hell is she doing?"

"Whatever she wants to do. She's always been that way. Forget about her, man. She's not worth it."

Shayla wasn't in class after lunch.

⭢⭠

Saturday morning Dad and I were making good progress on my truck. Dad had cut 16 inches off the new truck frame in a Z pattern and had welded it back together. He was making a few other modifications so the `56 cab and bed would fit the new frame. I was cutting the hump out of the floor of the new truck so we could weld it into the old cab to make room for the transfer case. It wouldn't be long before it would ready for the paint shop.

It was almost dark when Mom came out to the barn. "Scott, Sgt. Ortiz is on the phone. He wants to talk to you."

Dad walked out of the barn because of the noise and took the phone call. When he returned, he had a worried look on his face. "When was the last time you saw Shayla Stevenson?"

"Friday at lunchtime. Why?"

"It appears she's missing."

"Missing? What do you mean missing?"

"Apparently, she slept in her own bed last night but got up early and left before her parents were awake. They thought she had gone to a barrel-racing lesson until her instructor called to see if she was coming. She's not answering her phone. After she didn't come home all day and none of her friends had seen her, John Stevenson called the police to report her missing."

"The last time I saw her, she was with an older boy named Robert Willis. She didn't go back to school after lunch."

"All right. I'll make sure we check with Robert. I'm going to work until we find her."

"Can I go?"

"No. Stay here and finish cutting out that floor. I want to weld it in tomorrow. Keep your cell phone close in case I need to call you."

"Let me know if you find her, will you?"

"I will."

Dad left in his police cruiser. After he left, I started trying to think of where she might have gone. Figuring she was with Robert Willis, I didn't want to think about what they might be doing. It was hard to concentrate on what I was doing while wondering what Shayla was up to.

I pulled Dad's truck up next to the barn and turned on his scanner so I could listen to the police traffic. I heard Dad ask if anyone knew where Robert Willis lived. Sgt. Ortiz advised him that Robert was working at his parent's feed store and told dad where the store was located.

About twenty minutes later Dad came on the radio and advised that Robert hadn't seen or heard from Shayla since lunchtime yesterday. It was starting to get dark and I started getting worried. I called Jared and he told me the police had already come to Skeeter's asking about Shayla. He said half the town was out looking at her. He didn't have a clue where she might be.

A few minutes later, I heard Officer Goff come on the radio and advise that someone had reported seeing Shayla buying flowers at the store. Lt. Reinhardt came over the radio and said he was going to the cemetery to see if she was there. Dad answered him advising him he would meet him at the cemetery.

I knew they would be checking Bobby Patterson's gravesite. I remembered Colonel telling me that Shayla put flowers on the spot where Bobby had been killed. *Oh shit!*

I jumped in Dad's truck and headed south on the dirt road exceeding the speed limit by a long shot and leaving a dust cloud behind me. The road climbed rapidly up the mountain with ruts, rocks and steep banks on either side. I did everything I could to keep Dad's truck from bouncing off the road as I raced upward. Knowing this was about the time of year Bobby had been killed worried me. Shayla's truck wasn't in sight as I approached the shack. My headlights caught something on the ground next the tree where Bobby's marker was located. I skidded to a stop and put the truck in park.

Shayla was kneeing next the marker with something shiny in her hand. It was the big hunting knife used at the barn for cutting bale strings. I didn't see any blood. I got out of the car and approached her slowly. She didn't look in my direction or even acknowledge me.

I walked up next to her. Still holding the knife in her right hand, her left hand rested on her knees with her palm up. "Shayla."

"Go away, Andrew. This has nothing to do with you."

I took a couple of steps forward. "You want to talk about it?"

"No."

"It might help."

"Bullshit." She raised her voice. "I've been in counseling for three years. It doesn't help to talk about it. Go away."

I saw tears running down her cheeks. "This isn't the answer."

"How the hell do you know? You've never lost anyone you loved. I lost Bobby and then I lost Ruby. Go back to your perfect little fancy world and leave me alone."

I tried to think of the right words I needed, but I didn't know what to say. "Do you think this is what Bobby would want?"

"Shut up, Andrew." She looked at me for the first time. "You didn't know him and you sure don't know how he feels, or how I feel. Just go away, damn you."

"You're right, I don't know how you feel. But I think I know how Bobby would feel."

Her voice was calmer now. She sounded tired. "You didn't know him and you sure don't know how he feels. Just go away and leave me alone."

"Bobby was eighteen when he died. I'm eighteen now. He played football and I play football. And he loved you... and I love you."

Shaking her head and half laughing, Shayla said, "Oh come on, Andrew. You don't love anything but yourself. You don't even know what love is. Please go away."

"I might not know much about love, but I know Bobby loved you and gave his life trying to protect you. Is this how you're going to repay him?"

Shayla tilted her head and stared up at me, eyebrows narrowed. "What are you talking about? Bobby wasn't trying to protect me."

"Yes he was. Someone stole your phone and texted Bobby. The text said you were up here and needed help."

Shayla stood up and faced me. "What are you saying?"

"That's why Bobby closed the gym early and came up here. He thought you were in trouble and wanted to protect you."

Shayla shook her head back and forth. "You're lying," she screamed. "You're just making that up." Tears streamed down her cheeks.

"No I'm not. My dad had the police report at our house and I read it when he wasn't home."

"Why wasn't I told? Why would they hide that from me?" she yelled.

"I don't know. To protect you I guess. You were only 14 at the time. Besides, the police never release all the details about murder cases. They always hold back something only the suspect would know so they know it's him if he confesses."

"Damn them, damn them! I should have been told." Shayla threw the knife down and turned away from me sobbing. I ran to her and pulled her into my arms. "I'm sorry they didn't tell you. But you were just a kid. It wasn't your fault."

"You should have, Andrew. You should have told me."

"I'm sorry. I'm not supposed to be reading Dad's police reports. Besides, I just found out."

We stood there for a long time, her trembling and sobbing. I wasn't sure if it was from the crying or the cold. "Let's get in the truck, it's cold out here."

"Take me home," she said through her sobs.

I drove up to the shack to make sure Shayla's truck was locked. When I turned around, headlights were coming towards us. I stopped at the cross where Shayla had left the flowers, picked up the knife and put it on the floor next to my feet, then backed the truck up to the shack so the other vehicle could get pass. My father and Lt. Reinhardt came pulling up. "Are you kids alright?"

"We're fine, Dad. Shayla was putting flowers on Bobby's marker. I'm taking her home now."

Dad looked at us for a few moments without saying anything. "Why didn't you call and let us know you found her?"

"I just found her and was about to call."

I knew he didn't believe me but I'd explain later. Lt. Reinhardt notified everyone by radio that Shayla had been located and called off the search. Dad kept looking at me for a few moments as if thinking and then took a deep breath. "All right, Son, I'll drive Shayla's truck back to the ranch and meet you there. Call her parents and let them know she's all right."

Knowing he wasn't happy with me at the moment was one of my least concerns. He could see that Shayla had been crying. Shayla was quiet on the way down but when we turned onto the dirt road leading to her house, she said, "What am I supposed to tell my parents?"

"The truth. Tell them you put flowers on Bobby's marker."

"My dad will be pissed. He doesn't like me going up there alone."

"Tell him you were with me."

"I can't do that. Then he'd be pissed at you. Better me than you. I haven't spoken to him for months anyway." She looked down at the knife lying on the floor. "What are you going to tell them?"

"Nothing," I said as she started to cry again. "Are you thinking about hurting yourself?"

She shook her head no.

"Promise?"

She looked at me through tears. "I promise."

Her mother ran out to meet us as we pulled into the rear yard. Her father's truck was gone. I assumed he had gone looking for her. Shayla looked at me and took my hand. "Thanks, Andrew. I needed a friend." She reached over and kissed me on the cheek, got out of the car and ran to her mother. Dad pulled up in Shayla's truck and parked it by the barn. I slid the hunting knife under the seat. He gave Donna the keys to Shayla's truck and got in with me. He didn't say anything but I knew I had some explaining to do when we got home. I needed to think of what I wanted to tell him. But when we got home, he didn't ask and I didn't say anything. When Mom asked what had happened, Dad told her Shayla had gone to put flowers on Bobby's grave and that I found her and took her home. He never mentioned it again.

CHAPTER FORTY

Dad and I had no sooner got started working on the truck when Dad's phone rang. "What's up, Harvey?"

I could only hear part of the conversation but I knew the call was serious. Dad walked outside and the call lasted a long time. When he ended the call and came back into the barn, I asked, "What's up?"

Dad wiped the grime from his hands. "We have another body. I have to go."

"Who is it?"

"We don't know. It's a female. It might be Carrie Campbell."

Dad threw the rag in the bucket and started for the house. I followed. "Where did they find the body?"

"At an old Indian archeological site down by the river on the Baxter's farm."

"Can I go with you?"

"Sure, if you want to, but stay out of the way and don't touch anything."

On the way to the crime scene, I said, "I haven't heard about any Indian graveyards. What do you know about it?"

"There's not much left of it but a few walls and on old Indian gravesite. The body was found in one of the graves."

"I've never heard anything about any Indian graveyards around here."

"It's fenced off and has no trespassing signs posted around it. The only people allowed in there is some college professor form the U of A and his students. They come twice a year to excavate it as part of his class. They don't find much. They uncover the graves to record the sex and approximate age of the bodies. They don't disturb them any more than they have to and cover the graves back up once they record the information. While working the site this weekend, they discovered the body in one of the old graves they had already covered back up. It was buried under about two feet of dirt. Looks like the coyotes dug her up."

"How long has she been dead?"

"Not very long. About as long as Carrie Campbell has been missing. But, that's not for sure. The worms and beetles have done a number on her. I hear the stench is horrendous."

"Does her hair color or clothes match Carrie's?"

"They're not sure. Her head and hands are missing and she doesn't have any clothes."

"What do you mean, missing? Did the animals get them?" I asked.

"No, whoever brought her here cut them off before they buried her." Dad paused for a moment and then said, "He's one sick son of a bitch."

"Dad, that sounds like the same guy that killed the woman in the mine."

"Yep, it does."

"And this case belongs to us unless the Sheriff's Department can prove she was killed outside the city limits."

We continued to the Baxter's farm and down a dirt road besides the their barn. The road led between fields of crops right down to the river. Several police cars and a bunch of college students were standing next to a white bus with U of A painted on the side. Sgt. Ortiz had taped off the crime scene and was getting written statements from the instructor and his students. Bernie Baxter and his parents were there also. Ortiz said the coroner was on his way.

Bernie Baxter greeted us. "Thanks for coming on your day off, Scott. This is terrible. Her head and hands are missing."

"Yeah, I heard." Dad looked around the gravesite and the surrounding fields. "How many ways are there to get to this place?"

Bernie glanced around. "You can get here from several directions by using any of our farm field roads. They're all connected." He paused and looked around. "Or, you can get here by boat. There aren't many places to get a boat ashore in this area because of the thick brush along the banks, but there are a few places. We used to keep a boat down here when I was a kid. We used it for fishing."

"Is there a back way to Bennett's place from here?"

"Sure, just take any of these dirt roads west as far as you can go, then turn south. You'll come out right behind his store."

Bernie stared at the gravesite. "Scott, whoever who did this is one sick bastard. You need to catch him."

"He sure is, Bernie. Excuse me, I need to talk to Sgt. Ortiz."

"If you need anything from me or my family, please ask." Bernie said as Dad walked away.

We walked over to Ortiz and he briefed us. "When the students arrived at the site this morning, one of the graves they had already covered back up had been dug up by a coyote. When they started to cover it back up, they discovered the body."

The coroner arrived, raised the yellow tape and walked into the graveyard.

I could smell the corpse form ten yards away. Dad walked under the tape at the gate and joined the coroner at the gravesite. I stayed outside the fence to watch. The coroner was wearing a mask and I wished I had one. Dad introduced himself and asked the coroner what he could tell him so far.

"Well, she was white, in her mid-to-late-thirties. I don't see any bullet holes. But, she wasn't killed here. There's no blood spill anywhere. I won't know the cause of death until I get her back to the lab. And even then, I might not be able to unless we find the head. Do you have any idea who she is?"

"We have a missing waitress about that old. She's been missing for a couple of weeks now. It could be her."

"If you can get me some DNA, it won't take long to find out."

"That might not be as easy as you think. No one knows much about her, where she's from or anything about her family, and someone burned her house to the ground right after she disappeared. Forensics will come out here before they remove the body," Dad said.

"Are they on their way?"

"Yep. We had to call them out. They don't normally work on weekends."

The coroner scratched his head, "Well, find that head and hands if you can. I'll need something to work with."

"We'll do the best we can, Doc."

Dad told Sgt. Ortiz to get the report to him as soon as it was finished. He called Reinhardt and asked him to respond. He was already on his way.

There wasn't a fence on the north side of the gravesite. The two side fences ran right to the water's edge. Dad walked to the river looking down at the ground, obviously looking for something. He stopped to look at some bushes, then walked down to the edge of the water. He knelt down and studied the ground in several places where there were breaks in the thick brush.

Lt. Reinhardt arrived at my location and Dad joined us. "I think we found Carrie Campbell's body Lieutenant."

Reinhardt looked towards the uncovered grave. "I can smell her." He took a handkerchief out of his pocket and placed it over his mouth. "She's been dead for a while. Do you know what the cause of death was?"

"Not yet. But, the head and hands are missing."

"Missing?"

"Yeah, they were cut off before she was buried."

"Damn," said Reinhardt. That's like the woman in the mine, except they didn't take her head. Why would they do such a thing?"

"To hide fingerprints and dental records. The killer probably thought no one would ever find her and they sure didn't want them to know who she was if they did."

"Pretty smart to bury her in a grave that had already been dug up and re-covered."

"It would have been if he had buried her deeper. The killer probably thought the grave would never be dug up again. The coroner's going to need some of Carrie's DNA. Did you take anything from her house that might contain any?"

"No, we didn't know we had a crime yet. I didn't take anything."

"Is her car still parked behind Skeeter's?"

"Yes. And I believe they have employee's lockers in the back. If Carrie had a locker, we might find some there. If we can't, we'll get some from her car."

"We should be able to find DNA from either place. I'll stop by there on the way home. When forensic get's here, tell them there is a broken-off branch and indentions in the mud where a small boat pulled ashore."

"Is that how they brought the body here?"

"Yep, there are footprints in the mud in the water. I think the killer used a branch to cover his tracks."

Dad and I stopped by Skeeter's and Carrie's car was still parked in the rear lot. It was still locked. Dad called Claude's towing to come take her car to the police impound lot. Officer Goff waited for the tow-truck to make sure no one got inside. Skeeter told Dad that Carrie had a locker in the back but it didn't have a lock on it. Dad removed a comb, a can of hair spray, a toothbrush, some toothpaste and some feminine products. He placed the items in an evidence bag and told Officer Goff to put them into evidence at the station. We headed home. I could tell Dad had a lot on his mind.

"Andy, remember those lunch boxes you found in the mine and took photos of?"

"Yeah, what about them?"

"Boxes just like those have been showing up at truck stops. Drug sniffing dogs are finding them attached to the frames of Semi trucks."

"What's in them?"

"Heroin, pure heroin. They are putting them under cattle trucks headed to New Mexico and then to Denver."

"Why cattle trucks?"

"Probably because it is harder for the dogs to sniff them out with all the smells. Or, because they know the trucks are headed to the stockyards and know where to intercept them to retrieve their drugs. The drivers don't even know they are attached to their trucks."

I thought about that for a moment. "That's pretty smart. Someone else transports your drugs for you and there is little chance of you getting caught."

"And you know what else, Andy?"

"What?"

"Every one of those trucks stopped at Skeeter's to eat. I think that is where someone attaches the drugs to the trucks."

"Do you have any idea who's doing it?"

"Not yet. But I have a hunch the dope is coming in here from Mexico and then being hidden under the trucks. I also believe the drugs have something to do with these murders. And I intend to find out."

CHAPTER FORTY-ONE

Dad was rolling up his sleeping bag when I walked into the barn. I watched as he loaded his binoculars, a spotting scope, Power Bars, canned goods and a box of .308 shells into two saddlebags. Two canteens of water, a rifle and scabbard sat on the bench next to him.

"What are you doing, Dad?"

"I'm going varmint hunting."

"The four-legged or the two-legged varmints?"

"The kind that smuggles drugs and shoots at innocent boys."

I waited until he had packed the gear into the saddlebags, and asked, "Who's going with you and how long will you be gone?"

"I am going by myself. I'll be back in a day or two, three at the most."

"Can I go with you?"

"No." He stopped and looked at me. "Son, I'm probably chasing shadows. I have no idea if I'll find anything or not. I'm only working on a hunch. I'd rather you stay here and watch after your mother. Work on your truck and concentrate on the game."

"Whoever shot at me and Jared is still out there somewhere. I don't want you to be alone."

"I won't put you in danger, son. This is my job. I took an oath. I know he might be out there. If he is, I want to bring him in before someone gets hurt."

"What if he won't come in?"

"Doesn't matter what he wants. If he's out there, I'll bring him in one way or the other. Besides, I won't be completely alone. I'll have my phone and police radio with me."

"Cell phones don't work very well in those mountains, Dad. I could go for help if you couldn't get out on the phone or radio."

"I won't camp where I don't have service. I'll call you every day. I need you to stay here. All right?"

"All right, but you have to show me where you're going to be on the map in case we have to come looking for you."

"Okay, but I won't know the exact spot where I'll be camping until I get up there and see the area. I may have to move around to get phone service, but I'll call you if and when I change locations. I'll show you the general area of where I'll be."

"Where are you going to leave the truck?"

"At the Double J Ranch and ride out from there. If I left my truck on the mountain, it would scare off any potential suspects. I'm riding in on horseback. I'll be pulling out in the morning while it's still dark so I can't be seen."

The idea of Dad going into the mountains alone worried me but I had a lot of faith in him. I wanted to go but knew it wouldn't do any good to argue with him.

I didn't sleep very well that night. I woke up early and walked into the kitchen at 3:45 a.m. Dad was getting ready to leave out the back door. He was wearing camouflage and had his .40 Glock semi-automatic on his hip. He looked more like a solider than a police officer.

He looked at me as if he knew what I was thinking. "I'll be careful, Son. Watch after your mother. I left a map on the table of where I'll be. I love you."

"I love you too."

CHAPTER FORTY-TWO

I didn't sleep well the next night either worrying about my father. I got up early and studied the map Dad had left. I estimated he was camped about a half-mile west and a quarter-mile south of the mine where someone had shot at Jared and me. I could ride Mom's horse but Dad took the trailer and I wouldn't have anything to pull it with anyway. I'd have see if I could borrow one from the Double J Ranch.

I put my .270 Remington rifle and binoculars in the back seat of my car and left Mom a note telling her I was going to see Shayla. I drove to the Double J Ranch and parked next to Dad's truck. Shayla was riding the new horse that Mr. Patterson had loaned her in the practice arena. Thunderbolt pranced back and forth along the fence in his pasture. Shayla acknowledged me but kept riding. I walked into the barn and put the hunting knife back where it belonged. A few minutes later, she rode over to me. "What are you doing here? You're not working today are you?"

"No, I'm not working. I was just bored and thought I would come see you."

Shayla got off her horse, "What for?" She studied my face. "Are you feeling okay? Your eyes are red."

"Yeah, I'm fine. I was wondering if I could borrow a horse."

"What for?"

"I thought I'd go for a trail ride up in the foothills."

"By yourself?"

"I was, unless you want to go too. I thought I'd ride the foothills out to the southwest. I've never ridden there before."

"Are you asking me for a date?"

"Well... kind of."

"Are you, or aren't you?"

"Yes, I'm asking you to go riding with me."

Shayla paused and tapped her lower lip with her finger. "How long are we going to be gone?"

"Until you want to come back. Why?"

"Okay. We'll have a picnic. I'll grab some sandwiches and a couple of sodas. Go saddle one of the mustangs and I'll be back by the time you're finished."

I saddled the horse named Arrowhead that I had ridden on the roundup and filled a canteen, then walked him to the practice arena. Shayla watched me slide my rifle into the scabbard but didn't say anything.

She stuffed the sandwiches in her saddlebags while I studied the map and marked the ranch on my GPS. She placed the saddlebags over her saddle horn and we rode out the back gate and into the foothills following the fresh hoof prints.

"What's your new horse's name?" I asked.

"He's not mine. Mr. Patterson loaned him to me until Dad can afford to get me another one. His name is Stormy. He's Thunderbolt's son."

"Are you going to buy him?"

"I'd love to, but we can't afford him."

There was little conversation for the first mile until Shayla rode up beside. "Andrew, what do you think of me?"

"You're alright."

"No, really. What do you think of me?"

"I think you have grit, like the girl in the movie, *True Grit.*"

"What else?"

"I think you have a good seat."

"Meaning I sit a saddle well, right?"

"Of course. And you also have a nice ass."

She glanced at me from the corner of her eye and smiled. "And what else?"

"I think you're afraid of me."

She stayed silent for a long time before asking, "So you think I have a nice ass, do you?"

I laughed, "A great ass!"

"At least you're honest. You're not like most boys, you're a conundrum."

"I guess that's better than a '*dumb one.*' That's what you called me the first time we met."

"I wasn't very nice to you, was I?"

"Nope."

"Can I ask you something personal?"

"Sure."

"What did you do to Hairy Larry?"

"Just convinced him that it was in his best interest to play football."

"I know that, but how did you do it?"

"Promise not to tell?"

"I promise."

"I kicked his butt."

"Really?"

"It was long overdue. Then I made him an offer he couldn't refuse."

"I saw you guys and it didn't look like you were fighting."

"I didn't want it to look like we'd been fighting. I almost broke his ribs, his sternum, his wrist and his elbow. Then I told him I wouldn't tell anyone I kicked his ass as long as he stayed away from you and helped me with the football team. Of course, he was in a great deal of pain when he conceded."

Shayla shook her head. "I didn't think anyone could hurt that dumb ass, but thanks, anyway."

"I'm glad you came to save me."

"I didn't come to save you. I just didn't want anyone to get hurt on my account."

"No, you came to save me and I thought that was sweet of you."

I guess she knew she'd lose that argument, so she dropped it.

"You said I was afraid of you. What am I afraid of?"

"You're afraid of getting close to me or anyone else. That's why you don't date or go to school dances."

"I date. I'm on a date with you right now."

"That's different."

She paused to think about that. "Why do you think I don't date?"

"Because you withdrew after Bobby was killed, and I don't blame you. I might have done the same thing if I'd lost my best friend."

She stayed quiet for a long time. When she spoke, I could hear the strain in her voice. "Bobby was more than my best friend, he was like a brother to me. I really miss him."

"I think I understand."

I checked my GPS, changed directions, and headed due south. We rode into a saddle where two small mountains came together. Several large mesquite trees shaded thick winter grass covering the ground. It had a good vantage point of the valley below and the mountains above.

"This looks like a good place for a picnic," Shayla said.

I checked my GPS again and noted our position. I knew Dad was up there somewhere.

She asked, "What are you looking for?"

"A good place for a picnic and you found it."

We dismounted. Shayla got the saddlebags with the food and drinks. I searched the hills for movement, not expecting to see any. She unrolled a saddle blanket and we sat down.

"What are you going to do after graduation, Andrew?"

"I want to go to the one of the military academies. How about you?"

"I'm not sure. I'll either go to ASU or the U of A. I want to be someplace close so I can come home and ride my horse."

She lay back and closed her eyes. I had no idea what she was thinking. I scanned the mountains with my binoculars, not sure what I was looking for. I looked at Shayla and her eyes were still closed. I wasn't sure if she was sleeping or not. Her cheeks were turning pink from the sun and the freckles on her nose stood out. She reminded me of her nickname, Peaches. It occurred to me that she seldom, if ever, wore make-up. I saw the sweetness of a child in a woman's body. She opened her eyes and caught me looking at her. "What are you thinking about, Mr. Hanson?"

"Nothing."

"You're not a good liar."

"Sure, I am. You're just not as naive as most girls."

She smiled and shook her head. "You're so full of it."

I didn't answer. After a long moment, she sat up and asked, "Andrew, what do you want to do with your life?"

"Finish high school, go to college, get a job, get married and raise kids."

"Who are you going to marry?"

"I don't know."

"What do you mean, you don't know?"

"How could I know? I'm not a fortune teller."

She thought for a minute. "Do you think you might know her?"

"Know who?"

"Your future wife, that's who, and it's whom."

"I don't have a clue."

She lay back and put her hands behind her head. "Do you think there's something wrong with me?"

I turned my head side to the side up and down. "Not that I can see."

"I'm serious, Andrew. Do you think I'm screwed up?"

"I think you are as normal as anyone else I know. Why would you ask that question?"

"You know. I think my dad thinks I'm a little nuts sometimes."

"Are you still mad at him?"

"Not mad, just disappointed. I don't think he realized how much Ruby meant to me. I raised her from a colt."

"Colonel said she went to a good home."

"He may have said that just to make me feel better. I think she went to the slaughterhouse."

"Colonel doesn't lie."

"Yeah, right." Shayla closed her eyes again. After a few minutes, she started breathing deeply. I watched her breast move up and down with each breath. She had dosed off. My phone beeped letting me know I had a text. It was Heather. *What's up, big guy?*

I texted her back. *I'm having a picnic in the mountains.*

With who?

A girl and a horse.

Is she pretty?

She is.

Are you in love?

Yes.

With who?

The horse!

Shayla asked, "Who are you talking to?"

"No one. I'm texting, and it's to whom are you talking to."

"Whom are you texting, Smart Ass?"

"Heather."

Shayla sat up and placed her elbows on her knees and her face in the palms of her hands. "Is she someone special?"

"Yes."

Shayla looked surprised. "Oh… how long have you been dating?"

"We haven't. She's just a friend. She dates Cody Johnson."

"But you said she was someone special."

"She is, like a sister, not as a girlfriend. We grew up together on the same street." She seemed to understand but studied my face searching for something. My phone beeped again. *Send me a photo.*

I answered. *Of the horse?*

LOL, the girl, dummy. Is she pretty?

"What is she saying?" Shayla asked.

"She wants me to send her a photo of you."

"I don't believe you, Andrew." She grabbed my phone out of my hand. I reached to get it back but she turned away from me, held it with both hands close to her breast and started reading the texts. I let her. When she finished reading, she started texting.

"Oh no you don't." I wrestled her for my phone. She was laughing and rolled onto her stomach. Before I was able to roll her over and get my phone back, she had already hit the send button. I was lying on top of her. I sat up and checked the text. *Uglier than a mud fence.*

We both laughed. "Why did you tell her that?"

"So she wouldn't be jealous."

"She won't be jealous. I told you we're just friends."

"Okay then, send her my photo." She tossed her head back, stuck out her chin and posed. I sat up, leaned back and snapped her picture. It was a good one. She had the smirk on her face she gave me when she felt she was pulling something over on me. "Let me see it," she said.

I hit the send button and sent the photo to Heather.

"You didn't!" She pushed me backward and sat up. She grabbed my phone and looked at the photo. She was unaware her shirt had come undone during our wrestling match and that her bra and cleavage were showing in the photo. "Andrew, how could you? She'll think I'm a slut." She hit my shoulder, her lower lip sticking out, pouting.

I reached for my phone. "No. I want to see her response. Jerk!"

She moved closer so I could read the text but she held onto my phone. We waited, her staring at the screen and me staring at her. She hadn't buttoned up her shirt. The phone beeped.

She's gorgeous, Andy. Way to go!

Shayla looked at me looking at her. She blushed when she realized her cleavage was still showing. She handed me the phone, turned away and buttoned her shirt. I texted Heather. *Later.*

"Let's eat," Shayla said, as she got up to get the sandwiches. She obviously wanted to change the subject. I turned my phone off and put it in my pocket to keep her from erasing the photo. After lunch, we kicked back and took a nap.

I thought I heard the sound of a motorcycle in the distance. I searched the hills with my binoculars and located a quad slowly working its way up the mountain in a small ravine about a half-mile to the east. I watched the ATV for several minutes until it disappeared behind some trees and stopped. I kept watching and saw a man with a backpack and carrying a rifle walking up the ravine away from where the quad had stopped. The man hiked up the mountain passed through a small saddle, and disappearing over the next ridge.

Shayla was sound asleep. I walked away from her and attempted to call Dad, but he didn't answer. I kicked myself for not calling him earlier.

I watched where I had last seen the man for about thirty minutes. I located him coming back down the mountain the way he had gone. It appeared the backpack he was carrying was a lot heavier and fuller now than it was when he walked up the mountain. I woke Shayla and told her about the man with the rifle and backpack.

"What do you think it means, Andrew?"

"I don't know, but his backpack has a lot more in it now than it did when he climbed the mountain."

"Maybe he's a rock hound, collecting rocks."

"Could be, but I doubt it."

We sat in the shade as I watched him working his way down the mountain. He didn't seem to be in a hurry. I heard what sounded like a horse running somewhere behind and below us. I moved so I could see into the lower valley. My father was riding Big John hard from west to east at the bottom of the canyon. He was at a full gallop.

"Shayla, that's my dad and he's in a big hurry. I'm going to go see where he's headed. Why don't you ride back to the ranch?"

"No way, Andrew Hanson! You don't take a girl on a trail ride then abandon her. I'm going with you!"

"It could be dangerous."

"I'm coming with you." She had her mind made up and I didn't have time to argue.

I mounted my horse, dropped down into the ravine and made my way to the canyon where I had last seen Dad. I found his tracks and started following them. Shayla was right behind me. I knew I couldn't outrun her. She was a much better rider than I was.

We rode for about a mile before Dad's hoof tracks turned up into a big canyon. We followed the trail for a quarter-mile and found Big John tied to a tree. He was wet with sweat and there were boot prints angling away from him going north in an uphill direction. We attempted to follow Dad's tracks but the area was too rocky and we lost sight of them before we topped out on the ridge.

I wondered what I should do and thought of the time I had been shot at when I was at the mine. I was glad I had my rifle but didn't like Shayla being there. I checked my cell phone. It was useless at this location.

"What do you want to do, Andrew?"

"I'm going to the top of this hill and see if I can see my dad or the man with the rifle. I think his ATV is just over this hill somewhere. Why don't you ride back to the ranch, call the police and tell them we need help."

"I'm not going back to the ranch by myself. I'm staying here!"

"Alright then, stay with the horses and if you hear any shooting, haul ass back to the ranch for help."

"Why don't you ride back to the ranch with me and we'll call the police together?"

"I can't leave, my dad might be in trouble. I have to stay."

"Okay, I'll stay with the horses, but be careful!"

I took my rifle and climbed to the top of the small mountain. I inched forward over the top of the hill on my belly. I crawled through some thick brush staying in the shadows until I could see the man making his way down the steep slope to the south. He carried his rifle in his right hand and appeared to be struggling with the heavy backpack. He had to watch his step to keep from falling.

The quad was just below me in a small patch of cedar trees. I had a good view of the quad and I was well hidden. I couldn't see my father but I knew he was down there somewhere. The man made his way to the bottom of the steep hill and was now making better progress. He would reach his ATV within a few minutes.

I recognized the man as Bennett Nahche as soon as he got close to his ATV. He wasn't wearing the hat he normally wore but he had on the same high-top leather boots with the leather ties. I

279

also remembered what Colonel Lightfoot had said about Bennett. *"Avoid him at all times."*

Inching forward with my rifle, I watched Bennett while looking for my dad. My movements were very slow in case Bennett looked in my direction. I got the rifle up in front of me and watched him through the scope. He was about 50 yards away and I could make out every detail of his face. He had a pistol in a holster on his right hip.

When he got to his quad, he stopped and stood very still for a few moments, looking around. He looked back up the mountain from where he had come and into the wash full of cottonwood trees behind him. He removed his backpack and placed it in the ice chest tied to the back rack of his quad. He turned around very slowly searching the landscape as if he knew someone was there. He looked in my direction and I lay very still. He didn't act as if he had seen me. He continued searching the area for a few minutes and then put his rifle in the gun rack on the front of his quad. He got on it and started the motor.

I wondered if Dad had gone to the road to call the police. But that didn't make sense because it would have been easier for him to ride his horse to the road. It was at least another half-mile. He had to be down there somewhere.

Bennett put the ATV in reverse and started to back up. I noticed movement to his rear and saw my father approaching him from behind with his gun drawn. Dad yelled, "Don't move, Bennett. You're under arrest!"

I kept both eyes opened and my scope aimed at Bennett.

Bennett's handlebars were turned to his left. He floored the accelerator on the ATV. The quad launched backwards. Dad attempted to get out of the way but slipped on the loose gravel and the quad knocked him down and ran up on top of his left leg. Dad dropped his pistol. Before he could react, Bennett had his pistol out of his holster and pointed at him. Bennett jumped off the ATV and grabbed Dad's gun. The quad had Dad pinned to the ground and he couldn't move. Bennett turned the ATV off, picked up Dad's police radio. I could hear them talking.

Bennett put his pistol back in his holster and pointed Dad's gun at him. "Hello, Chief, what brings you out here?"

"I'm here to arrest you, Bennett!"

"And what where you going to arrest me for?"

"I'll start with drug smuggling and then we can talk about murder."

"Are you talking about Bobby Patterson?"

"And the woman in the mine, and Carrie Campbell."

"Carrie's not dead. She's just missing."

"No, she's dead. We located her body in the old Indian ruins behind the Baxter's farm."

Bennett hesitated and his voice hardened. "I didn't kill anyone. But don't worry about Carrie, justice will be done!"

"Why did you try to kill my son?"

"I didn't kill try to kill Andy and Jared. I shot over their heads. I was just trying to scare them off so I could get the drugs out of the mine."

"Give yourself up, Bennett. If you didn't kill anyone and cooperate it'll be much better for you in the long run."

"I don't think so, Chief. I'd spend the next twenty years in prison. You think you have it figured out, but you don't. You knew Bobby Patterson and the drugs were connected but you didn't know how. I only supplied one kid steroids and that is after he begged me. It wasn't my fault he hung himself. I knew you were onto me when I saw your officers staking out Skeeter's parking lot. Now you leave me no choice. I have to kill you."

I held the cross hairs on the center of Bennett's back and steadied my rifle. I heard Dad say, "Give yourself up Bennett. The entire Clarksville Police Department will be here any minute. There's no place to run."

Bennett looked around, "There's no one here but you and me, Chief. If they knew we were here, they would already be here by now." Bennett raised the pistol and pointed it at Dad's face.

It was as if I were watching them in slow motion. I watched Bennett extend his hand forward, aiming the pistol at my dad, and I knew he was going to kill him. I squeezed the trigger. The round hit Bennett in the center of his back. I heard his pistol fire at the same time and watched him falling on top of my father. I jumped up and ran down the hill as fast as I could.

When I got there, Bennett was still alive and talking to my dad in a raspy whisper. I heard him say, "Chief, dancing Kachina, Chief dancing Kachina… " The last of the air left his lungs in a low moan and I knew he was dead. His eyes were open staring at my father.

Blood covered my dad's face and hair, but he was alive. I wasn't sure if the blood was his or Bennett's. He wiped the blood from his eyes and looked up at me.

I knelt next to him and rolled Bennett off him. "Are you alright, Dad?" My hands were shaking. I had never shot anyone before or seen a person die.

"Where did you come from?"

"From the top of the hill." I said as I lifted the ATV off him.

He sat up obviously in pain, "I see you brought back-up."

'What?" I turned to see Shayla running up to us. "I thought I told you to go home if you heard gunshots."

"I was right behind you when you shot Bennett. I saw the whole thing. There was no need to go for help. Are you all right, Mr. Hanson?"

Dad felt his face. He had gravel in his cheeks and ear. "The bullet must have hit the rocks next to my head and sprayed me with rocks. I think most of this blood belongs to Bennett. I believe I'm alright."

Handing Dad his police radio, I said, "Call for help, we need to get you to a hospital and make sure you're okay."

Dad turned his the radio on and called Lt. Reinhardt and told them to come to our location.

Shayla went to get the horses. Dad tried to stand up but his knee wouldn't support his weight. I helped lower him back to the ground. "What were you doing out here, Andy?"

I wanted to tell him we were on a picnic but I didn't want to lie to him. "I was worried about you."

"I told you to stay home."

"I know. What the hell happened?"

"I spotted a rider on a horse leading a mule coming from the north on the old Indian trail. I called dispatch and had several of Clarksville's Police Officers stand-by at the Double J Ranch so we didn't scare him off. I had already called the Sheriff's Department by phone and they have men on horseback coming in from the south. I had to keep moving downhill to keep the rider in sight. By the time I located Bennett coming to meet the guy, I couldn't get out by phone. I decided to come arrest Bennett. By the time I got here, he was too close for me to use my radio. He would have heard it."

"Why didn't you go to his truck and arrest him there?"

"Because he would have seen me if I rode by on horseback and it was too far to walk. I wouldn't have made it before he took off. I can't believe I let him get the jump on me like that. I should have known better."

"At least you're alive."

"I should be mad at you, Andy, but I'm not. You saved my life, Son. I'm proud of you."

I looked at Bennett with no regrets. "He deserved it. He was going to kill you. I'm glad I shot him."

Shayla came back with the horses. Her hands were trembling and it was obvious she was frightened. She stared at Bennett for a long time and then said, "He killed Bobby Patterson, didn't he?"

"I'm pretty sure he did," Dad replied. Shayla started sobbing. I ran to her and held her tight.

CHAPTER FORTY-THREE

Mom wanted Dad to stay home but he insisted on going to work. I talked him into letting me stay home from school so I could drive him to work.

Chief Baker was sitting at his desk reading the morning newspaper when Dad and I made our way into Dad's office. Dad had a considerable limp as I assisted him to his chair.

Chief Baker got up from his desk and followed us into Dad's office. "Good morning. I didn't expect you to be in today, Scott. How you feeling?"

"Good morning, Harvey. We're alright."

"Want some coffee?"

"No thanks."

"How's your leg?"

"Sore, but I didn't break anything. Just bruised and skinned up. I'll be fine in a couple of weeks."

"Are you alright, Andy?"

"I'm fine, Sir."

"Scott, how in the Hell did you know they would be making that drug run yesterday?"

"It's a long story but mostly a hunch about moon patterns."

"Moon patterns? What did the moon have to do with it?"

"I checked the dates when the truckers came through Clarksville that had drugs planted on them. At first, I couldn't find any connections. They were on different days of the week and different times of the month. But when I listed the dates on my calendar, I noticed they all came through Clarksville during the third quarter of the moon. I wasn't sure if that was a connection or not but it got me to thinking. I figured if they were bringing drugs up from Mexico, as I expected they were, they had to be doing it by horseback during the half-moon. They needed enough light to travel at night to see the trail but not so much as to be spotted by a farmer or rancher. If they were on horseback and started on a half-moon, it would be a quarter-moon by the time they got to Clarksville and placed the drugs on the trucks."

Chief Baker rubbed his chin and thought about what Dad had just told him. "That was a mighty slim hunch you were working on."

"I knew I was grasping at straws. But after Colonel told me about the old Indian trail leading up from Mexico and finding hoof-prints on it, I figured that was what was happening. Besides, we really didn't have anything else to go on."

"Well, it paid off big time. But next time, you need to keep me informed, damn it."

"I didn't want you to think I lost my mind if nothing happened."

Chief Baker rubbed his chin. "I have to admit, that was a long shot. Have you seen the newspaper yet?"

"No."

Chief Baker laid the paper in front of Dad and the headlines read; *Star Football Player Kills Murder Suspect.* Dad started reading the rest of the story out loud. "Clarksville star quarterback, Andy

Hanson killed local resident Bennett Nahche who was attempting to kill the Assistant Chief of Police, Scott Hanson while he was being arrested for drug smuggling. Hanson's son shot and killed Bennett after Bennett ran over the Assistant Chief and was going to shoot him." The article went on to explain that Bennett was a major drug smuggler and had run Dad down with a quad ATV. The paper called me a hero and went on to say that Bennett Nahche may have killed Bobby Patterson, as well as the unknown woman in the mine and Carrie Campbell.

"Damn it!" Dad said as he lay the paper down.

"Damn it what? Andy is a hero."

"Not that, Harvey, the part about Bennett being the suspect that killed Bobby Patterson and the women in the mine and Carrie."

"Well, it makes sense, Scott. Bennett was a major drug dealer. Bobby obviously found out that he was involved in dealing drugs and Bennett killed him to keep him quiet. Bennett was at the gym on the night of the killing and could have stolen Shayla's phone and used it to lure Bobby up there with the text message. Also, Bennett was carrying a 270 rifle like the one that killed Bobby and he admitted to you that he had shot at Andy and Jared at the mine where the drugs had been, and where the woman's body was found. Hell, Scott, he was going to kill you-for Christ's sake. And, he was screwing Carrie Campbell. It all fits. Who else could it be?"

It made sense to me but not to Dad. He didn't answer for a long time, as if he was thinking about something.

"It still doesn't add up Harvey, there has to be someone else involved."

"Why do you say that?"

"Several reasons. Have you ever known Bennett to wear anything but moccasins? There were two other sets of footprints in the mineshaft besides Andy's, Jared's and the dead woman's. Bennett wears a size ten and a half and the boot print found at Bobby's murder scene was a size twelve and a half or thirteen as was one of the prints found in the mine. Bennett admitted to the shooting at the mine but claimed he was intentionally shooting over their heads to scare them away so he could get his drugs. Also think about the shot that killed Bobby. Do you think Bennett could have made that shot during the day, let alone at night?"

"I have no idea. I've never seen him shoot."

"I still think someone else is involved." Dad said.

"I don't know, Scott. Some of that makes sense, but it doesn't mean Bennett wasn't the killer. He could have worn larger boots when he killed Bobby just to throw us off his track."

"Bennett was going to kill me. He didn't have any reason to lie. Also, he seemed surprised and angered when I told him Carrie Campbell was dead. He told me not to worry, justice would be done for her murder."

"I still say Bennett killed Bobby Patterson, the woman in the mine and Carrie Campbell. He would have killed you too if it hadn't been for Andy. We should just leave it with that unless you get evidence to prove otherwise."

"Maybe, but you know what else bothers me, Harvey?"

"What?"

"Bennett's last words to me. He said, "Chief Dancing Kachina," not once but twice. Why would anyone use their dying words to talk about dolls? And I've checked and there is no Kachina doll called Dancing Kachina."

"Bennett spent almost all of his time making Kachina Dolls. Maybe they had some spiritual meaning to him that we don't understand."

"Could be, but he wanted me to know, as if somehow it had a greater meaning. I don't know, Harvey, maybe we'll find the answer when we do the search warrant on his store and home."

"How's that coming by the way?"

"Officer Goff has the store secured until Reinhardt gets the warrant. Then we're going over the place with a fine-toothed comb."

"Has anyone identified the body from the mine yet?" asked Chief Baker.

"Not yet, she's still listed as a Jane Doe."

Both men were quiet for a long time until Chief Baker broke the silence. "How are you holding up, Andy?"

"Fine, so far."

"It took a lot of nerve to pull that trigger," said Chief Baker.

"Are you going to execute the search warrant, Scott?"

"Nope, I'm going to stay right here and rest my leg. The Sheriff's Department and Lieutenant Reinhardt will conduct the searches. It was the Sheriff's jurisdiction, remember."

I stayed with Dad all day to make sure he stayed off his leg. Chief Baker took us to Skeeter's for lunch and Lt. Reinhardt joined us while we were eating. "How did the search go?" Dad asked.

"Not bad, we found $26,000 in his safe and 20 kilos of heroin."

"I would have expected a lot more money than that, since he was moving so much drugs. Does he have any hidden bank accounts we don't know about?"

"There wasn't any evidence of any, but the Sherriff's Department is looking into it.

"What else did you find?"

"We found several lunchboxes with magnets attached. DEA is going to love us. Bennett was taking old speakers apart and soldering the magnets inside the lunch boxes so they wouldn't fall off the trucks while being transported. And, he's been doing it for a long time."

"Any indication he had a partner?" Dad asked.

"Nothing to indicate an accomplice or that he was working for someone else."

Dad leaned back, closed his eyes and thought for a long time. He shook his head, "It doesn't add up Chief. There has to be someone else involved."

"If there is, we haven't found him yet. I think he acted alone."

Chief Baker said, "You did a great job, Scott. It is what it is. Just let it rest and enjoy your success."

CHAPTER FORTY-FOUR

I was sound asleep when I heard a soft tapping sound. Sitting up in bed, I looked around the room and the sound stopped. Just as I lay back down, I heard it again. I thought it was coming from outside. I went to the window and found Shayla standing outside my window smiling at me. I opened the window and felt the cold air rushing in. "Shayla, what are you doing out there?"

"I came to see you, Andrew."

"Why didn't you call first?"

"Because I don't have your phone number."

"Everyone else does, thanks to Jared. You could have asked any of your friends."

"And let them know I was interested? No thanks, it's none of their business."

"You want to come in? I'll open the door for you."

"No, I want you to come outside with me."

"It's cold out there."

"So, dress warm, I want to go to the barn. I don't want your parents to know I'm here."

I didn't want her in the barn because of Ruby. "Just climb in through the window. My parents won't know. Their bedroom is on the other end of the house."

Shayla smiled and climbed through the window. She was wearing a short jacket over a buttoned-up shirt and jeans. Several buttons of her shirt were undone and her low-cut bra did little to hide her breast as she climbed in the window. While I was helping her inside, she tripped and landed on top of me. She started laughing. With that all too familiar smirk on her face, she said teasingly, "Oh, Andy, what big muscles you have."

"Have you been drinking?" I asked.

"Maybe."

"I didn't know you drank."

"There's a lot you don't know about me, Andrew Hanson, but you're about to find out."

"Does that mean you're not the ice princess everyone thinks you are?"

Shayla smiled and pushed me back on the bed, "I'm cold, but I'm no ice princess."

Shayla crawled on top of me and kissed me firmly on my lips. Her arms were cool from being outside but her lips were warm and firm and her breath tasted of sweet wine. I could feel her passion as her breast moved up and down as she breathed. She sat up and removed her jacket and threw it on the floor. She smiled at me and slowly unbuttoned her blouse one button at a time. Her eyes were sparkling and she had a grin on her face. She took her blouse off and threw it on the nightstand.

I watched her as she unhooked the front clasp of her lace bar and opened it up just enough to taunt me. I smiled and reached for her. She cupped her breast in her hands and bent down to kiss me again. "I want you to want me, Andrew."

"I've never wanted anything more," I replied as I pulled her close and kissed her. I could see her watching me, her eyes sparking in the moonlight coming through the open window.

She moved forward, kissing my chest as I messaged her shoulders gently. I could smell her hair, the wine on her breath, and her sensual perfume. My heart was pounding in my chest and I was breathing hard.

I felt her warm tongue on my lips and tasted the sweet wine. She was in total control and I wanted her to be.

All of a sudden, I saw a bright light and heard a familiar voice saying, "Andy wake up, Honey! Andy, wake up son."

I sat up and looked around the room. Shayla was gone and my window was closed. I had my shorts and pajamas on and was sweating and breathing hard. My mother was sitting on my bed and my father was standing at my door. "What's wrong?" asked Dad.

"Andy was having a bad dream, Scott. He was screaming and thrashing around in his bed."

Dad had a very concerned look on his face. "Are you all right, Son?"

I got my bearings and pulled my sheets up on myself. "I'm fine. It was just a dream. I'm okay now."

"Do you want me to get you some water or a glass of milk?" Mom asked.

"No Mom, I'm fine, really. I'm alright, I just want to go back to sleep."

"I'll stay with a for while if you want."

"No, Mom, please, I'm okay. I just want to go back to sleep."

"Come on, Sherrie, let him get some sleep. We'll talk about this in the morning."

Dad took Mom by the shoulders and led her out of the room, turning off the light and shutting the door. I felt a warm fluid in my shorts. "Damn it!" I walked into the bathroom, removed my shorts, washed them in the sink and hung them on the hamper to dry. I washed myself off and put on a clean pair of shorts. I put my pajamas back on, climbed back into bed and fell asleep.... thinking of Shayla.

Mom and Dad were in the kitchen making breakfast when I walked in. Dad asked, "How are you feeling this morning?"

"I'm fine."

"Do you want to stay home from school today?" Mom asked.

"No, I'm fine, I want to go to school." I didn't want to say anything about the wet dream.

Mom asked, "Do you want to talk about it?"

"No, it was nothing, really." I could tell they were worried about me and I wanted to change the subject.

"We'll talk about it later," Dad said.

I finished breakfast and went to school. Later that evening, Dad joined me in the barn as I was working on the truck. He drank a beer and watched me bending a brake-line into shape. I screwed one end of the line onto the truck and marked the other end with a black marker, then removed the brake line, cut it to length and flared the end.

"How's it going, Son?"

"Great, Dad. This is the last brake line and I'm finished with that project."

"What else are you going to do?"

"Fill the master cylinder, bleed the brakes and then, she should ready to start."

I tightened the brake line, filled the master cylinder with fluid and started bleeding the break cylinders. Attempting to avoid the subject of last night's dream, I said, "Mom seemed to be in a good mood today."

"Yeah, she said she lost five pounds last week."

"Have you noticed how she always tells you when she's lost weight but never tells you if she gains any?"

"I know. I've been keeping track of all the weight she's been telling me she lost for the last year and she should have disappeared by now."

We both laughed and Dad said, "Remember, Son. What happens in the barn, stays in the barn."

"I won't say a thing." To keep the conversation away from the dream I asked, "Dad, how did you know Mom was the right woman for you?"

"What do you mean?"

"Mom told me you walked up to her and said, 'Hi, I'm Scott Hanson,' and she knew you were the one. Six months later you were engaged and were married within a year. How did you know Mom was the right one?"

Dad laughed, "That's mom's version, but there was more to the story than that."

"Tell me about it."

Dad looked back toward the house as if he wasn't sure he wanted to tell me. "I'll tell but you have to promise, what happens in the barn, stays in the barn and never say anything to your mother."

"My lips are sealed."

"What really happened was your Mom moved into the apartment complex where I was living. She had a roommate named Sara. I can't remember her last name. Anyway, Sara was hot. She had the body of a Playboy magazine centerfold and a bikini that was so small, she couldn't possibly keep it all in. Every guy in the apartment complex was chasing her like dogs in heat and wanted to go out with her. Every time Sara and Sherrie showed up at the pool, a dozen guys were out there trying to get a date with Sara. Your Mom was much more conservative, a real lady. She ignored them and did her homework or read books. Every time I started to put the move on Sara, two or three other guys would beat me to her."

"You wanted to date Sara, and not Mom?" I asked grinning from ear to ear.

"Yeah. Anyway, I decided I would go introduce myself to Sara's roommate figuring she would introduce me to Sara when Sara came back to the table. I was going to outsmart those other fools."

"So, what happened?"

"I just walked up to your Mom and said, 'Hi, I'm Scott Hanson," and offered her my hand. She shook it. We sat talking for about an hour before Sara came over and Sherrie introduced us. As soon as Sara started talking, I realized she was an airhead. She was as dumb as a rock. But your Mom was obviously intelligent and very nice, so I asked her out instead."

"So, what happened to Sara?"

"She got pregnant, dropped out of school, had an abortion and years later, came out of the closet claiming she was a lesbian."

"Mom lived with a lesbian?"

"Don't say anything, and remember, what happens in the barn stays in the barn. She never knew I introduced myself to her hoping to meet Sara."

I shook my head. "I won't say a word."

I tightened the brake cylinder I was bleeding and switched to drain another cylinder when Dad asked, "How'd you sleep last night, Son?"

"Good."

"You didn't have any more bad dreams?"

"Nope."

Dad got a real serious look on his face. "Andy, I want to talk about something. No man ever knows how killing another man will affect him. It's not easy to take another man's life. We can get you some help if you need..."

I held up both hands to stop him in mid sentence. "Dad, stop! I wasn't having a nightmare."

"What?"

"I was having a dream about Shayla. It had nothing to do with Bennett. If I had my way, I'd have one of those dreams every night."

Dad thought about what I was saying and then held up both hands. "Oh, one of those dreams!"

"Yeah, one of those dreams and I'm fine. Now it's up to you to convince Mom I'm all right without mentioning Shayla. Remember, what happens in the barn, stays in the barn."

Dad started to reply but didn't. He slowly shook his head absorbing what he'd just learned. "My lips are sealed," he said. Then he turned and walked back to the house.

CHAPTER FORTY-FIVE

Thursday morning I dropped Jared off at school for weight training. "Tell the coach I have something I have to do this morning but I'll be in the film room at lunchtime."

"You alright Bro?"

"Yeah, I'm fine, see you later."

To tell the truth, I just wasn't in the mood to work out this morning. I drove to the main parking lot and sat facing east waiting for the sun to come up. The parking lot filled up with vehicles and I didn't seem to notice. The bell rang indicating classes were starting in ten minutes. A few minutes later the parking lot became quiet again and I leaned my head back on my headrest, closed my eyes and let the warmth of the sun warm them. I was almost asleep when I heard someone knocking on my side window. Shayla was standing next to my car watching me. She had an arm full of schoolbooks. I smiled and she smiled back. I closed my eyes again. She attempted to open my door but it was locked. I ignored her and she walked to the passenger's side door and opened it, "Andrew, what are you doing out here?"

"Watching the sun rise."

Shayla looked at the sky, "It's risen."

"I know."

"Your late for class."

"So?"

Shayla closed the door and started to walk away. She stopped, walked back and opened the door again. She got in the passenger seat and sat there. After a minute she reached over and gently touched my arm. "Andrew, look at me."

I opened his eyes and looked at her.

"Are you okay?"

"I'm fine. How are you?"

Shayla thought for a few seconds. "Better. As a matter of fact, I haven't felt this good in years, but I'm worried about you."

"Why's that?"

"I don't know, maybe because of Bennett."

"He deserved what he got. By the way, Happy Birthday."

"It's not until Saturday?"

"I know."

"You knew my birthday is Saturday?"

"Of course. I've already got you a very special present."

"You did? What is it?"

"It is a surprise. What are you doing on your birthday?"

Shayla didn't answer for a long time, "I'm thinking about getting all dressed up and going to a nice restaurant and having dinner."

"Are you asking me out on a date?" I asked.

"No!"

"What are you doing?"

"I'm asking you to ask me out on a date."

"Okay, will you go out with me on your birthday?"

"Maybe. Where do you want to go?"

"Oh, for Christ sakes, Shayla, do you want to go out with me or not?"

"Andrew, this isn't easy for me. I've never been on a date before."

"All you have to do is say yes or no."

"Yes."

"Yes what?"

"Yes, I would like you to take me out on my birthday. But I would like to know where we're going so I know how to dress."

"Dress up and I'll take you to a very special place for dinner."

Shayla reached over and kissed me on my cheek. Her lips were soft, warm, and moist. "Thank you Andrew." She got out of the car and walked away leaving me sitting in the sun. I pulled my visor down, put my head back, smiled and closed my eyes.

The bell ran indicating the end of first period. I got out of my car and walked into the school and found Jared.

"Where the Hell have you been? You missed first period, are you alright, Bro?"

"I'm fine, Jared."

We were walking down the hall when Stephanie Miller and Kelsey Garner ran up from behind us and grabbed my arms on both sides, and walked with us. They were both smiling at me.

"Hi, ladies, what's happening?" I asked.

"Is it true?" Kelsey asked.

"Is what true?"

"We heard you have a date with Shayla Stevenson."

"Who told you that?"

"Shayla did. She said you're taking her out to dinner and have bought her a very special gift for her birthday."

"She told you that?"

"She told everyone that," answered Stephanie. "Cricket is in the bathroom right now having a mental breakdown."

"Oh, give me a break!"

"Well, maybe just crying."

"Or maybe puking," added Kelsey.

"Well?" asked Stephanie.

"Well what?"

"Oh come on, Andy. Are you taking Shayla out on a real date or not."

"Yes, I'm taking Shayla out for her birthday."

"What did you get her for her birthday?"

"It's a secret."

"We won't tell anyone," Kelsey said, "We promise."

"Yeah right." I said as both girls let go of my arms and ran down the hallway laughing. Jared looked at me. "Don't tell me you melted the ice princess! You're going to have to do something really special you know."

"Like what?"

"I don't know, eat a bunch of raw oysters or something."

"Yeah, Jared, like I need to be taking advice form you, Romeo."

My phone beeped and I saw I had a message from Stacey Miller. I turned it off and walked into my class.

By the end of the day everyone at school knew Shayla and I were going out on a date. You would have thought it the most exciting thing that had happened at Clarksville High School since the transformation of Hairy Larry. Rumors ran wild everywhere.

After school I returned Stacey's call. "I'm happy for you Andy. Shayla is happier now than she has seen since Bobby Patterson was killed. Please treat her good."

⇒⋅⋅⇒

When Dad got home and pulled his truck into the garage, he could hear our music blaring all the way from the kitchen. The song "My Girl" by The Temptations was turned up loud. When he entered the house, Mom and I were dancing and singing along to the song. We were being very animated. "Hi, Honey," "Hi, Pop," we said in unison. We kept dancing and singing.

Dad walked over to the refrigerator, got himself a beer, and sat on the kitchen counter watching us dance. When the song ended, Mom reached over and turned down the volume. Dad asked, "What are we celebrating?"

"Andy has a date Saturday night."

"With who?"

"With Shayla Stephenson."

Dad smiled. "Damn, dreams do come true."

I shot him a quick stare. He held his hands up in surrender, "I know, I know, what happens in the barn."

"What are you two talking about?" asked Mom.

"About having dinner in the barn. That's all."

"How'd he know about that?" Mom asked.

"Never mind, let's go," I said as I took her by the arm and led her out the back door.

"Hey, were are you going?" asked Dad.

"We're going shopping to buy Andy some new clothes. He's going to give Shayla the colt for her birthday. I want him to look special. Your dinner is in the crock-pot, the bread's in the oven and the salad is in the fridge, Dear. Bye." Mom said as she we walked out to her car and left.

CHAPTER FORTY-SIX

S tanding in front of the mirror, I studied the boy grinning back at me. *Not bad,* I though. The jeans, boots, and shirt with snaps looked somehow out of place. I put my Cowboy hat on, adjusted my new Western belt, and stepped back for a better look. "Heeehaw, Cowboy!" *Who would have ever guessed?*

I had waited for my truck to be completed before I asked Shayla out. The Ford pickup truck would round out my image. Besides, it was Shayla I want to impress, not myself.

"Andy, you're going to break a few hearts looking like that," Mom said as she walked into my room. "You look so handsome!"

"Thanks, Mom. But you'd say that no matter what I looked like."

"You think so? Wait till Shayla sees you."

Dad added, "That's a great look, Son. Does Shayla have any idea what you have planned?"

"She doesn't have a clue. All I told her was that I was taking her to dinner for her birthday. I didn't tell her where we were going, what I was giving her for her birthday, or what I would be driving. I want it to be a complete surprise."

"She's going to be ecstatic," Mom said.

Dad asked, "Have you named the colt yet?"

"No, I'll let Shayla do that."

"As soon you go into the barn, Mom and I will start bringing the food out. Then we're leaving to go meet Shayla's parents for dinner. If you guys decide to go dancing, meet us at the rodeo club.'"

"Thanks for helping me with dinner and the truck. I never thought it would look this good."

Mom had her hands on her cheek and a smile spread across her. I hugged her. Dad said, "You better hurry, Son, you don't want to be late for your date. We wish we could be here to see the expression on Shayla's face when she sees her present."

I didn't like the idea of driving the truck on the dirt road but I didn't have a choice if I was going to show it to the Stevenson family as promised. I drove slow, hoping not to chip the paint and trying not to get it too dusty. The smell of leather and the shine of chrome made the truck look brand new. Over 400 horses rumbled over the gravel road as the truck headed back to where I had found it.

Shayla had told me I was "dumber than I looked" for wanting this piece of junk. I wanted to see her face when she saw it now. I placed a CD from "Little Big Town" in the stereo and set it to the song, "Pontoon." I pulled into the ranch, parked behind the house and turned the engine off. John must have heard the rumble of the exhaust pipes and came out to see the truck. He raised his hands in the air and shook his head. "No, this can't be the same truck." He interlocked his fingers around the back of his head as he circled it. "It's looks brand new. No, it's better than brand new."

Donna came outside after a couple of minutes. "I can't believe it, Andy! The truck is beautiful." Shaking her head, "This can't be the same truck you pulled out of here."

Grinning from ear to ear, I said, "The body is the same but almost everything else is new. It has an automatic transmission, power windows, power door locks, cruise control, tilt steering wheel, air conditioning, disc brakes and four-wheel drive."

John walked around the truck with a look of awe. "I sure wish my dad were here to see this. He sure would be proud."

Donna replied, "He sure would. I can't believe what a great job you and your dad did on this old truck."

Donna noticed me looking towards the house. "She's still getting ready. Andy. I'll go see what's keeping her."

John and I were admiring the motor when Shayla and Donna returned. I hadn't seen Shayla until I heard, "Oh my God!"

Shayla stood staring at the truck with her mouth open and both palms on her cheeks. The expression was priceless. I had never seen Shayla with makeup before or wearing a dress. The ponytail was gone and her hair hung down over her shoulders. She was wearing a strapless black dress to the beltline and green from the waist down. The dress was tight with a slit up the side of her leg and she was wearing high heels. She appeared taller, older and more mature. I stared at her. She was even more beautiful than I had thought possible.

Shayla realized I was staring at her. Her cheeks turned pink. She broke eye contact and looked back at the truck. "Andrew, the truck is beautiful. I can't believe this is the same truck my grandfather drove. The color is gorgeous. You told me you were painting it blue."

"I changed my mind. I painted the truck to match your eyes!"

Shayla opened her mouth to speak but the words didn't come. She covered her mouth with her hand. We just stood there looking at each other.

John broke the silence. "Come on, kids, get outta here. I want to hear the truck while it's running."

I walked to the passenger's side door and opened it for Shayla. She walked slowly with her hands out to her side, unsteady in her heels. She found her voice, smiled and said, "You look very handsome this evening, Mr. Hanson."

"Thank you, Miss Stevenson, and you look gorgeous," I replied as I shut the door. I got in the truck, started it and slowly drove away from the ranch. I could see John and Donna hugging each other watching us as we drove away. When I got onto the dirt road, I turned the stereo on and the song "Pontoon" started playing.

"Oh Andrew, you remembered," Shayla said as she started swaying in the seat to the beat of the song. I silently thanked God for this night.

While swaying to the beat of the music, Shayla asked, "So, where are you taking me for dinner, Mr. Hanson?"
"It's a surprise, you'll have to wait and see."
Shayla kept dancing as if she didn't have a care in the world. It was wonderful to see her so happy and relaxed for a change. I drove to my house, pulled into the driveway, past the house and parked next to the barn. I turned the motor off, got out of the truck, walked around to the passenger's door and opened it. Shayla looked around and asked, "What are we doing here? Did you forget something?"
"Nope, I didn't forget a thing. We're having dinner in the barn."
Shayla hesitated and with a wrinkled brow stepped out of the truck. I walked over and opened the barn doors. Sitting just inside was a table fully set with plates, silver wear, crystal glasses, candles and a white tablecloth. There were two red roses in the center of the table and soft music playing in the background. Using the best English accent I could muster, I said, "Everything we are having for dinner tonight my dear, I made myself."
Shayla smiled and imitated the accent, "Well, Mr. Hanson, I didn't know you knew how to cook."

A horse whinnied somewhere in the barn and Shayla looked in that direction.

Still using the accent, I said, "That's because you never joined me in our creative cooking class, Miss Stevenson."

My parent's arrival with the food turned Shayla's attention away from the barn. I turned the music up a little.

"Happy Birthday, Shayla!" Mom said as she and Dad carried the food out to the table. "If you two will take your seats, we'll serve you and get out of our hair. We're meeting your parents for dinner."

I pulled Shayla's chair out for her and she said, "Thank you, Mr. Hanson."

"Your welcome, My Lady." I sat and my parents served us meat-loaf, mashed potatoes, sweet corn and homemade bread.

Mom beamed with pride saying, "Andy also made a peach pie for dessert and I didn't help him cook a thing."

Dad filled our glasses with ice tea and gave me a wink. Then he and Mom bid us good night. After they left, Shayla said, "I never thought I'd ever have a date in a barn, but this is very thoughtful of you. It's kind of romantic."

I stood up and walked over to a pile of hay and removed an ice chest. I pulled out two wine glasses and a bottle of red wine. A horse whinnied somewhere in the barn and again Shayla looked in that direction. I turned the music up once more. "You do like red wine don't you, Miss Stevenson?"

"Well, yes I do. But how did you know?"

"I know a lot about you that you don't know I know. And, I have a very special birthday present for you after dinner."

"Oh really, and what's that?"

"It is a surprise, you'll just have to wait."

We made small talk as we ate and drank wine. I hadn't seen Shayla so relaxed and talkative before. It was as if she didn't have a care in the world. "Andrew, this is the best meatloaf I have ever tasted, what kind is it? I don't remember us making meatloaf in class."

"It's elk meatloaf. It's my own recipe."

A horse whinnied again and then a small colt whinnied.

"That sounds like a colt." Shayla said as she looked back into the barn searching for the sound.

"Miniature horses make a lot of funny sounds."

"I didn't know you had miniatures," she said still staring back at the stalls.

I quickly changed the subject. "Are you ready for dessert?"

She smiled. "Well of course, Mr. Hanson, thank you."

"Do you like your pie a la mode?"

Pointing her chin upward, she said, "No thank you, sir. I'm watching my weight. I'll have mine plain."

After taking a bite, Shayla said, "This pie is as good as the ones Polly makes. You didn't sweet-talk her out of her family recipe, did you?"

"Only for your birthday, Miss Stevenson. But I promised her I would destroy it after I made the pie, which I did."

"Darn, I was hoping to get that recipe myself. How's your memory."

"Perfect, but I am saving the recipe for my wife."

Shayla smiled, "Well I'm sure she will appreciate it, whoever she is."

When we finished the dessert, I asked, "Are you ready for your present now?"

"Sure, what is it?"

"Stand up, put your hands over your eyes and don't look until I tell you to. Okay?"

She stood up and covered her eyes. "All right. I'm ready."

"Promise you won't look?"

"I promise, Andrew. What is it?"

I took her by her arm and walked her back into the barn.

I heard concern in her voice. "Where are you taking me, Mr. Hanson?"

"To your present, be quiet and keep your hands over your eyes."

I stood her in front of Ruby's stall, turned her towards it and opened the stall doors. "Okay, open your eyes."

Shayla opened her eyes and saw Ruby standing in the stall. Her mouth flew wide open and her hands went high into the air. "Oh my God, Ruby!" She ran to the stall and wrapped her arms around Ruby's neck. "What are you doing here?" she asked with tears streaming down her cheeks. "I've missed you so much!"

After a few moments she turned towards me with her head tilted to one side and palms outward and asked, "How did she get here?"

"I bought her at the auction."

She ran to me and wrapped her arms around my neck, "Oh, Andy, how can I ever repay you? You saved her life. I thought she had gone to the slaughterhouse for sure. This is the best present I could have ever dreamed of." She was literately jumping up and down. "Thank you. Thank you!"

She was crying, and laughing all at the same time. This was the first time she had ever called me Andy. When she calmed down, she turned and hugged Ruby's neck again. "Are you ready for your other present?" I asked.

Shayla looked confused, "What other present, knowing Ruby is alive and safe is the best present in the world!"

"Well, Ruby has a present for you, too."

I walked to the next stall and opened the door. A small colt just a few months old stood in the stall. I let him out and put him in with Ruby. The colt went to Ruby and started nursing. He was the same color as his mother but had a small jagged blaze across his forehead and one white stocking.

Shayla stared at the colt with her mouth opened and her hands on her cheeks. She looked back at me and then at Ruby. "Ruby had a colt? Who did you breed her to?"

"I didn't, she was in-foal when I bought her."

Shayla clasped her hands around each other and held them close to her breast. She narrowed her eyebrows, "Well who's the sire?" Shayla asked staring at me.

I crossed my arms, stood tall with my chin up, smiled and just looked at her. Shayla looked at me, then at the colt and then back at me. Then it hit her. Her mouth dropped open again and I could see ever tooth. "Oh my God. It's Thunderbolt's colt. Andy, do you know what this means? This colt is worth at least thirty thousand dollars, maybe more."

"I'm not sure how much he's worth but he is yours now!"

She melted before me. "Oh Andy, no, I can't! I can't accept something like this. I've been so mean to you and I don't deserve him." She started bawling. "Andy, I'm so sorry, you didn't deserve being treated that way. You have always been so good to me." Before she understood what she was saying, "I love you!" sprang from her lips. She ran into my arms and kissed me on the lips. I held her in my arms as she sobbed. I could feel her heartbeat pounding in her chest and her breast heaving as she breathed. She stopped crying and looked deep into my eyes as if looking for acceptances. I continued holding her tight and kissed her for the first time. It was a long slow warm tender kiss full of passion and desire. Fire burned in my soul. My knees felt weak and I was unsteady on my feet.

When we separated, tears were still streaming down Shayla's face smearing her mascara. She looked up at me and buried her face in my chest. We held each other for a long time. I could feel her body trembling and smelled her perfume and her hair. After a few moments, I broke the silence. "What are you going to name him?"

"Oh Andy, I can't. I can't accept something this valuable. He's worth a lot of money. I just can't."

"What am I supposed to do with him, take him to the Naval Academy with me?"

"Do your parents know you want to give him away?"

"Of course they do. They're telling your parents right now. So, what are you going to name him?"

Shayla turned and looked at the colt but she didn't let go of me. The colt had quit nursing and came to the stall door looking curiously at us. "He's beautiful, Andy. Absolutely beautiful!"

She rubbed him between his ears and traced the white blaze across his forehead with her finger. "It looks like a lightning bolt." She turned back to me smiling, "Lightning, I'll name him Lightning"

Shayla gave me another long passionate kiss while holding me tight. "His name is Lightning!" she said again.

Thinking of this night, I almost regretted having already committed to going to a military academy. I didn't want to leave Shayla and we wouldn't have much time together before I had to report. But deep inside, I knew I had made the right choice. If this was meant to be, she would wait for me.

CHAPTER FORTY-SIX

Ruby didn't want to load into the trailer. I loaded Lightning first and Ruby followed. I drove to the Double J Ranch. While putting Ruby and the colt in the pasture, Shayla, her parents and Colonel joined me at the fence. Ruby ran around the pasture kicking high in the air, obviously happy to be home. Thunderbolt pranced over to meet her and ran back and forth along the fence. I put the colt in the pasture and he ran around trying to catch his mother. Ruby went nose to nose with Thunderbolt and the colt joined them. Thunderbolt sniffed the colt for a long time. Then, he reared up and ran around the pasture as if celebrating his new son. The colt turned to his mother and started nursing.

Shayla put her arms around me and kissed me on the cheek, "Good morning, Andy." No one seemed to notice the kiss but me.

"If that ain't the best looking colt I've ever seen, I don't know what is," John stated. He looked at Colonel. "I suppose you didn't know anything about this, did you?"

"Who me? I didn't know a thing."

Donna winked at Colonel, "Yes you did. I know you, and thanks." Colonel winked back at Donna but didn't say anything.

I said, "I've never see a better-looking colt in my life. And you can't even tell Ruby was ever injured. She'll make you a great trail horse if you want her."

John looked surprised. "You'd sell her back to us after all the work you put into her?"

"I got more out this than Ruby did, Sir."

Shayla leaned into me and squeezed. John knew what I was talking about. "How much do you want for her, Son?"

"You can have her for free as long as I can ride her when I'm home on leave. Lightning needs her and I sure can't take her to the Naval Academy with me."

John walked over to me and held out his hand. "You are a good man, Andy." When I reached for his hand, he pulled me close and gave me a big bear hug and patted me on the back. Everyone else joined in for a group-hug. It made me feel like family.

As we were hugging, Bob Patterson and his wife pulled into the rear yard. Bob got out of his truck and walked over to us. He walked up to me and said, "Andy, I'm want to thank you for killing that snake, Bennett." He held out his hand and I took it. He didn't let go of my hand and said, "It took a lot of guts to pull that trigger, young man. I'm proud of you."

"I didn't have much choice, he was going to kill my dad."

"I know you didn't, but when you shot Bennett, you not only saved your father, you saved our marriage. Meg has snapped out of her depression and I think she is going to be all right. You never get over losing a child. You just have to learn to live with it. You made that possible for her."

"You're welcome, Mr. Patterson. I hope your wife will continue to improve."

"I'm sure she will, she wants to talk to you. Would you mind walking over to see her?"

I walked over to the truck and Mrs. Patterson got out and hugged me. She seemed weak and frail as she spoke. "All I wanted was to have my son back, but I know that's impossible. No one can bring Bobby home again." She paused and took me by the hand. "But you did the second best thing." She smiled and squeezed my hand, "You gave me my life back. I will always be grateful to you, Andy."

I hugged her. "Only time and God's grace can heal a broken heart, Mrs. Patterson. Give it time and He will do the rest."

She kissed me on the cheek, "I will, Andy. Come by and see us now and then, will you?"

"I will, I promise."

I walked back to the pasture. Donna joined Meg and they went into the house. Bob Patterson looked at the colt and said, "Looks like Thunderbolt has being doing a little moonlighting while my back was turned. How'd that happen?"

Colonel replied, "Thunderbolt jumped the fence one night."

"Who's does he belong too?" asked Bob.

"He was Andy's, but he gave him to me for my birthday." Shayla said.

"Damn nice present, Andy. You think she's worth it?' he asked with a smile on his face.

"You know I am, don't you?" Shayla said as she hugged Bob Patterson.

Bob hugged her and looked at the colt. "Sure you are, Peaches. When you get ready to register him, come see me and I'll help you with the paperwork."

CHAPTER FORTY-SEVEN

The Championship game against Safford was being played at a natural stadium at the Pima High School. Everyone from miles away would be there. The Cheerleaders had made a big sign above the Clarksville side bleachers that read, "RETURN TO GLORY."

Dad took Jared and me to lunch at Skeeter's. Lt. Reinhardt and Chief Baker were there and joined us.

"Ready for the big game tonight, boys?" asked Chief Baker as he pulled up his chair.

"I am," said Jared.

"Me too," I answered.

Dad was being abnormally quiet. "What's bothering you, Scott?" asked Chief Baker.

"Bennett's bothering me. I can't explain it but he sure has been eating at me. I keep thinking I'm missing something but I can't figure it out. What the Hell am I missing?"

"Nothing, that I can see," said Lt. Reinhardt.

Some customers were checking out and a lady asked Skeeter if the Kachina dolls were for sale. "Yes. I only have three left and I'm selling them for half-price," answered Skeeter.

The customer purchased one and left the store. Dad looked at the other dolls, walked over and picked one of them up. "What are these things made of anyway?"

Skeeter answered, "Most of the body is made from the root of the cottonwood tree. Bennett painted them and made all the clothes himself."

Dad read the label on one of the dolls out loud, "Hilili or Whisper Kachina." Dad put the Kachina doll back and picked up the other one. "Each one of these has its own name doesn't it?"

"Yes, each one represents a different religious belief and meaning to the Native Americans. It is forbidden to make a Kachina doll of any tribe unless you are a member of that tribe. That's why the Apaches wouldn't have anything to do with Bennett. He made Kachina Dolls from all tribes," answered Skeeter.

"Do they have one called Chief Dancing Kachina?"

"A lot of them are dancing Kachina Dolls but I have never seen one that is just called Chief Dancing Kachina."

Dad turned the Kachina Doll up-side down and read the label, "Kwahu Kachina." He turned to Reinhardt and asked, "Do we still have Bennett's place sealed off."

"Of course, why."

"Can you drive me out there? I want to check something out."

"Sure but let's do it early or you'll be late for the game."

"Let's go now. You boys want to go for a ride?" asked Dad.

As we started out the door, Skeeter reminded us of the victory party she was having after the game if Clarksville won. "Don't worry, we'll be there," Dad said.

"And we'll win," said Jared.

As we drove to Bennett's store, Dad called Mom and asked her to go to the game with the Stevensons and we would meet them there."

When we got to the store, Lt. Reinhardt took his key and unlocked it. We walked in and Dad turned on the lights. He stood in the middle of the store looking at the merchandise for a long time. "What are you looking for, Dad?" I asked.

"Bennett was trying to tell me something. I'm trying to figure out what it was."

There were about twenty Kachina dolls in the store. Three very large Kachina dolls sat in a glass case above the counter. A sign above the case read, "Not For Sale." Dad walked around the store picking up every Kachina doll and reading the label out loud. After examining each one, he put it back where he found it. The first label read, "Siyangephoya, Corn Mana, Ahote Kachina." Jared, Lt. Reinhardt and I stood watching him. When Dad was finished with the Kachina dolls that were listed for sale, he asked Reinhardt to climb up on the counter and hand him the three dolls from the glass case. The first one looked like a wolf and the sign on the bottom read, "Nataska Kachina." The one on the far right looked kind of like an eagle and the sign read, "Broadface Kachina." The center Kachina looked like a man and was dressed like Bennett with a big smile on his face. It was much larger than the other two and the sign read, "Dancing Kachina." Dad picked up each doll and examined it, and put it back down. He stared at all three dolls for a few moments and then picked each one up and shook it. The large Dancing Kachina had a definite rattle that none of the others had. "Do you have a knife, Lieutenant?" Dad asked.

Lt. Reinhardt handed Dad his pocketknife and Dad carefully removed the clothes from the doll. He turned it over and located a small door in the back of the doll. Dad opened the door and a tiny cassette recording tape fell out. He looked at the tape and said, "It's dated."

Dad shook the doll and several more tapes fell out all with a different dates going back for over three years. Dad smiled, "This is what Bennett was trying to tell me all along." He wasn't saying, Chief Dancing Kachina, he was calling me Chief and saying, 'Dancing Kachina."

"What do you think is on those tapes, Dad?" I asked.

"I don't know. But we are going to find out first thing tomorrow morning. We need to leave now or we're going to be late for the game."

"Scott, I've waited almost three years to find out who murdered Bobby Patterson. I think the answer is on these tapes. If you don't mind, I'd like to listen to them before I put them into evidence," said Reinhardt.

"That's up to you Lieutenant, but you'll be missing one Hell of a football game."

"I'll listen to the tapes first, then catch up with you at the game, if that's all right."

We walked out of Bennett's store and Lt. Reinhardt locked it. He dropped us off at the stadium and left to review the tapes.

CHAPTER FORTY-EIGHT

Lots of people were already inside the stadium when we got there. The school parking lot was almost full and fans were lined-up waiting to pay the admission fee. People lined the fence all the way away around the track with standing room only. Dad made his way into the stands where his seat had been saved on the 40-yard line half the way up. I went with him to say hi to Mom. Jared joined the team in the locker room. I was running late, but I knew I had time.

Dad sat between Mom and Harvey Baker. Chief Baker asked Dad if we had found anything interesting at Bennett's store. Dad told him no, which surprised me. I hugged Mom and headed to the locker room to get dressed.

"You're late, Andy," Coach Ford said as I entered.

"Sorry, Coach."

"Hurry up and get dressed. We need to get out on the field."

The team captains from both schools walked out to the center of the field for the coin toss. I noticed a difference in the attitude of the Safford team captains as they approached the center of the field. They didn't look so sure of themselves this time and had a much more serious demeanor about them.

Clarksville won the toss and we chose to kick off to Safford. The Owls received the ball at the 15-yard line and ran it back to the 23-yard line. Safford went three and out and kicked the ball back to Clarksville. The Cougars ran the ball back to their own 38-yard line. We ran the ball two more times but only gained two yards. Then, I hit our big tight end, Sonny Turner, on a screen pass for 25 yards and a first down. We continued to move the ball downfield to Safford's own 21-yard line and stalled on three downs. Coach Ford decided to try a field goal. The field goal was blocked by Safford's All American linebacker. Safford got the ball back.

Safford drove the ball 80 yards on nine plays, ending the drive with a 21-yard pass in the end zone for a touchdown. They kicked off and I ran the ball back 60 yards, giving us a first down on Safford's 34-yard line. I hit Sonny Turner in the end zone on the next play but he dropped the pass when two defenders hit him at the same time. He was slow to get up but not injured. He limped back to the huddle. I asked, "Are you hurt, Sonny?"

"No, I'm just faking it. Run the ball to the right side this time and I'll keep limping. It will make them think I'm injured. They'll move up close to me and I'll be able to get around them. Then you can hit me in the end zone."

The coach sent in a long pass play to the end zone and I had to scramble out of a full blitz to my right but was able to gain 6 yards on the play. It was third down and four. Safford gambled that Clarksville was going to pass and blitzed again. Our two wide receivers hugged the outside of the field and ran straight for the end zone. They were well covered. Sonny Turner faked a block and ran to the center of the field where the middle linebacker would have been if he hadn't blitzed. I hit Sonny with short pass and he carried two defenders into the end zone for a touchdown. The score was Cougars six Owls seven after Safford blocked the extra point.

The game went back and forth through the rest of the first quarter and almost to halftime with neither team gaining momentum. Safford ran a trick play on the last play of the first half. The end around reverse play had their wide receiver come back around on a hand-off and threw a pass to a wide-open receiver 20 yards down field who then ran the ball in for a touchdown. After the extra point, the score was 14 Owls to 6 Cougars.

Enthusiasm ran high for the Clarksville fans who seemed optimistic even though the Cougars had some making up to do. I noticed Lt. Reinhardt wasn't in the stands at halftime.

When we got into the locker room, we were tired, sore and disappointed at the score. I addressed the team, "Guys, I know the score isn't what we want it to be but we can beat these guys. All that work we put in during the summer will help us in the second half. We are in better shape than they are and we can win that championship if we don't give up."

Hairy Larry was frustrated and commented, "What the Hell do you know about winning a championship?"

Coach Ford walked into the locker room and everyone became quiet. The Coach responded to Larry's remarks, "A hell of lot more than any of you do, Larry!"

"What are talking about, Coach?" asked Larry.

Coach Ford looked at me and I shook my head indicating I didn't want the coach to continue.

Coach Ford said, "We only have a half of a game to get this right, Andy, and they need to start believing in themselves right now or we are going to lose this game. I think it's time for them to know. "I didn't answer.

"Know what, Coach?" asked Jared.

Coach Ford continued, "Andy knows exactly what it takes to win a championship. He started on the Superstition Mountain High School football team last year that won the 5-A state championship and broke all those records. He knows what it takes to win."

321

Everyone in the room stared at me. "Is that right Andy, did you play for the Bulls last year?" asked Larry.

"Yeah, I played for the Bulls. And you know what they had that I'm not seeing in this team? Heart, and belief in themselves. We get a little behind and you all start acting like we've already lost the game. I'm not defeated, and neither are you unless you believe you are. As a matter of fact, I haven't even started to fight yet. Now, are we going to cowboy up or just lie here and bleed?"

"We're going to get out there and kick some ass!" yelled Larry.

A big roar filled the locker room while the players jumped up and down while holding their fists in the air yelling, "Cougars, Cougars, Cougars!"

When they stop yelling, I said, "Good, now listen to the coach, he has a few surprises for Safford in the second half."

Coach Ford addressed his team, "Guys the problem with me and Coach Harris is that we both know each other too well. He was my assistant coach for many years and we almost know what each other thinks. Andy and I have worked out a few plays to run that Coach Harris won't expect us to run. I think we can catch them napping with their head up their asses if we run them at just the right time. Andy knows what these plays are and will call them when he feels the timing is right."

No one asked any questions so Coach Ford continued. "If we aren't ahead in the score with five minutes left on the clock, we're going to run a no-huddle offense. If we do that, you need to get back on the line as quick as possible after each play so the Safford players won't have time to adjust and neither will their coaches. Andy will call the plays at that time. It that clear?"

The whole team erupted in one big, "YES SIR!"

"All right then, let's get out there and kick some serious ass!"

The team ran onto the field with new determination and a lot of fight left in them. The crowd could tell this team hadn't given up by their attitude and enthusiasm. The Cougar fans responded with a loud roar welcoming the team back on the field.

Safford kicked off to start the second half. I caught the ball and ran it back to our own 45-yard line. The next two plays were running plays that only gained 4 yards. It was third and six.

I had a feeling the Safford linebackers were going to blitz. I called for a play where I would hand the ball off to the fullback running to his right and the receivers would be spread out wide along the sidelines. As soon as I handed the ball off to the fullback, I sprinted up the middle of the field where the blitzing linebackers had been. The fullback hit me with a short pass. I ran 60-yards to the end zone for a touchdown.

Jared moved off the line as a blocker in the backfield for the extra point and was able to stop the rush of their big All American linebacker. We made the extra point, making the score 13 to 14.

Both teams moved the ball downfield during the third quarter but each team hurt themselves with major penalties, miscues or fumbles ending long drives. The Cougars squandered another opportunity to go ahead when a tipped ball was intercepted in the end zone by Safford giving them the ball back on their own 20-yard line.

Safford drove the ball to the 48-yard line on six plays. Then they scored a touchdown with a 52-yard pass when our safety pulled a hamstring and had to leave the game. Sonny Turner blocked Safford's extra point attempt, making the score Safford 20, Clarksville 13.

Safford kicked off and I caught the ball. I got hit by two defenders at once and fumbled the ball on our 36-yard line. Coach Ford called a time-out with less that five minutes left in the game. "Their coach will want to run the clock out. He knows we'll think they will run the ball on every play, so he'll call for a pass. Be ready for it. Get that ball back and go to the no-huddle offense."

We faked a blitz up the middle and then backed off the line at the last second. They faked a handoff up the middle and the quarterback dropped back for a pass. We intercepted the pass and ran it down to their ten-yard line. Twelve seconds remained on the clock. Coach Ford called another time out. He had us huddled up and called for a pass-option play to the right side. I took the ball, faked the handoff and ran to my right looking for an open receiver in the end zone. When I couldn't find one, I cut back across the middle of the field. Safford's All American linebacker hit me on the five-yard line. I drove forward to the 2-yard line before another one of Safford's player hit me, stopping my progress. Before my knees touched the ground, the entire pile launched forward for several more yards.

When I hit the ground, I wasn't sure if we had scored or not. I heard the whistle being blown by the referee. As the players piled off of me, I saw Jared and Larry both smiling. I looked over and saw the referee holding both arms high in the air. I knew we had scored. The score was now 21 Safford, 20 Clarksville. An extra point would tie the game and we would go into overtime. When we lined up for the extra point, I called our last time out.

The team gathered on the sideline with Coach Ford and he asked, "Why did you call for a time out, Andy?"

'What are we going to do, Coach?"

"We're going to kick the extra point and go to overtime, that's what we're going to do."

"Is that what Coach Harris thinks we will do?"

"He knows damn well that's what I'm going to do. That's what he would to do too if he were in my shoes."

"And what will he do?"

"He'll send everyone he has dead-on to try to block that extra point."

"Then why don't we surprise him and go for two and win this game right here and now?"

Coach Ford rubbed his chin, "I don't know, Andy, what do you have in mind?"

"I think that All American linebacker is going to run right past Sonny and dive for the ball while it's in the air. I think we should fake the extra point. I'll pull the ball out and hit Sonny in the end zone for two points and we go celebrate the win."

Coach Ford thought about it for a few seconds then asked, "Team, you want to go to overtime, or do you want to try to win the game right here and now?"

Jared answered first, "I want to win it now."

Larry said, "Me too."

The coach looked at Sonny. "Do you want to try it, Sonny?"

"I think Andy's right, he'll run right past me and I should be wide open. If Andy can get the ball to me, I'll catch it."

"Alright team, go win yourselves a championship!"

The team broke the huddle and lined up for the kick. The big All American paced back and forth like a caged tiger. All of Safford's players were right up on the line. As soon as the ball was hiked, the big All American linebacker knocked Sonny out of his way and dove for the ball. If the ball had been kicked, it would have been blocked. But I pulled the ball back as the kicker's foot came forward and the big All American dove for air. I stood up and saw Sonny turning around in the end zone wide open. I threw him the ball as time ran out to end the game. Sonny caught the ball and we won the game.

The Cougars of Clarksville had won their first State Football Championship in four years. Larry and Jared hoisted Sonny onto their shoulders and the whole team joined in and carried him off the field. The fans went nuts, yelling and screaming. I saw Shayla jumping up and down and clapping her hands with a big smile on her face.

The teams lined up and shook hands. When Coach Harris got to Coach Ford, he wrapped him in a big bear hug. "I sure hate losing this game Dan, but I'm glad your back. I was worried about you, old Buddy!"

"Thanks, my friend, I needed this win."

"You forgot to teach me that last play. That was something I knew you'd never do."

"It proves, you're never to old to learn. I'll see you next year!"

All of the Clarksville fans stayed in the stands for the presentation of the trophy. After the presentation, the teams left the field and everyone started heading for the parking lot.

Dad, Lt. Reinhardt and Mom waited for me at the end of the stadium. Dad said he wanted go to Skeeter's with me. He told the rest of them to go on and we'd see them at the party.

Bernie Baxter walked up to Dad and said, "Hey. Scott, that boy of yours really turned our team around." He looked at me with a big smile on his face. "As a matter of fact, Scott, you turned the whole town around when you discovered who killed Bobby Patterson. Congratulations, Chief." He shook Dad's hand. "I sure regret not voting yes when we hired you."

"Thanks Bernie, I appreciate it. Are you going to Skeeter's for the celebration?"

"I'm headed there now."

Shayla came and threw her arms around me. "Andy, you did it. Isn't it wonderful?" She caught me off guard by planting a big kiss right on my lips. I saw Dad laughing while she was doing it.

"I've got to get to the locker room. We have a party to go to and I wouldn't want them to start without us."

"Hurry up," Shayla said. "I don't want to be late."

When I got to the locker room, it was one big party. I hurried up and showered so I could get to the party and see Shayla. When I got to my car, Dad was waiting for me but Shayla wasn't there. "Where's Shayla, Dad?"

"I sent her to the party with her parents. I need to talk to you and didn't want her to hear what I have to say."

"Okay, Dad but let's go. I'd hate to miss the party."

"We won't."

We got in my car and I drove. Dad started talking right away, "Son, Bennett didn't kill Bobby Patterson. He would have killed me if you hadn't shot him, but he didn't kill anyone else."

He went on to explain everything he had learned from the tapes he had found in Bennett's store. Everything except who the real murder suspect was.

"Dad, can I be there when you arrest the killer?"

Dad thought about that for a moment and said, "Yes, you can, Andy. You earned that right. But you must not say anything about this or the tapes to anyone until after we make the arrest. And Jared must not say anything about those tapes either."

"I'll make sure he doesn't say a word."

"Good. Reinhardt is trying to find the parents, brothers and sisters of Carrie Campbell and Sue Anne Bradley so we can get a positive match on their DNA."

He looked over at me and said, "By the way, Son, that was a great game. Let's go celebrate."

CHAPTER FORTY-NINE

When we got to Skeeter's, a big sign on the door read, "Closed for a Private Celebration." Chief Baker bought Dad a beer and Bob Patterson said he would buy he rest.

When Chief Baker and Bob Patterson left our table, Mom asked Dad, "What happened at Bennett's store?"

Dad whispered, "I can't say much yet, but we figured out who killed Bobby Patterson and the women. I can't say anything until after the arrest on Monday. I'll explain everything later."

The celebration was in full swing and more and more fans were crowding in. They gave the football players and coaches a standing ovation as they walked in. Coach Ford had to duck his head as Jared and Larry carried him through the door. Mom wiped the lipstick off of my face. It was the same shade as Shayla's and I noticed Mom and Shayla smiling at each other.

Skeeter had removed the tables from the center of the restaurant to make room for dancing. She dragged Henry Spillman out on the dance-floor for the first dance. It was "The Dance" by Garth Brooks. When the song ended, Henry climbed up on top of a table and asked everyone to be quiet because he had a special announcement. Skeeter scolded him and told him to get down before he hurt himself.

Henry ignored her and continued. "I have another announcement. All of you know that I work for the mine. What you don't know is that I am one of the owners of the mine. I didn't let anyone know that because I didn't want anyone treating me differently because of money." He stopped and looked at Skeeter then continued. "I've always wondered what I would do the rest of my life after my first wife passed away. Thanks to Skeeter, and her bucket list, I now know. I just sold my interest in the mine and I want Scarlet and me to spend the rest of our lives going to all those places on her bucket list."

Skeeter covered her mouth in disbelief. "Henry, you can't be serious, are you?"

"Yes I am, Darling." He turned towards her, dropped to one knee and opened a small box. Inside was a huge diamond ring. "Scarlet Manson, will you marry me?"

Skeeter's mouth dropped open. "Oh, Henry, of course I'll marry you. You're the kindest man I've every known." Tears streamed down her cheeks. She leaned forward and kissed him as he slid the ring on her finger.

Henry stood back up. "Now, I want you to get rid of this restaurant so we can travel, travel and travel some more. I want to see all those places just as much as you do."

Skeeter had her hand over her mouth turning in circles jumping up and down. "Oh my God! Oh my God! What am I to do?"

"Just give it away, Honey, we don't need it."

"Okay, let me see." She looked around at everyone in the room. "I know. I'll give Skeeter's restaurant to the one person who deserves it more than anyone else. Someone who will love it as much as I do. I'm giving Skeeter's to Polly Label because I know she will take care of it and Clarksville will always have the best pies in the country."

Polly was holding both hands over her chest. "Somebody pinch me, I'm dreaming."

"No your not, Mom," Jared said. "I heard her say it, and whatever Skeeter says is the truth."

Polly gave Skeeter a big bear hug. "Hallelujah, and thank the Lord Jesus. Jared, you are going to college!"

Everyone clapped and congratulated Skeeter, Henry and Polly. Someone started banging on the door. Some stranger was trying to get in. Skeeter said, "You better get that, Polly, it's your restaurant now."

Polly walked over and opened the door. "Sorry, we're closed for a private party."

"I'm Coach Peterson from ASU," said the man. "I'm looking for Jared Label."

"Well why didn't you say so, young man. That's my boy. Come on in here and let me get you a piece of my famous pie." Polly put her arm around the man and walked him to Jared's table.

"Pontoon" by Little Big Town started playing. I saw Shayla standing by the jukebox smiling. She walked over, grabbed my hand and led me onto the dance-floor. Skeeter, Henry, Donna, John, Sherrie, Scott and most of Clarksville's faithful citizens joined us. It was one Hell of a party. Shayla and I snuck out early and no one seemed to notice.

CHAPTER FIFTY

Dad woke me up much earlier than I would have liked but I didn't want to miss finding out who the killer was. He told me not to say anything to anyone about this case as we drove to the police station. Harvey Baker sat at his desk reading the newspaper when we entered. "Good morning, Scott, Andy. Scott, are you going to tell me what the Hell is going on?"

"Sure, Harvey, but let's go to Skeeter's and I'll buy you breakfast first. Andy is starving and this is going to take a while to explain."

We went to breakfast and I could tell Dad was in a very good mood. Chief Baker was a lot quieter than normal and we didn't say much during breakfast. When we returned to the station, Dad told me to go see Lieutenant Reinhardt while he talked to Harvey. I walked into Reinhardt's office and he had me take a seat. He was expecting me. He closed the door. Sgt. Ortiz came into the office and pushed a button on a tape recorder sitting on the desk and took a seat. We could see and hear everything that Dad and Harvey were saying in Chief Baker's office. Lt. Reinhardt put his finger to his lips indicating he wanted me to be quiet.

Chief Baker sat in his chair with his back to us and Dad sat in a chair on the other side. Dad put his feet up on Harvey's desk. "You still smoke those high-dollar cigars, Harvey?"

Harvey looked at Dad's boots on his desk but didn't say anything about it. "Sure, want one?"

"Yeah, we need to celebrate."

Harvey took out two cigars, clipped the ends and lit Dad's and then his own. "Now tell me what's going on before I pull my hair out."

"First I'll tell you how the three football players deaths are connected."

Chief took a drag on his cigar and blew the smoke out. "All right. How are they connected?"

"Dave Keller was taking steroids. Bennett was supplying them. Jimmy Turner found out that Dave was on steroids and talked Dave into giving him some. When Jimmy collapsed on the practice field and died, Dave thought he had killed his best friend by giving him steroids. He hung himself two days later."

Chief Baker took another puff on his cigar and blew a smoke ring into the air. "If that's true, what does it have to do with Bobby Patterson?"

"Before he hung himself, Dave Keller told Bobby Patterson what he had done and that he had been buying steroids form Bennett. Bobby confronted Bennett at the gym on the night he was killed. He told Bennett he knew about the steroids and was going to go to the police and have him arrested. Bernie Baxter saw them arguing, broke it up and made Bennett leave. Bobby was killed so he couldn't go to the police."

"Well, that makes sense. Bennett killed Bobby so he wouldn't get arrested. What about the two dead women? Why did Bennett kill them?"

"Bennett didn't kill them. As a matter of fact, he didn't kill anyone."

Chief Baker took his cigar out of his mouth and knocked ashes into his ashtray. "You're losing me, Scott. Back up and tell what the Hell you're talking about."

"Bennett wasn't smart enough to run a big drug operation and didn't have the money to front it. He had a boss that ran everything and his boss killed Bobby and the women."

Harvey thought about that for a minute while smoking his cigar. "Why did this boss kill the women?"

"He killed Carrie because he saw me talking to her and knew she would be coming to my office for questioning. He knew she would tell me that she was getting the truck driver's destinations for Bennett so he knew which trucks to plant the drugs on. And that information would lead me to Bennett. He knew that if I arrested Bennett, he would want to make a deal and trade the information about his boss's operation and the murders to get his charges reduced."

Harvey didn't say anything for a long time, then asked, "And the other girl?"

"She knew too much. That was sloppy for the boss because she was a druggie and he should have known not to tell her anything. I figure she was going to leave him so he killed her to keep her quiet."

Harvey leaned back and blew several smoke rings towards the ceiling. "I suppose you're going to tell me who she is, aren't you?"

"Sue Anne Bradley, a small-time porn star with three prior drug convictions. The boss figured if she left him, it would only be a matter of time before she was busted again for drugs. Being a repeat offender, she would be looking at a minimum of 14 years in prison for any felony convictions. She too would want to make a deal and rat out her old boyfriend and Bennett. The boss must have felt he didn't have a choice."

Harvey leaned back and blew a few more smoke rings at he ceiling. "You know, Scott, everything you just said is circumstantial. You don't have any hard evidence to prove any of that."

"I have DNA from both Carrie and Sue Anne to prove who they are. I'm sure I'll find a lot of money and probably more drugs during my search of the suspect's house. And, you know what else, Harvey?"

"What?"

"The suspect is going to make a full confession when I tell him what I know."

"You think so, do you? And how did you come up with all these theories?"

"Lots of little things. I got the steroid information from a guy in prison. The coroner's report on Bradley said it looked like a trophy had smashed in Sue Ann's skull. When I saw all those trophies in Bernie's gym, it got me to thinking."

"Bernie isn't going to admit to anything. His parents have megabucks and as soon as you arrest him, he'll lawyer up and you won't have shit."

"I'm not talking about Bernie."

Chief Baker stared at Dad but didn't say anything. "I also got to thinking about that long shot that killed Bobby. Not very many men I know could make that shot. Certainly, not Bennett. The first mistake you made, Harvey, was thinking Bennett was just a dim-witted Indian."

I turned and looked at Reinhardt and Ortiz. Reinhardt nodded his head indicating yes, I'd heard right. I turned to watch what was going to happen next.

Dad continued talking. "Bennett wasn't dumb after all. He didn't trust you and knew if you guys ever got busted, he would be charged with murder just as you would. So, he bought one of those small voice activated tape recorders like the ones we use in police work and recorded your conversations."

"You've got to be shitting me, Scott," Harvey said. "Bennett didn't even have a remote TV or a cell phone before I bought him one, let alone a tape recorder."

"I'm not shitting you, Harvey. He didn't know you killed Carrie until I told him she was dead. That's when he used his last breath to tell me where the tapes were hidden. I just didn't understand what he was trying to tell me a first. He hid the tapes in a Kachina Doll. And guess what?".

"You're killing me with suspense, Scott."

"I found the tapes."

Harvey just sat there smoking his cigar and looking at Dad. After a while, he said, "You said my first mistake was to think Bennett was an idiot. What other mistakes do you think I made?"

"For one, you hired me." Dad took a small tape recorder out of his pocket. "Bennett recorded twelve different tapes of your conversations. This is the one I liked the most." Dad placed the recorder on the table and hit play.

"Bennett, get your ass in here and shut the fucking door." You could hear a door shutting and then, "You dumb fuck! I told you not to give any of those kids steroids."

"I only gave them to Keller."

"Yes and he's dead and so is Jimmy Turner because Keller gave them to him."

"I didn't know he was giving them to Jimmy."

"It doesn't matter what you knew, you dumb ass. They are dead and if the police find out who supplied those steroids, you're going to jail for about 25 years for manslaughter."

There was a long pause.

"Well?"

"You didn't have to kill Sue Anne and Bobby."

"Think about it, you moron. Sue Anne was a drug user with three felony convictions. She was stealing my money and as soon as she got busted again, she would want to make a deal and tell them all about our operation. DEA would be on our ass before we knew it and we would both be spending the rest of our lives in prison. Is that what you want?"

"No, but why Bobby? He was a good kid."

"Yes he was, and it's your fault he's dead."

"My fault? I didn't kill him."

"Sure you did. As soon as Dave Keller told him where he was getting the steroids. If I hadn't killed him, you would be in jail right now. You'd be lucky to ever see the light of day again. From now on, listen to me and I mean it! Do you understand me?"

There was another long pause. "Bennett, are you listening to me, Goddamn it?"

"Yeah, Harvey, I'm listening to you. What do you want me to do?"

"Don't fucking call me Harvey, asshole. You call me Chief."

"Ok, Chief, what do you want me to do?"

"I want you to take that bag of shit and hide her in that old mine shaft you told me about."

"What if someone finds her?"

"No one is going to find her, that mine isn't even on the maps. Even if they do find her, they won't be able to identify her. I pulled her teeth and cut her hands off. No one even knows she is around here."

"Okay."

"Now get the fuck out of here."

Harvey listened to himself telling Bennett why he had to kill Sue Anne and Bobby. When the tape ended, Dad hit the stop button. "I thought about the shot that killed Bobby. Not very many men I know could make that shot. I got to thinking about all those shooting titles you won when we worked together at the Mesa Police

Department. I remember you getting the award for the best shot in the Academy and being a sniper on the SWAT team. You still have all those shooting trophies, don't you, Harvey?"

Harvey didn't respond. He blew more smoke rings in the air while staring at the ceiling.

"I bet I can match one of them to the indent in Sue Anne's scull. What do you think, Harvey? "

Harvey blew another smoke ring at the ceiling. "You know what your problem is, Scott?"

"What's that, Harvey? What's my problem?"

"You were always too fucking smart for your own good. Always figuring out things no one else could. You could have made Chief if you had tested for promotions. But no, you just wanted to solve crimes. You were always a fucking prima donna! But you know what, you're not that smart. You wouldn't have figured this out in a hundred years if that fuck-head Bennett hadn't taped those conversations."

"Maybe, but I did. What I really want to know is why did you do it?"

Harvey took a long drag on his cigar. "Money, what else? My ex-wife took half of my retirement pension when I left Mesa. Think about it, Scott. Guys like you and me spend our whole careers chasing criminals and risking our lives. If we're lucky, we retire and get a small pension and no one gives a shit. We sit around worrying about how we're going to pay our bills and then we die. No one cares about guys like you and me after we retire. I wanted more. I wanted a big house on the beach in Florida and an eighteen-year-old hooker once a week. Is that too much to ask? I'd have it too if you hadn't fuck it up."

Dad leaned back in his chair and blew smoke rings into the air. Harvey reached over and pulled his pistol out of the holster hanging on the hat rack next to him and pointed it at Dad's face. I jumped up but Reinhardt grabbed my arm and stopped me.

"Don't worry. He's all right, Andy. Stay here." I sat back down but was worried.

Dad looked at Harvey and smiled, "What you going to do, Harvey, shoot me?"

"I'm going to Hell, Scott, and I'm taking you with me. Do you think that pretty wife and kid of yours are going to appreciate how smart you are once your dead?"

"Oh come on Harvey, that's not your style. Put the gun away. You only kill helpless women and unarmed kids."

Harvey placed the red dot from the laser right between Dad's eyes. Dad just looked at him. "Go ahead, Harvey, pull the trigger." Harvey hesitated. "What's the matter, asshole? Afraid to shoot a real man?"

Harvey pulled the trigger. When it clicked, he tapped the pistol's magazine, rapped the chamber, aimed and pulled the trigger again. When it didn't fire, he ejected the magazine and saw the gun was empty.

Lt. Reinhardt and Sgt. Ortiz ran into the Chief's office with their guns drawn and I followed. When we came in, Dad said, "I had Reinhardt empty your gun while we were having breakfast. We also have this room bugged. We recorded everything."

Lt. Reinhardt said, "You're under arrest for the murders of Sue Anne Bradley, Bobby Patterson, and Carrie Campbell. You're also under arrest for the attempted murder of Scott Hanson. You have the right to remain silent. Stand up and turn around!"

Harvey looked at Dad and put his cigar out in the astray. "I guess you get that Chief's job after all."

"I don't want it, Harvey, that's Reinhardt's job. I'm happy right where I am. All I want is peace and justice. Book him, Ortiz!"

ACKNOWLEDGMENTS

As my disclaimer, this book is a work of fiction. Some of the towns and locations in Arizona are actual towns and places. The town of Clarksville and all characters and events in this book are fictional created in the mind of the author. Some of the names in this book are real and used with the permission of the person named. Colonel Lightfoot, Sonny Turner, Priscilla Zayas, and Scott Davison. I hope they like the characters I created out of their name. All other names are fictitious.

I'd like to thank my wife, sons and close friends for your patience and enduring the countless stories about my imaginary friends. And, to my son, Nathaniel, yes, I know they aren't real.

I'd like to thank retired police detective Jim Pomish for his assistance and encouragement during the early days when this book was only a dream and no one believed it would ever be written.

I appreciate the technical assistance given to me by Coach Dan Dunn on football coaching, Sierra Devaney for barrel racing and rodeos, Colonel Lightfoot for showing me what a real cowboy is supposed to be like and my son, Adam Bray, for helping me with my website.

I'd like to thank my first editors, Laura Harvey for telling me during her first edit that it was a good story but very poorly written. And for her advise on what I had to do to improve my writing skills. And for encouraging me not give up on the book. To Paul Soderberg and Cheryl Payne for their hard work on the final edits and their kind words of encouragement and suggestions.

I want to thank the Power Road Writers Group, Carlene and Anthony Eye, Craig Mazur, Randy Lindsay, Ruth Chavez and Don Wooldridge. With out them, this book would never been completed. A part them are hidden between each page of this book.

Elvis Bray is an American author specializing in crime and suspense fiction novels, short stories and poetry. He served as a helicopter crew chief during the Vietnam War for two tours and was a police officer and detective of over 35 years. Now retired, he lives in Queen Creek, Arizona with his wife, three horses, two dogs and a cat he doesn't claim.

To contact the Author, please go to elvisbrayauthor.com